# CROSSOVER

JOEL SHEPHERD

CROSSOVER

A CASSANDRA KRESNOV NOVEL

an imprint of **Prometheus Books**
Amherst, NY

Published 2006 by Pyr®, an imprint of Prometheus Books

Inquiries should be addressed to
Pyr
59 John Glenn Drive
Amherst, New York 14228–2197

ISBN: 978-0-7394-7700-7

Printed in the United States of America

*To my parents, for making
everything possible*

## CHAPTER 1

**S**unlight lay across the bare floor of the hotel room, falling rich and golden upon the smooth white sheets of the single bed, and the exposed pale arm of its occupant. Sun-dappled sheets shifted as she stirred sleepily, pulling smoothly to the pronounced curve of a hip.

Eyes blinked softly open. For a long moment she lay awake, listening to the morning. Distant traffic could be heard drifting up from far below. City sounds. The faint whine of the maglev line distinct above the rest. Then, past the window, the mournful, deep-throated whine of an aircar passing a skylane nearby.

Loose, dark blonde hair lay mussed and untended to her forehead. She brushed it back with a lazy hand. Rolled onto her back, sheet and mattress smooth and pleasant against her naked skin. Turned her head against the pillow to gaze calmly toward the broad, wide windows that counted for the far wall, tinted darkly gold against the deep glare of the rising sun. Another aircar passed with a sound like a throaty sigh. It moved on past the window, sunlight flashing from sleek, angular lines.

"Minder," she said, her voice thick with sleep. "Less tinting, please." The windows lightened, the sunlight grew brighter. "That's enough." The sun was painful to look at now, but her eyes adjusted, filtering the glare.

Outside were the city towers, tall, broad, and varied. An architect's delight, they were. An economist's dream. A technologist's marvel. The towers stood not so close as to crowd, leaving plenty of open space between, gleaming golden with sunlight on glass. Aircars curved gently between them, banking slowly, unhurried and safely guided by invisible automation.

This was the city of Tanusha in the morning light, viewed from a single hotel room on the sixty-first floor of the Hanaman building, where the Emerald Si'an Hotel made its residence between the fiftieth and seventieth floors. The woman blinked at the view, no longer sleepy. Calm. Her lips pursed slightly in what might have been a smile. The traffic hummed, a gentle cacophony of life, and she listened, searching for nothing in particular, as her eyes took in the view without really looking . . . just drifting. In the comfortable bed with the silky sheets.

The net traffic was increasing, too. She could hear it—or feel it, which was perhaps more accurate—a steady drift and flow of voices and machine-talk across an undulating landscape of static. It increased as she focused, snatches of words, broken, obscuring walls of encryption, action and counteraction on the early morning airwaves. People talking sleepily over breakfast, their bellies full of coffee or tea, a paper on the slate to read in the golden light through the windows, munching a pastry . . . And she let it go, having little interest at this moment, content to feel it as a constant murmur, pressing comfortably at the back of her consciousness.

It was 07:13 local time on the twenty-four-hour clock. She stretched, luxuriously, arching her back, arms overhead, fingertips brushing the wall. And sighed. Pushed the sheets to one side, swung herself easily off the bed and walked naked to the bathroom, fingers combing her hair into some kind of order.

Emerged from the shower at 07:26, having taken more time than she needed. But that was becoming her habit these days. She stood on the warm bathroom floor, her skin tingling from the drying cycle, small, fine hairs standing pleasantly on end. Ran a palm across her forearm, brushing at the hairs. Curious. Her forearm tingled. And she smiled at her own wanderings, and gave a slight shake of her head. Picked a brush off the bench, and began work on her just dried hair, watching the mirror as she did.

Pale blue eyes stared back. Attractive eyes, she thought. Yes, definitely attractive, as the hair began to fall into place. She put down the brush and leaned forward on the bench rim, gazing closely into those eyes. Ran the tip of her forefinger across an eyebrow, down to the tip of her nose. And trailed further down, pulling at a lip. Tried a smile, and liked how that looked. Content, she walked back out to the main room, still naked, sat down on the softly carpeted floor, and began to stretch.

After several minutes, the door chimed. "Room service," called a very real and unautomated male voice. The woman climbed smoothly to her feet, gave her arms one last swing, and reached for her white hotel bathrobe.

"Enter," she said, tying the robe loosely about her waist as the door light flicked to green and the door swung open. A smallish man entered, well dressed and with a bow tie beneath his collar, supporting a breakfast tray in one hand.

"Your breakfast, madam," the very unautomated hotel man said. His cart was in the corridor behind him, loaded with other breakfasts.

"Thank you." She smiled at him, and took the tray from his hands. He smiled back.

"I apologise for the slight delay, Ms. Cassidy. As you may appreciate, only the machines are never late." She waved a hand.

"Not at all. I prefer the personal service."

"I'm very glad." The man smiled again, and gave a small bow before retreating. The door shut behind him, and she was alone again. The woman carried the tray to her bed, placed it carefully upon the rumpled covers, and climbed up beside it. She ate her breakfast like that, cross-legged on the bed in her bathrobe, watching the airborne traffic weave and sigh amid the tall, strikingly modern and eye-catching buildings of Tanusha, gleaming in the sun.

She washed down a slice of toast with a fragrant mouthful of Chinese tea, for which she had developed a strong liking, and reached for the small, compact unit on the bedside table. Palmed it in her lap and drew from the side a long, slim powercord. Brushed aside the hair at the back of her head and inserted the slim metal connector into the receiver socket with a small yet profound *click*! that she felt rather than heard, deep in her inner ear. Touched a button on the hand-unit and began the interface.

She found her personal records and files, all safely contained within hotel barriers and encryption walls. Darted inside, sorting bits and pieces, checking her traps, records of access, authorised and unauthorised. Found nothing, which pleased her. Her luck was holding. Surrounding traffic was very strong, as she'd become accustomed to in Tanusha. Automateds darted this way and that, countering, interacting, doing whatever their programming instructed them to do, all with that familiar, mindless tenacity. Minds were slower, pondering, thinking. Walls of light and motion, shapes and textures, glowing, impenetrable yet transparent, branches and limbs of consciousness that grew and retracted with intent or otherwise . . .

She flicked through her records one last time, scanning the numbers, the names, the images. April Cassidy. Which was not her name, but it was the name she wore for now, while it suited her. Born 15th of May standard, 2521, on Octavia 3, city of Tillanna. A registered citizen of the Confederacy, subject to its various rules and principles, recipient of its evident benefits. Both parents killed in the war against the League. No brothers or sisters, or close family of any kind. Raised under the legal guardianship of a war orphanage now disbanded, owing to Confederacy cutbacks on repatriation expenditure, now that the war was over. There were other things, too—social security number, birth certificate, credit cards, records of employment and company details . . . she was a cognitive software expert, self-employed—a journeyman, headed wherever work was available. And, of course, she had plenty of money, and generous terms of credit from her bank.

It was an interesting life. She thought about it for a while, disconnecting the hand-unit and letting the coil retract inside. She wondered what such a person would be like, this April Cassidy, with her orphanage past and her software skills. Sometimes she fancied she empathised, particularly over the lack of parents, a home life, a childhood. At other times she thought the deception might well be beyond her, this woman, with her civilian thoughts and peaceful upbringing, no matter how disrupted. She sat cross-legged in the bright pool of sunlight that fell across her bed, thinking about this life she had borrowed, as the city awoke from a light, almost-slumber, and a new day began.

A good life, she thought, finding peace amid the myriad simple, everyday intentions, the people intent on work, and family, and children on their way to school. The priorities were simple here. Life was a tapestry of basic concerns, and basic needs, and people were happy. The war had never touched this place, although Tanusha's technology and its cash had driven the war's progress to no small degree. She could be happy here. And if not here then, well, there were many stars, and many planets, and many cities and places to see. But for now, there was today. And she had an appointment.

It was 08:19 when she was invited in for her first interview. She left the *Street Scene* magazine on the coffee table in the waiting room, followed the secretary down the corridor to the open door, and walked inside.

"Ms. Cassidy?" the small, Vietnamese-looking woman said as she entered, rising from the seat at her broad working desk.

"That's right," April Cassidy said, exchanging smiles as she shook the other woman's hand. "Nice to meet you, Ms. Phung."

"Likewise. Please, take a seat," indicating the cushioned chair before the desk. She took it, glancing once more out the office windows as Ms. Phung settled back into her chair. This office was not so high up as her hotel room, only the twenty-third floor. The streets were closer, as was the moving traffic, distinct beneath the shading trees.

"Lovely view," she commented. "Every office in the city seems to have a view like this."

"Yes, it's a definite plus to living and working in Tanusha, that is certain. You've travelled quite a bit, I've noticed, to look at your résumé." April Cassidy nodded, legs neatly crossed, hands folded comfortably in her lap.

"Yes, I love travelling. And I've never really found a place that I feel I could call home. Although this," and she indicated out of the window, "this feels very nice. I could certainly get used to this."

Ms. Phung smiled, and examined the datapad on the desk before her. "You graduated with full honours, I see . . . very impressive." April Cassidy sat patiently, not fidgeting, waiting for the next question. "How would you rate the Batista University? I've not encountered anyone from there before."

"It's extremely good. They're not overly theoretical, as a rule, and they have plenty of private sector involvement, so there are lots of practical, hands-on projects to get involved with. Plenty of job opportunities—I got a number of offers on graduating, but remaining on Octavia wasn't a high priority for me at that point."

"Hmmm." Ms. Phung nodded, appearing genuinely interested, eyes continuing to peruse the slate. "I've heard that the opportunities on Octavia are quite good."

"Yes they are, but I've always been a little more ambitious. I wanted to travel, and probably to work someplace where the environment is a little more cutting edge. Most of the best places on Octavia are already taken, and promotion doesn't come easily."

"I see." More study. "And what drew you to Wardell Systematics?"

"It was one of the medium-sized firms most highly rated for innovative work in Tanusha, with lots of R & D, plus some very interesting long-running contracts—that aroused my interest."

"You'd choose a medium-sized firm over a larger one?"

"Given the choice, yes, I would. I like the necessity towards creativity wherever possible. That's the kind of work that most excites me, and it's what I'm best at, too."

Ms. Phung nodded to herself. "Well, perhaps you could show me what you can do?"

"Of course." She reached into her inside pocket and withdrew her small black hand-unit, withdrew the cord, reached the end around behind her head, and jacked herself in. Thumbed the receiver button on the hand-unit, which set itself to the office frequency with a click and rush of data, a visual, sensual wave. Strong setup. But she was getting used to that in Tanusha. "What would you like me to look at?"

"This." Ms. Phung tapped a few buttons on her desk keypad, and a strong system appeared amid the corporate boundaries . . . solid, intricate construct, a very impressive piece of intelligence programming. "What can you tell me about it, at first glance?"

"Well, it appears to be a level nine cognitive function . . . in fact, I'd say it was a visual sorting function, the way the memory bands are branched with third level backups as they are . . ."

The analysis went on for a while. Ms. Phung gave no overt signs of approval or disapproval, but April Cassidy could tell she was impressed. Which was not surprising. April Cassidy, for her part, was similarly impressed with the level of engineering in Wardell Systematics' work—much of it was truly cutting edge and very creative, verging on custom design. Which was the one area where the smaller firms had a real edge over the larger ones, who were unable to get big enough returns from the smaller, custom contracts to justify their initial expenditure. And she doubted that this particular construction was the most they were capable of, either—much of that would be classified. Very interesting.

"I'll have a discussion with the rest of the group," Ms. Phung told her when they were finished and rising from their seats. "Obviously I can't promise you anything in advance, but I must say I've been very impressed with what I've seen here today."

"Thank you. You do know where I'm staying?"

"The Emerald Si'an Hotel, yes. I've got the room number recorded somewhere. That's a nice place, the Emerald. Try the Thai restaurant on the top floor, it's marvellous." She extended her hand, and April Cassidy took it in a firm, friendly clasp, and smiled.

"I'll remember that, thank you."

"You have other interviews today, I suppose?"

"Yes, three more today, and another four tomorrow. I intend to spend the time in between just wandering around."

Ms. Phung sighed. "Well then, I suppose that if we did decide we could take you on, we'd be lucky to get you, wouldn't we?"

April Cassidy's smile broadened. "As you say, I can't guarantee anything . . . anyway, it was a pleasure to meet you, and I'm sure I'd be very happy to work for your company if that is what eventuates. It all just depends. I'm sure you understand."

Ms. Phung smiled back. "I do. I understand very well." She walked to the door and opened it. "Just one thing," she said, and April Cassidy paused in the doorway. "Your old company on Reta Prime, Boushun Information in Guangban . . . why did you leave them, if you don't mind my asking?"

"Not at all. Well, I'm . . . ." She smiled, and gave a small, self-deprecating shrug. ". . . I'm a fairly restless person. Boushun were very good to me—and I to them, I'd like to think—but I just had a feeling that I could do better elsewhere. And Guangban isn't nearly as nice a city as Tanusha. I think it's more sensible to make a move like that when you're younger and don't have too many commitments and connections. So here I am."

"Indeed. I'm very envious." They both laughed. "Well, have a nice time in Tanusha, and I may be seeing you again sometime soon."

"I'd like that. See you later."

April Cassidy left the offices of Wardell Systematics feeling pleased with herself. Things were going very well. With any luck, within a few days she'd have the pick of the bunch, and a very impressive bunch they were, too. It was highly unlikely that they'd ever find a young technician with quite her degree of ability, although she'd been careful not to show off too much, just as they'd been careful with her. The work would be interesting, the pay would be excellent, and she might just make some friends along the way. It was a very agreeable list of positives. Yes, all in all, she was beginning to enjoy Tanusha.

She ate her lunch that day in one of the green parks between the roadways, on a quaint wooden bench under the spreading branches of a leafy tree. The meal was a couple of crisp vegetable rolls with a spicy dip, bought from a parkside vendor—it tasted delicious. The breeze made a pleasant sound through the spreading leaves, mingling with the surrounding traffic noise, though that remained muted even down here at ground level. Some nearby smaller buildings rose unobtrusively above the trees. Near and distant the towers rose, evenly yet randomly spaced, tall and gleaming against the crystal blue sky.

A remarkable exercise in city planning, Tanusha. Social modelling on a massive scale. "A Grade" office towers—or mega-rises—were about 400 metres high, as uniform in height as they were varied in imaginative, inspired design. They stood widely spaced, no two in close proximity, except for the occasional twin-pair, each marking a convergence of traffic and building density. Midsize buildings clustered around such centralised hubs—business districts, a crisscross of road and rail transportation, fanning outward. Midsize high-rises ranged from 100 to 150 metres and varied greatly, though evidently within zonal limits. Between the hubs lay suburbia, undulating to occasional multistorey flats penetrating the carpet of lush green trees that lined the many streets, parks, schools, temples, shopping districts, and sports stadiums.

She could see the patterns, even down here at ground level, though one had to venture high to truly appreciate the fifty-seven million people-strong scale of it all. High-density pockets amid a varied sea of human residence. Grand convergences, dropping low then rising once more. Computer modelling accounted for traffic flows, for services and the availability of, and distance from, Tanusha's multifarious attractions and necessities. High-cost and low-cost residencies blended together to mutual advantage. There were no bad locations in Tanusha. The planners had obviously seen to that. Such industrious civilianisms impressed her. And more to the point, the place was beautiful, with variation and aesthetic design wherever she looked. And so many trees. She took another bite of her lunch, and felt pleased at her choice of cities in which to start this new life.

Her interviews had gone very well, and she was confident she'd made a good impression. Tanusha's software tech was legend, almost certainly the best in the Federation, but still, she had certain capabilities she knew very well they would rarely have seen before. And she'd kept a lot to herself. An unfair advantage, no question. She'd been relying on it for going on a year now. It kept her comfortable, well paid, and secure. Among other things.

A commotion nearby caught her eye—children, perhaps eight or nine years old, running haphazardly across the green lawn between the trees, shouting and laughing. That building must be a school, then. Several of them were kicking balls or throwing Frisbees. They made a lot of noise, most of it unnecessary. Several nearby lunchers got to their feet and moved off, looking annoyed or bemused, their peaceful lunch-break now disturbed. April Cassidy sat on, eating the last of her veg-etable rolls and watching the children with intense curiosity, like a musician reading from a particularly interesting sheet of music. And smiled at their arguments, at trivial things elevated to such a ground-breaking importance.

She finished her last mouthful and got up, tossing her trash in the bin provided and strolling off toward the walkway that would take her to a lightrail stop, from where she could get to her next appointment. Not that she was intending to go the short way there. A gridiron ball hit the ground in front of her, a young boy running after it, still some way off. She picked it up with one hand and put her briefcase on the grass. The boy held up his hands expectantly, but she gestured not at him but at the girl he'd been playing with, some thirty metres away now. Eyes wide, she jogged backward, awaiting the throw. April Cas-sidy threw it not particularly hard, but the ball shot upward through the sunlit air in a huge arc, spinning madly and sailing on to land a good ten metres behind the girl even as she ran madly after it.

The boy made a loud, awestruck sound and grinned at her. April Cassidy grinned back, picked up her briefcase, and walked off toward her rail stop.

It was 18:32 when she got back to her hotel room at the Emerald Si'an, and outside the windows the dimming sky was streaked with shades of pink and orange. She placed her briefcase on the freshly made bed and began to pull off her clothes, folding each item onto a neat pile beside the case. That done, she walked to the shower and stayed there for a while. Then she crossed to the wardrobe to select another outfit from where she'd hung them on her arrival in Tanusha last evening. She pondered for a moment over the tight black dress, before deciding no, not on her first night out. And settled finally on the other dress-suit, which was formal but had flared hems and wide cuffs, flamboyant striping, and a low neck that revealed some skin beneath. That plus a black blouse, with a low neckline, and matching stockings.

She dressed with the fastidiousness of an utter egotist, examining herself in the mirror on the addition of every new article, but her expression was more curious than self-obsessed. Then for makeup, which she'd never entirely got the hang of—or the point of, come to that—but no matter. She sat herself in front of the mirror with her small cosmetic box and applied a touch to the lips, and eyelids and lashes, with not inconsiderable artistry for one so lacking in practice. And then jewellery . . . well, she had precious few items, save the silver chain with the star-shaped emblem that had some significance to one South Asian cultural group or another—she put it on, and it settled comfortably around her neck, the emblem only just visible above the vee of her jacket.

Finally, she gave her hair a quick brush and examined herself one last time in the mirror. She looked . . . formal. Formally attractive. She hesitated to suppose she looked more attractive than usual—they were only clothes, after all. But she thought she looked very nice. And found herself smiling at her own ignorance.

"What would you know?" she asked the woman in the mirror. The woman smiled back calmly. A controlled display of humour, but genuine. She possessed no other kind.

Tanusha had many popular nightlife districts, but the Fern Street district numbered among the ten most well known, a high ranking indeed for a prolific party town like Tanusha. Fern Street ran along the centre of a protruding bulb of land, isolated by a loop in one of many branches of the Shoban River delta snaking back upon itself. April Cassidy could certainly see where the nightlife industry came from, as she ambled along the curve of riverfront, gazing up at the nearest towers that soared above the riverbanks. Light blazed and flickered off the darkened waters, tossed by the wake of a passing cruise ship and several smaller craft.

A choice piece of real estate, it was. Particularly the isolated bulb on the inner side of the river's bend, where the towers grew especially thick and well lit. Mostly residential and tourist developments, she thought as she strolled, hands thrust deep into her pockets. With river views on all sides, it was hardly surprising that so many people would want to live here. And where people went, entertainments followed. But river views were everywhere in Tanusha—the megatropolis sprawled across the broad basin of the Shoban delta, where the runoff from the northeastern Tuez Ranges divided into hundreds of spidery arms that snaked across the flat, forested ground. The riverside topography had obviously given the city planners ideas. People-centres sprang up, lining the banks. The original trees had been kept wherever possible, leafy greenery flanking the gleaming waters in a most un-urban fashion. And she wondered again at the priorities of a city whose designers would devote such care and attention to frivolous fancies.

Couples strolled by, arms about each other as they walked, their way lit by muted pedestrian lights. Music echoed through the air from a multitude of random sources. Fragments of conversation drifted across the water from a passing cruise ship as a jazz band played and glasses clinked.

Most of the attractive young women out on that night, April Cassidy noted, were in the company of attractive young men. Several people glanced at her as she passed, and several of the male glances lingered. Possibly she looked a touch unusual, not in that she was well dressed and attractive, but in that she was alone. But then someone had to be alone, she supposed. How did people become couples without first being singles? She'd been reading the signs for nearly a year now, learning on the job, as it were. Sex was easy. Relationships less so. Courtship was downright confusing. And romance eluded her entirely. She preferred her orgasms uncomplicated and frequent. But then, what would she know?

Further on, the peaceful riverside walk changed. The open space and occasional tree gave way to a row of compact old-fashioned brick-and-mortar buildings, four storeys high and with flat, colourfully painted fronts, narrow windows, and attractive wooden shutters. All about were tables, crowded with diners and the roar of mingled conversations, music, and laughter. She picked her way leisurely among the crowds, watching the waiters with their loaded trays and the people gathered about the tightly packed tables, intent on conversation. The entire waterfront now was bars and restaurants, with new premises every few steps and signs by the walkway advertising the local specialty. It smelt delicious. Everything did.

She finally found an empty table right by the riverside, in a slightly quieter section of the row. A well-dressed waiter took her order, which she selected entirely at random, and moved off purposefully. Nearby, a melodious saxophone was playing, unaccompanied and very pleasing to the ear. From further along, a lively techno-rhythm was thumping, dimmed by the waves of conversation.

Her meal, when it arrived, was . . . different. Callayan seafood, from the fish farms along the neighbouring coastline. The waiter, having no other customers to attend to, assured her that it was a local delicacy. April Cassidy wasn't sure—it was certainly rich, and strong, but very, very unusual. By the time she'd finished it, and half of the glass of fruit wine that accompanied it, she'd decided that she liked it. Which was her usual conclusion about unusual things. She ordered dessert and started on the second half of the wine, gazing out across the water.

A man slipped into the seat opposite her. "Do you mind if I sit here?" he asked.

"No, of course not."

He smiled easily.

"I'm Joachim." Extended his hand, and she took it.

"April."

"April. That's a lovely name."

Conversation with Joachim proved interesting, if not spectacular.

Obviously he wanted to get her into bed. She looked him over as they talked, surreptitiously, and decided that his chances were pretty good. Thus decided, she enjoyed her fruit ice cream dessert and a second glass of wine that Joachim bought for her, and enjoyed the company.

"So what do you do for a living, Joachim?"

"I work for a small communications firm, Hsu Communications— you probably won't have heard of them since you're so new in town." She shook her head, sipping her wine. "So, you know, I've got this great view from my office in the Mohan building . . ."

She learned a fair few things about Tanusha from Joachim that evening. Mostly small things, like where the best entertainment arcades were, and who the most famous martial arts star was, and how to get a line of credit when you were seriously overdrawn from too many late-night benders, doubtless with an assortment of single, attractive women of whom she was only the latest. After half an hour, she thought she'd probably have preferred her own company again, but she fancied she was getting a feel for the typical Tanushan resident, which had to be worth something. And besides, she rather had her heart set on sex.

12:37, and April Cassidy stood naked before the broad, clear windows of Joachim's apartment. Tanusha at night was a spectacle to behold. She had never seen so many lights, such variety of light, probing, strobing, fingerlike or centred patterns and colours intentional or otherwise . . . she placed a hand to the cool window, palm splayed, and trailed her eyes in a lazy sweep across the never-ending horizon of blazing lights.

The central mega-rise of this region soared up to her left, this one shaped like a sail, glass and metal in a mutually enfolding embrace, ablaze with corporate signage that conformed to the architectural intrigue. About its skirts fanned the middle high-rises, an irregular jumble of disparate shapes, crowded and clustered unpredictably above streets ablaze with neon and nose-to-tail late-night traffic. One of Tanusha's hubs. One of hundreds. Beyond, the buildings faded to parks, trees, and a vast expanse of forested suburbia broken by the bend of yet another branch of the Shoban, gleaming in the electric night. And beyond them, other mega-rises staked out additional hubs like flags, sometimes grouped close together, sometimes forming corridors along strategic stretches of river or road, sometimes isolated and alone, but always purposeful. Aircars in their hundreds wound between. A trained and patient eye could discern the invisible skylanes, watching the drifting, bending masses of blinking airborne lights. Like swarms of fireflies in a forest, stretching away across the vast, urban distance.

Her eyes followed as one of the airborne transports whined mournfully by, a shimmering reflection slipping across its gleaming shell like mercury, running lights blinking. Voices played at the back of her consciousness, a building pressure, then receding with tangible, physical sensation. Machine traffic, people traffic, sharemarkets, transport guidance, personal calls . . . all blended smoothly into one clear presence. Thus the city spoke to itself, and thus to the other cities about the globe, and to the station above, and the planets and the people beyond even that. The net was huge. Vast. And many, many things beyond . . .

She turned to look at Joachim, who lay naked amid the comfortable tangle of sheets, limbs splayed amid the fall of night light from outside. Sighed, softly, and began to pull on her clothes from where they'd fallen 107 minutes before. Joachim did not stir, having had perhaps one glass too many in the evening past. And she had worn him out—107 minutes was apparently much longer than he was accustomed to.

Well, she thought, as she fastened her belt about the waist of her jacket, she had no complaints. It had been a while, that was all. A week, at least. She checked that her wallet was still in her pocket and that her various cash and identification cards were still where they ought to be, and then finger combed her hair back into some kind of order in the gleam of window light before Joachim's bedroom mirror. Her hair was slightly strewn, but she liked the effect and she smiled at herself in the mirror. The mirror smiled back.

And then, because she harboured a secret ambition to one day become a hopeless romantic, she walked to Joachim's bedside and kissed him gently on the lips. Joachim's breathing may have altered slightly, but his eyelids never so much as fluttered. April Cassidy moved softly to the door, opened and closed it silently, and walked off down the empty corridor, the soft remnants of a saxophone melody running gentle circles through her mind.

That night, alone in her hotel bed, she dreamed.

She was surrounded by cold, dark metal. Loud, mechanical noises echoed and crashed, and heavy forces crushed her into her seat, then tossed forward against the restraint bar. Her thickly gloved right hand clasped the grip of a rifle, locked into a heavy brace. Her body was encased in armour, lightweight but hard, and a helmet strap pulled tight beneath her chin, visorplate open, systems temporarily offline in the predrop.

Other soldiers sat on the benches around her, similarly armed and armoured, secured by their restraints as the forces slammed them this way and that and the engine noise whined in their ears. She knew their names, these soldiers. There was Tran, child-faced and slight. Rachmin, cold-eyed and narrow-jawed. Chu, tongue protruding from a corner of her mouth in nervous habit. Dobrov, dour and grim. Mahud, with barely restrained eagerness. The man sitting opposite regarded her darkly. Sergei. Or Stark, as he was more often called.

"Not long now, Sandy." She could see the target image on the forward scan uplink, drawing closer. She looked about her. Another sudden lift slammed her hard down into the seat, blurring her vision. Her discomfort grew.

"My name's not Sandy. I'm April Cassidy now."

"Wha's tha', Cap'n?" asked Chu.

"My name," she repeated. "I'm not Sandy any more. My name is April Cassidy." The return stares were blank, uncomprehending. Tran yawned.

"Approaching the target, Captain," said Stark. His stare was ominous, as always.

"I can't lead you," she told him. "I'm not supposed to be here. This is a mistake." The discomfort grew worse. There wasn't much time, and she was unprepared, so unprepared. How could she lead them without her plans? Where were her intelligence reports? She always had intelligence briefings before an operation, but she couldn't remember receiving one.

"Thirty klicks," said the pilot. She didn't know the pilot's name. Or was it Marsh? No, it couldn't be. Marsh had been killed in the Riemus op. She felt a surge of panic. She had to know the pilot's name. How could she let her people be flown into a firezone by a pilot she wasn't checked out on? No, this was a bad op, she couldn't let this continue . . .

"Abort," she snapped into her mike, "abort mission. This is Captain Cassandra Kresnov ordering an abort of . . ." Good God, she'd forgotten the mission codename. That was impossible. She stared helplessly at Stark, who stared back, offering little comfort.

"What's the matter, Cap'n?" Mahud asked her from further along, grinning. "Cold feet?"

"Twenty klicks," said the pilot, and another thrust of G slammed her helmet against the headrest. Fire ripped past, targeting acquired and Cover replied with violence, tracking and tagging . . .

"I'm not meant to be here!" she shouted at them desperately. "I'm not your captain any more, I'm April Cassidy. I'm a cognitive software technician . . ."

Mahud broke into sneezing laughter.

"You're a what?" Dobrov asked her, mildly interested.

"Target approaching, Sandy," Stark intoned warningly. Oh hell, they were all going to die, in a firezone that she hadn't prepared for, in an op without a proper intelligence briefing, because she didn't have her counterpoints locked in and she hadn't a clue what the primary objective was, let alone the withdrawal procedures, and she was going to have to wing it, which meant that they were all going to die. Just like the last time, they were all going to die . . .

. . . And she awoke in fright, bolt upright in bed, dripping with sweat and gasping for air . . .

For a long, long moment, Cassandra Kresnov sat upright in bed, sweat cooling in the mild room temperature, the sheet fallen to her hips.

Sandy. Her name was Sandy. She'd thought that to change it would be simple, and that would be that. Her official records swore blind that her name was and always had been April Cassidy, but the official records were fake. Captain Cassandra Kresnov, Dark Star special ops. As if she could ever have escaped it.

Outside the window the sun was rising. It was 6:24, and she'd had slightly less than six hours' sleep, but anything over four hours was an indulgence really. Sleepiness was not a common affliction for April Cassidy. For Sandy.

She screwed her eyes shut in frustration. Cassandra Kresnov. Sandy, to her friends. If friends they really were. Hard to tell with that bunch of two-dimensional personalities for whom "kill or be killed" was not just a survival strategy but an entire moral philosophy. Perhaps she'd been a bit like that herself, once. Perhaps. But they were all dead now. And she got up, not wanting to think about it any more.

Emerging from the shower, dry and somewhat recovered, she sat on the floor, and stretched. Muscles that had not been seriously exercised in over a week creaked and groaned their displeasure. Stretching helped, but she knew she would be well advised to do some more serious exercise soon. Which would be difficult, considering that most exercise in a place like Tanusha was done in public. But she thought she could probably find something that would do her some good while not frightening the locals too much. Or alerting the authorities.

Breakfast was still seventeen minutes away when she finished, so she sat cross-legged on the bed and jacked herself into the net. Her files were still very much in order within the hotel's protective confines, although they had been accessed several times, as she'd thought they would be. All four accessors were the companies she'd had interviews with yesterday. She sorted through their various data trails in thoughtless reflex, following leads in about twenty directions at once, seeing where they'd been, and what they'd done with the information. Company names, address numbers, access codes formal and not so formal, encryption, bypass pathways . . . it all went flashing past at high velocity, sorted, scanned, and abandoned, each with equal thoroughness. There were a couple of mental question marks, but otherwise, nothing. And her security tripwires, in case anyone started searching down other, telltale avenues, were still in place.

But there was nothing like that. Just a bunch of interested companies running the standard legal background checks on a prospective employee, like any good company should. They'd find nothing but glowing recommendations, too, not least from Boushun Information, for whom she'd done a genuinely excellent job, adding nearly thirty percent to their annual profit figures while she'd been there. But Boushun were upstarts, willing to take a risk on a relative unknown who could possibly have been a security breach for all they'd known, and from what little they could glean from her education files.

She could have been, too, if money had been her motivation—Boushun would have been none the wiser. But she wasn't, and had left Boushun with her bank balance looking very healthy and her much-needed glowing recommendations on file, without which she wouldn't have much chance of getting into one of these Tanushan tech majors. She'd turned down a big pay raise offer on leaving, too, but Boushun couldn't have been too unhappy—she'd left them with a couple of basic design patents that would be raking in at least fifteen percent profit growth per year for the next six or seven years. At least. She felt good about that, too. Boushun had done her a good turn, and she'd done them one in return. It was such a simple thing, this friendly, civilised business of being nice to people. A simple pleasure. She liked it a lot. And besides, there was plenty more where those software patents had come from.

Breakfast was three minutes late again, delivered by the same hotel employee with the bow tie, who again apologised for the slight delay. He seemed friendly even beyond the usual hotel-politeness, and delayed for a few more words, no doubt making the next breakfast even later. Possibly he'd noticed the casually drawn bathrobe and deduced from appearances that she was in the habit of walking naked about her apartment. Probably he wanted to nail her, too.

She smiled wryly to herself, shucking off the bathrobe to eat her breakfast sitting naked on the bed, watching the magnificence of the rising sun among the towers. Screwing room service would certainly not do—he was late enough already. Although he had to get off work sometime. And then there was that man who'd spared a second and a third glance at her in the elevator yesterday morning. He hadn't been bad looking either. She wondered if she'd see him again this morning. Life in Tanusha for a single woman with decidedly pronounced sexual tastes seemed like a pleasant prospect.

"Anything that moves," they'd said in the military, and they hadn't been talking about shooting things.

Sandy, or April Cassidy, or whatever your name is—you are definitely not a one-man woman.

The thought thus composed, she smiled broadly to herself and attacked her breakfast with renewed vigour. All in all, she was feeling much better.

The Tanushan Heritage Gallery was an experience. She wandered slowly across the polished wood floors, interested as much in the setting as the art itself. The walls were long, white, and smooth. Small lights illuminated each exhibit from calculated angles, and the ceiling light was soft and muted. People strolled, and stood, and talked in low, considered voices, studying one canvas or another with serious intensity.

Sandy paused before one such, a tall, rectangular frame that covered much of one wall. It was a mess. Paint everywhere. Red paint, blue paint, green paint, splotted and splashed in thin, seemingly random lines. But not random. She looked closer, eyes narrowed in concentration. Looking for the calculation that must surely exist behind a work like this. It was exhibited in one of the major galleries on the planet, after all. But it was difficult to tell.

But maybe, she thought to herself as she pondered, that was the artist's intent. To make you look. And think. Which struck her as very strange—that an artist could be considered such by challenging the notion of art itself. Possibly even devaluing it. She wasn't sure that she liked the idea.

And straightened before the painting, looking around her at the other people, all considering other pieces of equally abstract work, and taking it all very seriously. What were they seeing? she wondered. Something she could not see? Merely the differences between individuals, perhaps? Or was it something specifically to do with her?

She looked back to the painting and altered the visual signature upon her retinas. It only looked cold and flat. A piece of dead canvas with some paint on it. Changed spectrums, and the colour mix only became even more chaotic. Back to standard light. Same old painting. And still a mess.

She remained in the gallery for some time, enjoying the hushed, thoughtful atmosphere. People moved slowly, and no one rushed. Her comfortable walking shoes squeaked pleasantly on the polished floorboards, and if she tried, she could almost ignore the gathering, grating stiffness that was accumulating in her muscles from lack of recent exercise or massage.

Four hours later, following a pleasant lunch in one of the gallery's restaurants, Sandy moved on. The morning sun above the city streets had given way to thick cloud and rain, steady and persistent. She walked briskly along the footpath from the five-storey, anciently styled gallery building, an umbrella in hand, her overcoat wrapped firmly around her legs to keep the moisture from her casual jeans. Wind gusted through the roadside trees and traffic hissed by on road-wet tires. But it was hardly unpleasant and she walked happily enough, shoes splashing in the puddles as the rain continued to fall.

Lightning flashed nearby through a gap between the massive towers. Then boomed, a deep, guttural rumbling that echoed strangely off the buildings. Huddled under their umbrellas, people looked up. A couple of teenage girls laughed and chattered, hurrying on to where the pedestrian cover made a sheltered walk, safe from the rain save for the occasional driving gust.

Up ahead, a man and woman hurried from cover to a waiting aircab, clambering quickly inside as the doors swung closed—then a building whine, clear and loud above the rush and hiss of the road traffic, and the lights along the pedestrian walk flashed red. People stopped behind the yellow lines, watching as the aircab lifted smoothly away from the cross-striped landing zone and into the air. Sandy stopped too, feeling the familiar static charge prickling at her hair, like pins and needles, then fading as the engine note changed and the aircab accelerated up and away, and the pedestrians walked on again. The next cab in line rolled forward, and the next behind it, rain spilling and beading on slanted windscreens.

In the air above, through the water-stained glass of the ped-cover, Sandy could see the next one coming in to land, taking up the final place in the queue, and the lights at that end began to flash yellow. She had a clear sense of the descending aircab's landing frequency, talking simple, directional binary, up and down the scale as she stepped back quickly to clear the next yellow line. An interesting binary, though, she thought as she walked. A different basic notation from most machine languages. It stood out very clearly.

Thunder crackled, high pitched and racing haphazardly across the sky, then plummeting to a deep, booming rumble that shook the air for several long, ponderous seconds. She fancied she could smell it in the air, that warm ozone smell of a thunderstorm, alive with energy. Behind her, the aircab settled to the ground with a whining thrum of engines.

Again she sensed the binary tone. Reflexively she broke the signal down as she walked, segmenting it into parts. Visualised the odd branches off the third-phase interactive modulators, and the compressed storage segments that they serviced. . . . She sidestepped through the oncoming traffic beneath the long ped-cover, seeing her way without really looking, eyes distant and unfocused. Yes, that was a high band, big meg carrier. It had levels that she could not penetrate, as brief as her reception had been. Probably it was the lightning. Interesting.

She sensed it twice more on the lightrail train, a faintly ghosting presence against the background traffic. The carriages hummed smoothly past rain-wet streets and the occasional flashing light of an intersection. From her seat by the window, she saw several more lightning flashes, gleaming brightly off the tower windows. Above the train's electric whine could be heard the faint, suggestive rumblings of thunder.

It failed to stop the air traffic, though, she noted with an upward glance out of the window. Aircars moved in smooth, curving lines among the towers, obscured briefly by a passing flurry of wet greenery, then visible again. Tower glass reflected an overcast grey, grim, and silent beneath the darkening sky.

"Not much of a day, is it?" the woman sitting beside her said, peering past into the bleak, grey light. Sandy mentally disconnected herself from the net connections she hadn't even realised she'd been using, and smiled.

"I like the lightning," she said. "It makes a day interesting."

The woman gave her a thoughtful look. "That's one way of putting it." And was silent.

Content that there would be no further conversation for the time being, Sandy reestablished her connections. Frequency input involved necessarily less interactivity than a direct linkup, but it served the purposes of a basic search. As before, she went straight to her records. All was in order. No new visitors. She wondered idly how long it would be before one of her interviews resulted in a job offer. And wandered down one of those pathways while the train pulled into its next stop and people began to get up. Found herself at the Wardell Systematics site, which was very solid and professionally intricate, as she expected. The train stopped, doors opened, and those disembarking squeezed past those getting on. Umbrellas were folded, and the new, mildly wet passengers moved to empty seats.

Again that binary signal, and Sandy lost her connection to a momentary rush of static, regaining it almost immediately. For a long, long moment, she stared blankly out of the window, watching as the trees and the roadway and pedestrians began to slide past the windows at an accelerating pace. Her attention was focused instead on the reflection of a man sitting four rows behind her, in a seat by the aisle. He was carrying some kind of communication gear. Its transmissions were somehow linked to that binary signal. That was what had blanked her connections. It was possible, she knew, that it meant nothing. It was even possible, she thought very, very calmly, that it was a total coincidence.

April Cassidy might have had the luxury of believing in coincidences. Cassandra Kresnov did not.

Her eyes roamed the carriage interior, across the broad rows of comfortable seats and the spacious central aisle. A man sat facing her across the space around the carriage doors. He wore a transparent plastic raincoat over his clothes, beaded with moisture. In its distorted reflections of light it held an image of the entire carriage behind her where she could not see without turning her head.

Sandy snap-froze a brief image and stored it. Focused inward on that internal copy, zooming and then scanning. Sections flashed by, faded and blurred. She began sorting, millisecond fast, finding and discarding. Settled on the clearest, and began enhancing it, clarifying the colour fades and reorienting the warped sections. It left her with a final, moderately clear image of a middle-sized Asian man in a dark overcoat, wet about the shoulders and hem. The wet hem caught her attention. It was darkened like puddle-splashes. Like the man had been walking a long way. Most Tanushan business commuters would catch transport. And this man was no tourist.

Sandy pursed her lips gently and exhaled a single, soft breath. Knowing she had no choice but to assume the worst. For now, at least. If she was wrong, well, she would find that out later. A single, panicked thought at the back of her mind wailed despairingly about her dreams of a peaceful life here in Tanusha—all shattered in this brief instant. Blackest despair threatened.

No. She was jumping the gun. Typical military paranoia. She had known that adapting to civilian life would be difficult. This was one of those difficulties—she could not go around assuming the worst at every slight alarm. This might be of little importance. In civilian life many things often were.

So. She resolved to find out.

She climbed to her feet as the train approached its next stop, grasping the overhead handle by the door. Spared the carriage a casual, disinterested glance. The Asian man was reading a magazine. But that meant little.

Out, then, and walked under the pedestrian cover of the small station, by a road intersection. A major tower stood on the street corner opposite. Adjoining that was a large shopping mall, perhaps nine storeys high and sporting external, glass escalators and walkways in a shameless display of architectural ostentation. Sandy jogged towards the mall, the weather giving her an excuse for speed. Leapt quickly up the stairs of the overpass, then walked the covered length above the roadway. A number of people were on the overpass with her, headed in both directions. Scan vision showed them as flowing, multifaceted displays of light, red fading to blue in many subtle shades. Nothing magnetic or electronic, save for the woman with the prosthetic right eye whose neural cordings curled back toward the interface. And the young boy with the headphones, but that signature was slight and inoffensive. Traffic flowed by below. Huge lighted neon proclaimed the superstore chain's name in letters five storeys high. Thunder grumbled, rolling over the traffic and store-music sounds like a wave across a sandy shoreline, and fading gently away.

The mall was enormous. Shops fronted onto open walkways around the central atrium, the full nine storeys high. The transparent roof overhead let in the light. There were glass elevators and escalators by the dozen, all buzzing with people, voices echoing together in their hundreds and thousands, competing with the speaker music.

The red-to-blue flowing shapes now slid past Sandy on all sides. She moved purposefully, her strides even, processing data. The crowds were a distraction to her and a cover for her enemies, if they existed. But they offered protection, too.

She stopped by a databoard and pressed some icons at random. Directories flashed up but she spared them little attention, scanning instead through her peripheral vision, searching for followers. Nothing but the crowds of shoppers, carrier bags swinging. Somewhere within the open atrium an amusement ride was operating, an echoing clatter of machinery and the screams of excited children. Her finger found another icon and the floor display changed again.

And felt a faint flicker of recognition at the periphery of her consciousness. Her eyes flicked up, scanning the open atrium. She immediately registered the spectrum disturbance, a faint shading upon her retinas . . . and found the source a moment later, a man standing at the opposite railing, wearing dark sunglasses. Indoors.

Sandy turned and walked on, her stride now a fraction brisker. Her throat was tight. She'd been found. Who or how was not important, she was certain that they intended no good. They never did. She pushed impatiently past a dawdling couple admiring the window displays. Shrieks from the amusement-riders echoing off the high atrium roof. She tucked her folded umbrella into her overcoat pocket, leaving her hands free, and turned right, stepping quickly across the path of oncoming pedestrians and into the adjoining corridor.

Only now realising that something didn't make sense, that if someone had wanted to get her, their best bet would have been at her hotel room when she was asleep. Not in a crowded shopping centre. Unless, of course, they'd only just found out where and who she was. And had decided not to waste another hour. It was possible that they thought her that important. It was very possible.

Her datalinks were running as she walked, sifting through the regional database, through the official traffic flows that hinted of police movements and security alerts . . . and thought, as she pressed briskly through the corridor crowds toward the road overpass, to check back to her hotel records. Found them barricaded from just beyond the public perimeter, and her presence triggered an alarm . . . she fried the trigger system in a burst of anger, and sent her killer systems speeding out, scanning for electronic target IDs.

Frightened now at the speed things were deteriorating. She knew only too well what was happening. And she knew that moving slowly would gain her nothing—they had her pinged, and no casual pretence would make it otherwise.

She sprinted straight for the overpass opening in the wall ahead. And inside, colliding hard off the railing through the nonexistent gap past some pedestrians, bodies sprawling as she raced onward up the tube, weaving fast through the traffic as yells and shouts broke out around her, ordinary people, startled and angry. She hurdled a small child at nearly thirty kph, and saw through the merging bodies that the narrow exit was blocked by a random convergence of shoppers . . . planted a foot and leapt—astonished, frightened faces ducking for cover as the woman in the long coat went flying low overhead. Collected someone's head with her hip, then hit down on her legs and backside, skidding hard into another two pedestrians in a heavy impact of falling bodies . . . and felt the targeting sight brush her scalp, grabbed the pedestrian for a shield (*don't panic man, they'll never shoot a pedestrian*) then releasing and running backward, darting across to keep the dazed man between herself and the low, crouched figure with the small, black hand weapon . . .

And off up the next hallway, broad and marble, people in suits whom she blew past at inhuman velocity, coattails flapping. Skidded into a painful, controlled collision with an adjoining corridor's side wall then flying up the broad stairway eight steps at a time, turning the top corner at speed as a single shot cracked loudly off the side wall.

Stun shot, was the thought that registered in her mind as she sprang up the next flight. They wanted her alive.

Around the next corner, and the next, sending another pedestrian crashing to the ground as she skidded up the steps . . . and registered double movement up ahead, planted her next foot and leapt hard at them. And hit, grabbing her target right-handed as he dodged, and threw him hard into the back wall while bracing her own legs, slid and hit, then threw herself back at the other man. *Crack!* and her left arm leapt back, Sandy spinning with the shot to collect him with a roundhouse hit to the ribs that smashed him hard into the wall two metres away then sliding limply down the steps up which she'd come.

Running again, checking her linkups to confirm there *was* an aircab stand on this level, and scanning the layout ahead for possible tight points. Her left arm hung limply at her side, numb from the bicep down. She knew from the queasy feeling that it was chemicals. They knew what she was all right. She had to hold the arm as she ran, to stop it from flapping about. It slowed her down.

Past more staring pedestrians, most now alerted to the commotion in the building and standing well back, except for one brave fool who tried to tackle her and bounced off like a rubber ball when she dropped a well-timed shoulder. Then hurtling down another corridor in time to see the safety door sliding to the ground at the far end, cutting her off from the waiting cab rank. She accelerated, was caught five metres short as the door came down, hitting it with full force. Crunch. Rebounded, half stunned, looking around dazedly, trying to regather her linkups and sort herself a new way around. Found there wasn't one—she'd have to retrace her steps or be trapped.

She turned back to the door, wound up her best sidekick, and unloaded with an almighty *boom!* that echoed down the corridor and rocked the half-ton alloy door in its tracks. Swivelled and repeated it, twice, and again, and again. The fifth time, and the left side railings broke away with an explosion of sparks and twisted mechanisms. The sixth half-ripped the entire door from its right-side runners. She squeezed quickly through the gap, torn metal clawing at her coat.

And found herself in an empty cab rank, an open space in the wet, gathering wind. Now about seven storeys up, looking back at the shopping complex. But no sign of aircabs—all the ranks were bare, yellow-striped spaces spattered with rain. Her linkups assured her the rank was still operating—she even had an ID signal from an incoming cab moving about the tower's far side . . .

She scanned further, cracked the signal coding down with furious determination . . . and found the feeder mechanisms, and the alternate subroutines that made it look so real for someone without the time to check it further.

Doors opened on opposite walls, armed men and women walked out, weapons trained on her. Sandy stood and watched them, shoulders heaving, clutching her dangling left arm with her right hand. Realising all too well that there was nowhere left to run. Her legs felt weak, and she was frightened.

One man in particular caught her attention, walking to the front. His face was young, his dark hair fell loosely about his shoulders and his eyes were hard. The weapon in his right hand was fixed unwaveringly on her breastbone. He stopped four metres in front of her, too far, and she knew it. He knew it, too. And grinned at her unpleasantly.

"Let's see you get out of this one, Skin."

And he shot her in the chest.

# CHAPTER 2

arkness. The chemicals stung, and she fought them. Established an active barrier. Failed to get immediately further, which was frightening. She should have been waking up. Unless there was a deliberate blockage, which was more frightening. She focused hard and felt that awareness trigger a response. It grew stronger. Through the tangled pathways of colour and light she found her bearings, and felt the pathways opening up on all sides.

Sounds, faint and distant, now growing stronger. Beeping. It sounded like an audio mechanism for a monitor. Human voices. Indistinct. The whining of something mechanical. Electrical.

". . . can't you . . ."

". . . much I . . . insufficient penetration . . ."

And other things.

Light, multispectrummed and unidirectional. She always saw that first, before the rest. Then brighter, and clearer, and she discovered her eyelids, and blinked. Lips parted, and for the briefest instant she felt them tingling.

She was staring at the floor, she realised. Lying prone on something, face down. She couldn't feel the rest of her body. Yet. Again the whining noise. Then a thick humming. She could smell more chemicals then, rich and cloying. Antiseptic. And suffered a jolt of terror, knowing that smell intimately under different circumstances.

"Nearly full consciousness. Damn that's fast."

". . . not going to be able to shut it down for a while yet . . . the intricacies of those barrier matrixes mean a long, hard time before the infiltrators get close enough."

Sandy tried to speak, but her voice wouldn't work. Just a slight, ineffectual movement of her lips. She was nearly completely paralysed and numb, and was aware of something nibbling, working deeper, somewhere deep inside. She focused inward, searching for her linkups. The connections were sluggish, but they worked. And they told her that something was eating away at her barrier elements.

She searched further. It had a power source, an external link, which meant it was plugged in somewhere. That was bad news. As for what it was . . . and she recoiled as it shocked her, blanking her newly acquired vision back to darkness.

"It's probing. Ran into the barrier elements just then. Probably try again in a moment."

"Right, keep working. Don't get impatient . . ."

It had left an impression when it shocked her, that invader. Sandy pondered over it for a moment. And when she figured she knew what it was, she began to drop a section of her elements, slowly, fading in and out.

". . . here, you see that? That's progress . . ."

"Try it slowly, see what happens . . ."

The invader moved in, sucking in the codes, breaking them down, bit by bit, eating away . . . and greedily bit deeper than it ought.

Sandy raised her elements hard as she could, feeling a surge of fury as she trapped the thing momentarily, and hit it with as high an attack burst as she could muster, right where she thought it most vulnerable. For a moment, it was a complete energy whiteout.

"Shit!" There was a popping noise, and she could suddenly smell something burning, like cabling. "What the fuck was that . . ." and a confusion of activity.

Her vision was clearing. Small muscles in her face, neck, and throat, and down her spine, chemicals cleared out in that energy burst, down the main neural pathways. Down her back and into her legs, a tingling rush of sensation.

"Damn, that's wiped the chemical blockages. She's regaining contact."

"Increase the dosage . . . get that damn unit replaced, it's completely fried, you'll never restart it . . ."

"That's the most powerful neural attack pattern I've ever seen from a Skin . . ."

"Dammit, I told you not to underestimate it."

More commotion, and the movement of equipment. The smoke smell lingered. Someone pulled the cable connection from the back of her skull, only to replace it with another . . . she tried to send another charge up it, but the barriers were too strong, and in her present state she was unable to find the necessary frequency modulations.

She could feel her arms now. Numb, now that the chemical dosage was being reapplied, but she could feel them all the same. She could feel her whole body, except for her left leg below the knee. Numb, but feeling. And she had those connections firmly secured now, she knew her systems well, and knew that once reestablished, no chemicals would entirely displace them. She had adapted.

Another burst of concentration and she had her voice back.

"Where am I?" The sound was little more than a croak, but the words were clear enough. There was a silence, except for equipment shifting.

"Hello Cassandra," said a male voice, after that slight pause. Bemused sarcasm. Coming from somewhere above and behind her. "That is what you call yourself, isn't it? Cassandra?"

The buzzing sound resumed from behind, and something in her right knee tingled faintly, sensation running up and down her leg. It grew stronger, and not at all pleasant.

"What are you doing to me?"

"Joe, can you shut it up?" No audible response.

"Tell me!" She could hear the fear in her own voice, bad as it was. The right leg sensation got even worse. Reflexes tried to move, but nothing happened. It was the drug, and the restraints. And that damnable cord in the back of her head, probing away. She hadn't the strength to hit it again. And it wouldn't make the same mistake twice.

"We could gag her." Sandy realised that she was hardly even breathing, the oxygen was coming from elsewhere. And something in her knee gave way with a hard pop that she felt jamming through her teeth.

"It's not a her," that same male voice replied. "No one calls it her. Got that?" More deep concentration, and Sandy gathered another breath.

"What are you doing to my leg?" An unsteady rasp. Pain, then, of a deep, horrible kind, far from the superficial torment of skin and flesh wounds. Conversational murmurs, working conversation and something crunched agonisingly through her knee, the buffers overriding then, making it numb. Which told her it must have been very, very bad.

Movement, then, to one side of her head, people walking. She rolled her eyes to that side as far as she could, unable to move her head. But in her excellent peripheral vision, she saw one of the lab-coated workers was holding something in his hands, placing it carefully onto a synthetic trolley surface . . . the bottom half of her right leg, amputated at the knee.

That, obviously, was why she couldn't feel her left foot either.

Sandy screwed her eyes shut. Tears leaked through the lids, spilling

onto her eyelashes. She tried to draw a deep breath but found it difficult. This couldn't be happening. It couldn't.

"Stop it," she croaked. No one listened. There was more conversation about other things, and the sounds of more equipment. "You can't
do this. Please. Please stop."

"I'm getting very sick of listening to that." Distracted, and bad-
tempered. "Shock it."

"We'll move faster on the barrier elements if she's conscious . . ."

"I don't care, shock it."

There was a white flash of energy, and more pain, and then darkness.

Awoke with a jolt. And found herself in a living nightmare. Vision
blurred in and out, and the antiseptic odour stank foully. A crushing
pressure weighed upon her consciousness. She felt herself squashed into
a small, cramped corner, forced by something incredibly heavy. She felt
desperately for her elements, finding shards of broken code and jum-
bled, staticlike mess. Her balance was shaky, and things floated.

Sounds came to her as if from a great distance. Voices, once loud,
then soft again. She fought the pressure, panicking, and made herself
a little space amid the nausea, grabbing at the old, steady connections,
squeezing desperately at the clogged pathways . . . and nearly wished
she hadn't. Hard pressure midway up her back, jabbing deep. A popping, hammering vibration, rattling her skull. A sickening wrench
from her right shoulder, one way, then the other. The harsh whine of a
power tool in her ear. A limp weight being shifted. Her arm. An
impossible, grinding agony through her middle, buffers not coming to
her rescue. . . . A frightened, agonised gasp from her lips, air spilling
into empty lungs. Murmurs of consternation from nearby, echoing
through the fractured sanity in her mind.

"*STOP!!!*" she screamed, pure terror wrenching back control of
lungs and vocals. "*OH FUCK, I can't feel my legs, fucking STOP IT!!!*"
Drew another great, sobbing breath, something popping hard up her

spine in an explosion of static pain. *"Oh GOD!!! I'm SCARED, don't DO this to me!!!"* That shrill whining in her ear, hard, crackling pressure through her shoulder joint . . . she couldn't feel her left arm either, it was gone, like her legs, like her entire pelvis . . . *oh Jesus, cut in half, they'd cut her in half and were working up her spine . . .*

*"PLEASE!!!"* she sobbed hysterically, shuddering breaths fighting past the growing, rasping tightness of her throat and chest . . . *"Oh God, I'm begging you . . . NO!!!"* as with one final *crack!* something in her shoulder gave way, then that awful, zero-sensation of something just missing, simply not there anymore. To her right, something limp and heavy was lifted away. Her arm.

She would have screamed. But a scream was insufficient. And then she lost her voice completely, and the pressure crushed her flat and sprawling.

"Got through," she heard a voice, faintly. "That's the final one, it's all downhill from here . . ." And nothing more.

The pressure bore down, hard, cold, and invasive. She fought. The effort was enormous—the pressure consumed, it drank down light, and thought, and everything that was hers and hers alone. It took her space and her thoughts, and her hope. It was despair. It could not be fought.

But she could run. Sandy drew back, retreating down familiar pathways, cross-connections, withdrawing further and further into the deep, dark recesses that only she knew, hiding, making herself small. The darkness followed. It pulled, and it gnawed, and it bit. It threatened to suck her down, into oblivion. Instant by instant, it consumed those last deep pathways, snatching her hiding places, pushing her backwards, further and further, deeper and deeper. There was no hope. But she fought anyway, pointlessly clutching to the last, barest strands of what was hers. It was what she was. And it was all that she'd ever been.

The thing on the operating table was a curiosity. It was a torso, although only barely recognisable as such. A human torso. Separated skin hung in great, thick folds over the table rim, draped like rubbery cloth. Musculature glistened in the theatre glare, thickly structured and coloured a reddish grey. White bone showed in places, the curvature of ribs. Sensory implements protruded from the spinal column like a back-ridge of slim bristles. Below the lowest rib there was nothing, only the glistening cavity where the intestinal tract had been. The spinal column ended abruptly at a single, nubbed vertebra of the middle spine. Rounded bone at the shoulder joint, smooth and glistening. Musculature trailed loosely where it had been separated.

Above perched the black, angular arm of a scanner, waiting and watching, vulture-like. Cabling trailed down from attachments, connections inserted into that mass of wet, red-grey tissue. Systems analysed, took data, stored it. Some emitted pulses and measured the response. People in white coats looked at their monitors and pushed their buttons, absorbed in their tasks.

Beneath a ragged mop of dark blonde hair, the woman who knew herself as Cassandra Kresnov stared sightlessly at the spotless floor, her head held in place with a metal brace, fixed tightly across the forehead. Once expressive blue eyes were blank and unmoving. Eyelids still. Her lips were pale, held slightly apart, as if frozen at the beginnings of a word, or a sentence. From a corner of her mouth hung a thin strand of saliva.

". . . absolutely incredible sophistication," one of the whitecoats was saying to the man with the shoulder-length dark hair. His voice was a hushed murmur in the morgue-like silence broken only by the beeping machines. Screen light reflected off the viewing windows, rapid scrawls of numerical data chasing infinity. "It'd take our biomechanics industries another hundred years to match this level of sophistication."

"I know." The dark-haired man stroked his chin, gazing intently at his monitor. "It makes you wonder."

"Sure does. Hell, I've seen Skins before, but this is something else. The neural integration is just . . ." He let out a small whistle and shook his head. "Absolutely mind-blowing. Seamless growth interface.

There's no telling where the neurology leaves off and the technology begins. She processes datalink information like you or I process a punch in the arm—it's all reflex. More than that, if you or I had to process all the sensory input she receives we'd go mad. But she seems very stable."

"Don't call it she," the dark-haired man said, still watching his monitor. Screen light scrolled across lean, handsome features. The eyes were watching. Cold.

"Force of habit." Ran a hand through short clipped hair. "How long do we have?"

"Long enough." The other man nodded. Cords and cables roamed across the floor. A central screen projected accumulation graphics. Levels rose. The database grew. "Just keep working. No protests when they get here—we'll look after you."

Another nod, though less assured. "With any luck, we'll get a couple of hours." The dark-haired man's lips drew together in a thin line.

"Not the CSA. I'd give you ninety minutes." The second man went back to his work, looking grim. The dark-haired man merely watched his monitor, calculating. If he was worried, it did not show.

What remained of the woman named Cassandra Kresnov merely stared at the floor, hearing nothing. The thin strand of saliva broke, falling unnoticed to the floor. Her eyes registered no response.

Forty-three minutes later, SWAT Lieutenant Vanessa Rice crashed explosively through the main doorway as the doors went flying across the room, propelled by an armoured kick.

"CSA!" she yelled over her helmet speakers, advancing fast with weapon levelled. "Don't move!" One of the startled whitecoats in the decorous office ran for an electronics bank—Vanessa twitched her gun to taser and nailed him with a vicious burst of blue light. The man went down screaming. More shouts and confusion as she ducked through office doors into the surgery proper, more doors and windows

splintering as the rest of SWAT Four crashed in, yells of "CSA!" split-
ting the air, then howls of protest.

"What the hell do you think you're doing!" a bearded whitecoat
shrieked at her as she stormed into the central office, several of her
people barging through adjoining doors. "You can't just come in here
and terrorise people . . ." He got right into her way, and Vanessa threw
him one-handed across the room—propelled by suit armour he crashed
and rolled, nearly hitting the wall.

"I said don't fucking move!" she yelled at the continuing commotion
of whitecoats about their banks of hastily erected electronics, and around
the gear beyond the transparent wall to the side, which appeared to be
an operating theatre. They stopped their fiddling reluctantly . . . one
woman kept working and Vanessa shot her too in a convulsive burst of
blue light and flailing limbs. "Are you morons hard of hearing?"

As her people grabbed those still standing and thrust them
ungently against the walls, wickedly dark, fast armour amid helpless,
stunned technicians, Vanessa strode into the theatre, weapon levelled
at the several techs there . . . and stopped in horror, seeing what
appeared to be a dismembered corpse on the central table, skin peeled
back, spine bristling with monitor needles. The theatre floor was a
convulsive mass of cables and wires, and tubes to siphon blood.

"Oh Jesus." For several long seconds, she couldn't move, immobilised with shock.

"GI," said Hiraki, moving in behind her. Circled about the theatre,
checking the various monitoring equipment through shaded helmet
visor, ignoring the whitecoats who stood aside with forced, nervous calm
. . . not particularly surprised, Vanessa reckoned, in stunned disbelief.

And stared back at the grievous mess on the tabletop . . . GI, of
course it was a GI. That was synth-monitoring gear, even she recognised it, having seen something similar when she'd had her own
enhancements done. A GI . . . oh shit, so that was what this was about,
the FIA were after a GI . . . good Gods, had there been a GI running

loose in Tanusha? How the hell had that happened, and why hadn't the FIA told them like they were supposed to when dragging Federal business into Tanushan territory? And what the hell was all this gear? She directed a stare at the nearest whitecoat, hovering nearby.

"Is it alive?" The whitecoat shrugged. "What did you do to it?"

"LT," said Hiraki, examining a readout on one of the electronics banks, "looks like they're compiling a database . . . I think it's just been transmitted into the net, could be anywhere. This copy just erased itself." He hooked a connector from his suit and plugged it with clumsy armoured fingers from helmet to insert socket. From outside the theatre came the sound of more protest at rough treatment.

"What," Vanessa asked the whitecoat icily, "are you pricks doing here?" Another shrug. "That's not good enough. You don't infiltrate Tanushan security and start a gunfight in public with a GI then just shrug at me when I ask you questions. I'm the law here, fucker. Where did this GI come from, and what are you doing with it?"

The whitecoat just looked at her, lips pressed to a thin, stubborn line.

"It's alive," Hiraki said, staring at another monitor, "I have brainwave function. They've got it hooked up with an infiltrator virus of some kind. . . . I'd guess it's been conscious for some of the time they were cutting."

Vanessa swore, and strode fast to Hiraki's console.

"That's this plug here . . . it's still alive all right, but I don't know how long they can last without life support . . ." She spun around on the whitecoat, who had not moved. "Someone come and get these fuckers out of here," she snarled, disconnecting her helmet lock in a hiss of escaping air and deactivating visor graphics.

The three whitecoats were pushed toward the door, where Sharma and Devakul, weapons steady, awaited them. Vanessa collared her helmet, shouldered her weapon, grasped the sensor plug in the back of the GI's head and removed it.

"Someone get me a chair!" she shouted, raw vocals to the empty air, and in the space beyond the transparent wall someone scurried to oblige . . . Vanessa unwound her own connector from her armour webbing, wrinkling her nose as she realised that something smelt very bad here, a pungent, chemical stench that might have been biosystems-based disinfectant . . .

"LT," said Hiraki, voice muffled behind helmet breather, "what are you doing?"

"I'm going to dive," Vanessa told him, as Bjornssen arrived with a chair. She sat, finally getting the thigh pouch open to unfold a small headset, settled it tightly over her head, made the plug-ins, and jacked herself in with a heavy, eye-blurring click . . . so much for seamless interface, she thought sourly, unfolding the longer connector cord as members of her team gathered curiously about her.

"LT . . ." Hiraki's voice was clearer, having removed his helmet, ". . . that's a GI there. I don't think you should dive without . . ."

"I can set for automatic disconnect if I'm branched," she replied, carefully feeling through the GI's soft, blonde hair for the socket insert . . . found it, and inserted. Felt the familiar, humming buzz somewhere deep, loading and interface programs kicking in, establishing connections, powered by her suit's internal source.

"Vanessa," Kuntoro said warningly from across the operating table, helmet removed, hair flattened and sweaty, "you should wait just five minutes, we'll get an expert team . . ."

"It'll be dead in five minutes," Vanessa retorted. The buzzing pulse grew stronger and she could see the construct now, unfolding before her eyes. She pulled the headset visor down . . . rookie necessity, but Kuntoro was right, it wasn't strictly her specialty. Bright, glowing textures and shapes, nothing like the raw datalines of external VR . . . conceptually compatible graphical-construct, CCG. "The Feds evidently won't talk, and if we lose this GI we'll never know what they wanted with her. This is too big to let go. Now shut up and let me concentrate."

An expert jacker would not have needed that last. She concentrated anyway, and with the visor down, the netscape unfolded more clearly before her eyes, uncluttered by genuine vision. The earplugs gave her sound, a gentle, thrumming pulse.

The GI was there. A large, intricate field . . . spherical and glowing, but only dimly. Light pulsed within the interior, golden and deceptive past the deadened outer layers . . . she moved closer and the spherical field grew enormously in her vision, revealing details. Barrier systems. Interface. Protected, interlocking detail . . . good Gods, it was massive. She stared in bewilderment, unable to conceive how a single consciousness could maintain a field this large in cyberspace . . . all these systemically capable structures.

She reached—an awkward, mental reach with dubious control—a light, probing arm through the emptiness of that simulated space . . . touched. Nothing. The barriers did not respond . . . and they should have, being that massively powerful. There was no conscious response, no lighting of nearby structures . . . just deadness. An intricate mass of outer functions, branches, and junction nodes . . . just dead. Like a ball of rolled-up steel fibres, complex but lifeless. How to proceed? She was baffled. And wondering, then, if she wouldn't have been smarter to listen to her teammates and awaited the experts . . . but caution was not her habit, and never had been.

She chose a pathway and entered. A long, complex passageway with a multitude of branches . . . more than dead, they appeared scraped clean, of a bare and unnatural clarity, like bone parted from flesh. Some connections had been severed, and she could see the gaps where connections ought to be. Internal systems could not communicate. Suddenly, an audio channel clicked open . . .

"*LT?*" Hiraki's voice, tinny and artificial. "*I've got a backup lock on you . . . what do you see?*"

"*Unbelievable,*" she replied breathlessly. "*The field's so far integrated it seems to go all the way into the main brain. Whatever infiltrator virus was hooked up on that cord, it's gone in a long way . . . everything's dead here in the outer systems. I'm going to go in deeper to see if there's something alive in there . . ."*

*"Ricey, I really don't think you should. GIs have neural interface so smooth they can even branch a regular human with basic augmentation. This isn't your average brain-hack we're talking about here . . ."*

*"If it dies, we'll never find out what the FIA were up to. This is huge, Hitoru, I can feel it."*

*"Which will do you no good if it kills you."*

*"Thank you for your concern, now get stuffed."*

She probed further, along mazelike systems of baffling complexity, only now coming to understand what it meant to say that GIs integrated to the networks far more efficiently than a mere augmented human. Human biological augmentation required translation between artificial and organic systems. GIs were entirely synthetic, and translation was only a matter of language, not of diametrically opposed systemologies. Every function of a GI's brain could interface with great independence, thus the complexity of the network field. She herself had to translate everything through a biotech modem, which filtered down the communication efficiency dramatically. But now, she thought as she probed even further into the dead, severed construct, it had proven a vulnerability. The infiltrator virus had hacked its way in, as all data-flows could go both ways. Greater access meant greater reverse vulnerability. And so . . .

She stopped. Before her, a node was dimly pulsing. She remained a long way from the construct's centre, and the node seemed peripheral. But there it was, a dimly, glowing light, where all about was dead. She thought furiously. She had access to programs that could restore and assist these systems, if she could find a way to interface with the GI's still functioning systems, if it had any. She called up a selection panel in the bare, still air before her, and sorted through the varied icons . . .

*"LT,"* came Hiraki on audio, *"you found something?"*

"*Might have. I'm going to try to analyse, see if it's alive or not . . . it's got a lot of life systems to keep functioning . . . some of these nodes have to be functional. Hold on.*"

She selected an icon . . . cautiously. Thinking it was probably the right one, and wondering once more if Hiraki was right and she was being a fool. . . . Her own implant was nowhere near as extensive as this, but there were enough ways into some of her own basic systems if the GI was powerful and clever enough, and she was leaving herself awfully wide open . . .

She activated the icon. Nothing. The node just pulsed, a chaotic, spiderlike junction point of many twisting arms and connections, many severed, but still pulsing dumbly, with stupid, unthought reflex . . .

Abruptly her selection panel vanished and the node ceased pulsing in favour of bright, alarming energy. In the walls and passages about her, strands sprang to life, bright paths of gleaming colour streaking across the walls. About her, the simulated air appeared to crackle, a dense, prickling sensation like static electricity on a humid day.

"*LT?*" came Hiraki's voice. He sounded alarmed. "*LT, get out of there right now, I read a huge reactivation sequence right in your region . . .*" and abruptly cut, in a burst of frightening audio static. Vanessa tried her cutoff sequence . . . it should have pulled her out, retracing her path at high velocity, but nothing happened. She backed up, forcing a flying retreat, but the air itself seemed thick as sludge, and prickling static leapt like bad pins-and-needles across her imagined, virtual skin . . .

Something probed her audio sequence . . . she could feel her heart hammering, back in some corner of her brain that continued to monitor such things, real fear at the power of this entity that now glowed in the air about her, and lit all space with brilliant curls and coils of light. Her last audio barrier fell, and it had her frequency with alarming ease . . .

"*. . . who are you . . . ?*" A small, quiet voice. Distant but not mechanical, not artificial as Hiraki's had been. Not simulated. A real,

weak, pain-filled voice, as real as a warm, gentle whisper in her ear.
"... *what are you doing here* ... *?*"

"I'm Vanessa." Her own voice sounded somehow clearer, on this strange alien channel. Things seemed thick and clear, as if under water. "I'm with the CSA. I'm here to help you."

"... *help* ... *me* ..." Which could have been a repetition, or a plea, she wasn't sure. "... *no* ... *structure* ... *no support* ..." A pause that might have been a sigh. Or a gasp, straining for strength. In the space about, the gleaming construct lines flickered and danced alarmingly. "... *too* ... *much damage* ..."

"I can help you," Vanessa said urgently. "Let me help you. Stop resisting, let me establish a linkup, you're too badly damaged to re-establish your own systems, we can feed you the programs externally that will rebuild your pathways ..."

"... *trick* ..." said the voice. Small, weak ... and scared, Vanessa realised with shock. She could feel the emotion clearly, could smell it in the simulated air. The construct reverberated with thick, cloying fear and pain. For a moment it was almost overwhelming.

"It's no trick. I'm with the CSA. We've arrested the people who've done this to you. If you don't let me in, you're going to die anyway. Let me help you. I want you to live."

"... *why* ... *?*" God, an honest question. An innocent, hurting question from someone with no reason at all to believe her ... *someone*, good Lord. She could feel the presence, could feel it probing weakly, trying to feel, trying to live ... Someone. This wasn't a machine. This was a person. It hit her with a force of revelation that almost left her speechless.

"Because," she said after a brief regathering, "we want to catch the people who ordered this done to you. And no one deserves this."

A moment's indecision. Fear. Reluctant, for reasons Vanessa could only too well understand, now that she'd seen, and heard, and felt. It thought she was going to finish it off. It did not want to be powerless. And it had no reason to believe that anyone would consider it worth saving.

Then, "... *go* ..." And the light about her began to fade, retreating down broken, fragmented pathways, a distant pulsing left in its wake. In haste, Vanessa recovered her selection panel, and activated the correct icons ... another gathering, humming sensation, her programs unfolding, a gleaming, latticework link unfurled, shooting up the deadened pathway down which she'd come, establishing hooks and feelers into the walls as it went. Past and over her, reaching for the pulsing node ... ripples spread, as if on the surface of a still pond. Interface accepted, established, and did not reject. The node glowed, and the glow spread, gathering to accumulate in many branches around, pausing at severed links, rebuilding as it went. The interface grew, assisted now by the GI's own systems, which merged smoothly with the growing flood, directing, mapping, showing the way ... with greater direction, the flow continued, and the surrounding universe began to gleam with pulsing, spreading energy. It was only a small portion of what needed to be rebuilt. But it was beginning.

Vanessa retreated, wanting to be clear of the construct's depths before it restored to anything like full power, feeling that she might not normally be so welcome here.

But, "... *thank you* ..." a soft voice whispered, weak with emotion and fading among the gleaming, broken strands.

... And she surfaced, eyes flashing open to reveal a glaringly bright operating theatre, and a cluster of worried armoured SWAT personnel gathered around, and someone shining a penlight into her eyes ... she batted him aside, unplugged herself, and leapt to her feet, mind spinning, breath coming hard as she strode across the room and stared sightlessly into space for a moment.

"LT?" came a cautious voice from behind her. Armoured footsteps approached, doubtless concerned that she might not be entirely together. Or sane for that matter. "Are you okay?"

"Jesus Christ," she said breathlessly, slowing her racing heartbeat with an effort. Spun about, to find a half dozen anxious faces staring at her, and Singh the one venturing close, the one with medical training. He held up four armoured fingers.

"LT, how many?"

She ignored him, and strode about the table, staring at the half-torso that lay there, stripped of skin and bristling with monitoring implements . . . most recognisably not human, at this range—incredulously similar, but she had seen autopsies firsthand and they were nothing this neat and precise. . . . She still held the headset in her hand, a trailing cord along the floor to the GI's head, connected to her suit's exposed collar. Continuing to feed the code, and make corrections and adjustments as it went.

"LT?"

"She's alive," she said breathlessly, staring at the GI. "She's taking code. I think she'll be okay but not if she doesn't get fixed up . . . Christ, we've got to get the paras here. Those look like clean cuts—they should be able to reattach easily enough. They do it to humans all the time if the cut's clean enough . . ."

"She?" asked Sharma, frowning. Vanessa stared at her, wide-eyed and slightly dazed.

"Yes, she. Her name's Sandy." How the hell did she know that? The GI hadn't told her. "She's scared. And confused. She doesn't know what she did to deserve this."

Stares from her guys. They thought she'd gone crazy. It happened sometimes to people who dived too deep, or stayed too long, or poked their reckless noses where they weren't welcome. Something bleeped on her inner-ear frequency. That was backup arriving, landing on the roofpads. She made a connection.

"*Naidu,*" a voice acknowledged in her inner ear, "*go Vanessa.*"

"We have to get the best biotech surgeons and specialists available. There's a GI here and she's in bad shape."

"*A GI?*" Pause. "*Shit, that explains a few things. I'll get everyone. I don't think they'll have to be asked twice.*"

Vanessa strode back around the table, ignoring her gathered team and careful not to entangle the cord. Knelt down by the GI's immobilised, blonde-haired head, an uncomfortable move in the bulky armour, and gazed at her face. The eyes stared unsighted at the floor, loose hair framing features that might have been beautiful under other circumstances.

You'll be okay, Vanessa thought, remembering the sensation of hurt and fear, and despair. Remembering the voice, distinctly female now that she remembered it, whispering in her ear. We'll fix you. Whatever you are, and whatever you've done, no one deserves this. Not even a GI.

# CHAPTER 3

Several times she woke. It was exhausting, being awake. Sleeping was just as bad. Her interface rebuilt itself, no longer needing the external feeds, and her sleep was delirious. She dreamed dreams that made no sense, of dark, shifting shapes and flooding, incoherent emotion. It washed her like a tide and left her scoured and bare. She lost all track of time, and struggled for sanity.

Awoke once more, and discovered after several searching minutes that she was face down on a bed. She had no access to her links, completely shut out, and something was hooked into her access. Reading responses, private things, like pain, and basic sensation. It registered that she was awake.

"Ms. Cassidy?" came a voice, distantly, from across a vast, unbridgeable distance. But that was not her name and she ignored it.

"April?" the voice tried again, many times. Something was pressing at her feet, she was vaguely aware . . . and found time to wonder at why feet should be significant enough to trigger a surge of unthought relief.

"Cassandra?" the voice tried again. Finally, the right name. She applied some effort, and tried to open her eyes. Her vision was dark and she shifted spectrums, trying for regular light . . . shapes remained indistinct. Further adjustment, and light drowned everything. She could find no in-between and moved instead to infrared, merged with motion-sense . . . it hurt her eyes to hold it there, but she could at least make basic sense of her immediate surroundings, as regular light alone could not. Sounds echoed badly. Of smell or taste she had no hope, her tongue swollen and dry, her sinuses blocked. "Cassandra Kresnov?"

She tried to speak, but nothing came out. Forced air from her lungs with an effort, and managed . . . "that's me." A small, dry whisper.

"Can you feel your feet, Cassandra?"

". . . a little . . ." Pause.

"Does that hurt?" Stupid question.

". . . never does . . . short of bullets . . ." She felt terrible, all over. She wanted to go back to sleep.

"Cassandra, you're going to be fine. We've fixed everything, the incisions were very precise and everything fit back together very easily. It was much easier than a normal human. So don't you worry. You're going to be perfectly okay."

She didn't feel perfectly okay. She felt like shit. Being patronised made her feel worse.

"We're going to put you back to sleep now. I'll see you again when you wake up." She had just enough time to decide she didn't like being turned on and off like a light switch, before the darkness hit her once again.

The next time she woke she was alone in a room. A big room with big, sunlit windows. She realised she felt much more clear-headed, and could see better. She could certainly see the sunlight. It was beautiful.

The windows went all the way around the room, and everywhere were the spires of tall buildings in a gleaming blue sky. Aircars passing. Light reflecting from glass. Light splashed over the lounge suite and pot plants, and she realised that it was not a regular hospital ward. More like a live-in apartment, her bed settled over in a corner behind the chairs, a dresser at her side. And an IV drip, with computer monitor.

After an indeterminate time watching the sunlight, some people came in. She heard a double-lock clack before the door opened and deduced with light-headed surprise that it was a secure room. Like a prison, really. But a nice prison.

"Cassandra?" said a man. She shifted her head minutely to look, and discovered that there was a plug in the back of her skull, connected to a cord that ran to the computer bank. She stared at it stupidly for a moment, feeling no real surprise. "Cassandra, these men are from the CSA. That's the Callayan Security Agency. They would like to have a word with you. Do you mind talking to them?"

A question. Questions required answers. She remembered thinking so. How to answer . . . she strained her memory. Do you mind? It wasn't much of a question, really. Since when did it matter if she minded or not?

"Cassandra," said a different man with an interesting accent. The sensor plug cord on the pillow beside her head finally lost her interest, and she looked at him. A heavy, brown-skinned man. Indian, she recalled. Long, unruly hair. That was unusual. "We are directing a very important investigation, Cassandra. We are trying to catch the people who did this to you. They were FIA, Cassandra, Federal Intelligence Agency. Would you like to help us catch them?"

Another question. It was asking too much of her, in this state, to answer questions. And they were blocking her view of that lovely sunlight through the windows. She wished they'd move a little, all three of them.

"Cassandra," the man said after a moment, more forcefully this time, "what are you doing in Tanusha? Why did you come here? Why did you leave the League?" Pause. "Do you understand me?" Then aside to the doctor, "Can she even hear what I'm saying?"

". . . are you a Hindu . . . ?" she asked the man, in the soft whisper that was as much of a voice as she could muster. A moment's consternation.

"Yes. Yes, I am a Hindu. Cassandra, this is very important . . ."

". . . I like Krishna . . ." she whispered. ". . . he's a good god . . . and Ganesh. Do you have a favourite . . . ?" Another pause. She wondered if he could hear.

"I've always been very partial to Lakshmi, myself," came the reply after a moment.

". . . if I ever had a religion, I think I might like to be a Hindu . . ." It seemed an important thought. She had often wondered what it felt like, having a religion. Believing in something. Belonging to it. Now, of all times, it felt important.

"If you could answer my questions," the man replied, "maybe I could help you to become a Hindu. Would you like to answer my questions?"

The doctor, she saw, was checking some readings on the bedside screens. Said something to the men. Something about drugs, postoperative procedures, and it really being too early . . .

"Cassandra," the man persisted, coming very close then, "I have an extremely important situation on my hands here, I am trying to catch the people who did this to you. These are very dangerous people, Cassandra, and they're loose in my city. Please help us catch them."

". . . it's not my war any longer . . ." she whispered. Her vision was all a blur, and she closed her eyes. ". . . it's not my war. It was never my war . . ."

"Cassandra." A hand descended hard upon her arm, her reflexes jerked in fast override of the drugs and someone yelled, a rush of jostling commotion, people surrounding the bed, grabbing the Indian man. Attempted vainly to peel her fingers away from his arm, a steel-hard grip through a handful of bedcovers. She realised dimly that she was still holding on, and let go. The Indian man staggered backward, assisted by alarmed colleagues. The room was filled with much alarm.

". . . I'm sorry . . ." she murmured, ". . . don't surprise me . . . too many drugs . . . bad reflexes . . ."

"I'm okay," the Indian man said, shaking them away, "I'm fine. She didn't hurt me."

"I think we'd better put her back to sleep," someone said warily, and there was movement to comply.

". . . no . . ." It was as much of a protest as she could muster, dazed and half blind on her back. ". . . no . . . please . . ."

When she awoke again it was dark. Night light shone through the windows. City light. Tower tops gleaming in the surrounding dark, and the blinking passage of aircars. Time had passed. She wondered how much, before remembering that she hadn't known the time the last time she was awake either.

She felt stiff from lying too long on her back and made to roll over. And found she could not. Her wrists were bound to the bed. Her ankles too, she discovered when she tried to move her legs. Her pulse rate rose and immediately sedative was flowing into her, she could feel it, a cold, creeping numbness from the tube in her arm, up the shoulder and into her chest. Her muscles were going limp. She breathed deep, calming breaths and tried to remain awake.

Succeeded, though barely. Through her bandage-wrapped body, the cold feeling remained, eating at her nerves. It scared her, both the cold and the bandages. Her bedside machine read the fear and pumped more sedative. It left her dazed, numb, and only barely conscious, struggling vainly for awareness, for some sense of where she was, and what had happened to her. She remembered, vaguely. Remembered horrible things. But she did not want to remember more now lest the machine put her entirely to sleep.

The discomfort was acute, all through her body. Not pain. Tightness. Wrongness. Damage, slowly repairing itself and being repaired. She needed to move, to get blood flowing, to loosen the stiffness. But she could not. Not struggling was an effort. Staying awake was. She did not want to sleep—she had slept far too long already. But waking was agony. And life itself promised little better. She was scared, and trying to repress it because of the machine, not wanting to sleep, not even free to feel her fear lest it drag her back to an oblivion of delirious dreams and turbulent darkness. Tears rolled from her eyes, wetting her temples. She lay in the light-strewn darkness for a full five minutes, in soundless tears, before the effort grew too great and she surrendered to the machine, and the darkness it granted.

"Lieutenant," said Naidu, rising to his feet as Vanessa passed the security door, restowing her badge in her jacket pocket. Behind her, one of the armed security guards saw the door securely shut and locked. Another man was present, she noted. He also stood. It looked like a waiting room, with comfortable chairs, a potted plant, and paintings on the wall. An adjoining doorway was open, revealing a complex battery of monitors, multiple screens and displays, watched by several seated operators. "I hope we did not spoil your evening. Did you have something planned?"

"Why me?" Vanessa asked him, fixing him with a very hard stare. Yes, she had had something planned, something intended to help fix her marriage, no less. Now her work had intervened yet again, and she was not impressed. Naidu perhaps read as much in her expression and got quickly to the point.

"She has been unresponsive," he said. He looked troubled, his longish, grey-streaked hair in a greater state of disarray than usual, his open-collared shirt rumpled beneath the jacket. "Obviously she is suffering from shock . . . the doctors recommend to leave her alone, but right now I don't have that luxury. The evidence suggests the FIA presence in Tanusha may be far larger than we had first anticipated."

"How much larger?" Arms tightly folded, and not at all surprised at the confirmation of this particular rumour . . . it had been making the rounds through CSA circles ever since the GI had been recovered three days ago. Intel, of course, had difficulty admitting to a large, undetected infiltration. And she watched, with merciless satisfaction, as Naidu shifted uncomfortably, ran a weathered brown hand through his hair.

"A lot larger," he admitted. "There are some very weird things going on in this city, Vanessa . . . some of them we are already on top of, and a lot more we're not. Obviously it's connected to the GI somehow, but she won't talk. And we no longer have the luxury of allowing her time to get over her trauma. We need answers."

"Which goes back to my question," Vanessa said impatiently. "Why me? I'm a SWAT lieutenant . . ." She held up a hand, forestalling Naidu's predictable response. "Yes, I know, I made contact with her, you think she might trust me, et cetera, et cetera . . . I'm not an analyst, Rajeev, I don't know what questions to ask. I'm not trained with interviews, I'm not a biotechnician and I'm sure as hell not a psychoanalyst . . ."

"So much the better. She appears to react very negatively to anyone smelling of 'establishment.' You are the closest thing this city has to an indigenous combat soldier, Vanessa, and I feel you might be our best chance of getting her to talk right now."

"It's just another piece of manoeuvring," Vanessa retorted. "She'd be stupid not to see it. You think she's stupid?"

"That remains to be seen, but her false identity documentation would suggest otherwise—it was quite flawless, probably the best I've seen . . ."

Another man entered from the monitoring room, a small man of Indonesian appearance in a dark brown suit.

"Ah, Lieutenant Rice, I am Dr. Djohan, the biotech surgeon. Mr. Naidu has briefed you on the situation, ah?" He came to a brisk stop before her. Small as he was, he was taller than Vanessa.

"Yes," Vanessa drawled.

"Good." He clapped his hands together. "Now firstly, when you are in the room with her, do not get too close. Mr. Naidu did that and she grabbed him, not hard . . ." as Vanessa shot Naidu an alarmed look, ". . . but harder than we'd thought possible with the repressant drugs. Evidently she has some sort of short-term reflexive resistance, so we've felt it safer to keep her restrained and heavily sedated. It also lessens the chance of self-inflicted injury and allows her more time to heal free of unnecessary movement.

"Now, you do know what she is, don't you?"

Vanessa frowned. "You mean she's not a regular GI?"

"Hmm . . ." The little doctor spared himself a small, amused smile. "From what little she has told us, her designation is GI–5074J-HK. Now, that is a most unusual designation. The first two digits typically designate the design type. Most GIs range from the twenties to thirties. Anything higher than a thirty is very advanced, and from the literature I'd read I hadn't been aware there *was* anything higher than a forty. But even a cursory examination of her interface capability suggests that her story is probably true—her neural interface patterns are simply extraordinary. We suspect she is an experimental model, which would perhaps explain her erratic behaviour in being here in the first place. Dark Star, as you know, is the most specialised and lethal of all League Special Operations units—their GIs aren't in the habit of wandering off, usually.

"Oh . . . and the HK at the end is standard League abbreviation for Hunter Killer." Vanessa blinked. "Just so that you know what you're dealing with here. Always bear it in mind, Lieutenant—this is a killing machine, designed to replicate human biological function in so close a mimicry that it is most difficult, without close examination, to tell the difference. But however apparently close to humanity she may appear, make no mistake, she is artificial, and she is most indisputably designed to kill.

"Are you aware of synth-alloy myomer?"

"I know they use something like it in combat armour suits,"

Vanessa replied cautiously. "It's the most advanced form of mechanical myomer available. It generates enormous power under contraction and can contract to densities in the body-armour range."

"Indeed," said Dr. Djohan, with an impressed little smile. "She's made of it. It substitutes for her muscles. Bone is ferro-enamelous, roughly equivalent in strength to spacecraft hull ribbing . . . it needs to be to withstand the enormous power generated by those muscles. Make no mistake about it, Lieutenant, even drugged she can kill. Undrugged, the restraints would be as worthless as tissue paper, and she could happily rip us all limb from limb. Now, do you have any questions?"

The secure room was spacious and attractive, Vanessa saw as she entered. A regular apartment, under other circumstances, with wide bow windows following the curving contour of the external wall, a lounge suite and coffee table, and an inset kitchen off to the left. The view of the Tanushan nightscape was typically spectacular, ablaze with sprawling, towering light, alive with moving traffic. The GI's hospital bed was pushed against the partial wall for the kitchen, a bank of life-support equipment beside it. Vanessa approached, feeling distinctly uneasy.

The GI appeared to be sleeping, her shortish loose blonde hair across her face upon the pillow. The full length of her beneath the covers, Vanessa saw, remembering all too well the horror of the last time she had seen her, this GI, this artificial whatever-she-was, if she could even be called a *she* with any degree of accuracy. . . . The GI rolled her head upon the pillow, and looked up at her. Soft blue eyes in a broad, pale face. Blinking blearily in the soft light. Gazed at her sleepily amid the sprawl of light hair. She looked, Vanessa thought, a most unlikely killing machine. Nearly as unlikely as she herself was as a SWAT lieutenant, she thought wryly.

"Hi," said Vanessa. Folded her arms defensively, uncertain. The GI simply looked, registering no expression. "I'm Vanessa Rice. You remember me?"

A flicker of response in the large blue eyes. God, Vanessa thought, startled . . . she was gorgeous. Stupid to be surprised, was her second thought, of course she was gorgeous—she was artificial, and it would take no more effort to make an attractive GI than an unattractive one. She guessed. And looks were good for socialisation, and thus confidence. Probably that mattered, somehow.

". . . Vanessa . . ." A small, hoarse whisper, the blue eyes studied, steadier than the voice. Up and down, with effortless, pondering attention. Vanessa stood, and continued to feel uncomfortable. ". . . I remember you . . ." Very quietly. ". . . you were there . . . when it happened . . ."

"Yeah," said Vanessa. "I was." Wondering if she had, in fact, done the right thing in saving this woman. Or whatever she was. Wondering if she'd come to regret it. The GI turned her head slightly, softly grasped a thin plastic tube between her lips, and sipped liquid. Rested back on the pillow, and stared at the ceiling.

". . . I thanked you, then . . ." came the small voice. Hushed in the quiet room, ". . . now I'm not so sure . . ."

"I can imagine," Vanessa told her, eyeing the faint bulge beneath the tucked bedcovers that indicated the restraints. There were a lot of tubes running from beneath the sheets.

The GI looked at her obliquely. ". . . you took a risk . . ."

Vanessa shrugged. "We needed you. The CSA. We needed to know what the FIA were up to. Why won't you help us?" A pause. From somewhere came the faint whirr of ventilation, and behind it the distant hum of nighttime traffic beyond mostly soundproofed windows.

". . . I don't know . . ." the GI said after a moment. ". . . I guess I'm not feeling very helpful . . ." Her eyes appeared damp, staring at the ceiling. Vanessa frowned, looking more closely. Did GIs cry? She'd never heard so.

"You're talking like it's all over," Vanessa said, frowning. "Like your life's gone and you'll never get a new one."

". . . well I won't, will I . . . ?" Still the small, quiet whisper. ". . . not in the Federation . . ."

"You always give up so easily?" The GI did not reply for a moment, then glanced across at her, a curious shift of gaze. Less impressed, with that comment. It was at least a response. "What do you think this city is? You think there's no free debate here?, No due process? If you defend yourself, not everyone is going to want you locked up . . ."

". . . I've seen the news shows . . ." A cool, firming of the whisper, the damp eyes hard. ". . . I know what people think of GIs. What did the doctor tell you when you came in? Nice Dr. Djohan? Watch out for the GI, she'll kill you when you're not looking . . . ?"

Vanessa frowned at her. Pondering that. Snorted in humourless laughter.

". . . exactly. What's my legal status? There's no precedent for GIs in Federation society. Even the League wasn't real keen to let me mix with civvies. Lobby groups here will flip their lid. Rainbow Coalition . . ."

"So you're just going to let them win? You're not even going to fight?" Challenging. Feeling herself increasingly irritated by this irrational defeatism. She couldn't understand it, had never understood defeatism in any form. It baffled her. "Dammit . . . Cassandra." It was, she recalled, the GI's name. "Cassandra . . . Tanusha is a weird place. Politically it's like a madhouse sometimes . . . not everyone will automatically hate you. Some may even like you, if you give them a chance. But you've got to help us, you've got to tell us what's going on, and what you know. Right now you just look like you're protecting someone."

The damp blue gaze was now slightly incredulous. Vanessa exhaled a hard breath, wondering how she could explain this city to a GI, a noncivilian by birth, who had never known civilian life and had no concept of what ordinary people thought.

". . . what makes you think I'm likeable . . . ?" Vanessa blinked, surprised by that. The GI was wondering why she, Lieutenant Vanessa

Rice, was defending her. No doubt thinking it was a ploy to win her cooperation.

"Aren't you likeable?" Which got a cool, effortless stare from the GI. It was unnerving. There was something in those eyes that was not . . . not entirely human, she supposed. But it did not feel malicious. Not even particularly dangerous. Just intent. But it was strange, and gave her goose bumps. "Prove it to me. Prove to me you're a likeable person. Prove to me you're decent. You might not be, I've no idea. But I'll listen. That's the point, Cassandra. Opinions are formed through experience. If you can show people that there is at least *one* GI in the known universe who *is* a decent person, then who knows?"

". . . there's more than one . . ." the GI whispered in reply. Took a slow breath, and sighed. ". . . there's so much more . . . or was . . . but people have no idea. People never do . . ."

"Hey, don't write me off. Convince me." She grabbed a chair from the end of the bed, and placed it alongside. Not at all certain of what the hell she was doing, or if it was the slightest bit sane . . . except that she remembered that dive, in the operating theatre, and remembered the presence that she had felt. Overstretched as she'd been, vulnerable in cyberspace, in the midst of a neural structure that was so much more powerful than her own, even in that weakened state . . . and she was still alive. That in itself had to count for something. "Why did you come to Tanusha? You were on Reta Prime before that, right? We traced you back that far."

The GI stared at her for a long, unblinking moment. Vanessa sat, arms folded, awaiting a reply with stubborn determination. Then, ". . . you've seen my software skills. Tanusha's the largest software and infotech centre in the Federation, outside of Earth . . ."

"You were looking for a job, is that it?"

". . . a life . . ." came the soft, gentle correction.

"What was wrong with the life you had? You must have been pretty important in the League."

". . . far too important. They were so careful of me . . ." A distant look, remembering things past. ". . . officers needed a security clearance just to talk to me. Psych analysis. They were never that careful with the others . . ."

"Why? What made you special?"

". . . GIs aren't bright, Vanessa . . ." The eyes refocused on her own with tired resignation. ". . . not real smart, as a rule. You've read the combat reports. Feds always said their greatest advantage against us was brains. GIs can be smart in straight lines. Rarely laterally . . ." Vanessa nodded, she had indeed read as much. Combat reports were a great source of useful material for any SWAT commander.

"And you are?" she guessed.

The GI sighed, softly.

". . . yeah. For all the good it did me . . ."

Vanessa blinked, realising something. A possibility. It unfolded before her like a map. She caught her breath.

"Is *that* why you left the League? You decided you didn't like their war?" Silence from the GI, not protesting the assertion. "Hang on, let me get this . . . the League created a GI capable of lateral thought process as . . . as what, an experiment?" Still no argument. "But the result is that you think *too* laterally for them, and decide you don't want to fight any more. Why would they risk creating a GI who wouldn't agree with their philosophies?"

A faint, almost imperceptible shrug beneath the covers. ". . . that's freedom of thought for you. That's the risk you take when you allow people to think entirely for themselves . . ."

"So why take that risk?"

". . . as an experiment. To make me more dangerous. GIs were always getting outsmarted by Feds. GIs were never as effective as people on either side seem to think. Lost thousands in stupid ambushes, kids' stuff. They figured they wanted a GI with all the perks but smart. Ought to be unstoppable . . ."

"Did it work?"

". . . oh yes . . ." With great sadness. ". . . an unqualified, extraordinary success . . ."

Vanessa suffered another chill, more severe than the last. Her mind switched back to what she was supposed to be asking. The information wanted by Intel, and Naidu in particular.

"So you came here with no ulterior motive whatsoever," she said. And let the implied question hang there for a lingering moment, slowly revolving. "The League's expansionist biotech policies had nothing to do with it?"

The GI breathed deeply through her nose, a gentle rise-and-fall of her chest beneath the covers. Flicked a glance up past her toward the ceiling behind, and the walls.

". . . they're watching me. I feel like I'm in a zoo . . ."

"Cassandra, why won't you . . ."

". . . I don't like these restraints, Vanessa. They're driving me crazy . . ." There was pain in her eyes, emotional pain, lips pressed thin. ". . . the drugs alone are enough, you don't need the restraints. I need to move . . ."

"You grabbed Naidu."

"Christ, it was a reflex . . ." With hoarse exasperation, her thin voice trying to rise above its forced whisper. ". . . I didn't hurt him. I was drugged stupid, I could hardly think. Look, you can put a guard in here with a tranq, if I move he can drop me . . ."

"You're avoiding the question," Vanessa told her.

Light flared in the deep blue eyes.

". . . damn right I am. You think I'm going to help people who treat me like this? With this damn machine feeding me sedative every time my pulse goes up, until you come in for an interview of course? Fuck you . . ."

It was desperation, Vanessa thought. And fear. She thought about taking the restraints off. Thought about trusting her, despite what

Djohan had said. It not only meant disobeying instructions. It meant getting close, bending down to undo the straps. Trust or no trust . . . synth-alloy myomer, Djohan had said. Unbelievably powerful stuff. Undrugged, GIs could crack a human skull like a nut, barehanded. Human physiology was nothing to them, fragile like gossamer, to break up and fly away on an errant breeze.

". . . look at you . . ." the GI whispered. ". . . you can't do it, can you? I've made love with straight humans, Vanessa, they never knew the difference. They enjoyed it. But just one piece of knowledge, and everything changes. I'm still the same. It's you who's different. You're doing it to yourself . . ."

"I don't know what I can do about that," Vanessa replied. Shaken, in spite of herself, by the GI's calm, quiet appraisal. The worst bit was that it sounded like truth. "How do you measure trust, Cassandra? I mean . . . how much risk is worth it? Look at it from my perspective. If I'm wrong, I die. Is that worth *any* risk? For someone I don't even know?"

". . . you already risked it once . . ." Again, it hit her, unexpectedly hard. Not having expected this calm, thoughtful logic from a GI. She was rattled and uncertain how to proceed.

"That was different," she said after a moment.

". . . impulsive . . ." whispered the GI. ". . . illogical. Now that you've got time to sit and think about it, you realise it was a stupid risk to take . . ." Vanessa blinked, not knowing anything to say to that. ". . . and you wonder why I don't like my chances here . . ."

A long silence. The GI gazed at the ceiling, sad and still. Vanessa watched, trying desperately to think of something that would fix it, and make it all better. But there was nothing.

"I'm sorry," she said after a moment. "I really am. If you are who you say you are . . . I'm really sorry. But I don't know."

". . . you remember the dive . . . ?" Glancing across at her. Almost hopefully. Vanessa caught her breath, remembering the VR immersion, the GI's huge, damaged field, the glowing lines and strands. The danger she'd been in, within the GI's structure. The presence, weak, but enough to finish her if it had wanted, in her tenuous position. It had not. And she remembered emotions, pain, desperation, determination, longing. . . . The memory assailed her once more, as powerful as a first grade tactile interface, triggers in the brain that recalled the experience as real, which it sometimes did on really deep dives.

She remembered a lot. And she wondered, then, how much the GI remembered of that necessary mutual embrace.

". . . I know enough about you, Vanessa . . ." the GI whispered. The blue gaze was back, holding her attention, mesmerising. ". . . I know you're a good person. I forgive you . . ."

"How much do you know?" Vanessa whispered, half in shock, her eyes wide. For the briefest of moments, a faint smile touched the GI's lips.

". . . not enough to scare you. Just enough to know you from a vegetable. But that's enough . . ."

Vanessa stared at the GI.

". . . and Vanessa? I know all about the League's biotech infiltration policies, I even helped on a few of the implementations. They do have ties with Callayan biotech firms, I know that much. Encryption here is lax, freedom of network information and all that—it lets the underground shuttle things around out of sight, but you already know that. I never learned the names. But penetration into major Tanushan BT firms is at least eighty percent—that's from League Intel reports I read three years ago.

". . . no, my being here has nothing to do with it. I knew it was the best place for software, and I wanted a good job. I made such a good civilian. I was better at that than I was even at soldiering . . ." With faint humour. ". . . and none of it explains the FIA. Although I do know of a few FIA secrets and about their own secret research into very illegal biotech that most Feds won't know. Would you like me to tell you?"

Vanessa stared. Turned and looked once over her shoulder, at the cameras there, recording everything. Imagined Naidu, Djohan, and half a dozen other Intel operatives gathered about the monitor screens next door, leaning forward in tense, nervous anticipation, biting fingernails. And she turned back to the GI, patiently waiting.

"Yes," she said. "Yes please."

It was an hour before she emerged, blinking wearily, and wondering if Sav would still be awake. Her husband had become increasingly tired of these late nights. The hopeful part of her mind pictured him asleep and unworried. The realistic part showed him awake, watching TV, and grinding his teeth between repeated glances at the time. Naidu and others were clambering out of the monitor room as the secure door shut behind her, Naidu looking very pleased, his eyes alive and smiling.

"Vanessa." He grasped her small hand in his broad one and shook it repeatedly. "I think you have the wrong line of work, Lieutenant, you should be in investigations. You were superb ... ." Pause to take a deep, disbelieving breath. "I don't know how much you know about League biotech policy or the FIA, but some of that was just . . . explosive. This is *really* going to keep us busy. Of course, I don't need to remind you that nothing you heard in there is to leave this building . . ."

Vanessa waved him away wearily, detaching her hand from his and strolling tiredly across the floor. "You should know better, Rajeev. I'm a grunt. I have the attention span of small winged insect." Massaging her face, feeling somewhat unsteady, for reasons that went well beyond the mere lateness of the hour. "Call me again if you need me."

"She's growing on you, I see," Naidu said, with the glint of a mischievous smile. "She *is* very pretty. For a European." Which was facetious too, that a GI should even be credited with an ethnic identity beyond the cosmetic. She frowned at him, as more Intel filed past from the monitor room, deep in hand-waving discussion, examining their copious notes and oblivious to anything else.

"I am still married, Rajeev," she retorted in dry humour, "I'm still in the middle of my five-year heterosexual cycle. It's not due to end for another thirty months. *Then* talk to me about how pretty she is." Naidu looked dubious.

"Lieutenant," white-coated Dr. Djohan interrupted with a perky, pleased smile. He shook her hand rapidly. "An excellent job. You appear to have established a level of interconnection with her that I hadn't expected possible for a human. Well done. You do realise, of course, that had you tried to remove her restraints I would have triggered a sedative dose from the monitor booth. I had a finger on the button the whole time, so have no fear, you were never in any danger . . ."

"Don't you think that's missing the point?" Vanessa said sharply. Djohan frowned, cocked his small brown head.

"And yes, how so?"

"Does trust actually occur to you as a concept?"

Djohan's frown remained. He blinked rapidly.

"She is a GI, Lieutenant. My own personal opinion is that the arbitrary application of human psychological concepts to a nonhuman is fundamentally flawed and potentially dangerous, and so . . ."

"Then what the hell was going on in there?" Vanessa demanded, pointing back toward the closed door. Another pause of rapid blinking by Djohan.

"I would say that you did manage to establish a degree of mutual understanding, Lieutenant. Considering the fundamental similarities in your professions, I don't consider that to be particularly improbable . . . but I would be very hesitant to ascribe the description of 'trust' to the interaction, merely because she did choose this time to share some of her information, much to her own benefit, I might add . . ."

"Jesus," said Vanessa, and turned away to stretch, running her hands through her short hair in fuming irritation, "if we left the world to doctors and technicians, it'd be in a real bloody mess, wouldn't it?" She turned back to the puzzled Dr. Djohan. "Here's my advice: if you want cooperation out of her, take off those restraints. And take that damn monitor plug out of the back of her head—that's gotta be shitting her."

"Lieutenant . . . I fear you fail to understand just how dangerous this particular GI is . . ." Pointing a sharp finger back at the door. "You heard what she said, and it appears to be true from her degree of intellectual and linguistic response to abstract concepts. She is an experimental GI with an advanced capability to process lateral thought, and that makes her dangerous to the most *extraordinary* degree . . ."

"I disagree!" Angrily. "I think it makes her ten times *less* dangerous!"

"That in itself is a very dangerous assumption, Lieutenant. This is not a human being to be judged according to human values . . ."

"You think *I'm* not dangerous?" Incredulously. She had no idea why she was so mad. At that moment it failed to matter. "I'm not an entirely natural human either, doctor. I have interface and physical enhancements, not to mention my training. Dammit, *I* could kill both you and Mr. Naidu there right now if I chose to, with my bare hands, and there's not a damn thing you could do to stop me. So why aren't you scared of *me*, huh?"

"You're CSA. You are sworn to serve and protect the citizens of Callay, like me."

"She's not League," Vanessa retorted, pointing at the door. "She left them. She's now giving up their secrets or what she knows of them. There's no evidence she's done anything bad while she's been here. We've got her records, we know where she's been, what she's done . . . she's been trying to find a job, she's gone sightseeing. She's very unlikely to be a spy since she could easily have gone for a higher security level job if she'd chosen, with those qualifications . . ."

"Well, we don't actually know that," Naidu cautioned.

"Give her the benefit of the doubt, why don't you?" Incredulously. "Face it, there's no reason to suspect her other than that she's a GI . . . it's bias, it's discrimination . . ."

"Based on extremely sound reasoning," Djohan retorted. "Have you any idea what she is capable of?"

"Capability doesn't equal intent, Doctor. Do you want what she knows or not? Because if you keep looking at her like the caged lab rat, she'll keep looking at you like the evil bloody scientist with the big syringe."

"Your point is well taken, Lieutenant," Dr. Djohan said coolly, in a manner that suggested he no longer had time to stand around and humour this small, excitable SWAT grunt, "but I am in no position of authority to recommend such a course. If you don't like it, I suggest you take it up with someone else. Good day." And he strode off, white coattails flying.

Vanessa glared at Naidu. "Well, who the hell *is* in authority?" Naidu only shrugged. Vanessa folded her arms and glared back toward the door. The whole thing was stupid. She felt claustrophobic enough to sympathise with the GI. Naidu watched her slightly from beneath raised brows, until she spared him another smouldering look.

"You were saying," he said, "that you hadn't noticed how pretty she is?" Vanessa snorted.

"Get a hold of your rampaging imagination, Rajeev," she said disparagingly as she strode toward the outer door, "you'll split your pants."

## CHAPTER 4

The Callayan executive courtroom was more or less
what she'd expected. It was small, bare, and functional, but not in any way that suggested insignificance.
Quite the opposite. It was simplicity born of security,
tight, hard, and impenetrable. There was no seating for an
audience, or for a jury. Three judges sat behind a bench of
plain, smooth wood, faces cast in blue light from the inset
monitor screens before them, below line-of-sight. All were
reading, studying. None spared her so much as a glance.

Preparing, Sandy noted. Listening to feeds from outside audio sources, scrolling through legal files, intelligence updates, accessing technical and medical analysts,
and—no doubt—various political advisors and go-
betweens. Seated alone on her single, barely cushioned
chair, Sandy allowed her gaze to wander along the blank,
featureless walls. Security shielding prevented her from
pinpointing the telltale emissions of the surveillance cameras, but she guessed there would be at least ten or twelve

individual units in a court like this one, covering every conceivable angle.

People were watching. Important people. She thought she could guess who.

Shan Ibrahim, chief of the Callayan Security Agency. His deputy . . . she scanned her memory to retrieve that elusive name . . . N'darie. Ulu N'darie. Their department heads, all four of them. Names followed. And Benjamin Grey, the State Security Chief, and his aides and seconds. Politicians, unlike the CSA, who were civil servants. She'd seen enough in the League to know the difference.

And then there was Katia Neiland, most prominently. Most prominently of everyone, in fact. It was a good bet that the Callayan President would be watching in person, whatever her tight schedule.

Security advisors, and their various key insiders and connections. The Secretary of State, Yu Weichao . . . no, he was on a diplomatic visit several light-years away. The ministers for Internal Security and the Armed Services and their aides.

And finally, Confederacy-Governor Dali. The thought gave her a mild but thoroughly unpleasant chill. Dali was the central Confederacy Government's representative on Callay. He was the communication conduit, the mediator, the bearer of the central administration's stamp of approval. Officially, he wielded no power, and resided in the Federal Embassy with his numerous staff. Officially, he was just another ambassador, despite the fancy title with its imperial-hangover overtones. But in the corridors of power, people who mattered knew better.

All the organs of power. All of the shadowy, distant people of whom she had only been aware in the abstract . . . all here, watching her. And the information would be recorded. People in the Federal Administration would see those tapes. All the way up to the top.

Capable as she was, Sandy could scarcely conceive of the scale of the predicament in which she was caught. Her mind was spinning, trying to take it all in. She felt numb.

The judge in the middle looked up at her. The woman to his left leaned back in her chair. So, it was beginning.

"I, Supreme Court Adjudicator Sandeep Guderjaal, declare this closed session open," the judge intoned. "Records will indicate that the time is 10:23 local, and clearance is registered triple A."

Sandy sat alone in the middle of the room before the judges' bench, wrists manacled in a heavy, triple-reinforced brace, legs bare from the calves down beneath the white robe she wore. A man from CSA Intel had given her a pair of slippers to wear on her bare feet. They were too big, but they were warm. She guessed they might be his, Intel had been nice to her, on and off. There were techno-geeks in Intel, it was obvious. Their interviews had been long and frequent, and she had answered their questions as best she could, mostly. Some of the interviewers had been very friendly, particularly the men. It had surprised her, and it had given her hope. Only a little, but any hope at all was a precious thing.

"So," the central judge said, studying her, a slight crease to his forehead, as if surprised to look up from his contemplation and find that he was not alone. "You call yourself Cassandra Kresnov, do you?"

"I don't call myself anything. My *name* is Cassandra Kresnov." Her voice remained hoarse, but it was clear enough in this bare, silent room. If she listened hard enough, she fancied she could hear the faint whirr of air conditioning. Beyond that, nothing.

"In this courtroom," said the woman to the right, "you should address each panel member as Your Honour. Will this be a problem?" Her eyebrows raised expectantly. A derisive retort would have released some tension.

"No, Your Honour," Sandy said instead, meeting the woman's gaze.

"And you do realise why it is that you are here?" the same woman asked.

Sandy nodded. "My case falls within the guidelines of several articles of State Security law," she replied. "CSA must have judicial approval in order to proceed with . . . whatever it is that they might wish to do with me."

"That is more or less correct, yes. How does that prospect make you feel?"

"Nervous." A short, heavy silence.

"Why does it make you nervous?" Sandy held the woman's gaze. Then allowed her eyes to stray about the room. And to one side, as if indicating the guards who stood against the wall behind her. Back to the woman.

"Because I feel I have a lot to fear. I'm hoping that you can tell me otherwise." There was no immediate reply. The woman looked down at her screen.

"Captain Kresnov," said the man on the left. He was a big, stern-looking man. His look was serious enough to be almost menacing. "What are you? How would you describe yourself?"

A deep breath. It hurt her gut, and pulled tight at her bandages. "I suppose the simple answer is that I am an artificial human being, Your Honour."

"Designed for what purpose?" Trap. Sandy felt her stomach tense. Her throat was dry again. She wished she had a table on which to rest a glass of water.

"I feel I should remind you that the original design purpose does not necessarily correlate with the precise nature of the finished . . ."

"Just answer the question, please. What did your designers have in mind when they made you?"

"Money, probably." The man's face darkened.

"Are you not prepared to answer the question?"

Sandy took a breath. "I was created to be a soldier. As you well know, Your Honour."

"But you're much more than that, aren't you?" The man's tone was hard, darkened by some unnamed emotion. "Your official designation is GI for General Issue, but your unofficial League designation is HK, isn't it? GI–5074J-HK. Can you tell me what the HK stands for?"

Sandy stared at him. "Do all Supreme Court judges waste time with rhetorical questions?"

"HK," the man continued forcefully, "stands for Hunter Killer. Does it not, Captain Kresnov?"

"It does, Your Honour. But someone else invented that label, and its relevance . . ."

"Someone else invented *you*, Ms. Kresnov. Someone else invented you for the sole purpose of killing as many of us flesh and blood human beings as technologically possible, didn't they?"

Sandy blinked slowly. Her nerves were settling surprisingly fast. Her vision fixed unerringly on the big, square-jawed man with the ruddy face. Eyes half-slid unconsciously into infrared, tuning through the spectrums. Targeting.

"And so the next question, Your Honour, is how should I achieve this objective that you have set for me?" Very calmly.

"Please explain what you mean," Judge Guderjaal cut in before the big man could respond. Sandy's gaze did not waver even a fraction.

"I mean that creating the perfect 'killing machine' has been attempted before, in a literal, technological sense. But most artificial intelligences cannot tactically coordinate and process abstract data on the same level as humans. The robot soldiers I've seen in perhaps a dozen TV programs and movies since I've been a civilian in reality are little more than cannon fodder.

"I am not a 'killing machine.' I was designed specifically to think laterally and creatively, well beyond the level of basic abstraction. The only biomechanical entity known to humans that can achieve this is still the human brain. My brain is a copy, an imprint, of the original article. I have the tactical skills required of a soldier, but as an automatic side effect I also have emotions, and personality, to the same extent as any person in this room. In fact, I do not believe I could be the tactician I am without that emotional input. That is my creative side. Without creativity, I'm just a target."

"You mean to say," the woman asked, "that emotions such as fear are actually of assistance to your combat performance? I'm not certain that that makes sense to me." Suspiciously.

Sandy looked at her, vision still tracking. Closed her eyes softly, restoring normal vision. Took another deep breath. Don't let the combat instincts take over, she told herself. Don't intimidate them. Be harmless.

It wasn't easy.

"I have good control," she replied. "I process a lot of data in a combat environment. I tend to get lost in it, and the fear does not register. But then, many human soldiers have reported precisely the same thing."

"How many people have you killed?" the big man asked her coldly. Sandy's train of thought was diverted for a brief instant, wondering at his allegiances, his connections, his supporters. Wondering who it was that the datalink in his ear and the comp feed on his bench were connected to, outside the courtroom. They were feeding him information even now. And probably, she realised, he would be trying to get a particular response from her, later to be used for his own purposes. Or theirs.

"I have no idea."

"No idea? You, the product of the highest technological capacities the human race has ever devised, have no idea? Is your memory deficient, perhaps? Your recording processes damaged during recent events?"

Sandy blinked slowly, her eyes calm, blue, and steady. "That is four questions, Your Honour. Shall I answer each of them individually, or take them as one single rhetorical outburst?"

The man's gaze deepened to a glare. "How many people have you killed, Captain Kresnov?"

"I believe I have already answered that question. I said that I had no idea. My accurate recollection of events is limited to those matters that I find necessary or helpful. A body count will serve neither purpose."

"You don't feel that the lives of the people you have killed are worth your bothering to recall?"

"I am quite certain I did not say that. I said I do not find those recollections helpful to my present situation. On the contrary, I find them extremely disturbing and depressing."

"You don't look particularly disturbed or depressed from where I'm sitting, Captain Kresnov."

"Respectfully, Your Honour, as a supreme court judge, you should know better than to judge by mere appearances."

The big man continued to glare at her, eyes hard within the shadows of his brows in the dim light. Sandy shifted spectrums slightly, saw hot blood pulsing in his neck veins, spreading through his temples and cheeks.

The female judge interrupted. "You were operating with Dark Star for nine years, is that correct?" Sandy tuned back to standard visual, looking at the woman. She had light brown skin, black hair, and a prominent nose. But not Indian. Arabic, Sandy guessed.

"That is correct, Your Honour. I joined when I was five at the starting rank of lieutenant, was made captain when I was six, and went AWOL when I was fourteen. That was one year ago."

"And over that nine-year period," the woman continued, "how many operations did you personally conduct?"

"Twelve as a lieutenant, nine of those as second-in-command. Seventy-eight as captain."

"And in how many of those operations did you come into direct contact with the enemy?"

"Approximately half, Your Honour."

The Arabic woman's frown was slightly quizzical. "Approximately?"

"Definitions of 'direct contact' vary, Your Honour," Sandy explained. "Kills can be made in an operation without the other side's commanders being entirely aware of it. Degrees of contact vary. I estimate that on approximately forty-five occasions direct contact did occur. But I leave out of that total several instances open to variable interpretation."

"Either way, Captain, that's rather a lot of firefights, wouldn't you say?" Sandy nodded slowly. "Yes, Your Honour. It is a lot."

"You are good at firefights, I presume? You handle yourself well?" Sandy nodded again, this time reluctantly. "Yes, Your Honour." She sensed no overt animosity from this woman. And yet Sandy had no doubts of which judge she found most intimidating, between her and the big man to the right.

"I see." The judge briefly studied the screen before her. Blue light played across her tanned features. "You and your assault team coordinated through neural linkups, did you not?"

"We did, yes."

"I'd imagine that given your other physical, sensory, and psychological advantages, this single unit coordination must have made your team extremely difficult for most mere human soldiers to oppose effectively, in a combat situation. In fact, it seems to me that your unit would have almost an unfair advantage. Would you agree with that assessment?"

Another reluctant nod. "That is the design purpose of most military technology, Your Honour."

"Indeed." A pause. The woman continued to read off the screen before her. Sandy's mind raced over the possible implications of what she was asking. Or what she might be reading from the screen before her. Intelligence, no doubt—mostly military. Intelligence on Dark Star. Then she looked up, her expression mild and purposeful. "Will I have heard of any of these operations?"

If your security clearance is as high as I think it is, Sandy thought, you can read about any of them whenever you wish. But she didn't say it. And said instead, after a moment's thought, "My unit was very active around Goan just three years ago."

"Which operations exactly?"

Sandy shook her head, wearily. "For the same reasons I gave to my CSA interviewers, I refuse to give any answers regarding my past military operations that are any more specific than those I have already given."

"Your continued refusals to cooperate have been noted, Captain," the big man said coldly.

"I'm very happy to respond to any questions directly relating to Callayan security," Sandy continued, addressing the Arabic judge as if her compatriot had never spoken. "My wartime record is a matter for Federal Intelligence, however, and does not directly involve Callayan security issues at all. I fear that sharing wartime information at this moment might entangle me directly in a lot of Federal politics I'd really rather avoid at this time. I appear to be in deep enough water as it is."

Guderjaal in particular, she noted, appeared to concede that argument. She guessed that, in his position, he knew a thing or two about Federal politics. He leaned forward, elbows on the bench before him, and looked at her from under serious, underlit brows.

"What have you done here, Captain?" he asked, changing the subject entirely.

The question caught her off guard. "Your Honour?"

"Here in Tanusha. What have you done here since you've arrived?"

"Well . . ." Still puzzled. "I believe my job interviews have already been documented by the CSA agents . . ."

"No, no." Guderjaal shook his head with a faint trace of impatience. "Aside from your work. Hotel records show that you spent a great deal of time away from your room, more time than would have been required merely for your interviews. What information we have gathered about FIA activities indicates that your tail was first obtained while visiting the Tanushan Gallery of the Arts. Do you like art?"

Guderjaal had thrown her completely. It was not the line of questioning she had expected in this place. Her pulse rate accelerated and she forced herself to calm, remembering the sensor plug and the monitor readings. Civilian judges, civilian law, Federation concepts. At any second, she was in danger of straying far out of her depth in these treacherous, unfamiliar waters. It scared her.

She blinked, forcefully refocusing her attention. "Yes." Unable for a brief moment to keep the puzzlement from her face. "Yes, I do like art."

"Why?" She blinked again. Guderjaal seemed perfectly serious. He had a live, cooperative GI before him. Command level, at that. An unmissable opportunity. Fear flared, and she forced it back down. The judges, however, all looked at their monitor screens, as if on cue.

"This line of questioning disturbs you?" Guderjaal asked, looking up through narrowed eyes. It was the sensor plug. It was reading her reactions. It was unpleasant and invasive and there was nothing she could do about it.

"This entire courtroom disturbs me, Your Honour. Your probe in the back of my head disturbs me. Everything, in fact, about the past few days disturbs me very, very much." Her voice, which had been rock steady, now held the faintest of quavers.

"Why do you like art, Captain Kresnov?" Guderjaal was evidently not in any mood for mercy. His eyes bored deep, like the hidden lenses, laying her bare.

"I don't know." She took a deep breath. Focusing. "Does anyone know why they like art? I'm sure you don't either."

Guderjaal nodded, as if accepting that answer. Or at least, she realised, it was now logged on tape. That was all they wanted. A taped, recorded reference of responses. Content was secondary. "So you visited the art gallery. What else did you do?"

Sandy shrugged, forcing herself to relax further. "I went sight-seeing. It's a beautiful city."

"You claim to have had sexual encounters with straight humans. Did you do so here in Tanusha?" Sandy stared at him. Remembering, suddenly, a claim she had made, talking with Vanessa. God, the ultimate xenophobia trigger. Not Vanessa's fault, that admission. But it had all been on tape.

"On one occasion, yes." Lying was not a safe option. She had no idea how far the FIA's surveillance of her had stretched, and how much of that surveillance the CSA had since recovered. If they caught her lying, in this environment, it would mean trouble. "A one-nighter."

"And he, of course, assumed you were a regular human?" Sandy managed a faint shrug. Uncertain of just how ridiculous this was going to get, or how worried she ought to be about it.

"Of course."

"This sounds to me like callous dishonesty, Captain." Guderjaal's tone was deeply disapproving. "Do you always behave in such a predatory fashion?"

"As a matter of fact, yes." Very bluntly.

"Misleading your partners with your cover story, luring them unknowingly into a sexual encounter with a person who is not, by your own admission, even legally human? Do you think this particular young man would have chosen to perform this act with you had he been fully aware of your true nature?"

"I could not presume to speak for him, Your Honour. But I can assure you, even with such prior knowledge, it is impossible to tell the difference." She paused, her gaze very direct. "*You* would not be able to tell."

For the first time, Judge Guderjaal looked slightly unsettled. To his right, the Arabic woman may well have smiled. Or maybe not. "You feel no remorse at your deception?" he asked after a moment.

"No one was hurt," Sandy replied. Utterly bewildered at the line of attack. "Ignorance is a key element in all one-night stands."

"What if he was a conscientious objector to League biotech? What if he had lost a relative in the war and hated GIs?"

"Then I probably did him a favour." Stares from the judges. Sandy shook her head faintly. And said, because she could not help herself, "Your Honour, if more people had sex more often with more different kinds of people, the universe would be a better place, I'm sure of it." It certainly made sense to her. She had no idea why more civilians didn't agree with her.

"Why is it that you even possess such appetites, Captain?" the

Arabic woman asked. "Are they not inconvenient, considering your line of work?"

Sandy exhaled shortly. "As I have explained in previous interviews, my own nervous system is in function no more and no less an imprint or copy of your own. Sexual urges are a side effect of this replication in exactly the same way that emotions and personality traits are. Yes, they are sometimes inconvenient. But to remove them is to upset the psychological balance. Sexual urges relieve tension and stress, among other things. Without them I would be incomplete, and that would jeopardise the efficiency with which I complete my duties."

"And why are you humanlike at all, Captain?" Guderjaal asked curiously. "I've heard artificial intelligence experts argue that the entire GI concept is flawed, that by imitating humans, League biotechnologists have in fact limited the capabilities of their creations."

Sandy nearly rolled her eyes. Not that old crap again.

"Your Honour . . . experts deal with theory. The rest of us live in the real world." Again a smirk from the Arabic judge. "In theory, they're right, of course. In reality, experimental models are incredibly expensive and a perfectly workable model already exists—that being a normal human being. GIs are the most financially practical option, they can integrate with the existing military infrastructure without the need for major adjustment, and they don't scare the political conservatives as much as some less-human creation would . . . to the extent that there is such a thing as a political conservative in the League. I'm just a human copy. Structurally, I'm just like you, nervous system included. I'm just made of different stuff."

"I put it to you, Captain," the big man said, "that your nervous system is nothing at all like my own. My nervous system does not have upward of seventy-five meta-synaptic implants and sensory branches to handle nearly a seven hundred percent additional load of combined sensory data input beyond what a normal, unaugmented human can handle." He was reading from the screen before him as he spoke, eyes hard and determined in the wash of blue computer light. "My nervous system does not have an integrated motor-skills function that is clearly biomechanical and focuses all synaptic reflex response into such a narrow perimeter field as to guarantee a completely machinelike precision in the execution of all physical activity. My own nervous system is far more erratic and imprecise in its execution of learned-response reflexes, I assure you. And neither does my nervous system possess what appears to be a dedicated data-storage/processing centre in the primary short-term memory sections that would appear to serve primarily to enhance the visualisation, recollection, and computation of rapidly unfolding and chaotic tactical situations, such as are frequently found on a battlefield." He looked up. "Do you deny that your nervous system possesses these nonstandard characteristics, Captain Kresnov?"

Sandy shook her head. "No, Your Honour." She could not argue those points. She was only happy that he'd missed a couple.

"And most, *most* importantly," the man continued, still looking at her, "my nervous system developed, grew, and evolved naturally from a state of immature childhood to what it is today. My experiences were random, controlled only by the systematic nature of my city-bred environment, and the troubles to which my parents went to expose me to certain kinds of stimuli. I am a random personality. If I had a clone made of myself, and raised in exactly the same manner, it is nearly statistically impossible that it would turn out to be exactly like me in every degree. The randomness makes it so.

"Your nervous system, Captain Kresnov, had no such developmental process. You came into the world fully formed and structured in most respects, except for your lack of direct worldly experience. This experience was replicated on tape, to be fed into your brain with a precision completely unknown in everyday experience, and completely lacking that random, unpredictable quality that has shaped each and every one of the fifty-seven million people who live in this city. Your developmental experience, Captain, was constructed, purified, and controlled

by the agencies of League military science in order to create exactly the
finished product that we see sitting here in this courtroom today.

"You, Captain Kresnov, are purpose built, and purpose designed,
by the will of a government that has already shown the greatest disre-
spect for the most basic of human dignities and moral values. I put it
to you that you are, and have always been, exactly what they wanted
you to be. This, when combined with your evident martial capabilities,
should fill any sane, law-abiding citizen of Tanusha or anywhere within
the Democratic Confederacy, with dread."

Sandy gazed blankly at the front of the judges' bench. There was
no identifying symbol on the front of that bench, as she had seen in the
courtroom TV dramas. Just bare wood, plain and functional.

She could see where this was headed. The cameras were rolling.
The spectators had gathered. The various sides and interests would
have their say. This was more than a trial. This was a hearing, where
positions could be set out, opinions stated, recorded, and marked for
future reference. These people here before her, these judges—they were
the mouthpieces, nothing more. This entire courtroom was little more
than a glorified, camera-infested soapbox. Or a pulpit.

And so . . . what was the debate all about? This man was arguing
. . . what? For her unsuitability for integration into common society?
For her continued incarceration? She knew from Naidu and CSA Intel
that the judges had viewed all her interview tapes, and had been
briefed on what she'd revealed of League and FIA biotech machinations. She knew there was a push from sections of the CSA, particularly
Intel, to keep her on Callay, where she was useful.

They hadn't told her how much resistance that concept was
meeting in the corridors of political power. Somehow they had always
found a way to be evasive when she had asked. Now she was coming
to understand why.

She looked up and found all three judges awaiting her response.
The cameras were rolling.

"Then why am I here?" she answered the big man's assertions very softly. The big man shifted in his seat.

"That is what we are here to determine," he replied.

And that, Sandy nearly replied, is bullshit. But she didn't say it. She didn't want to frighten anyone.

"Ten to fifteen years ago," she said instead, "what you describe may well have been true. I ask you to understand that ten to fifteen years can change a person beyond recognition, particularly when lived at the intensity that I have experienced. Those, more than the foundation tapes that you describe, were my formative years. That was my childhood." She paused, as the thought crystallised in her mind for the very first time. And looked Judge Guderjaal calmly in the eye.

"Now," she said, "I have grown up."

There was a pause. Glances dropped to monitor screens. Attention diverted, briefly, receiving a fresh input of data. Sandy sat and watched, shoulders and back beginning to ache from the sustained upright posture. The bandages felt especially tight about her middle, restricting her breathing. She recrossed her legs, settling herself to wait. The Arabic woman looked up first.

"Your childhood has been filled with the horrors of war, Captain Kresnov," she said. "For most of your life, you have known only violence, and violent death. You claim that this formative experience has made you a better person. How can this be?"

"I know the true value of life." Sandy's voice was very quiet. "I know the true value of beauty. Judge Guderjaal asked me earlier why I liked art. I think that I like art because it has little purpose other than the simple pleasure of its own existence. I do not mind political art, but I prefer simple, pleasurable art. A great comedic writer named Oscar Wilde once said that all the best art was essentially useless. I think I agree with him." There was a brief, slightly mortified silence.

Judge Guderjaal leaned forward. "You are familiar with Oscar Wilde?" Disbelievingly.

Sandy gave a faint smile. "I discovered *The Importance of Being Earnest* in a Naval library archive when I was nine years old. At the time, I had never laughed so hard in my life." Which was, she realised as she said it, not saying very much. But it was true.

"Your superiors allowed you access to such works?" Guderjaal seemed to be having great difficulty with this.

"The League military structure is not the fascist dictatorship that Confederacy propaganda might have you believe, Your Honour. I was an officer among other officers, some human, others augmented like myself. Our every thought was not war, death, and destruction. We had our entertainments, like any military. Most watched the vids, or did VR simulations, direct interface or otherwise. I roamed the library archives." Another faint smile, mildly self-deprecating. "I'm rather well read, actually."

"Then you would know Shakespeare?" Guderjaal pressed. "The *Ramayana*?"

Sandy nodded. "Yes . . . and Pushkin, and Tagore, Narayan, and the Mughal poets from your own culture too, Your Honour." Guderjaal blinked in utter astonishment. "I used to quote lines, occasionally, in my periodic general reports. Confused the hell out of the psychs, I'm sure."

"A chimpanzee can read Shakespeare or Oscar Wilde, Captain Kresnov," the big man interrupted. "Understanding them is another matter."

Sandy blinked, somewhat taken aback. "Your Honour, if manners maketh man, as someone once said, then I am surely more human than you."

The Arabic woman grinned outright, repressing it with difficulty. Guderjaal just looked at her, eyebrows raised high, as if lost in thought, or a sudden realisation. The big man merely glowered.

"Captain Kresnov," he said after a moment of narrow-eyed reflection, "I do not doubt your sentience. I doubt your right to exercise it."

Sandy's eyes narrowed in return. "My right?" she said disbelievingly.

"Your right," the judge repeated, firm and hard. "Callay is a civilised world, as are the other worlds of the greater Federation. Our respective constitutions are founded not only upon the responsibility of the State toward the individual, but the responsibility of the individual toward the State. Some individual freedoms must be sacrificed for the good of the whole. For this reason, ordinary civilians cannot own or purchase weapons without special permits, about which there are rigid regulations. For the same reasons, ordinary civilians cannot gain surgical augmentations beyond a certain level, because some of those capabilities may legally qualify their own bodies as lethal weapons.

"But you, Captain, you *are* a lethal weapon, with or without firearms. There is no single part of you that has not been designed with that single purpose in mind."

"Your Honour . . ." Sandy began.

"Tell me what my current body temperature is, Captain," the man continued. "Tell me now."

Sandy's lips pursed to a thin line. The other two judges watched impassively. She tuned her vision, shading to reds, golds, and blue. "From what I can see, it's thirty-seven point two five degrees."

"Good. Where did I last have surgery, of what you can see?"

"You have broken your left collarbone. It's an old injury, fully healed."

"Except for the faintest of joins and blood vessel displacements where the residual effects of bioengineering have lowered that region's ambient blood temperature, yes. I broke it playing football when I was twelve. How many residual energy emissions do you perceive currently operating within this courtroom?"

Sandy shook her head, her jaw firmly set. "The shielding is too strong."

"I did not ask you to judge their strength, Captain, merely to give a number."

"Your Honour . . ." looking exasperatedly at Guderjaal.

"Please answer the questions, Captain," Guderjaal said. Sandy exhaled hard.

"More than ten."

"Such modesty, Captain. You know very well there are in fact sixteen, don't you?" She gave a flat, disinterested shrug. "And finally, please show the court your little trick with your trigger fingers? Both, if you please, since you are ninety-nine point eight percent ambidextrous."

Sandy stared at him. Angry. It showed in her eyes, despite her control. To his credit, the big man appeared not to notice.

"Whenever you're ready, Captain."

Reluctantly, Sandy raised both arms, wrists bound before her and tightly encased. Spread the fingers on both hands. And moved both index fingers in a hard, tense reflex. They blurred back and forth so fast as to vanish before the naked eye. And she stopped, resettling the brace on her white-robed thigh. The other two judges were watching with eyebrows raised. Sandy continued to stare at the big judge, totally unimpressed.

"At that speed," he said, "I'm reliably informed that you could empty a twenty-five-round pistol clip nearly as fast as an automatic assault rifle—all twenty-five rounds in less than a second. Provided you did not wear out the trigger mechanism first, that is. And at a wild guess, I'd suppose that all twenty-five rounds would pass more or less through the same impact hole, wouldn't they Captain? Even from range."

"And your point is?" Sandy asked.

"My point, Captain, is that you are dangerous. That particular index finger reflex has no other purpose than to assist you in the operation of modern firearms. It does not exist on any of your other fingers. It is a custom design, specifically tailored to suit your purposes.

"And I need not remind my colleagues of the reinforced alloy blast door that you ripped from its hinges during your headlong flight from the FIA agents with only five well-placed kicks. You possess skills and capabilities that no member of any civilised society should possess, even its soldiers. Here in the Confederation there is legal precedent for this. The laws of the Confederation make every effort to uphold the notion of 'humanity' as more than just a word, and to preserve it against the encroaching tide of synthetic technology.

"You, Captain Kresnov, clearly fall outside of this definition. The very act of your creation was an insult to the morals and principles that Confederation law holds dear. In a truly civilised society, Captain Kresnov, you would not exist."

The big man was clearly far, far more than mere threat and bluster. He had succeeded in doing something that she had not thought him capable of. He had frightened her.

Again, the judges glanced downward. They were monitoring her fear. Doubtless expecting some explosion of mindless violence, despite the drugs, the restraints and the guards nearby with their stunners.

"You may well be right," she replied instead. Her voice was not holding out so well now—hoarse, and with a hint of a quaver. She needed a drink. "Don't think that I haven't thought of that." She paused. Feeling their eyes upon her. Studying her. Not for the first time, she wondered what they saw, or thought they saw.

"But here I am. I had no more say in my own creation than any of you did. I exist. I am sentient. And given the chance, I would claim before the highest ideals of your legal system that I do, in fact, have rights." Deathly silence. She fancied she could even hear the guards behind her as they breathed. "In what brief time I had to myself in your city, I was enjoying life. I searched for a job, a job I would have done extremely well had I got it. I saw some sights, and enjoyed the art gallery. Once I threw a football with some children. And once I made love."

She looked at the three of them, one after another. Her eyes were hurting. Not leaking . . . just hurting. "I have no desire to hurt anyone. And I have no political motivation left. I am no danger to anyone or anything. And it is your fear, not my reality, that makes you think otherwise. I only wish to be left alone."

"Captain . . ." Guderjaal broke off, glancing down at his screen. And back up again, his expression sombre. "Given what you are, and where you are, that hardly seems likely. Does it?"

"No." Her voice broke, and she recovered it. "No, Your Honour. I don't suppose it does."

# CHAPTER 5

There was nothing on TV. Nothing much anyway. She surfed channels, uplinked to room central. Images flashed by, millisecond fast. Dancing. Colourful costumes. More dancing. Martial arts action. She paused for a second and studied a scene. Two fighters, both men, hammering the crap out of each other to apparently little effect. Ludicrous. And they were so slow. Not to mention ridiculously flamboyant. Looking good, apparently, was more important than getting it right.

She continued surfing, seated legs out on the sofa, cushions propped with great care to support her sore, stiff, heavily bandaged body. Heavy bandage wrap showed thickly beneath the hem of her robe, further stiffening knees that were already near impossible to bend. She kept her arms folded with determination, whatever the pain, unwilling to allow the elbows to stiffen straight. It hurt, drugs and all. Days partly or mostly unconscious. More days since the courtroom interview. Follow-up questions from CSA reviewers. Court-appointed psych-specialists. Biotech experts. Even an NGO head on prisoner rights.

Do you have any complaints about your treatment, Ms. Kresnov? Sure. The door's locked.

Not like she was in any shape to walk out of it, even if it wasn't. She knew she should be happy. The pain meant she was healing, as did the stiffness. Djohan was incredulous at the speed. Had wanted to take blood samples and scan measurements. Had come, in fact, between interviews, just an hour ago and begged for her permission. She'd told him she'd tell the next government biotech reviewer who came in, and then he'd find himself investigated for collecting illegal research data. He'd retreated. After all, that was exactly what the FIA had been doing to her. Collecting illegal data. Things they weren't supposed to know. Things no Federation person or organisation was supposed to know. Wilful, legally enforced ignorance. Djohan evidently found it hard to swallow. So, she knew for certain, did much of the Federation private sector.

Her left hand was numb. She abandoned her channel-surfing for a moment and examined it, lifting it to the golden sunlight that flooded from the windows behind the sofa. Her shoulder creaked like a rusty iron hinge. Flexed the fingers, one at a time. Coordination was down. Sluggish. Just the drugs, Djohan had said. They went after the left side of her body more, for some reason. He'd wanted to do tests on that, too. Fat fucking chance.

She knew the basics, roughly. Artificial proteins, enzymes, hybrid-cells, microengineered biology and self-regulatory mechanisms . . . basic biosynth tech. Federation was already pretty good at most of those basics. She doubted Djohan could really learn much from her. There were plenty of legal applications here, from disease and injury treatments to life-extensions, to all forms of augmentation from cosmetic to medical to performance enhancing—all legal in the Federation. Consumers did vote, after all, and every year new laws pushed those self-inflicted boundaries. A bloody mess, all those laws. Terror at the prospect of artificial people. And difficult to find anyone in the League who didn't think it'd all collapse eventually. League foreign policy already focused on that expectation, she knew only too well. In the meantime, her limbs stiffened, her tendons reknitted, and any idiot knew synthetic materials fixed themselves ten times faster than organic—it was another of those advantages that so scared the Feddie lawmakers. Lucky her, to be so advanced. Lucky girl.

She flicked to network uplinks—and winced in extreme displeasure as the insert plug overrode her browser software. As good as an iron cage, the whole vastness of the network was lost to her, inaccessible. Frustrating as hell, automatic censorship plugged into the back of her skull, more effective than a pair of handcuffs. But for a few select links . . . she scanned on automatic, vaguely interested to see what they'd left open to her of all the possible selections. Library functions. Basic entertainment. No high-level VR . . . no loss, it didn't work well on her anyway. Live newsfeeds from various sources, though largely official and generalised, and thus heavily processed for commercial tastes. Waste of time, might as well watch TV. Games. Tourist info. Adult entertainment . . . God, they shouldn't have put that up, it only frustrated her further. Celibate for over a week now. A real suicide-trigger, that was. She couldn't even bend her legs, let alone spread them.

Parliament hookup. She shoved sardonic humour to one side and accessed. Got an internal visual of the main Parliament chamber, a broad semicircle of ascending benches facing a Speaker's chair and middle table. Lots of politicians, lots of suits, salwar kameez and saris, and other traditional dress she didn't recognise. There appeared to be a debate in progress. Tax reform, she found with a link to adjoining text-database. Curious as she was about civilian political process, she wasn't *that* curious.

She chose a camera angle instead and scanned the Government front bench. Came to rest on the red-haired woman in the big chair. President Neiland. Zoomed closer. Neiland's features were pale, handsome, and strong. Thoughtful now, as she leafed through some documents, half listening to her colleague's speech at the podium beside her chair.

Sandy accessed another text-link and more info sprang up. Katia Neiland. Forty-two years old, Doctorate with Honours in Communications Law, Ramprakash University . . . Class Dux. That meant best in class, she gathered. Youngest ever Union Party leader. Youngest ever Callayan President. Due for reelection in twelve months. An opinion poll graphic showed job approval at 78 percent, personal approval at 51 percent (curious discrepancy, she thought), and likelihood of re-election for Union under her leadership at 64 percent.

She watched for a long moment, internal visual. Wondering what Neiland had thought of her interview before the Supreme Court. Or interrogation, more precisely. The Union Party was the mainstay of Callayan politics. There were factions, but on issues like biotech they mostly stood together. The Progress Party was the main opposition. Not League-sympathetic, that was misleading. Just "progressive," whatever that meant. She could expect more sympathy, ideologically speaking, from Progress. Union had the voters, by a wide margin. And Neiland was a technocrat, doubtless the present tax-reform debate held her attention longer. She'd take her advisors' advice on security matters, no doubt. So who advised her?

She switched cameras again and found a better angle. Panned until she found a tall man in a blue suit, clipped dark hair, and bland expression. Benjamin Grey, secretary of state. The CSA answered to him—he'd have the last say on this kind of thing. She scrolled through the text-link . . . and abruptly lost the whole feed, a sudden, disorienting collapse to static confusion.

"You fucking morons!" she shouted to the empty room. "How can I become a model Federation citizen if you won't let me learn about the political system?" Glaring at the space where her emissions-detection knew one of the numerous cameras to be, high in a corner. No reply. "Fools."

She'd complain about it, when she got the chance. It was her only resort, complaints. It made her feel cheap. She slumped back against the cushions, arms folded tightly, trying to ignore the wrenching tightness across her bandage-swathed shoulders and back. Microsystems at work, repairing her tormented body. But she didn't want to think of that. She was a special ops commander, not a technobiologist. And the memories hurt far too much.

She flipped on the TV again, desperate to take her mind off other things, bothering things. Normally she preferred music, but she wanted to keep her eyes occupied. Found a sports channel . . . tennis, she remembered the game was called. And spent the next ten minutes marvelling that even augmented human nervous systems were so imprecise that top players needed to hit the ball so far inside the lines to stay in the points. There was obviously no room for GIs in sport either. Ninety-nine out of a hundred tennis points wouldn't get past the serve. No matter where she looked, she couldn't help but find evidence of how unwelcome she was here. Funny how a week could change that perception so drastically. It had all looked so beautiful a week ago.

"*Cassandra*," announced an unexpected voice over the room audio, "*you have some visitors here. Please be courteous.*"

"Sure," she muttered, not taking her eyes from the screen. "I'll refrain from bodily tearing them limb from limb." The door opened with a heavy clack of reinforced locks, and a pair of CSA guards entered, stun pistols in hand. She ignored them. A man and a woman followed them in.

"Hello Cassandra," said the man, with surprising confidence. "I'm Aw Sian Thiaw. I'm an advisor to President Neiland." *That* got her attention. "And this is Mahudmita Rafasan, the President's senior legal advisor." Doubly so. She stared in wary surprise. "Can we take a seat?"

Her usual sarcastic affirmative failed her this time. Thiaw sat anyway in one of the two opposing single leather chairs, and Rafasan took the other. Sandy stared at Rafasan in particular. She was one of those immaculately dressed Indian women only rarely seen in the League, where such ostentatious cultural displays were hardly vogue. Her sari was a blaze of red, orange, and gold, intriguingly patterned. Gold bracelets and bangles chimed on her wrists, and a simple stud gleamed on the side of her nose. Saffron daubed the centre spot of her forehead. Brown skinned and dark eyed, hair tastefully arranged beneath the sari's veil, she was the picture of South Asian feminine elegance. Sandy blinked again. In the League, senior government officials simply did not dress like that, be they Indian or otherwise. Tanusha, she was gathering, was different.

"So, Cassandra," Thiaw said, leaning forward from the edge of his chair, elbows on knees, his face a model of well-practised, professional charm. "How are you being treated here? Well?"

A small man—Rafasan had stood an elegant half head taller. Also brown skinned, but East Asian features. Which could have meant anything. Guessing ethnicity was one of Sandy's favourite distractions, and here in the Federation ethnicity was so much more pronounced. And celebrated. Thiaw's suit was bland and flawless, his hair neat and short. Young, she reckoned, especially for such an important position. And very confident for someone in the presence of a GI for the first time. Rafasan fidgeted with her many bangles, and chewed on the inside of her lip.

"What does the President want with me?" Sandy asked. Thiaw pursed his lips, considering her. Spared Rafasan a meaningful glance. Rafasan's return look was wary. Thiaw straightened, still perched on the edge of his chair, hands on knees.

"Cassandra . . . forgive me if this sounds condescending, but there's no other way for me to ask this question of you . . . How much do you know about politics? And how much were you exposed to in the League?"

It rang an alarm bell immediately. The courtroom. It had to be.

"What kind of trouble has that interrogation landed me in?"

Thiaw stared at her for a moment, almost surprised. Rafasan's fidgeting increased. Thiaw exhaled hard, a big heave of small shoulders.

"So you *do* know politics. What do you know about Callayan politics?" Not enough, and she knew it. Military reflexes kicked in, the need for a wider briefing.

"Enlighten me. Please." Guderjaal, her racing mind assured her, had most likely been safe. Ditto the Arabic judge. But the big, heavy-set man with the ruddy face . . . who backed him? How were judges appointed in Tanusha? What had that hostility been about, specifically? And why had these two senior advisors suddenly dropped into her lap? She didn't like the implications one bit. Her ignorance made it worse.

"Okay," said Thiaw, leaning forward even further, hands mobile before him, "I'll try and keep it simple, not because I think you're stupid, but because otherwise I'll be here all week." That, Sandy thought, was not a comforting beginning. "First thing: Union Party." A firm, definite indication with both hands. "They're the big deal. Sixty percent support base, they control the legislature. Now, being so big, they've got factions. The left are the cultural conservatives, anti-League, anti-biotech, anti-GI, all the religious groups are behind them—that's the core of Union support, probably half. The right are more moderate. The Centrists don't give a shit either way—they practise what the inner circle refers to as 'pragmatic indifference.' President Neiland's a Centrist. Generally. You copy?"

Sandy nodded slowly. Finding something more than vaguely incongruous in the situation—herself, bandaged and mostly immobile on the sofa, wrapped only in a bathrobe, being briefed on the Callayan political establishment by two of its more prominent insiders. Like a pair of religious preachers, attempting a conversion of a most unlikely neophyte. Not merely a GI, but a grunt-in-general. But Thiaw was clearly headed somewhere. Surely he hadn't risen to his present position at such a young age by not being headed somewhere every time he opened his mouth.

"Progress are the other main mob. They've got factions, too . . . all you really need to know is that they're the ones who are usually accused of being too close to the League. Settlers' spirit, advance or bust, Earth has too much influence, Callay for Callayans . . . you get the idea, all the usual self-indulgent euphoria. Of course, they're not allowed to indicate direct support for the League, even though some of their factions clearly sympathise, but they're not so big on central restrictions, including biotech restrictions . . . it's basically a League-ish platform. And I'm sure you're pretty familiar with that, right?"

"Sure." And because she figured a greater show of understanding might be called for . . . "League was founded on those principles. Fifty years of debate on whether or not to settle the border stars created a huge divide between expansionist idealists and cultural conservatives. Idealists went League, cultural conservatives stayed Federation, thus the split."

"Of course, sure. Great." With hand-heavy emphasis on each, apparently relieved to know he wasn't completely wasting his time. "Now, Cassandra . . . here's the problem. The CSA needs you, Cassandra. Director Ibrahim has especially put in a good word for you. He's very alarmed at this FIA infiltration and wants all the help you can give him. But now we've had the official court hearing, and your case is running around in legal and security circles within the Parliament, Cassandra . . . that's not the whole Parliament, your case is still very restricted, but the number of people now involved has increased . . . well, it's increased a lot."

"And the Opposition . . ." she paused uncertainly, ". . . the Progress Party, are going to give the President trouble for allowing the CSA to harbour me?"

"No," a vigorous shake of the head, "no, Cassandra, that's not the point. That would be manageable. Progress don't have the numbers in the House anyway. And Progress are League-inclined anyway . . . they don't like the biotech restrictions much at all. In fact, if you were going to find support within any major party in Tanusha, you'd find it in Progress." Sandy blinked, not liking the implications of that.

"You mean the Union Party factions . . . ?"

"Exactly. The President's own Party, Cassandra. Cultural conservatives. Religious groups. Anti-biotech in general. Probably the essence of what makes the Federation different from the League . . ."

"That Judge." As the connection quickly came clear in her head. "The big guy. Which group is he?"

"Oh, oh, wait, wait, wait . . ." waving both hands with an exasperated smile, ". . . no, really, Cassandra, you don't want to get into that territory now, that's judicial appointments, the bureaucracy's all different, the Judiciary's a whole 'nother cricket match. No, the important thing to focus on here is that it's out now, and there are officials and bureaucrats who are alarmed. They're figuring it's only a matter of time until this whole thing becomes public, in which case they'll be answering to their various constituencies at the next election . . ."

"No, wait, hang on a moment," Rafasan interrupted for the first time. "I think she has a point." Sandy raised her eyebrows at the legal advisor, surprised at the decisiveness of the interruption. From the delicate appearance and nervous fidgeting, she hadn't figured Rafasan for the decisive type. "I mean, Judge Pullman is at issue here, and the Judiciary, at least to some extent . . ."

"Sure," Thiaw said with exaggerated calm, "but I'd like to keep us focused on the key question here . . ."

"Oh enough with the constant *spin*, Thiaw, let's tell it to the woman like it really is." Thiaw shrugged defeat and withdrew defensively. Rafasan recrossed her legs and turned her dark-eyed attention upon Sandy, the fingers on her right hand playing with the bangles on her left wrist. "Judge Pullman—that is the man who showed such displeasure toward you at the hearing—was elected to the bench on the advice of the President's attorney-general as a sop to the various vociferous mouths in the Union Left who felt they were underrepresented in the Judiciary. I, of course, advised her against the move . . . ," with a self-conscious tilt of her head, and a vague motion of manicured fingers, ". . . but, for better or worse, the President is not always inclined to accept the more pragmatic advice ahead of the purely political."

She sounded, Sandy reckoned, somewhat miffed. Her accent was perhaps more Indian than many Tanushans. Sometimes, she'd gathered, accents became institutionalised within certain professions and colleges, further reinforced by educational tape-teach. Perhaps law was one of those culturalised institutions within Tanusha.

"So you are right in your assumption," she continued, hurrying through the sentence on nervous energy, "Judge Pullman was merely pleasing his constituency before the cameras as any politician would— more of the pervasive politicising of the Judiciary that I and some others have been campaigning against most strenuously . . . but, well," she coughed briefly into her hand, "now the Senate Security Council are onto your case, and certain of their members are closely connected to the aforementioned Mr. Pullman, and that is basically why we are here." In a rushed, nervous finish. Sandy frowned. Turned that frown upon Thiaw. Thiaw took an exasperated breath.

"As I was about to say, Cassandra," he said, "the Senate Security Council are charged with the broad purview of all Callayan security matters. They have an investigatory branch, the Special Investigations Bureau, or SIB, directly attached to them and answerable only to Security Council review. Now," he cricked his neck, with emphasis, "this is the Senate, Cassandra, not the Legislature. They're elected by different means, proportional representation, which means . . ."

Sandy raised her hand. Thiaw stopped, hands frozen in midsentence. When she was sure she had their complete attention, Sandy spoke. "The mindless, headkicking grunt portion of my brain just lost you. How does any of this affect me and my situation?" Rafasan, she noted, cocked her head in curiosity at that turn of phrase. As if impressed, and surprised to be so. Thiaw took another deep breath and threw Rafasan a brief, reproachful look. It had all fallen apart since her interruption, obviously, all his carefully planned explanation. The technocrat and the spin-doctor. Not a good match. But they seemed to know each other well.

"Cassandra," Thiaw resumed with long-suffering patience, "the Senate Security Council are concerned at your presence. You are a GI. Right?" Eyebrows raised expectantly. Inviting revelation. Sandy frowned. "Cassandra, you're in the Federation now. People here don't like GIs much. We fought a war about it with the League, precisely to stop the spread of GI-oriented technology. In many ways it's the fundamental ideological split between the Federation and the League . . ."

"No it's not," Sandy replied calmly, "it's just the most obvious manifestation. League progress-or-bust triumphalism goes all the way to the bone. GIs are only the main area of dispute . . . if not for that, there would be others."

"Fine, right, sure, whatever." Rafasan, Sandy noticed, was eyeing her colleague with increasing bemusement, some of the nervousness fading. "The point is, Cassandra, that the President's own party are putting pressure on her, since that courtroom hearing, to hand you on to the Feds. Over Director Ibrahim's objections. If you don't prove more cooperative than you have, then we're going to run out of excuses to keep you here on Callay, and then you'll get handed over to some Federal party who'll take you to Earth, where old mentalities are strongest, and where the FIA has most power, and where you're no damn good to Callay or the CSA in trying to find the bastards who've penetrated our security and could easily do so again. Does that make sense to you?"

It did. She stared at Thiaw for a moment, perched on the edge of his chair, eyebrows raised expectantly, looking pained. Rafasan, too, looked subdued, glancing at her lap with a resumption of bangle-fiddling.

"I've already given you a whole stack of information from League Intel on the FIA's own biotech research," she challenged half-heartedly. "Mr. Naidu was very impressed."

"Yes, and I thank you for that, Cassandra, that's valuable background information . . . much of it we already knew, but it certainly filled in the gaps. But we need operational detail. We need to know the specific operational details as to how the League is infiltrating local biotech firms, how the FIA are doing it, and on the possibility that they might be working together on this. And you've refused any detailed questioning on those matters, haven't you."

Sandy gazed back at the TV. A tennis ball spun backwards and forwards over the net. She *had* refused it. Repeatedly. And if they were speculating on complicity between the League and the FIA, supposedly the worst of enemies . . . then they were evidently quite advanced in their research. She sent the TV a mental signal, and the screen went blank. But still, she had her reasons.

"Okay," she said, quietly. "How do I know that if I help you, I'll get something for it? That I won't just get carted off to wherever as soon as you've milked me of everything I know?"

"We're working on getting you a firm guarantee from Justice Guderjaal," Rafasan said. "If you cooperate, we can . . ."

"You're working?" Fixing Rafasan with a firm, hard gaze. Rafasan looked desperately at Thiaw.

"Cassandra," Thiaw said earnestly, "it's the best we can do under the present circumstances. There are legal precedents for services rendered to Callay. Asylum of sorts has been granted under those circumstances, right?" At Rafasan. The legal advisor nodded quickly.

"Of course, absolutely. There are numerous cases, most of them regarding far less vital information than we presently require from you . . ."

"You'd grant asylum to a GI?" Staring very directly. The lawyer met her gaze with commendable conviction.

"Legally . . . well, it would, um . . ." flick at one elaborate earring, ". . . it would be an adventure. But Callayan law on the recognition of artificial sentience is actually very advanced. I'm . . . I'm actually quite confident, in all honesty, that if the process went to trial, you could definitely achieve asylum. Of some kind." Rearranging bangles on the other wrist. Despite the fidgets, Sandy nearly believed her. Nearly.

"And that," she said dryly, "is of course why all the cultural conservatives are so scared of letting me stay on that long, isn't it? They're scared I might win."

Dead silence from them both. Evidently not having expected that much insight. She didn't know the details. But she could think. And she could guess. It had always been her strong point. Now, a whole range of unpleasant possibilities were opening up before her.

"Do I really have a chance?" she asked, into that silence. "If I cooperate?"

"If the information you provide leads directly to the capture of some of the FIA infiltrators," Thiaw said, and shrugged, "of course, definitely, your chances then are extremely high."

"Despite the fact that my revealing League military secrets will attract the attention of all the top Federal military, political, and security apparatus, FIA and otherwise, who will all demand access to me and my knowledge, and will use some overriding Federal security law to get past any temporary asylum that Callay might offer me. They do have those kinds of overriding security laws, don't they?" she asked Rafasan. Rafasan glanced distractedly out the broad windows, and the sunny sprawl of the metropolis beyond. Nodded, reluctantly. "Then I'll want something more watertight than what you're offering before I tell you anything. Otherwise, opening my mouth any further is only going to land me in even bigger trouble."

"Cassandra," Thiaw pressed, "your trouble doesn't *get* any bigger. If you don't cooperate fully, Cassandra, then the political implications for you are . . . well, they're not good. Right now it only looks like you're protecting someone . . ."

"Damn right I'm protecting someone," Sandy cut in, with a hard stare and cooling voice. "Me. I know some basics about Federation security laws. Like Federal security in general, it takes precedence over the security of member worlds like Callay. That means they can declare me a Federal security asset or risk at any time and whip me off to Earth, and there's not a damn thing you or any of your puny local laws can do about it."

"And," Thiaw shot back, "you'll end up there anyway if you don't help us. Your one chance is to help us catch the FIA infiltrators here, and hope that that builds up enough local support for you in the corridors of power that . . ."

"With all respect, Mr. Thiaw," Sandy said coldly, "but you can't be fucking serious." She could feel her stomach tightening, a painful cramping through the bandages. "Politicians here are going to overlook the mass anti-GI panic out there because they feel *grateful* to me?"

She hadn't wanted this at all. To become a political pawn. To get caught up in the doubtless labyrinthine machinations of the Callayan corridors of power, and all the populist nonsense that went with it. To be backed into a corner, forced to tell more of what she knew, knowing this would cause trouble . . . so much damn trouble that she didn't want to contemplate it, it went too deep, and stretched too far into matters that she knew far too little about. She was feeling increasingly lost and threatened in the whole calamitous mess . . .

Thiaw sighed, oblivious to her growing anxiety, shoulders slumping.

"Cassandra . . . why don't you just think about it, huh?" He gave her a wry, winsome smile. "I'll be frank. We need to catch these FIA. The Security Council is increasingly alarmed, as are the President's more predictable opponents . . . and we need to catch them soon. You think about it. I'll call on you again soon, once you've had some time to consider your options."

He rose to his feet, looking deflated, and Rafasan made to follow . . .

"Wait." They both paused. Sandy gazed past them at the far wall. Uncertain of what she was doing. She was confused. Frightened even.

But not just for herself. "Sit down." They sat. Sandy gazed at the wall for an indeterminate moment. Wondering if she was about to sign her own effective warrant to bureaucratic hell. But she was running out of alternatives. Had, in fact, run out of alternatives long, long ago. Only now was she starting to realise it. She hated bureaucracy. Here, with its links to alien, populist politics in a society that actively disliked and distrusted GIs and advanced synthetic-replication biotechnology itself, it made her nervous in the extreme. But she was here now. She could not escape it. She was in the game, for good. Once in it, she had to learn to play within the rules. It was a slim chance. But it was the only chance she had. She switched her gaze to Thiaw. Thiaw looked back expectantly. Poor guy, she thought. You're in for it now.

"This is how it works," she said quietly. "The League have an official policy of changing the Federation from the inside. League theory on modern human evolution dominates all policy, including security. Market- and demand-driven forces cannot be challenged, cultural resistance just creates temporary hiccups. They're all convinced the Federation will embrace advanced biotech eventually, it's just a matter of time. They try to push the process along by feeding advanced biotech to various plants within the Tanushan BT industry. But you know all that.

"The FIA benefit from this too—they're pragmatists, they view GIs in particular as the League's primary strategic advantage and thus the Federation's primary threat. Federation biotech restrictions mean they're unable to carry out their own research . . . legally. And so, in this case, and several others I've read about on League Intel reports, they've teamed up and are effectively working together—the FIA gains invaluable data, and the League gets to spread the advanced biotech gospel through the Tanushan private sector, which is where all the illegal research is based. Got that?"

Thiaw blinked. Doubtless he'd heard it all hypothesized before. To hear it direct from someone who knew . . . the cameras were recording.

Everything she said was being recorded. In this room, everything always was.

"Now the FIA have abducted me. Whole stacks of research right there. I'm experimental, obviously. Something of a gold mine for them, I'm sure." She took a deep breath, not liking where these conclusions were logically taking her. "Only in doing so they've brought the CSA down on their heads. Their mission could easily have been compromised. The way they planned it, with the whitecoats you captured, it looks like they figured being caught was inevitable. Which means they're prepared for it. Which means they'll start shutting things down before the CSA gets to them, now that the CSA knows where to look. When the mission gets compromised, there's a withdrawal procedure. It's what the Intels call an MEK application . . . Most Extreme Kind. If it gets activated here, in this city, you'll know about it. Believe me. If the League's here too, I'd look for something heavy. Possibly GIs. But I'm just guessing, I've never been involved with anything like that myself. My superiors kept me well away from covert stuff . . . probably they were worried I'd be contaminated by too much civilian contact and wouldn't want to fight any more. And they'd have been right too."

Thiaw stared at her for a long moment. Rafasan too. No one spoke.

Then, "Heavy?" Thiaw asked, cautiously. "You think the League has a presence here too? For this . . . this escape clause? How heavy?"

"The FIA would be orchestrating it," Sandy replied tonelessly. "They're the ones with the inside knowledge. As for how heavy . . ." She shrugged. ". . . it's the FIA. Go figure."

"The FIA are . . . are . . ." Rafasan waved a beringed hand in search of the appropriate term. ". . . well, they're not exactly civilised, and I know they've been out in the dark for a long time, what with the war and the secrecy legislation enforced over such wide distances and dubious regulatory mechanisms . . . but, I mean, they're a legal entity!" With some indignation, although at precisely what, Sandy could not tell. "Surely there are *some* limits on their behaviour?"

"Ms. Rafasan," Sandy said dryly, "I've been privy to things that go on in areas of space no Federation official ever sees reports on or is encouraged to care about. You'd be amazed. Truly amazed, I assure you."

The assertion met with no response. Outside the room, Sandy was certain there would be commotion, calls being made. Doubtless a whole further mass of officialdom would descend on her in short order. Well, at least she'd done something. Tired of being drugged and prodded, she'd kicked back. Now let them panic, she thought darkly. She only hoped that throwing the proverbial shit so directly at the fan did not spray too much of it back into her face. But it was a civilian city. Anything seemed possible.

"There," said Dr. Djohan, cutting away the last bandage from around her knee. Probed and prodded at the joint for a moment, tapping the kneecap experimentally, fingering recently separated skin. It would show him nothing that sonic-mapping had not already displayed through the bandages, Sandy knew. He then stood back to examine her from a greater distance, arms folded with some satisfaction. Flat on her back, fully restrained and totally naked, Sandy was not entirely sure exactly what he was looking at.

"Can I get up now?" she asked mildly. Djohan actually blushed. She saw it on heat scan.

"Yes, yes, of course." He rapped himself absently on the head and stepped quickly to the door on his small legs. Sandy watched him go. Strange little man, she thought, partway between sarcasm and curiosity. The door closed behind him, locks snapping. A moment later the restraints automatically released and she eased herself up on the bed.

Her joints hurt. Most of her did, a dull, aching, multilevel pain. She stretched a leg out before her and looked at it. There was a clear red line about the knee, around the top of the kneecap, raised in a small ridge. She touched it. Probed with both hands. Nothing hurt. Everything was more or less where she remembered it to be. The underside tendons were sore and twinged unpleasantly when she flexed. Her other knee was much the same.

And it hit her, suddenly, what had happened . . . she squeezed her eyes shut, very hard, attempting to fight off the surge of horrid memory. She had been a special forces soldier. She had seen terrible things in the war. Operating theatres were not strange places to any GI, least of all one with her experience, for both battlefield injury and surgical upgrade as League biotechnology had improved. She recalled the familiar, antiseptic stench, remembering previous occasions when she had smelt the same . . . she had to cope with it. She had no other choice but to cope. She was a GI, after all, and unlike a regular human she *could* deal with such things. Physically, at least. Mentally . . . was another question. But she knew her physical nature. She knew she could endure, and recover. She knew that even the physical scars would be gone in time. She held to that thought with firm determination and resolved to be what she was and do what she knew best. To be a soldier, and cope.

The procession of CSA interrogators had receded at last, finally convinced she had nothing left to tell them. Which was good, because she didn't. She stood now, legs wide apart and cautious of her balance, before the apartment windows. She ached. A strange, all-over ache that throbbed and pulsed through her very bones. That was good. Very good, in fact—it meant that the systems were knitting together once more, responding to each other as any organism's would in full health. If she shifted balance from one leg to the other too fast she would get a shooting pain through a knee, or a hip, sometimes racing with electric reflex up her spine and shoulders. But that was good, too. Dr. Djohan told her so. And she believed him.

Outside, it was another stunningly clear, blue-skied, sunny day. She was located, she'd gathered, in the district of Largos, just south of midwestern Tanusha. One district looked more or less like another, however. Only the bends in nearby river tributaries and the location of distinctive building landmarks told the difference. Her building was just beyond the periphery of a business-district hub, she'd gathered, but facing outwards. Before her sprawled an unobstructed view across open, low-density suburbia swathed in spreading greenery. Several kilometres beyond, another hub, a rising cluster of buildings haphazardly flanking a huge, gleaming mega-rise. Mid-rises sprawled about more built-up urbanity, following a river course, and another soaring mega-rise, then gave way to suburbia again. And on and on the patterns stretched, across all the visible cityscape. There was a lot of cityscape visible. In Tanusha there always was.

The questioning had been intense. She reflected over the day's interrogation, since her revelations to Thiaw and Rafasan yesterday. Evidently she'd made some people nervous. And right that they should be. But even *she* did not know what was coming. If anything. It was all a mystery to her too, this covert ops—as she'd told Thiaw and Rafasan, and all subsequent interviewers, she only knew as much as she'd gathered from a distance. And a disinterested distance at that. She'd had better things to worry about back in Dark Star. Like keeping her team alive from one mission to the next.

She needed to move. Desperately. Thankfully, someone had set up an exercise bike further along the windows for exactly that purpose. She slipped carefully out of her bathrobe and into the comfortable tracksuit that that same person had thoughtfully slung across the bike seat, then climbed on.

She was still pedalling a half hour later when Naidu walked in.

"Cassandra," he announced, loudly over the noise of the African rhythms thumping from the stereo, "I need to talk to you."

"Sure." Leaning on the handlebars, legs going round in steady circles in time with the rhythm. "Turn the music down if you like." Naidu went and did that—some straights had hearing augmentation, she knew, but it usually failed to reach her extremes. The music faded and Naidu walked back over. He looked as rumpled as ever, jacket open, longish hair straggling about the collar. Age was of course always difficult to tell, thanks to technology. She judged he could be at least eighty. He had that slightly worn, weathered look about his broad, brown features. He stopped by the sofa, arms folded as he gave her a critical looking-over.

"How are you feeling?" She managed an absent shrug, still pedalling.

"Sore. I'm nearly fully flexible again, just a little slow. Miracles of League engineering and all that." A corner of Naidu's moustachioed mouth twitched, recognising, she reckoned, that jab at Dr. Djohan. "Itches like buggery. I'm sure I'd heal faster if I weren't full of drugs, too."

"Dr. Djohan assures me otherwise," Naidu replied, with understated irony, deep in his throat.

"Don't get any closer," Sandy said with bland disinterest, still pedalling, "I'm just a half hour away from my next repressant shot. You know how I get then—all slavering and bloodthirsty." Naidu just looked at her a little reproachfully, restraining a smile. A full day of interrogation on suppressant shots (self-administered, of course) and a constant wary armed guard had worked on her temper. "Are there any innocent virgins in the CSA? I eat those, you know. Three a week, when I'm not dieting."

"No," said Naidu, with that expressive flick of the head that was peculiar to Indians, she'd noticed. "I'm afraid the CSA is the wrong organisation to be looking for innocent virgins. Particularly Intel." The bike wheel whirred, forcing looseness back into her legs. It felt good just to be moving and free of bandages. And she needed the exercise, like any normal human. Her heart was beating again for one thing, with great, thumping beats that felt suspiciously like relief. Blood flowed. Temperature built up, a warmth upon her brow. After so long it felt wonderful, and well worth the occasional, inexplicable shooting pain.

"Cassandra, some of our agents discovered an apartment a couple of FIA agents appear to have been using as a part of their network. No arrests, they're far too slippery for that. But we did find a pair of very nonstandard weapons there. Tobra twenty-twos, and forty full mags. Full works."

More information. She'd been granting information to anyone who asked for the last full day. The implications scared her, when she thought about them. Generally she tried not to. She could only trust that it would get her somewhere and not merely land her in even greater trouble. She sighed, still pedalling. "What do you want to know?"

"Do you have any knowledge, in your field experience, of the FIA having cause to use the Tobra? Or anything of that magnitude of fire-power?"

"The FIA have about twenty branches that I know of," she said wearily. "You probably know them better than I do—this is just League Intel reports I read. About five are field branches. Two are effectively special ops. Only one officially exists."

Naidu nodded. "I know, Green Section are the registered lot. We understand they're actually more of a training and development base for the main black ops, but even we don't know what *they're* called. They're labelled in our reports as 'FP'—it's an ironic acronym for FIA 'Foreign Policy.' It can also stand for 'Fascist Pigs.'" Sandy made a face at that—League Intel had much the same opinion. "We think it's almost certain that it's this FP branch that we're up against here. But none of our Intel are very clear on their operating procedures. We thought you might be."

No. She wasn't. Not really. Just one damn report she wasn't supposed to have read, and whatever "clause Z" was . . . drastic, she remembered thinking. And the FIA had Tobras in town. Her mouth was suddenly drier than usual. It had only been speculation before. Now it seemed suddenly real.

"There's only a few instances I can definitely say I had experience with them," she said finally. "They're very good. But Tobra twenty-twos—that's not a covert weapon, that's an assault weapon. You can't exactly hide it in your pocket."

"Exactly," Naidu said grimly, arms folded tightly. "They may have acquired it here, or they may have brought it with them."

"Not through customs, surely?"

"No. If you were planting a covert team on Callay, how would you do it?"

"Well . . ." The old mental reflexes were unfolding, like an old, creased sheet-map long disused but still perfectly functional. ". . . What's this solar system's defence grid like? A place as important as Tanusha, you'd think it'd be pretty solid?"

Naidu grimaced, a pained twist of pepper-streaked moustache. "Private system. No separate military function, it's all integrated . . . high quality as far as it goes, but . . . well, you'd know the 'but' with any integrated system. Callay never came under direct threat during the war—it's too far away. The very idea is unthinkable."

"Jesus." Sandy was staring at him in genuine disbelief. "But, I mean, it's a good system? I've seen the technology here. It's as good as anything I've ever seen in League, and they've got some killer systems."

"It definitely deters casual raiders. But it's Federal security codes, Cassandra. Fleet security for any solar system is a Federal matter—all military is Federal. Individual worlds don't have anything independent. So the FIA . . ."

"Of course." Her legs continued pumping, her attention now entirely elsewhere. "Like a knife through butter. So they came in, landing somewhere out there in the wild, and hiked in to Tanusha, weapons and all. No customs."

"No customs. We don't know what else they brought, besides the Tobras. We don't know how many agents or weapons. We can't monitor their activity because all their communications are tapped into the local network, which is heavily shielded from government monitoring, because that is the grand Tanushan code—free enterprise, free communication, minimal government interference. Now you see the scale of the problem."

She did indeed. It was crazy. How crazy? . . . that depended on one thing.

"Now you just need to know what they need the Tobras for. Have the whitecoats talked?"

"No," said Naidu, with frustrated resignation. "They claim not to know anything more. Just that it was an operation to gather data on you. How they knew you were here, and what the data was for . . . they say they don't know. And we can't threaten them to make them talk, they don't fall under our legal system—as Federal agents in an FIA operation, they're automatically answerable to Federal law. We can't do a thing."

Sandy bit her lip, considering as she pedalled. Escape clause. She didn't really know what it meant, not in the way it'd been used. League Intel had their little games, and she'd kept her attention entirely focused on her own operational concerns. She could only guess. Until now she'd had no firm hints with which to guide her guesses. Now, there were the Tobras. The FIA rarely did things by halves. And now the firepower. She didn't like it. She didn't like it one bit.

"Look," she said, on a sudden burst of inspiration, "while you've got me, why not let me in on the investigation? Just hook me up to a terminal, and let me see everything, realtime." Naidu's frown deepened. She wasn't entirely sure herself why she offered. She was in enough trouble already. But Tobras were serious . . . any assault weapons in a civilian city were serious. And lately she'd had the unsettling suspicion that maybe this was all at least partly her fault. Her fault for coming here. Her fault for being so naive that she hadn't bothered to consider the other things that Tanusha was known for, besides infotech jobs, nightlife, and scenery. Naidu's expression, however, was not positive. She stopped pedalling, leaning heavily on the machine armrests, and studied Naidu's dubious expression. "Why not?"

"Cassandra," Naidu sighed, "I am under specific instructions to limit your involvement. Instructions from Secretary Grey, you understand. The President's administration, Director Ibrahim answers to him."

"You want me to help you," Sandy said slowly, "but you don't really want me to know too much. So obviously you don't want me to help you, in which case there's nothing else I can do."

Naidu looked frustrated, ran a hand through his long, dishevelled hair, grimacing tightly. It was politics, she thought. Obviously it was. Factions within this Senate Security Panel, among others, were leaning on the CSA, and on Neiland, and on everyone connected to her. So they were not allowed to trust the GI on anything, even if they'd previously been inclined to.

"Do *you* trust me?" she asked. Naidu looked at her through narrowed eyes.

"Yes." The answer almost surprised her. "As a person. As an ex-League special forces soldier, however, there are political considerations to be weighed before sharing sensitive information. It's not personal."

"But you agree with it?" With increasing desperation. She couldn't see a way to help—neither her way nor theirs. She was trapped. Naidu just looked at her, pondering. "What if I applied for asylum? Citizenship?" Naidu let out a sharp breath. "Ms. Rafasan said she would try to arrange it."

"You're very game, aren't you?"

"Why not? Where else am I going to belong, if not to this place? I can't go back now. Where else is there for me? Where else can I be useful?"

"Cassandra . . ." He looked uncomfortable. ". . . I feel I should tell you, the atmosphere at present is against it. Not within the CSA . . . Politically."

"I can't stay here," Sandy told him. The desperation grew worse. "I can't just stay here indefinitely, in this room. This can't be my *life*, Mr. Naidu. I'll go crazy."

"Cassandra, we'll do what we can . . . it may take some time, it's true. There are political considerations, security secrets, Federal issues . . ."

"Naidu, my own side don't want me, the Feds cut me into little pieces, now Callay . . . God, I could be so much help here, you know? I'm good at these information systems, I have expertise no one else in the CSA has . . . but shit, I'm running out of options here." Her voice held a faint quaver, and she swallowed with difficulty. Naidu appeared distracted, a flick of the eyes suggesting he was receiving . . . he backed up a step, watching her. And she realised.

"Oh Christ . . ." and glared up at the nearest camera inset in the ceiling, "Djohan you fucking fool, I'm not about to attack him. I'm upset, dammit. I'm allowed to be upset, just occasionally." Looked back to Naidu. He backed up another step. Her eyes hurt. "Oh come on," she told him, with shaky exasperation. "I'm drugged, my joints hurt . . . Christ, I wouldn't hurt you anyway. Please."

"Cassandra . . ." His voice was level, not at all frightened. Just very, professionally wary. "Maybe I should come back some other time and discuss this with you. You're obviously finding this upsetting right now."

"Look, for God's sake . . ." She climbed off the bike in exasperation . . . white, blinding light hit her, flashed at agonising intensity through her skull.

Then she was lying half sprawled on her back, one shoulder propped against the bike stand. Her head hurt like hell, and her vision refused to come properly clear. The shoulder wound ached, presumably from the fall. Her back did. Her vision gradually cleared to normal light, and the humming in her ears receded. She raised her head, looking blearily about. The room was empty. She lay alone in a golden patch of sunlight beside the bike. A potted plant frond floated nearby, a translucent, dreamy green against the glowing blue sky. She got an elbow beneath her and raised herself carefully. Pain shot through elbow and shoulder joints but she ignored it, propping her back against the bike stand. And sat there, stupidly, knees up and surveying the empty, comfortable room that was hers. Naidu had gone. She had no idea how long she'd been unconscious. It felt like a few seconds. It could have been longer.

The sensor plug had shocked her. Triggered by Djohan, no doubt, who had been reading her impulses. She wanted to damage the man . . . and put a very fast, tight lid upon that impulse, the sensor plug still monitoring her more extreme reactions, reading her temper. No doubt Djohan had set a predetermined threshold above which she was to be considered "unsafe." Evidently she had crossed it.

God. She put her face in her hands wearily. Wishing it would all go away. Wishing there was a conceivable way out of this system, for whom she was useful but could never be accepted as an equal. That was what had upset her. That Naidu, intelligent, open-minded man that he evidently was, himself still had trouble seeing beyond that barrier. Whatever else he was, he was a professional. However personable he may have appeared in conversation, he never forgot what she was . . . doubtless he'd read all the Intel reports, all the technical analyses, wanting to know what he was dealing with, conversing with. He trusted her as a person, he'd said. She'd believed that much. She still believed it. He simply did not know what happened to GIs when they were angry. Doubtless most straights assumed that a being designed for combat would necessarily become aggressive when angry, aggression and combat instincts being intrinsically linked in straights.

Well, they were not entirely disassociated in GIs either. God, she *did* get angry sometimes, and it *did* trigger combat reflex. . . . That was the worst part—in some respects, they were nearly right in their assumptions. They were right in thinking anger and combat reflex were connected. But to assume she would lose all control, all sanity . . . ludicrous. But how could she prove it? How could she prove intent? There were only words, and words proved nothing.

She pulled her hands away from her face and looked at her arms. Rolled up the tracksuit sleeves, examined the red marks, a single red line up the centre of her inner forearm. Rubbed an aching, twinging shoulder. Felt at the invisible incisions there, also, and received an unexpected jab of pain. Felt, then at the back of her head, and the sensor plug that nestled in the insert socket . . . one tug and it would shock her again, if she tried to remove it. She felt like a wreck. Hunched on the floor, monitored, drugged, shocked, recently mutilated, and still aching from the scars. Imprisoned. Humiliated. Hopeless.

She could feel the tears coming. She welcomed them, for the release they brought, and the escape. She sat beside her exercise bike, curled in her soft grey tracksuit, and sobbed into her hands. High in the walls, the cameras watched, and monitor technicians watched the screens. She knew they were watching. She hoped they were confused as hell. But that was not why she cried.

# CHAPTER 6

The wheelchair glided down corridors, rubber wheels squeaking around the corners. A blindfold obscured all vision. She could sense the movement on either side, could hear the footfalls of accompanying guards, measured and lightly shod. The drugs held further perception back, a dimming fog drawn about her senses.

Com-gear. She could sense that clearly, registering the coded frequency bursts at regular intervals. A clear fix was beyond her but it was there, and heavily coded. It triggered old reflexes. Wrists flexed against restraints, bound firmly in her lap. Ankles similarly bonded so her thighs touched. Immobilised and blind, she was wheeled helplessly down invisible corridors amid watchful armed security who spoke only in electronic code.

Into an elevator, a soundless pulse as the doors closed. Silence. A pulse of sharp energy nearby. Positional beacon. Tracking their upward flight to an outside monitor. Then slowing.

Stopped, and they were out. She could feel a cool breeze on her face, its source distant, further ahead. Getting nearer, and then they were outside, and the breeze was strong, snatching at her hair and drying her lips. A whine of engines, thickly reverberating. Data flowed strongly, sensory, authorial, Intel and autos . . . signals scattered through her drug-dimmed brain without care for order.

The engine whine grew very loud, right alongside where something was blocking the wind. The wheelchair stopped, and the blindfold came off.

Sandy blinked, eyes adjusting to the glare. It was a rooftop landing pad, many stories above the ground. A forest of similar-sized midlevel buildings about them, the local mega-rise soaring massively to one side, nearly a half-kilometre tall, marking the centre of the Largos district. Alongside on the pad, the smooth metallic flank of an aircar, open drivers' doors swung skyward, a suited man leaning down to talk with the driver above the engine whine. Inside, a quick glimpse of lean manual controls, all moulded handgrips and polished, lighted displays, the aesthetics of function.

Keys worked at her chair restraints, which came smoothly away.

"Up, please," one of her escorts said. The foot rests dropped and the toes of her shoes were suddenly touching the ground. She wriggled forward, and managed to stand, moving slowly. The aircar's rear door cracked open at seamless joins, swinging upwards.

"You all right?" the other guard asked her. It was one of her regular CSA guards from the room, and he sounded concerned. She nodded slowly, sliding another sideways glance to the driver's seat and the controls there. Fancy car. Government, no doubt.

And turned, a casual shuffle of bonded feet, to look beyond this aircar and across the broad, open space of the landing pad. Several more aircars parked nearby, engines whining and doors open. Five more, in total. Milling security in dark suits, rigged for network. Her eyes narrowed slightly, hair whipping across her brow in the freshening breeze.

Why so many vehicles for such a simple trip across town?

"Get in," her other escort instructed. Sandy turned her head slowly and gave him a long, hard look. Reflective sunglasses glared back at her, expressionless. "Get in," he repeated, waiting by the open door, fingering a familiar-looking control in his hand.

"Please," the other guard added, smiling faintly. Sandy favoured him with a slight, gracious nod and shuffled around to slide backwards into the car.

The interior was sleek leather. Spacious, she noted with mild relief, stretching her legs. Muscles strained momentarily against the ankle restraints. Without the drugs, breaking them would have been simple. With them, her muscles failed to solidify to critical tension. The restraints held, comfortably.

"Stiff?" her guard asked, sliding onto the seat beside her.

"A little." Not being able to stretch properly didn't help. Relaxed again as the second guard got in on the other side, her left. The doors swung down behind them, locks clicked, and suddenly there was silence.

"So that you know," that man said without preamble, "any sudden move on your part, and I'll hit this button." Gesturing with the small, black device in his hand. "It activates the shock sequence on the probe in your input socket. It will knock you senseless.

"In the unlikely event that you did overpower us, this entire rear compartment is sealed." Gesturing around them. The drivers up front were isolated behind a smooth, transparent shield. Despite appearances, Sandy knew it was very, very strong. "They'll gas you, and us along with you. And the car can be flown on remote if necessary, even if the drivers were coerced. CSA don't deal in hostages, period. If you took one of us hostage, the others would act without concern for our safety. We all understood the risks when we joined.

"Do you understand?"

Sandy didn't even bother looking at him. She was much more interested in the goings on outside. The guard sat back, content that his point had been made.

More activity up front, people getting in and doors swinging down. Some glances at her car from nearby personnel. The driver began touching controls and the display screens flickered with graphical response. Smooth vibrations through the leather seating and backrest.

Suddenly it hit her.

"This is the President's convoy, isn't it?" No immediate response from either side.

Then, "What makes you think that?" From her friendly guard.

"The President's the only one who warrants a security presence like this," Sandy replied, watching curiously, "except for foreign dignitaries, and there aren't any here right now. If you put this show on for anyone but the President, people would ask questions. You've just hidden me in the President's regular convoy."

"You can believe whatever you like," said the man on her left. "It makes no difference."

So which one was the President? That was her next thought. Not the lead car, and not the rear car. Other than that, it could have been any of them. A lot of effort for a Senate Security Panel hearing. More bureaucracy. She seemed mired in it, a never-ending circus of interviewers and department interrogations. What to do with her when news reached the official Federation heads? The sane ones—meaning anyone but the FIA, who doubtless hadn't told anyone official what they were up to.

Callayan officials certainly hoped not. Callayan rights had been violated. If it was tracked back to official Federation complicity, all hell would break loose. She figured that that was one piece of information many Callayans would happily do their utmost to avoid finding. The calamity would be too great. Separatist movements within Callayan society were not to be encouraged—even the Progress Party lived in fear of them, she'd gathered, and they were supposed to be the most "League sympathetic" ideologically. Get rid of the GI. She provokes too many questions. Hush it up, let it pass, and we'll take out our grievances with the Federal Government committee in a month when it arrives in person to examine these developments. In *private*. All Federal-level politicians lived in terror of the spectre of the League. That, they claimed in shrill voices, was what happened when separatists have their way. Conflict, mad scientists, ideology out of control. Separatism must be defeated, and don't mind the mess.

So she was not expecting much encouragement from her meeting with the Senate Security Panel today, but rather an interrogation designed to create plausible excuses to get rid of her, ship her off to Federation jurisdiction. Earth. Where the FIA's influence was strongest. She did not want to contemplate it. Not at all a hopeful scenario.

Up ahead the first car was lifting. Signalled communication, coded frequency and tracking. Another car began to rise as the first moved out, accelerating slowly out into open sky.

Then their own. A smooth throbbing vibration, the landing pad dropping gently away below, faces of attendant security turning upward to watch. And easing forwards, the tower wall abruptly plunging away beneath them, breathtakingly. Out then, beyond the highrises of Largos and over the green of lower-density suburbs . . . she stared left, and saw how the highrises had clustered to follow yet another bend of a Shoban delta tributary, huddled buildings arcing to follow that gleaming trail of water. The rivers broke up the Tanushan topography, made it unpredictable . . . a stray tail of towers here, a cluster there, a junction at a river fork, an alignment for multiple bridges and calculated traffic flows. Her windows were large, and she could see a long way. Flying at altitude was a whole new experience. And the sheer, visual spectacle was simply stunning.

She thought to look up ahead, where the next aircar in line was travelling one hundred and sixty-five metres in front. Gliding left now as they picked up speed, rounding the architecturally curious, curve-side of the next mega-rise tower, the pivot of some unknown hub-district, their driver's hands tilting slightly on the controls to follow. The tower side glided past—a transparent side atrium ten storeys tall with gardens and hanging plants. Tanusha was full of such curiosities, and the perspective was breathtaking. Then fading behind, the car straightening, the forward screen showing their airlane prescribed in a lighted, gridwork passage in the sky ahead.

"Haven't you seen Tanusha from the air before?" her guard asked.

"No." She shook her head, faintly. Still staring. Sunlight reflected from the towers, visible beams spilling through the clouds, angled lines of light amid vertical high-rises. Trees below. Air traffic curving by, a spattering of moving dots, like small birds amid tall forest trees, their trajectories unnaturally smooth and full of curves. "It's beautiful."

It was indeed beautiful. The towers went on forever. Another slow turn to pass another tower, and still more beyond. The clouds made a ceiling, broken by the wind, fractured sunlight spilling through. Fifty-seven million people. For the first time since her arrival Sandy found herself confronted by the sheer size of the place.

Tanusha was simply monstrous, in every dimension. A gleaming jewel in this half of human space. A treasure of unimaginable proportions. A generator of wealth on a scale that the human species had never before seen. It was awe-inspiring. And, in the same moment, frightening.

"How'd you come to arrange the President?" she asked her guard. He shrugged.

"We arranged it. She makes occasional stops at all kinds of government posts. It's no big deal." No doubt they wished to make it appear that way to any outside observers. Just another Presidential flyby. Nothing to arouse suspicion that there was anything in that particular building that required a separate security presence. Just include her in an existing one. The guard spared her another glance. "The monitors read your dosage as marginally beyond parameters. How do you feel?"

"Fucked," she murmured, gazing out at the passing towers.

"I'm sorry. It can't be any fun."

"No, it's not." And left it at that as the car banked again, the driver's hands moving on clear manual control. It was a tightly controlled manual, though, fixed within safety parameters. A security measure. If every car was auto, then the system was vulnerable to attack. Constant, regulated manual control solved the problem of vehicles falling from the sky if the system crashed.

Both guards remained silent. Sandy was glad. It meant the replication counter she was running through her interface was working, and no one suspected it for anything more than it looked like—drug suppression. In truth, she hadn't felt so clear-headed in days. Their fault for not doing their homework. It took some effort though.

A particularly large tower loomed self-importantly to their left, multiple wings tapering to a glass-domed summit. The Tanushan Trade Centre. Probably the most expensive piece of real estate in the human galaxy. It looked the part. Sandy focused briefly, and found a com-net simply jammed with constant transmission, a living flow of banded waves, like a giant river.

Another building was the central bank—a more austere, unostentatious building by Tanushan standards. And the giant names soaring by atop their massive structures of glass and steel—corporate names, names recognised through all of human space. Nearly governments in their own right, some of them. Nearly nations.

She saw at least one big biotech name she knew. And suffered a cold shiver. What was their interest in this? Had any of the database the FIA had compiled on her ended up in one of those buildings, hidden in some secret sub-bracket within the manifold data-storage systems? They were what it was all about, ultimately. Technology. Profit. Corporate leaders of course denied any laws were broken. But all tech corps were hives of independent-thinking groups—that was where the innovation came from. No single boss knew everything that happened within his organisation. And how did you stop innovators from innovating? Profit-seekers from being profitable? A losing battle, the League said. But then the League said a lot of things. "We shall win the war" foremost among them. Neither side, it seemed, had a monopoly on truth. Both competed fiercely, however, for a competitive edge in bullshit.

They were losing height, she realised then. Glanced through the transparent shield in front, and saw the flight path display winding gently downward around another pair of looming towers. An altitude display ticked downwards, slowly unravelling. An aircar cut by close overhead, very fast.

"Do they ever leave their lanes?" she asked her guard, indicating overhead with her eyes.

"No. If you try to fly outside the parameters, not only does the autopilot take over, it appears on the screen of some cop monitor in some office. Tamper with the parameters and you could end up in jail."

Sandy nodded slowly, watching the car's reflection suddenly running parallel alongside. Then gone as the tower passed. Open space ahead then, and a massive, low structure looming up before them. Everyone knew that building, even those who lived many, many light-years away. With its architecture harking back to an earlier time, with grand arches, domes, and spires . . . it was unmistakable.

It was the Callayan Parliament. And for some strange reason, she hadn't got around to seeing it earlier, when she was taking in the sights. Maybe the trappings of power reminded her of too many sinister possibilities.

The flight path dropped further. Lower buildings below gave way to green parkland and trees, winding paths and glints of water. Glimpses of people out strolling as they cruised by overhead—the Parliament botanic gardens, nearly as famous as the building itself. Far ahead, the faint speck of the first convoy vehicle was curving around, still descending, towards the rear of the building's right wing.

Sandy gazed at the building as they neared, a red-brown sandstone structure, impossibly large for such primitive materials. It was modern underneath, obviously. Perhaps ten storeys high with great arching balconies supported by columns opening onto grassy lawns, the famous gardens beyond. The roof domes were perhaps Islamic by inspiration, although the teardrop windows and deep, earthy finish were more specifically Indian. The rest was colonial European, with alternate influences everywhere, baffling and pleasing the eye.

Such were the grand symbols of power that the first settlers of Callay had built, reflective of their hopes, dreams, and aspirations. Callay was a new world, and Tanusha was its capital, but in their hearts and souls the Callayan settlers had never forgotten their roots. In the League, they built great, modern edifices of grandiose, imaginative, totally original design within which to house their elected representatives. All semblance of historical nostalgia was to be purged, a new beginning made, a fresh start, free of all the historical ills that had plagued the human species.

Not here, or in the Federation generally. The great domes and reddish arches rose magnificently above the brilliant green lawns, a triumphant pronouncement of all that humanity had achieved, built, created, and brought *with* them out among the countless stars. In the League, history was a page in a textbook. In the Federation, it was everyday life, rich, varied, ever-present, and celebrated at every available opportunity. And Sandy knew, in that moment, exactly why she'd come here and abandoned the place of her creation. And she knew why, whatever the difficulties, she could never go back.

The side wings, workplace of much of Callay's civil service, sprawled out below. The aircar turned steeply left now, presenting a stunning view of pillars, domes, and open lawns out of the left side window.

Sandy looked ahead as they levelled out, saw that the first two aircars were already down on the broad sprawl of landing pads below, a third making its approach. The pads were atop another impressive structure, arrayed in a broad rectangle across the top of the rear-wing building's nearside flank, which loomed impressively above an outdoor arrangement of gardens, pools, and tennis courts . . .

Some strange frequency signals then, and the copilot's head jerked upwards as if in surprise . . . old reflexes jumped, and Sandy's heart missed a beat. The guards on either side had stiffened, leaning sideways, scanning the skies.

"What's happening?" Sandy demanded, forgetting herself for a moment. The pilot's hands shifted, the engine throbbing beneath them as the car changed attitude. Scanned hard out the windows, vision snap-shifting in unconscious reflex. Only towers. Ahead, people were running, one car preparing to lift again, the other aborting its approach . . .

In the front seats, the pilot was shouting something, but she couldn't hear what. Her pulse was pounding now, a familiar hard calm settling as the car rebuilt its speed . . . realising only too well this was the only time a Presidential convoy would be vulnerable. It fitted too, too well . . .

"Incoming!" she shouted then as a flame trail erupted from up ahead . . .

"Fucking hell!" from her left, and a violent twist from the pilot, throwing them all sideways.

"Five bogies!" Sandy announced, tracking that launch to the five widespread bodies on high V approach, hurtling out of nowhere. A huge double flash from the landing pads, someone's frightened voice yelling "They hit the fucking President!" then a very nasty tracking signal that had Sandy grabbing hard for the handles overhead.

"Brace yourselves guys," she said calmly, pressing hard with her feet into the forward shield, "that incoming's got us totally nailed." A wild, downward manoeuvre threw them against the restraints, her companions fumbling wildly for their handles as the tracking signal suddenly dopplered, badly, and getting worse extremely fast. Then everything blew up.

. . . A wild nightmare trapped amid smoke and flaming wreckage, rushing wind and tumbling, falling, over and over . . . a brief glimpse of rushing green grass and landing pads . . . *wham!!!* everything smashed forward. Bounced, tumbling over with a violent, terrible momentum, then *bang!!!* hit something else and spun around.

Sudden awareness, a horrible, crushing pressure, bending her neck . . . realised she was upside down and twisted violently, limbs tangled with what might have been wreckage, and might have been other limbs. Something was burning, the smoke filled her nostrils. A last heave tore her legs free, curled and sprawled beneath hard pressing leather, someone's bodyweight pressing into her side, trapping her further. Her brain snapped into gear with an electrifying jolt. The car was upside down, and she was lying on the ceiling. Everything had been flattened, and the seats were trying to crush her from above. Beyond the immediate vicinity of the rear seat compartment she could see nothing. She didn't even know if the front of the car still existed.

There were sounds from outside, explosions and gunfire, very distinct. She had to get out.

Twisted around with a desperate, trapped wriggling, grabbing the body by the suit lapels and pulling around . . . he was dead, there was blood everywhere.

"Cassandra!" The other guard, in pain and sounding trapped. "Cassandra, wait . . ." Definitely in pain. A massive explosion nearby, vibrations through the wreckage. "Don't move . . ." Thunder of crossfire, rounds smacking ferociously off the sides, everything shaking.

Sandy pressed herself past the guard's body, found a small space to see out from. Landing pad beyond, a scattering of wreckage. An armoured flyer landing, crossfire ripping every which way, scattering crazily off the tarmac, a door gun traversing to fire back . . . more shots hit them, and the entire wreck shuddered and rocked as she ducked back.

"Get my cuffs off and I'll get us out of here!" she yelled at the CSA man. She couldn't see him, unable to turn about further.

"I can't . . . !"

"Are you hurt?!" *whumph!!* A grenade hit them, shockwave blinding, wreckage tearing. For a moment she couldn't see for the smoke. "Are you hurt, dammit?!"

Something fumbled at her ankle cuffs, and her legs were suddenly free. She shoved a knee hard upward, straining against the drugged weakness, then a crunch as something gave way and she could turn, wriggling about sideways.

"Wrists!" she yelled at the agent—he looked in bad shape, face covered with blood, but she had no time to ponder it, got a brief look out the shattered window beyond, saw the pad perimeter, walkways and barriers rapidly getting cut to hell, things burning ferociously beyond.

Her wrists came loose, and she slithered forcefully over the agent, tearing his heavy calibre pistol from the shoulder holster, then ammo from the pocket, the man protesting weakly, a hand pawing her arm . . . good thing about the calibre, if this was what it looked like, she was going to need it.

"Stay here!" she told him, and slithered out the shattered window opening.

Rolled flat on the tarmac, rounds zipping past, the full roar of battle assaulting her eardrums. Heard another grenade shot and covered instinctively, exhaling hard as the shockwave hit and the ruined car lurched aside. Shrapnel scattered and she was up, target scanning through the covering smoke.

Two flyers, larger than standard aircars. Troops in defensive positions, military patterns, gone straight through the side doors and into the building where the fighting was corridor by corridor. Between them was another aircar, burning furiously. Bodies of security personnel. On her exposed side, surviving security were pressed to the walls, five of them, returning fire where they could.

The screaming whine of engines brought her head snapping about, a flyer arcing about to one side, level with the pads. Fire erupted from a door mount—KW-laser cannon flaring staccato blue light that blew across the security's remaining positions, bodies falling amid flames and erupting masonry.

Sandy sprinted away from the grounded flyers and toward the walkways and barriers of the pad perimeter, the airborne flyer twisting about to acquire her as she raced across its path, angled her right arm out at full sprint, and spraying ten rapid shots from the corner of her eye, blowing the door gunner's head off. Fire cut past from behind, shattering transparent barriers ahead—she threw herself, hit shoulder first, and smashed through in a scattering of broken shards.

Quick crouch to gain her bearings, heavy rounds streaking across the pad in pursuit, past her ruined car . . . more shattering barriers and she ducked and rolled, three times, propped up and fired four quick rounds to drop two of three runners headed for her car, the third diving for cover. The airborne flyer was twisting to acquire her with the other side gunner—she killed him, too, five rounds through the right eye from fifty metres.

She ran, burning wreckage on the pads beyond these to her right, and more people shooting, then into the building and what would have been the reception foyer in saner circumstances—patterned tile floor and corridors off to the sides. Used the smooth tiles to come to a sliding halt on her rear, back pressed to a side wall. Quick check of the magazine—sixteen rounds left—*chack!* Levelling that arm back the way she'd come, scanning the corridors around—*bang!* as a pursuer grenaded his approach for cover, then two figures diving through the smoke . . . she dropped them with a rapid volley whilst barely looking their way, which gave her the warning to dive-roll explosively left as someone burst around a left-hand corridor and sprayed that spot with bullets, Sandy already returning fire from a left-handed tile-slide, up and still shooting as the body snapped backwards, and blew his partner three metres down the corridor as the recoil thumped comfortingly through her arm.

Quickly recovered his weapon, scooping left-handed while emptying the pistol's remaining rounds down the corridor to keep it clear. Saved a last pair for the wounded man at her feet, two shots point-blank to the head, necessary precaution with GIs. Sidestepped the corridor mouth, pumped a grenade from the newly acquired rifle into an adjoining corridor, then another back the way she'd come. Then she ran.

She was not frightened. She saw no people, only targets. Her world held no straight lines, only the shifting stains of colour and movement, heat and vibration. Everything blended together. Everything made sense. Pieces fit into place, like a giant, moving puzzle. The corridors, landing pads, and intervening walls seemed abstract, as if seen from a distance, or in a VR sim. And within it all, she was now confident that she knew what was going on. Someone was trying to kill either her or the President, or both. That narrowed down her options, because she could take care of herself. The President was another matter.

They hit the convoy during landing with a mobile attack force—the only way it could be done, considering the nature of permanent ground security. How they had got so far, and past the Parliament perimeter systems, was something she did not have time to ponder. Equal forces down on both landing pads, one airborne to provide cover . . . ten troops in each flyer besides the crew, that meant forty on the ground.

She had seen where the convoy cars had landed. Knew how the security would be stationed, and how they would react. And most importantly, she knew how the attack would go, if she had planned it herself. The relevant question was simple: if she was going to screw up her own attack plan, what would she do?

When the attacking craft had first broken standard flight patterns, Shigeru Mishima had failed to believe what his security posts, defence grids, and his own eyes were telling him. This state of disbelief lasted a touch over five seconds. Those five seconds proved fatal.

Mishima was head of Security detail Alpha. There was no detail more important than Alpha. Alpha meant the President, and Mishima was the best that the Callayan Special Service had to offer. His capacity to handle technical detail down to the last microdigit on his command override frequencies was nearly inhuman, even for rare augmentations of his type. And his capacity to handle his job, while simultaneously juggling all of these details, had got him his position as the President's senior bodyguard.

Mishima ran a tight ship. He tolerated no oversight among his juniors, no matter how small. On this particular day, the Parliament Building's aerial defence grids had been functioning perfectly. All transgression coding had been altered and secured according to the random numerical programming that Mishima himself had provided. Emergency interlink channels with all security, administrative, and legal units throughout Tanusha, and over all Callay, were fully established and locked out.

His people were On. They were focused. They had left no procedural, technical, or conceivable stone unturned. And so, when his feeler networks had relayed an air-traffic control alert regarding five Andra-model transport flyers suddenly breaking away from established airlanes at a number of random points, Shigeru had made a microsecond judgment of the possible reasons.

It may have been a hardware-related problem—the model of all five bogies was identical, making a manufacturer-specific cyber-glitch seem entirely possible. And then there were various hitches and cyber-echoes the controller systems had been suffering at the interface levels recently—electronic figments of the system's own imagination emerging from cyberspace as object reality.

Even when it became plain that they were diving at the Parliament Building in a loose but rapidly assembling formation, Mishima had hesitated. Stickler for detail that he was, he simply could not perceive of the incredible range of factors that would need to have been manipulated in order for this to actually be an attack. Without the knowledge of those factors, he was dealing with an unknown quantity. In order to take effective countermeasures, he had taken the time to assemble those factors in his mind.

It was a full five seconds later when he realised that not only did he not have that time, he had never had that time to begin with.

Code Red was issued, effectively activating every security measure in Tanusha, right down to the lowliest police officer on his downtown beat. The President was grabbed and rushed inside at a sprint. The grounded aircars, Alphas One through Three, began to lift to draw attention and possible fire. Alpha Four had aborted landing, accelerating and evading. Alphas Five and Six changed to intercept. The ground security grid went up, armed and active. It should have meant death to anything airborne and unidentified crossing the perimeter.

Everything went wrong. The security grids failed to recognise the attacking flyers as Threat ID Positive and did not fire. The first incoming rounds destroyed Alphas Two and Three on the pads. Alpha One was riddled by door-cannon fire ten metres off the edge of the building, exploding in the utility personnel parking lot below. Alpha Four was struck by a homing projectile which blew the front end apart and sent it skidding into a tumbling collision with the wreckage of Alpha Three. With no fire support from the grids, Alpha Team's small arms had little effect on the armoured flyers, and the mounted weapons had cut them to pieces. Mishima was inside before that happened, sticking with the President while his men were slaughtered outside, fulfilling their oaths as they'd sworn they would.

Additional pad security was armed only for escort and watch duty, not for an armoured frontal assault with air support. Two landers grounded on each of the two main pads, disgorging heavily armed and armoured troopers who moved in precise, military patterns. As Mishima ran with the President and her remaining personal guard through the inner corridors, listening to the helpless, panicked shouts and screams of the outgunned, outprepared Parliament internal security staff, he knew very well who was after him. It could only be Dark Star. Only Dark Star could have got this far in the first place. And his estimations of what they might be after altered yet another notch.

Inside was chaos. Frightened staffers ran every which way, bull-dozed and flung aside by the running wedge Alpha team had formed around the President, half carrying her as they rushed down the corridors while the forward and rearguard support yelled at staffers to evacuate to the ground floor. Behind them was shooting, and things exploding. The whole building shook, bits and pieces fell from ceilings, screaming, panicked staff colliding in doorways, blocking the exits.

Alpha Team found a deserted office three levels down, bundled the President in, and began securing their perimeter. Her senior advisor, Aw Sian Thiaw, had been accompanying her in the convoy car—he crouched near the corner in which she sat, hovering protectively, face drawn and frightened.

"Thiaw," Neiland gasped, watching the frantic activity of Alpha Teamers running out of corridors, weapons ready, covering approach points and shouting in an unintelligible code that sounded like tactical geometry. The hastily fitted vest was very tight, restricting her breathing. "Thiaw," she grabbed his arm hard, "what are we doing here, why don't we go to ground level and get out?"

"They've got transports, they can cover ground level." Swallowed hard, eyes darting about, a crash of overturning desks and cabinets. "They'll come up and meet us in the middle. We need to buy enough time for Central Security to reach us, or SWAT—they're only down the road." He grabbed her hand, tightly. "Don't worry, we'll nail these fuckers. We just need a few more minutes."

"Thiaw, for Christ's sake, what about the staff?" Neiland was panicked, red hair sprawled in disarray, eyes wide and wild. "They're heading downstairs, they'll get run over . . . !"

"It'll buy us some time. We just need a few minutes . . . !"

"*No!!!*" Leaping to her feet, starting forward as Thiaw grabbed her, bodily restraining her as she screamed, "*No fucking way* do we leave them to die!" Fighting him desperately. "Mishima! You fucking get them back here! Don't you fucking dare . . ." *Umph!* Another body hit them, knocked them to the ground, pinning her.

"Ms. President!" the man shouted in her face, pinning her from above. It was Johnson, Mishima's second. "We don't have time for this bullshit! We're going to keep you alive, and that's *it!* Do you hear me! I'll break your damn legs if I have to, but you're going to do what we say! That's final!" Neiland stared up at him, stunned.

Johnson pulled himself off her, ripped a pistol from his belt, grabbed Thiaw's hand, and stuffed it in. "Last resort," he told him, eyes blazing with controlled fear and adrenalin. "If you use it, make sure it's them you're hitting." Thiaw nodded wordlessly, eyes wide, and Johnson darted off.

"Oh my God." Neiland was sitting up again, huddled, shaking, and terrified, her voice quavering. "This can't be happening, this just can't be happening . . ."

Gunfire snarled nearby, answering pops, then an explosion that made everything rattle. More commands from Alpha Team members down the corridor, suited and crouched, guns levelled and searching with muscle-trembling intensity. Mishima was nearby, crouched, talking fast into his throat mike. More gunfire, and screams. Shots intensified, a two-way firefight, rattling explosions and more shooting. Still the screaming.

Neiland whimpered, still shaking. Five steps up the corridor the ceiling exploded, and everything vanished under flying debris and smoke. Then gunfire exploding all about, shattering the senses. Someone grabbed her arm and hauled, half carrying her through the chaos and screams. Blue lightning ripped through the side wall, turning all to exploding flame.

Running then through the next doorway, Johnson dragging her like a sack of grain as she tried to find her feet to assist, vaguely aware that people were following, fighting a retreat. Into another, bigger room with scattered desks across an open floor and windows that let in the sunlight, running hard as Johnson dragged her nearly to the far wall, then shouts of warning and throwing her flat and sprawling, bullets striking about with impossible force, splintering desks and kicking over chairs, return fire answering, and then it was on, and hell broke loose for the second time.

Neiland scrambled on hands and knees to the wall beside a filing cabinet and stayed down, Johnson crouched behind a splintered desk and returning fire with the remainder of Alpha Team, a deafening roar of small arms fire. One man fell into a wall painting and collapsed over the potted plant below, leaving a bloody smear down the white wall behind. The glass partition to the adjoining executive office disintegrated beside Neiland's hiding place, the conifer-timber door kicked open by multiple strikes. Johnson lurched backwards in a spray of blood as a terminal screen exploded. Neiland screamed and lunged forward to where he'd fallen as a grenade went off and blew everything to hell, knocking her flat.

Johnson was up and shooting again left-handed, right arm dangling as dark shapes leapt through the smoke, guns blazing. An Alpha Team woman made a defiant dive for new cover amid a tracking hail of fire, popped up to return fire and was blown back two metres into a bookshelf that collapsed on her. Another stood his ground, refusing to cover, dropping one attacker and wounding a second before a third blew his guts out. Neiland scrambled backward over shattered glass, into the exposed executive office, watching in a mesmerised, unnatural calm as Johnson covered long enough to reload with his damaged right hand, then up again to keep firing. He was still shooting when the shots found him again, and what remained of his bloody corpse thudded limply to the ground.

Suddenly silence. Neiland huddled backward, beneath the big desk of the executive office, staring through the wall-to-ceiling frame where the window had once been and across the shattered main office, desks and chairs askew, obscured by drifting smoke. Johnson's body barely three metres away in a thickening pool of blood. Time slowed. Each heartbeat, each passing moment, lingered to eternity.

A human figure appeared, cradling a heavy rifle. Looked at Johnson. Looked at her. And raised his weapon.

And vanished as the ceiling exploded for the second time, debris collapsing in a confusion of smoke and dust. Too stunned to cover herself, Neiland stared straight into the confusion and saw something dark and human-sized fall straight down through the opening. Gunfire roared in rapid, staccato bursts, a fast, dark shape that moved like a ghost in the wind.

A brief moment of chaos, and the room was suddenly empty. A burst of fire from down a corridor, moving away. And another, and a thud like a body falling.

Moving suddenly of her own accord, Neiland was scrambling out from under the desk and into the main office, feet crunching over broken glass. Looked wildly about at the destruction, the sprawled, bloody corpses . . . saw several new ones with large weapons. One's head was mostly missing. Another had a fist-sized impact hole through the chest.

Her stomach churned and she was suddenly on her knees, vomiting helplessly. Her head spun. Nothing seemed real. None of this could possibly be happening, and in her mind it refused to register. Another painful, stomach-cramping retch. And gasped, desperate for clean, clear air. A deep breath, gasping, her ears ringing, nausea passed for the moment. Eyes unfocused, seeing only a blur.

And began to come clear again. On a pair of bare feet and grey track suit leggings. Stared, not having heard the arrival. The owner of the feet crouched alongside, and Neiland looked up, hardly daring to breathe. Untidy blonde hair, burning blue eyes. Cassandra Kresnov. The GI. The one whom all of her closest advisors were telling her to sentence to bureaucratic hell.

"You okay?" Kresnov asked her. It was unthinkable that anyone should sound so calm in the midst of this nightmare. Everything was insane. She managed a faint nod, unable to speak. "Are you going to be all right here? There are some people I'd like to kill on the lower floors—they were shooting running civilians, last I saw."

Utterly serious. There was no malice in her voice, only a statement of fact.

"Be my guest, please," Neiland rasped. "Kill them all."

The GI nodded. "Thank you, I will."

More shooting from downstairs, then, before she could get up, an explosion shook the floor. The GI listened, expressionless but for a slightly raised eyebrow, as if hearing something of mild but not enthralling interest.

"Hmm. Reinforcements just got here. No point now, they'd just shoot me into the bargain. And they'll be down on the roof in another minute."

"Who will?" The Presidential mind was refusing to function. The Presidential mind was registering a wetness between her thighs, and a warmth that just had to be urine. The Presidential mind didn't care.

"SWAT, if I recognise the signature. They started taking out the flyers two minutes ago—you were probably too busy to hear. I'll stay here and make sure no stragglers get flushed this way."

Explaining herself calmly as she knelt in firing position on the floor, covering the ruined, bullet-ripped corridor entrances. Sitting helplessly on her knees, Neiland stared at her. The right forearm and hand, now gripping the trigger handle, were red with blood. Her white T-shirt was torn and bloodstained. And she was utterly, utterly calm.

Neiland got to her feet, swaying slightly. Staggered through the strewn wreckage to the first of her Alpha Team men, finding him messily, unpleasantly dead.

"Don't bother," Kresnov said from behind her. "There's no one alive in this room but us. I can tell." Neiland stared down at the dead man. Lim, she remembered his name was. His face was intact, young, Asian, and handsome. So young. Oh God. Tears blurred her eyes.

"I'm sorry," Kresnov added.

Neiland fell to her knees by the body of the young man named Lim, whose first name she had never learned, never thought worth bothering to learn, although she saw him nearly every day, every time she travelled certainly. . . . She cried without restraint, while the GI who by all rights should want her dead guarded the corridors to her back, and waited for the fighting downstairs to stop and help to arrive. She was still crying when the confused thud of heavy boots sounded in the outside corridors, and Kresnov called out. Laid her weapon down on a desktop in full view, and stood, hands on her head.

Armed figures burst in, weapons levelled. Took in the scene.

"Down on the ground!" one of them yelled at Kresnov. "Now!" Kresnov complied, as calmly as before.

"It's the President!" shouted another one, rushing forward and shouldering his weapon while the others covered him. "We've found her, we've found her!" Crouching alongside, then, in awed concern . . . "Ms. President, are you hurt?"

"It's the fucking GI!" another shouted as Kresnov's hands were bound behind her back. Planted a boot on her shoulders, pressing the gun barrel to her head . . . "I should blow your fucking brains out right now, you fucking bitch!"

Neiland staggered to her feet fast, rounding on the troopers who were suddenly gathering around where Kresnov lay face down on the floor, weapons held ready. Too fast. Everything faded, and noises dimmed.

"Bind her feet man, she's fucking dangerous!"

"Don't move, bitch!" The thud of a boot landing, hard. And again.

"Ms. President?" someone spoke very clearly from nearby as everything else faded away.

It was the last thing Neiland heard before she passed out.

# CHAPTER 7

"**M**s. President, the doctor said that you ought to rest."

"I don't want to rest, Ms. Rafasan, I'm perfectly capable of holding a meeting."

Mahudmita Rafasan gave Benjamin Grey a despairing look. Half seated on the hospital bed that the President ought to have been occupying, the Callayan State Security Chief shook his head, lips pressed to a grim line. His shirt and tie were uncharacteristically askew, and a suggestion of stubble darkened his jaw.

Seemingly oblivious to them both, President Katia Neiland sat between the far wall and the large desk, facing them both. Chi Haotian hospital reserved exclusive sections for important, busy people. This room was one such, and the hospital bed was accompanied by the inevitable working desk. If either of the President's aides found the irony of this pairing amusing, they kept it to themselves.

Neiland was fully and properly dressed, refusing the

white bed robe that the nervous attending nurse had offered. How anyone could possibly expect her to lie in bed and stare at the ceiling when the entire city, indeed the planet, had just been turned on its head was completely beyond her. She could only assume that certain of her advisors did not take her responsibilities as seriously as she did.

She flicked from one shielded channel to another, checking on her latest advisory reports, reading most and internalising some through the direct link. With a practised eye, she noted the signs of frantic haste—the contextual ambiguities, the grammatical errors, the incomplete analyses. The bureaucracy was going nuts. Reports were being churned out, instructions overlapping from a dozen different departments, queries misplaced, security restrictions imposed . . . it was chaos of a sort that modern, infotech administrations were supposed to have been cured of long, long ago.

Good Lord, Neiland thought glumly as she scanned quickly through the mess, have we let things get this far out of hand? She remembered reports, warning documents urging caution in the face of unbridled expansion and administrative indulgence. . . . You never notice the problem until the crisis hits. She shook her head tiredly. It all seemed so predictable in hindsight. But at the time there had never been enough reason, and the administrative demands had been so enormous, the pace of change so much faster than any comparable administration had ever had to handle. . . . She'd thought she'd been doing a good job on this kind of thing. It dismayed her to discover otherwise.

The door to the private ward opened, and Neiland looked up.

"Ms. President?" It was Ulu N'darie, the deputy chief of the CSA. Small, black, and compact, she was a ball of seamless efficiency. "Everyone is here except for Mr. Ramos and Mr. Ibrahim . . . should I have them wait?"

"No," Neiland sharply cut off the two advisors present, who stared at her with consternation. "I'll see them now, thank you. I don't have time to wait for the unpunctual." It was a harsh assessment of both absent men, who were no doubt entangled in their own procedural nightmares on this most singular of Tanushan evenings. N'darie merely nodded and vanished from the doorway.

"Ms. President," Grey tried again, "don't you think it would be better to wait . . . ?"

"No." The word was sharp and tactless, with little regard for feelings. Grey had no response. Doubtless, she thought, he believed her unreasonable. That suited her fine. She was in no mood for reasonable. She wanted answers.

The main door opened once more and stayed open, as a file of important, anxious-looking people entered the room. Neiland absently disconnected the shielded plug-in from the back of her skull and leaned back in the deep leather chair. Unlike her office chair, it was not moulded to her body, and the cushions felt all wrong. Another incongruous wrongness on a day of wrongnesses. It gave her a strange feeling, and she had to blink herself back to attention as the greetings flooded in on her.

"Ms. President," Governor Dali was saying, "I cannot express my relief at your survival, I was truly terrified for you, truly terrified." He loomed over the desk, his face a picture of dark-skinned, long-nosed concern. With his deep, sallow eyes and languid wrists, he reminded Neiland of a long brown goldfish. He talked on for a time, but she missed what he was saying. Which was frequently her habit with Dali.

And the others—Sanjay Golpanath, the Vice President, some of the senior cabinet members, the head of Tanusha's IT network (a bureaucrat), Ulu N'Darie in her boss's absence and the head of the Secret Service, among others. Neiland did not perform a head count— she knew these people, and worked with them constantly. She was pleased to see her Treasurer, Claudio Rossini. Not that this was a matter concerning treasurers, but she considered Rossini a friend. For Katia Neiland, real friends were rare indeed.

"Right," she said when all of the condolences and expressions of relief had been dispensed with. And took a deep, hard breath, sitting back in the unfamiliar chair and looking about at the serious, worried faces that ringed the desk. "First off, as you all no doubt know, my senior advisor is dead."

There was a long, silent pause. Neiland remembered Thiaw's face, drawn and frightened, trying to protect her. Grasping the pistol that he did not properly know how to use, the ceiling collapsing, and the chaos that followed. It had been explained to her, in her moments of recovery, that it was a fairly common tactic among special forces these days to come in through the ceiling—modern sensory technology did not require a direct line of sight to track an opponent. They'd dropped in at several points using grenades to clear space, and then killed everyone in sight. Including Thiaw. How they'd got him, without hitting her in the process, Neiland had no idea. He'd been right beside her. Right alongside. . . .

And she blinked, dragging herself back to here and now.

"Thiaw's loss is a tough one for all of us," she continued, "both personally and professionally. I hope sometime soon we will have the opportunity to properly grieve his loss. But as Thiaw himself would be the first to tell me, were he here, we don't have that time right now."

She paused, brushing strands of long red hair back into order. She did not understand what it meant, Thiaw being dead. It would make a difference to her job, surely—she had always valued his advice and his candour. She would miss his forthright appraisals and his occasionally unflattering assessments. Beyond that she could not say. Could not think that far, at this moment. Just seeing beyond the enormity of this moment, of this entire day, was too much to handle. She took another deep breath and straightened her jacket. It did not feel right, like the chair. Nothing felt right.

"First and foremost," she said, gazing about the room with as much meaningful authority as she could muster, "what I require of you, and of all my department heads, is common sense. The shit has just hit the fan in this city in a way that has never happened in its entire history. The media is going crazy. There are conspiracy theories by the thousand, business is being disrupted, and ordinary people who have never given a damn about politics before in their lives now feel themselves personally involved.

"Tanusha has never been considered a political city, neither have we considered ourselves as such. Possibly that was naive, considering our central importance in the scheme of so many different things. I feel we are about to find out." From about her, there were sombre, silent looks— powerful, intelligent men and women lost in their own thoughts.

"And so," she considered after that brief pause, "I require all of you to be independent, and to manage your affairs within your own department with as much restraint and simple common sense as possible. Pull your heads in. Break channels if needs be. Do whatever is necessary and nothing that is not. And the first person," a jab of a warning finger, "to resort to bickering or infighting of any kind, over any matter, will lose their job, I guarantee it."

Another considering silence. Some looked alarmed. Several looked approving. She looked at N'Darie.

"The investigation is progressing?"

A short nod. "It is. There are many leads. All of the attackers' bodies have been recovered and are being examined. They're all lower-model GIs, less advanced than our Captain Kresnov, but advanced enough. We think that they're almost certainly Dark Star. You'll have a full private briefing when Mr. Ibrahim arrives—the investigations are distracting him, as you'll appreciate." That much support for her boss. N'Darie was loyal, Neiland had no doubt of that.

"Any final casualty figures?" Neiland asked.

"Sixty of the attacking GIs," N'Darie replied. "That appears to be all of them. All that were involved in the attack, anyway—it does not appear that they expected to survive the assault. Parliament security plus Alpha Team plus several of the responding SWAT units lost seventy-three dead and twelve injured. Parliamentary staff, seventeen dead and twenty-five injured. That's a total of ninety dead and thirty-seven injured, although that number could change over the coming forty-six hours."

Murmurs of disbelief from those assembled, some mutterings of consternation and sad headshaking. Neiland repressed a swallow, trying to keep her expression even. It was a lot of people dead for an operation that ideally should have resulted in only one death.

"How many more GIs might be out there?" she asked quietly.

"That is what we are attempting to determine," N'Darie replied evenly. "It depends how they got here, and how they're managing to stay hidden. And it depends on the nature of any possible connection between the attack on yourself and the presence of Captain Kresnov in government custody. I don't say that such a connection exists, but it is a possibility we are investigating."

"Are we certain," one of the gathered officials asked, "that our space lanes are secure?"

N'Darie took a deep breath. "No," she said reluctantly. There were more murmurs of consternation.

"You mean that the greatest human civilisation outside of Old Earth itself can't even guard itself from infiltration?" asked the Vice President, Golpanath. His voice was incredulous.

"Sir," N'Darie said, "even Old Earth can't completely guarantee space lanes. The solar system is a big place. Most spacecraft have stealth designs that are undetectable by active scanning, except at close range, and nothing in space is close. We see them only when they manoeuvre, scan, or fire. Standard covert military tactics is to enter a system at far nadir or zenith jump points, run silent through the equatorial plane, dump velocity with jump engines, which produces no actively detectable pulse unless you happen to be focused directly on that region of space when it happens, and release a landing shuttle. The shuttle needs no directional adjustment and uses the atmosphere for deceleration alone. And once inside the atmosphere, well, ninety-eight percent of Callay is uninhabited.

"Furthermore, we have clear evidence that the Plexus grid sensory system has been compromised from within. We do not know how, and we have no guarantee that it will not happen again. Until we uncover the means of this infiltration we must consider ourselves vulnerable to outside infiltration of this nature. Be assured that we have assigned this matter top priority."

The expressions on the many assembled faces reflected general dismay. We complacent city-folk, Neiland thought sourly, thinking ourselves so secure. Of course everyone knew the basics of solar-system physics, but no one ever bothered to think about what it actually meant from a security standpoint.

"If you wanted more information on how it's done," she said to N'Darie, "I'd suggest Kresnov. I doubt you'll find anyone more experienced in the matter." N'Darie nodded shortly.

"I have done that personally. She has been most helpful."

"We're certain that Kresnov did save the President's life?" asked Benjamin Grey, from off by the foot of the hospital bed.

N'Darie gave him a short, appraising glance.

"Very certain. Present investigations show that Kresnov accounted for at least twenty of those GIs. Which also serves to demonstrate just how dangerous she actually is, but nevertheless it does perhaps give some indication as to her loyalties, such as they are."

Grey nodded, appearing to give that some serious thought. He did not look entirely pleased. Neiland turned back to the gathered faces before her.

"All right," she said, "I want a status report from each of you. This is the last time we'll do this face to face—I merely wanted this one occasion just to make certain that everyone understands everyone else. After this, I'm certain we'll all be far too busy. Begin."

When President Neiland pushed her way through the door of the isolation hospital ward, the two guards on duty there snapped to rigid attention.

Neiland ignored them and walked down the long, open room, beds lining the wall upon her right and broad, open windows to her left.

Many-coloured lights strobed and gleamed in the outside dark. Media cruisers were hovering at the required distance, searching for a camera angle. Trucks and trailers with big antennae had surrounded the hospital, and cameras blocked every exit. Police, SWAT, and Secret Service made up the security, preventing intrusions. Somewhere amid the mess, regular hospital staff tried desperately to go about their job of treating sick people. It couldn't have been easy. Outside the room the hospital corridors were jammed so full of stern, armed security staff that it was difficult to move.

On the very end of the last bed a woman sat in a white bed robe, fully upright as if contemplating the view. As she drew nearer, Neiland noted that her ankles and wrists were bound separately, the ankles in turn connected to the bed end with unbreakable cord. Cassandra Kresnov sat with her arms over drawn-up knees, and gazed out at the play of moving light beyond the one-way windows.

Neiland stopped by the neighbouring bed. Folded her arms. Kresnov did not spare her so much as a glance. She looked calm. Flares of blue and red light deepened the natural highlights in her fine blonde hair, gleamed in dim reflection in her eyes, played along the smooth curve of her jawline and over a cheek. Strong features, Neiland thought, watching her in that timeless moment, quiet but for the faint wailing of a distant siren, and the floating expanse of city sound beyond. Strong, broad, and wide-browed . . . and the most beautiful, wide, expressive blue eyes. Serene and calm, watching the lights.

Neiland found herself unaccountably nervous, in a way that dealings with important politicians or bureaucrats never made her feel. She did not, at that moment, know what she was going to say. It was an unaccustomed feeling.

"I'm sorry about the restraints," she said then. Her voice sounded strange in the quiet, subdued hush.

"The restraints don't bother me so much as the drugs," Kresnov replied. She spoke in a soft, mild voice that somehow carried an authority far surpassing its volume. Neiland forced a soft, painful sigh.

"I'm sorry about the drugs, too," she said.

"The drugs don't bother me as much as the sensor plug in the back of my head," Kresnov added. There was a subtle note in her voice that might have been wry, sarcastic amusement. But it was difficult to tell.

Neiland gazed at her for a long moment. And on a sudden, frustrated impulse strode forward to Kresnov's side, and felt for the insert socket beneath the tail of blonde hair. Kresnov frowned, but did not move. And let out a small, sharp gasp as the sensor plug came out, the shock sequence deactivated in the presence of hand restraints. Neiland pocketed it, and sat beside Kresnov's drawn-up knees on the edge of the mattress, looking back at her face. Kresnov gazed at her, eyes puzzled . . . more than puzzled. Alive and aware, all of a sudden, where they had been distant before. The change was remarkable. And always lurking, that subtle, indefinable gleam of intelligence, in the faint narrowing of eyes, the minuscule change of expression. It was several more moments before Neiland realised she was staring.

Kresnov raised a mild eyebrow and cast a meaningful sideways glance back up the length of the room. Neiland looked. One of the guards was standing with his rifle levelled, a clear shot to the side of Kresnov's head. The other was speaking into a comlink, tense and worried.

"Son," Neiland said loudly, "you've got three seconds to put that rifle away before I personally walk over there and shove it up your ass." And on the next thought, "And tell your backup to stay where they are. This woman risked her life to save mine, dammit. If she was going to hurt me, she'd have done it already."

She had no idea if it would work—arguing with Mishima on security matters had often seemed as useful as banging her skull against a bulkhead. But Mishima was dead now, like all the others. The thought abruptly hit her, like a hammerblow between the eyes. For a moment the room seemed to spin, and her heart accelerated to a racing panic. And eased, just as quickly, as her control restored itself—more an act of habit than an assertion of will. At the far end of the room the guard had lowered his weapon. No support arrived. Which surprised her. She had said that Kresnov would not hurt her. Maybe someone in security actually agreed with her.

But they would be watching her. In this ward more than any other, the security cameras were very active.

And she looked back to Kresnov. The GI was watching her, blue eyes narrowed with sombre consideration.

"I take it," Kresnov said calmly, "that you've never been shot at before?" Neiland moved to shake her head, but thought the better of it. She felt weak, and the neighbouring bed looked very inviting.

"No," she replied. And on an impulse, "I take it you have?" A faint shift of reaction in Kresnov's eyes. And her lips pursed lightly with faint, considered humour.

"Perhaps," she said. "In my youth." Glanced down at the small space between them, seated together on the same mattress. And back up. "You do know that you're making the guards nervous? I could probably kill you where you are now, even drugged."

Neiland blinked. "And why would you do that?"

Kresnov frowned. "You really think I'm that harmless?"

"Aren't you?" To which Kresnov gave a sharp tug at the restraints, achieving nothing.

"Why these then?" she asked mildly. Neiland sighed, and glanced back towards the windows. Then back again, to find that Kresnov's gaze had not wavered a millimetre. It was disconcerting. But somehow, surprisingly, it was not threatening.

"Security provisions," she said tiredly. "You know how it is."

Kresnov gave a faint shake of her head. "No," she said, gazing back out of the windows. And sighed, eyes suddenly distant, tuning away to the colours and light beyond. "I don't know."

Neiland pursed her lips, not knowing what to think. Kresnov confused the hell out of her. She remembered seeing her that first time in the staff office that the media were now calling "the final stand" in their countless, repetitive, and mostly inaccurate computer sim reruns of the attack, or what they knew of it. Barefoot, clad only in grey tracksuit leggings and a white T-shirt supplied by her security for the transfer to the airport. Covered in blood, most of which Neiland now knew had not been her own. Eyes narrowed beyond the dead-steady rifle, but only a little. Alert, aware, and lethal.

Kresnov in combat had not swaggered, had not yelled with bloodlusting fury, had not made strong, heroic gestures or even looked fierce. She merely killed everything that came within reach that she deemed to be threatening, and killed it fast. The debriefing simulations had shown four Dark Star GIs in that room, with the last of Alpha Team dead. Kresnov had blown the ceiling with a shaped charge stolen from a dead GI and dropped through the hole with a pistol in each hand and the rifle slung over her shoulder.

Point two nine seconds later all four Dark Star GIs were dead or incapacitated. They'd simply made the fatal mistake of being in the same room as Kresnov when she had a weapon in each hand, initiative on her side, and was looking to kill them. That being so, numbers were of no relevance. Twelve point four seconds later the last of the Dark Star GIs on that entire level was dead. As one of the Secret Service people who had analysed the tapes had said, at the risk of stating the obvious, the performance was simply inhuman.

And yet here, sitting on the bed alongside Kresnov, Neiland sensed nothing of threat or intimidation. Only a mild, intelligent woman with a subtle sense of humour whom she suspected would much prefer to be at a concert, or smelling flowers, or making love, than gunning down marauding hordes of her ex-comrades in arms. There were those among her staff who believed such simplistic analyses were misleading. That it was dangerous to judge a GI in human terms. Neiland truly did not know—it only confused her more. And she was almost surprised at herself for reaching out a hand and resting it upon the GI's white-robed forearm. Kresnov looked at it, as if it was some strange kind of butterfly that had landed upon her arm and aroused her bemusement. Then looked up to Neiland, her eyes seeking an explanation.

"Captain," Neiland said softly. There was some deep, heartfelt emotion welling up from somewhere inside, but she was not certain what it was, or where it came from. "Captain, you saved my life. I . . ." and she swallowed hard. Kresnov watched, unblinkingly curious. "I know you didn't do it just for me, that it's just for my office and I shouldn't take it so personally . . . but I can't help it."

She gripped the arm tightly. It was firm and human feeling beneath the robe. "I suppose I'd just like to say thank you," she finished lamely. Much to her amazement, Kresnov smiled. It was a small, sad little smile, and for a brief moment the fifteen-year-old GI looked as old and wise as the Louban Sea.

"You're welcome," she said.

"Why did you do it?" Neiland removed the hand and used it for support as she twisted round on the mattress.

Kresnov's smile slowly faded. "Why?"

Neiland nodded. "You're so good at tracking targets, you could have just avoided them. You might even have used the confusion to escape, possibly shoot your way out. You might have been free right now if you'd done that."

Kresnov's brows drew together in a pained expression. "And where would I have gone? Lived in some alley somewhere? Stolen some money, gotten some illegal surgery to change my appearance? I sure as hell couldn't get off the planet if everyone was looking for me, face or no face. I'd be stuck here. So I'd have to try and make a life of it."

"If anyone could have done it," Neiland countered, "I bet you could."

Kresnov shrugged. "Sure. I could have been a fugitive, always on the run, always looking over my shoulder. I couldn't have got a real job, or done any of the things I wanted to do. I'd have nothing."

"You were a fugitive before." Kresnov shook her head.

"No," she said quietly with the dawnings of a faint, sadly wistful expression. "I wasn't a fugitive at all. I was April Cassidy, cognitive software technician. I was going to have a nice job, and a nice apartment, and I'd go out nights and see bands, and meet people and make ordinary friends who knew all kinds of interesting things. Maybe I'd even get a boyfriend . . ."

She trailed off, gazing with sad, blue eyes at the blinking motion of lights beyond the windows. Neiland felt her breath catch in her throat, watching her. And she had no idea why Kresnov should affect her so greatly, except that the expression she wore now was as sorrowful as she'd ever seen on someone without the presence of tears. Not upset. Just deeply, deeply sad.

"And so you thought what?" Neiland said quietly into that silence. "You thought that if you saved the President, you'd get a pardon?"

Kresnov sighed, a short, silent heave of broad, white-robed shoulders. And shot Neiland an unreadable sideways look.

"You can't pardon me from being a GI," she said. "It's a life sentence."

"No," Neiland agreed, "but hell, it's got me sitting this close to you without having a division's worth of security dragging me away by the armpits. Your popularity rating among some of the people I've spoken to recently has skyrocketed."

Kresnov snorted. "I *was* bottom-dwelling river sludge," she retorted. "Now I'm only pond scum."

Neiland fought down a smile.

"That as may be," she said with what she hoped was a reassuring touch of humour, "but people are beginning to accept the possibility that you might not be evil. A lot of them thought you were. Or otherwise just not to be trusted. But you've got them wondering. So if that's what you were intending, I'd commend you for picking a good option."

Kresnov thought about it for a moment. Her lips pursed, twisted slightly to one side. Neiland found that intriguing, and again could not say precisely why. It was like in those movies of first contact she'd occasionally seen, back in that earlier life when there had been such a thing as leisure time, where the alien and the human finally met face to face, and discovered that they shared a common facial gesture. An awe-inspiring point of similarity, of togetherness. Neiland's brain said that Kresnov was not human. And yet everything, *everything* she saw in Kresnov said utterly otherwise.

Which simply did not make any sense. There was not a single organic cell in Kresnov's body. There was a strong thread of philosophical argument, particularly common in the wartime Federation, that GIs were not even life-forms. They were imitations. Reflections of humanity's self-perception made real through the organs of commerce, technology, and politics. The philosophers claimed that as such they had more in common with works of art than genuine life-forms.

But damn, how could you argue with a deadpan sense of humour, an active libido, and that damnably subtle little wrinkle above the left eyebrow that she got whenever she considered something difficult? Neiland watched that wrinkle now, an intelligent narrowing of the eyes, considering her last statement. Then she shook her head as the conclusion arrived.

"That's not why I did it," Kresnov said. And looked at her, as if slightly puzzled by her own conclusion. "I think I did it because I could." Neiland frowned. And Kresnov sighed again, in that very human way of hers.

"I know, it probably sounds a little odd. But they were trying to kill the President of Callay, and I was in a position to stop them. And . . . I don't know, maybe that's just what I am, and the way that I operate. Maybe I just need to be useful. I just can't imagine having found myself in that position, knowing that I could stop them, and not doing anything." She shrugged helplessly. "That's just the way I am."

"And I'm very glad of it," Neiland added with feeling. Kresnov glanced away, eyes calmly scanning. Her report said that she enjoyed sensory pleasures, Neiland remembered. Certainly she seemed reluctant to turn her eyes away from the view.

"I don't know if you should be thanking me for that," she said a little sourly. "I'm probably just designed that way."

"Oh God," Neiland sighed painfully, getting to her feet and stretching, "no more philosophy of human free will, please. I'll die." Walked two steps to the head of the neighbouring bed, took a pillow, and settled it against the end frame. Climbed gingerly up, and leaned back, half seated against the pillow, long stockinged legs stretched out before her. Kicked off her shoes on an impulse, and settled properly with a long sigh, tugging the dress hem firmly to her knees.

Looked back to Kresnov, and found her watching, looking surprised. And a little amused.

"You're just like me after two days with no exercise," she said. "I creak like a rusty gate every time I sit down."

"You don't mind if I stay here for a moment, do you?" Neiland thought to ask her. As President, she wasn't much in the habit of asking. "This is probably the only room in the hospital I can go to without being mobbed by panicking administrators or officials wanting to show their unutterable relief that I'm still alive."

Kresnov shrugged. "I could use the company, I suppose."

"Good." Neiland nodded to herself absently. Thinking about what she'd just said, and how lucky she was to actually be alive. Very, very lucky, she supposed. It ought to have been a thought that stuck, and stuck hard. But it floated, and was impossible to pin down, however hard she sought to focus.

It had yet to fully strike her, she knew. But she knew that it would, sooner or later. She was not looking forward to it.

"How badly were you hurt yourself?" she thought to ask Kresnov then.

"A few bits of shrapnel," Kresnov replied, gazing off out the windows again. "Mostly grenade fragments from the landing pads. Dug them out with tweezers, no trouble." Like a gardener talking about trouble with insects in her rose garden. No trouble. Just routine really.

"You've had those before, I take it?" Flash, an impact of explosions, driving breath from the lungs and sense from the brain. . . . She blinked, and took a deep, shuddering breath.

"A few times," Kresnov replied, not appearing to notice. Or choosing not to, more likely. "My muscles work like body armour. Two things make them harden to critical pressure—one is signals from my brain, and the other is a hard, high V impact. Pressure like that triggers the hardening reflex. Most shrapnel doesn't get much further than skin deep. Not with personnel grenades, anyway."

"Interesting material," Neiland said.

"Your muscles work on the same principle," Kresnov told her. "Mine just take it to an extreme." Neiland nodded, trying to think on that. Flash, and the grenade went off again, and a glimpse of a body flying, violently torn and everything going sideways . . . her heart was suddenly racing again, thudding violently against her ribs. A stuttering roar of gunfire, shots thudding home in murderous succession . . .

"Take deep breaths," Kresnov calmly advised her. Neiland held up a reassuring hand, blinking her vision clear.

"I'm all right," she said a little dazedly. "The doctor gave me tape to lessen the shock. It hasn't really hit me yet."

"It will," Kresnov said. "Tape can only cover for so long." Like she was speaking from experience. Neiland gazed at her, heart settling in unpleasant, heavy thumps against her ribcage. Wondering if Kresnov, too, suffered from post-traumatic stress, or if the League doctors had taped it all over, and made her forget. Or if her brain was structured differently to help her deal with such distractions.

And yet Kresnov professed to have a conscience. She claimed to have been disturbed by the things she'd seen and done. Neiland did not see how that was possible without a clear memory of those individual, violent incidents. And now she'd recently killed twenty or more of her former colleagues, and appeared completely untroubled by the experience. Although, then again, she claimed not to have liked them very much. The thought gave Neiland a cold, sharp chill.

Kresnov just watched her, blue eyes unblinking. If the restraints or her seated posture gave her discomfort, she gave no sign. Her eyes were startlingly clear.

"You're staring at me," she said.

Neiland blinked. Glanced reflexively away to the blank wall by the end of her bed. And looked back, irritated at herself for being so flustered.

"I suppose I am. You must get that a lot."

Kresnov smiled wearily.

"No. It's a totally new experience for me. Nobody here seems to understand that."

It was another hour before Neiland emerged from Kresnov's hospital ward. Benjamin Grey was waiting for her.

"Ben, I want to talk to you." A sideways glance showed that the corridor was empty. Grey nodded, thin brows drawn downward in concerned concentration. His dark eyes appeared too large for his unremarkable, soft-chinned face. Neiland impulsively took him by the arm and drew him several steps away from the doorway, where scrupulous agents, doubtlessly with enhanced hearing, stood guard.

"Ben," she said in a low voice when she was sure he was paying attention, "what are you planning to do with her?" Neiland was tall, but Grey was taller. She spoke to a point somewhere level with his shoulder, leaning close, looking up at him from under serious brows without tilting her head.

"Well," Grey said slowly, "I'm not sure it's entirely up to me, Shan's investigations are under way now and I'm not certain that I want to preempt . . ."

"So you're going to leave her cuffed to the bed and drugged to the eyeballs until Shan says that it's safe to release her?"

Grey frowned in surprise. The wall was behind him, and retreat was impossible. "Release her? Who said anything about releasing her?"

Neiland took a breath. "Ben," she said with forced calm, "she's not dangerous—to us. Any idiot can see that. She shouldn't be locked up like this."

Grey stared down at her from beneath furrowed brows. "That may be so, but many of the people and the groups she's connected with are most certainly *very* dangerous . . ."

"That's no damn reason to lock her up, Ben. We should put her to work for us, dammit. She'd be a real help in Shan's damn investigations if you let her . . ."

"Wait wait wait." Grey shook his head, hands raised in defence. Neiland stopped, arms folded, her stare burning. Grey took a breath. Doubtless he realised that his position had just become precarious, interrupting Katia Neiland in midflight. "Ms. President, this is a *GI* we're talking about here. Now, I know she just saved your life. I'm as grateful to her for that as you are, believe me. But to make the leap from there to saying that this is our ally and comrade-in-arms is . . . is a very big step, and one I'm not convinced is supported by the avail-able evidence."

"Why would she save my life, Ben? Twenty-four hours ago you'd have been grateful if she'd just refrained from killing me, given the chance. Not only did she pass up that chance, she purposely and with forethought placed her ass in the middle of a hail of bullets with no other intention but to *save* my life."

Grey was frowning. Neiland knew what he was thinking—that his beloved President was letting her emotions run away with her. Again. Neiland liked Benjamin Grey, but sometimes she wanted to hit him.

"Just for once, Ben, you quit that damn bureaucratic poker face you like to pull and try looking at things from her side. She does *have* a side, you know, it's not all just cogs and gears turning in there. You tell me, why would she give a damn what happens to me, given everything that my administration's done for her so far? Why, huh?"

Grey stared at her for a long, troubled moment. Then shook his head, conceding defeat.

"Because she's not half as bloody rational as you are, that's why." Grey blinked. "You heard me." Neiland's balance was restored, and she was beginning to feel like herself again. Strange how a verbal barrage could do that for her.

"She's got feelings, Ben," she continued, just as forcefully, staring up at him with unwavering intensity. "I'm not talking touchy-feely here, I'm talking politics. She believes in things. That's how damn advanced those fools in the League finally got with her. They created a GI who is not only capable of free and independent thought, but who is actually capable of forming her own ideology independent of her creators and superiors.

"She didn't save me because she loves me—she didn't even know me. She just doesn't think people have the right to go around assassinating democratically elected Presidents, that's all. Now what does that tell you?"

Grey still looked puzzled. And baffled, as if trying to guess an answer that might possibly placate her, truthful or otherwise. Neiland felt a surge of exasperation.

"We're talking about *principles* here for God's sake, Ben. I can recognise it very easily because it's so damn rare among my colleagues and opponents. Kresnov is naive, inexperienced, and *principled*. That means she's either our worst enemy or our best friend. Now given recent events, which do you think is most likely?"

Grey scratched at the side of his nose with a finger and grimaced. "What are you suggesting we do with her?"

"Do with her?" Hadn't he been listening? "I'm telling you that she's not our enemy, and given a little friendly persuasion she might even be a friend. How would you normally treat a friend, Ben?"

Grey just looked at her. Obviously, he didn't have a clue what she was talking about. Neiland exhaled hard.

"Look," she said, "just give her to me." She pretended not to notice his startled look. "She'll need a high-security place to stay, and the Presidential Quarters are probably the only place in the whole damn city we could put her that wouldn't arouse suspicions. She'll be invisible there."

Grey was staring. "You're serious," he said then, like it had only just occurred to him that she might be. The muscles in Neiland's jaw tensed, very tightly.

"I'm not a comedian by nature Ben," she said coldly. "Give her to me. She might even be grateful."

"Ms. President, I'm not sure that I can authorise something as . . ."

"I can," she snapped. "I'm the President of Callay and Tanusha. That's got to count for something."

# CHAPTER 8

Sandy stood head down in the shower, hands against the shower wall, leaning into the jets as the water coursed hotly over her head and down her body. The flowing water plastered hair to her face, clung thickly to her forehead, her closed eyelids, her ears and cheeks. She breathed deeply, thick, pleasant lungfuls of steamy air.

Her head felt unnaturally clear. The dim bathroom lights flooded her brain with white, artificial light. Water thundered and drummed against her skull. The heat against her skin was somehow both sharp and numb, a confusion of sensation. She tilted her head back, face up to the water jets. For the first time in days her system was free of drugs. It felt strange, to say the least. Perhaps, she pondered, this was what it felt like to be hung over. She didn't like the sensation.

No drugs. No restraints. No guards . . . no, that wasn't true, the security perimeter of the Presidential Quarters was crawling with guards. But no personal guards. No watchful armed presence hovering over her shoulder, alert for that one hostile movement. A movement that now, by all appearances, was no longer expected.

"Christ," she murmured to herself tiredly, and dropped her head so water fell over her shoulders and down her back. Suddenly she was trusted. Trusted by President and Presidential security alike. It was too fast, far too fast. Her head was spinning from too much awareness, echoing like an empty room, and she was in no condition to process such political machinations. No condition at all.

Something twinged in her side, and she removed a hand from the wall, trailed light fingertips over the incision above her ribs . . . light penetration. Would have ripped the lung of an unprotected straight. The hand trailed down, over a flat, bare stomach, probed lightly at a second and third incision, already healing. Sighed deeply, eyes still closed beneath the cascade of water.

Bad fight. Bad situation. What the analysts at DS Intel would have called a defensive counter. Grunts called it a fuckup. That covered any situation where the enemy held more cards than you did. A big, *big*-time fuckup. Not quite the biggest in her experience. But close.

Dark Star they'd been, all of them. It was possible, she knew, that she might know the unit. GI 23s and 25s. She'd never liked the designations, personally. Had never really known why, until she'd lived among civilians. 23s and 25s were just people, really. Kind of. Different from herself, obviously, but then she'd never met a GI who wasn't. And then, they were all different from each other too.

But they were predictable. She'd always found them so . . . and had known that Federation soldiers always said that their one advantage against Skins was creativity. Fixed mind-sets could only improvise so far, however creative their tape training. Sandy had found them painfully obvious. And not just in their combat patterns, either—their personalities were just as bad. Sometimes she'd spent time wondering if that was the model designation or the environment, or the tape. Or all three combined. She'd never really figured that one out, but somehow she'd never got too upset when some group of midtwenties walked into a Federation ambush and disappeared for good. God knew, it had happened often enough. Not like her guys. Her lips pursed reluctantly, suggesting a smile. Not like Tran. Not much, anyway.

She remembered Tran asking her why she bothered reading those old books. Reading a few pages herself, before losing interest and going off to clean her weapons. Tran asking her if all wars had been as boring as this, once when they'd been stuck in systems patrol and recon for the better part of a month without having seen a station, let alone a planet.

Tran wanting advice over weaponry interface adjustments, moments before she was due to go under the scalpel for an upgrade. And Tran once challenging her to explain what an orgasm was, interrupting her and Dobrov in the act on Sandy's bunk to get an answer. They had not been alone to begin with—in ship berth you never were—and Dobrov hadn't bothered stopping for her to deliver an answer. Her explanation had become more of a moment-by-moment demonstration than a technical answer. She and the half-dozen others in the berth had found that very amusing.

Tran had looked up to her. They all had, to one extent or another. She was the Captain. She had an unusual designation. She was, in their own personal opinions, by far the best Dark Star unit commander ever. Which she was. She kept them alive, where other commanders expected heavy losses. They appreciated that, very much so. Worship was too strong a word, and was too emotive anyway. But they obeyed her utterly and without question. The Captain was always right. Sandy knew best.

Tran had taken this very much to heart. Unlike her compatriots, Tran had a mind full of questions. The Captain was the holder of all truths, the knower of all answers to every question ever invented. She always asked Sandy first. It had been occasionally irritating. But it was character, a rare trait among her underlings, and she was loath to discourage it. Tran without questions would not have been Tran at all. And by God, did Tran have questions. Sandy smiled, finding it amusing even now.

And was surprised at herself, standing head down beneath a private shower in a Callayan Presidential Quarters bathroom, for even thinking of Tran. She hadn't before, when things had been going well. Assuming that things had ever truly been going well . . . but that had all been an illusion, hadn't it?

She had so little choice in any of it. Leaving had been her choice . . . but in the painful glare of hindsight, even that seemed perhaps inevitable. Certainly she could not have stayed, not feeling as she had felt, and knowing what she had known. Surely she could not have stayed and remained sane.

And perhaps, she considered further, she had no more choice now than she had back then, when things were as they were for no particular reason and there was no way to question any of it. She remembered lying on her bunk and thinking thoughts of other places, other things she might want to do . . . if one day, perhaps, the war would end.

Which was what Tran had thought. God. Had she ever been that naive herself? As naive as Tran? And she smiled faintly as she remembered what she had told the small, dark-haired GI—"The war will never end, Tran. Not for us."

Tran had frowned. "But when we win, they won't have any need for us any more, will they? We'll get leave, maybe even a discharge. . . . Don't know what I'd do if I got discharged, but there's gotta be something. You're smart, Cap'n . . . tell me what I could do. Security maybe?"

It gave her a cold shiver, even now, beneath the pleasant wash of warm water. No, Tran. When the war ends, they won't have any need for us at all. Not until the next one anyway.

Dammit. She squatted in the shower, suddenly unsure of her balance. Hamstrings and buttocks pulled tight as the water coursed down and she steadied herself against the water-soaked tiles. Beneath the warm water she felt suddenly cold, her stomach tightened with knotted dread.

Only now was it setting in. The shock, and the fear. The things she hadn't shown before the President. And Neiland had been understandably self-absorbed at the hospital, given recent events.

The firefight had been bad, but she could deal with that. Had dealt with countless others, though perhaps not under quite such drastic circumstances. What scared her was the organisation. The precision. The specific movements, some of which she'd practically pioneered herself, the timing moves, the coordination signals on the integrated assault network she'd been unable to hack effectively during the attack, what with the sensor plug still in place in the back of her skull, blocking selected transmissions. But she'd just known. Her Dark Star minders had frequently failed to understand the effectiveness of many of her assault techniques. Analysts often refused to believe in instinct in straight humans, let alone in GIs. But she hadn't known what else to call it. She just knew.

And she knew that no straight human had planned that raid. No straight human knew those moves. No straight human could have planned and executed them in that fashion . . . straights never commanded GIs, they lacked the familiarity, the gut instinctual knowledge of a GI's capabilities. Only GIs commanded GIs. She was the highest-level GI in existence. But often other, midrange levels would suffice.

She dropped her forehead into her hands and let the hot water course carelessly over her head. Feeling that her balance might go if she stood upright again. Some revelations were too big for even a sane, rational, stable GI like herself to handle calmly. And she knew, with an absolute certainty that shook her to her bones, that a high-level GI had planned that raid, and was here, right now, in Tanusha. A very high-level GI. One who knew her moves. The number of possibilities was not high. They were frighteningly, terrifyingly small.

Oh God. She slumped to her knees on the tiles, and sat on her heels, gazing with helpless dread at the blank tile wall before her face. She'd thought they were all dead. She knew they were. And now, it seemed, at least one of them was not.

And she had no idea what she was going to do about that now.

She emerged from the bathroom in the dark blue bathrobe she'd been provided with. Clothes were available too, she'd been told—civilian clothes—but the shrapnel wounds would heal faster if unconstricted.

Even so, walking down the main corridor of the Presidential Quarters in a bathrobe felt decidedly strange. The polished wooden floorboards were cool beneath her feet. The portraits on the walls were of faces that Sandy felt she probably should have recognised but did not. Former Presidents, she guessed, pausing to examine one work, and then the next. There were no name tags on the works. Presumably visitors were expected to recognise the faces at first glance. Pity she hadn't read up more on her Callayan history before coming here. But she hadn't paid much attention to the past back then. That had been her intention, anyway.

She sighed, moving slowly on aching feet from one portrait to the next. She could hear footsteps and voices on the far side of a door further down the hallway . . . her hearing improving with the drugs now gone. She fancied one of them was Neilands, but too much concentration made her head hurt. From the other direction a TV could be heard, and the sounds of someone in a kitchen. And all about, on various unobtrusive frequencies, were the security channels, leaking vague, watchful emissions. It felt very solid, though. At least something was working properly today.

The TV channel sounded like the news, which aroused her interest. She walked unhurriedly down the broad, high-ceilinged hallway and emerged into a luxurious setting that could only be the President's living room. Everything was old-fashioned. A pair of French doors led to a balcony beyond shrouded by gauze curtains. The wide, open floor was of polished wood, gleaming to a doubtless synthetic, mirror finish. Wood-carved and deep-cushioned furniture gathered about a large rug of intricate Indian design. There was even a real fireplace, with a real fire—doubtless the smoke was processed to harmless vapour some-where up the "chimney." Tanushan zero-emission standards would not abide unrestricted log fires.

Intrigued, Sandy strolled about the room. Intrigued further that it was empty. She had expected a guard . . . or a guide, at least. But it seemed she was free to wander, watched only from the usual closed-circuit TV.

Decorative ceiling, wall paintings (landscapes here). Christ, there was even a bar set into the right wall behind the furnishings. And, out of place amid this nostalgic prehistory, a broad, flat-screen TV in the far corner.

". . . no clues as to the whereabouts of the assault unit's Command and Control element, or C-and-C, as the CSA investigating officers are calling it," the man on the TV was saying. "It now seems almost certain that the 'brains' behind the Dark Star suicide attack did not participate directly in the assault itself—indeed, when one considers all the covert, organisational activities required to position such a unit for an attack of this nature in the first place, it seems just . . . utterly incredible . . . that they got as far as they did."

"Kim, many of the experts we've heard from tonight have expressed similar disbelief not so much at the nature of the attack itself, but that it could have got as far as it did undetected. Many of them have been questioning the CSA's effectiveness. What questions have you been hearing, and is there any truth to the rumours about an investigation into CSA and other regional and national security procedures in the wake of this unprecedented attack?"

"Su-Li, it's impossible to say at this time. Things are very confused down here . . ." On the TV screen, red and blue lights were flashing behind the reporter's position. Engines whined and nearby voices added to the confusion. It made for very good television, Sandy supposed, ignoring the reporter's words as she had come to ignore much of Tanushan news reportage, what little experience she had had of it. But the TV package was much better than the direct net access that TV was always fighting with for viewers. TV packaged information for viewer convenience. Direct access required interactivity, and most viewers lacked the time, expertise, or inclination to interact usefully, particularly when something like this was going on. The old medium was alive and well in Tanusha, and doing better by the minute, by all appearances.

Footsteps from the hallway . . . she turned, and saw a small, dark-haired woman swagger in, stride adjusted for the weight of the heavy canvas gearbag she had slung over one shoulder.

"Hi-ya," said Lieutenant Rice with forced cheerfulness. Sandy wondered how the woman managed to operate outside of her armour—she was too small for heavy, unsupported armaments. Strength had never been a problem for GIs of any size. Rice dumped the gearbag onto the plush antique sofa. She wore operational gear, fatigue pants and jacket with unit patches. SWAT Four, a prominent shoulder patch read. Others denoting university and training school. A lieutenant's shoulder pips. And a few more assorted patches. Rice appeared to have collected quite a few. She folded her arms and gave Sandy a wry once-over. "So y've been busy, huh?"

"Could say," Sandy replied. "What are you doing here?"

"I've been dragged." With glum exasperation. "Ought to be sleeping with the rest of my guys . . . they just pulled me out of the debrief and said they'd like me to give you a rundown . . ." A baffled shrug. "So I say 'hey, I'm SWAT, not security,' and they say 'tough luck lady,' and they give me this bloody great bag of crap, don't even offer to lend me some strapping young hunk to carry the damn thing for me, and here I am."

Sandy's brain remained fixed on "debriefing." "You were at the Parliament?"

Rice let out a long, hard sigh.

"That's my job. And a great, wonderful fucking job it is too." Looked her hard in the eye. There was an energy about Rice, Sandy saw. Lively most times. Darkly unhappy right then, and forcing wry humour to cover it. "Lovely mess your friends made."

"They're not my friends."

Rice cocked an eyebrow and nodded acknowledgment.

"I know. Lovely mess you made of them, too."

"Is your team okay?" Sandy asked. If Rice was a good SWAT lieutenant, it would be the only question she truly cared about, at that moment.

"*My* guys are fine," Rice replied with a hard stare, "but a friend of mine lost three in three seconds, all dead. I knew them all."

"I'm sorry," Sandy said quietly.

"And it *really* fucking shits me," Rice continued, barely controlling the anger that suddenly writhed to the surface, "because I saw the space on the debrief, I went through about three just like it when we came down on the roof. There were only about fifteen damn GIs left by then . . . it could have been me or anyone but now this friend of mine's banging his damn head against the wall thinking how he could have avoided it . . ." She caught herself, and exhaled hard. Shrugged. "Anyway." Again fixed Sandy with a firm stare. "We would have lost a hell of a lot more if you hadn't been there. Including the President. They said you got twenty."

Sandy shrugged. "Roughly."

Rice snorted. "So Dr-fucking-Djohan was right, you *are* a dangerous wench."

"I never claimed otherwise."

"No. No, you didn't, did you. Well fuck it, you're not drugged now, you're not restrained, I'm standing five metres away, and I'm still alive. It'll do me."

Her dark eyes were intent with the lingering fire of the day's events. Sandy knew that different people dealt with it in different ways. Rice, it appeared, went into energy overload and had trouble calming down. Only she did so now, just a little, as her brain appeared to catch up with what she'd just said. Her eyes narrowed further, looking Sandy up and down. As if only now realising the significance of standing in a room alone with an undrugged, unsecured GI. And realising that only yesterday she'd not have thought it at all prudent.

"So here you are," she stated, recovering some lightness with an effort. "Upright."

"Bother you?" Sandy asked her.

Rice met her gaze. And did not flinch when she held it, unblinking. Which was rare, among straights. And rarer still in these circumstances.

"Not after today," Rice replied.

"And that's why they sent you," Sandy guessed. Having just added that piece for herself. "Because they think I might need a chaperone."

"Oh no," said Rice, "it's far, far worse than that, I'm afraid." She turned and unzipped the canvas bag on the sofa. Pulled out a black, angular firearm—a Chesu PK–7, Sandy saw—and presented it to her, held crosswise in her hands. "You've been appropriated."

Sandy just looked at her. And at the Chesu. The PK–7 was a close-quarters model—low on firepower compared to what she was used to, but concealable, compact, and efficient. A nonmilitary weapon. The grip was angled towards her invitingly. Circumstances as they were, she wanted to take it. It was logical that she should be armed, after all that had happened. But she did not move.

"What's the deal?" she asked quietly.

"Congress just passed emergency powers," Rice said, folding the weapon to a comfortable hold at her side. "CSA has overriding juris-diction on just about every security issue going. Priority being on finding who did this and stopping it from happening again. So this is your lucky break, populist politics just went down the disposal and you just got yourself declared a security asset."

"And that means arming me?" She was not at all sure of the implications. The logic made sense. But it was freedom-through-despera-
tion. It was the CSA cutting her restraints with a gun to their head. It
was not by their own free will, and she distrusted that entirely. Evidently her suspicion was showing.

"They're trusting you, Cassandra," Vanessa said earnestly. "They
know they're not going to get cooperation out of you until you feel
accepted. They're putting you on the team. So yes, that logically means
arming you. I mean hell, you're dangerous enough without weapons.
They'd drawn a line on just releasing you before. Now they're crossing
that line, they reckon they might as well go all the way."

"No more politicians leaning on the CSA to block me out?"

"They've been overriden." With evident pleasure, a gleam in her
eyes. "It's no longer a matter for politicians. This is where the profes-
sionals come in. On emergency legislation, we can tell the politicians
to go jump."

Sandy sighed, a short, reluctant heave of robed shoulders. They felt
stiff, aching with unreleased tension. Vanessa waited for a reply.

"What'll I do?" she asked eventually. Reluctantly.

Vanessa shrugged. "Help. Anyway you can. Who knows? Cassandra . . . this city just fell to pieces. Psychologically. It's chaos out
there, the media's going completely crazy, there are lunatics on all
fringes preaching war and insanity. . . . This is the party town, Cassandra. This isn't a political hotspot, people aren't political here. No
one realised there was a problem . . ."

"What *is* the problem?" Sandy asked. Wondering if they knew yet.
Or if they'd guessed.

"Well, Ibrahim's guessing it's your precious 'escape clause.' Only it
doesn't appear to make any sense . . . unless they were after you, but postanalysis doesn't indicate that at all. He'll be along to talk to you about it
shortly. He thought he'd give you a chance to rest for a half hour first."

Sandy ran both hands hard through her hair, trying to clear the lingering fog from her brain. She did not yet feel entirely steady on her feet. She felt disoriented. Being asked to make commitments. . . . She wasn't entirely sure what she felt. Or where her loyalties lay. Or if she had any loyalties at all. The deal sounded like progress. Technically. She'd told them about the escape clause, and now, unhappily, something appeared to have come of it . . . and that, she guessed, had done her credibility no end of good. No more drugs, no more restraints . . . trust. Or something like it, if only motivated by panicked desperation. But she wanted . . . hell, she didn't know what she wanted.

Perhaps it would be enough, she thought, to know that these people were worth helping. The CSA, Tanusha and Callay more broadly. They had yet to do anything for *her*. She was uncertain if they ever would, unless their own immediate concerns were at stake. She looked at the angular, snubbed weapon in the lieutenant's hand, and wondered if she would ever feel whatever it was that one needed to feel in order to commit oneself to such obligations. Service was her habit— was, perhaps, her truest nature. It was certainly the reason she existed. But she wanted more. More than the unthought reflex, in the Parliament ambush, to protect those obviously in the right from those obviously in the wrong. Then, she hadn't had time to think it through before acting. She wanted to know she could think, and still act, aware of all implications. She wanted to know it was worth it.

"What?" Rice asked, watching with dark, sombre eyes.

"I don't know." She shook her head wearily. "I don't know why this is happening. I don't know if it's my fault, I don't know if I owe anyone here anything, I don't know what I ought to do about it. I don't know, Vanessa. I just . . . don't know anything."

Vanessa considered her for a moment. Turned and placed the Chesu back on the sofa. "Look," she said, folding her arms tiredly, "we've got some clothes for you in the other room . . . and some other things. Why don't you get dressed, we'll have something to eat, and we can talk for a while. About Tanusha. And other things."

Sandy blinked, wondering, as she gazed at Vanessa, just how much she understood of what she was feeling. Vanessa raised an eyebrow, waiting.

"Fine." She managed a small smile. "Food would be good."

The food, in fact, was excellent. The Presidential Quarters had its own staff, divided into housekeeping and catering—Alpha Team took care of all security regarding the President, including household security. One staff member brought them dinner on laptop trays, with the same careful presentation afforded genuine VIP guests. Outfitted in her new, comfortable jeans and CSA regulation heavy leather jacket, Sandy marvelled at the tray setting, with silverware, separate little magnetically adhesive bowls for sauce and spices, and a main meal of steaming Thai curry, one of her many favourites. And crisp, steaming spring rolls with soy sauce dip . . . she *loved* spring rolls.

"I could get used to this," Vanessa commented on the sofa opposite, devouring a mouthful of her spaghetti. "Ever since I met you, I've been moving up in the world. I haven't been waited on since my honeymoon."

"You haven't been here before?" Sandy asked.

"Here?" Incredulously. "Hell no. SWAT-rats don't get found in places like this. The closest I've got to political power before was when the Vice President gave me my university degree . . . but that was Abdul Hussein, he was several administrations ago."

"How old are you?"

"Thirty-six." Winding up another spaghetti mouthful around her fork. One of the household staff put another log on the open fire, sparks showering up the chimney. "Graduated fifteen years ago. Want to know what I studied?"

"Mmm." Sandy nodded past her mouthful.

Vanessa smirked. "I did an MBA." And popped the full fork into her mouth.

"You wanted to get into business?" Sandy asked with amazement. Vanessa nodded, chewing heartily. "How well did you score?"

"Uh-uh," Vanessa waved a finger at her reproachfully, "don't cast aspersions upon my academic achievements, young lady, I was third in my year . . . that's at Jayasankaran University too, that's prestige for you. I had about twenty headhunters chasing me then, big firms too. I'd be rich if I'd stuck with it."

"Why didn't you?" With fascination, her meal temporarily forgotten. Even the shock of recent ground-shaking events faded, in such surroundings, in company she was admittedly beginning to find of increasing interest. Not forgotten. Just postponed. If she hadn't learned that skill early, in Dark Star, she would have gone insane long, long ago.

"I did, for two years. One of the least emotionally satisfying things I've ever done. They're a pack of self-centred bastards, I'm telling you . . . it's this city, they have their corporate ladders, their damn expensive dinner parties, trophy girlfriends and boytoys . . . they don't talk about anything but work. They've got their own little egocentric world. They spend their entire lives immersed in this trivial bullshit and nothing touches them. After two years I was climbing the walls."

"But why SWAT?"

Vanessa rolled her eyes. "You know," she said, jabbing her fork for emphasis, "that's the really weird thing. . . . When I was young and stupid, I just thought I wanted independence and power. You know, I reckoned I'd make a stack of money, buy my own stuff, sleep with whoever I wanted . . . y'see I'd always been overindependent if there's such a thing, had screaming rows with my parents since before puberty even, that kind of thing. If you'd suggested SWAT or even CSA to me when I was in school, I'd have laughed in your face—I thought authority only existed to give decent people the shits.

"Then I saw the alternative. There's a broad section of people in this city that just don't give a shit. War with the League? That's light-years away, doesn't affect anyone here, who cares? Spreading underworld activity? Natural side effect of liberal-market policies, just grin and bear it. I mean, it's not like I thought business circles would be full of humanistic enlightenment or anything, I just didn't realise they'd be that *hollow*. And I didn't realise how activist I actually was until I went somewhere where I was starved of it . . . it drove me mad. So I started looking around for ways to get involved in things that actually interested me . . ." Pause for a sip of her drink. ". . . and I soon discovered that the only major organisation that has any real influence over issues I thought were important was the CSA. So I joined."

"Just like that?" Sandy was still gazing, chewing slowly on her food.

Vanessa smiled crookedly. "Just like that. That's my motto. I'm not much on deliberation."

"They wanted people with MBAs?"

"Sure, financial crime's the ten-headed monster here, not to mention someone has to figure out their own budgets. Only I'd listed martial arts, scuba diving, and general sports among my proficiencies, so they gave me the full physical and found reflexes and coordination in the top two percentile, so they sat me down and politely asked me if I'd ever thought of SWAT. So I thought, heck, accountancy, tax evasion, special weapons and tactics, what's the difference?"

Sandy actually managed a grin, much to her surprise. "You ever regretted it?"

"Sure, heaps of times. Like today. But the day after, I always find myself feeling kind of proud that I'd been there, however horrible it'd been at the time. I need that . . . I need to feel I actually matter, that I'm doing something useful, whatever it is. I didn't really realise that until I went into corporate business. I didn't realise just how useless ordinary people can get. And . . . God, there are times I just feel *so* superior to all of them." She grinned at Sandy, an abrupt flash of lively energy. "It's a huge ego thing but I love it. We have these public open days sometimes. You get all these suited wonders coming and gaping when we show 'em armour drills and demos. I ran into an old business

acquaintance there once, real popular bigshot, queen of the in-crowd
. . . we spent fifteen minutes chatting about all the things I'd done
since then, and all the things she'd done, and Christ—she walked away
from there feeling absolutely, totally inadequate, it was wonderful."

Sandy took another mouthful, still smiling. And sighed. "I wish
we'd had a few open days. We rarely got to see civilians."

Vanessa frowned. "You got leave, didn't you?"

"Sometimes. My team didn't think much of civilians. Never
understood my fascination certainly. And there wasn't anyone else to
go with . . . GIs needed monitors, too."

"Even you?" Vanessa asked with a deeper frown.

"I don't officially exist, Vanessa. Regular GIs needed it—officials
said they might get confused, it was for their own good. And no one
wanted to admit how different I was, so I got treated like the others.
With apologies, of course."

"Must have been tough."

"I suppose." She swallowed another, thoughtful mouthful, and
washed it down with some hot tea. "I didn't think about it much until
the last few years. It was just life, I hadn't known anything else. And
my team was more important than anything straights might do. I was
with them mostly."

"Where are they now?" Vanessa asked. Sandy's eyes flicked up
briefly. Met Vanessa's curious gaze for a moment. She didn't want to
tell Vanessa now. It was the wrong moment, and Vanessa was not an
analyst. She would leave it for Ibrahim. And besides, it didn't answer
Vanessa's question. She turned her attention back to her meal.

"Dead," she said softly. "All dead." There was a silence, filled only by
the crackling of flames in the fireplace, where the new log was burning
nicely. The warmth was pleasant on her face, even at this range.

"How?" Vanessa asked. Not "I'm sorry" or "how tragic," Sandy
noted. Vanessa was not certain if such comments were fitting. Vanessa
would not bullshit her. She appreciated that, as much as she had appre-

ciated anything since she'd been in Tanusha. She sipped at her tea, and released a deep breath. And told Vanessa something that she had not been willing to divulge to any investigator up to this point.

"My superiors had them killed," she said quietly. "All but me." She looked up, in that silence that followed. Vanessa looked shocked. And she was the wrong personality, Sandy guessed, to make a good actor.

"What happened?"

"The war was winding down," Sandy said quietly. "My commanders separated me from my team—put me under the knife for an upgrade while my team was sent on a new mission under a different captain. It was the first time in five years any of them had been on a mission without me. They never came back."

She closed her eyes. Memories assailed her. Arguments with Colonel Dravid, a ferocious shouting-match. She'd broken his desk, smashed it clean into two pieces. Never before in her life had she snapped like that. It had been a revelation to her . . . and to Colonel Dravid, too, she had no doubt.

Dravid, who had always been civil enough, in a distant kind of way. A Fleet Man to the soles of his shiny black shoes. No way had Dravid volunteered for administrative duty over a bunch of steely eyed killer-skins. With the others, he was cool, direct, and totally devoid of emotion. With Captain Kresnov . . . the same, only tentative.

Sometimes, Sandy could have sworn he was frightened of her. But then, every officer behaved differently around her. With some it was simple curiosity. With others it was sidelong looks and nervous, unthinking finger-tapping. Dravid hid it well. But after so long, and so many administrators, guardians, commanders, and seniors-in-general, she could always tell.

She remembered Dravid's face, white and trembling with anger and fear, threatening her with court-martial. Which would have been funny if she hadn't been so furious. Try explaining a court-martial to her minders. To the platoon of navy psychs who analysed her debriefing reports. To the biomeds who tested her reflexes and upgraded her functions. To Captain Teig, who sometimes invited her up to bridge level for dinner and conversation—often politics, or books, or music, or of places Teig had visited in her long navy career.

They couldn't court-martial their multibillion-dollar test subject. They had far too much riding on her. But they were evidently concerned by her sudden lack of emotional restraint. Her outburst earned her a fast trip to Lieutenant-JG Ghano's couch.

"How does this make you feel?" he'd asked when she'd explained the reasons for her fury. For a psychologist, Ghano was not at all bad. He did not patronise . . . much, anyway. He was direct. He even had a sense of humour. And he was Sandy's personal shrink, since she found all the others so annoying.

"How the fuck do you think I feel?" she'd retorted. "It's a fucking light metals ore-refinery, Sevi. Why do they need *my* team to hit a damn ore-refinery? Do they think the Federation will collapse because they suddenly don't have enough foil covers for their microwave dinners? The target selection doesn't make sense!"

"Sandy, Sandy . . ." Sevi Ghano had held up his hands, as if to fend her off. "I'm not a strategist, Sandy. I don't know what to say about that . . ."

"Oh come one, since when am I wrong? They fucking designed me. They should damn well know what I'm capable of, and I'm telling them they're wrong!"

"They designed me?" Ghano had looked pained. "Sandy, that sounds like seriously retrograde thinking to me. You know perfectly well that *no one* designed your thought processes, you're as much an individual as me or anyone else on this ship." Deathly silence from his patient. "Now I'm a smart guy, I can see you're upset. You don't usually get upset like this. It's more than just the target selection, isn't it?"

"Of course it's more than the target selection." Shortly. "Intra-orbital insertions are dangerous, whatever the pinheads say." Pinheads were the intelligence number-crunchers. Mission planners—mathematicians, mostly. And every grunt's favourite target for derision and contempt. Algebra warriors. Armchair generals. Pinheads. "My team hasn't operated without me for five years. I need to be with them."

"Sandy, do you or do you not need that surgical upgrade?"

"It can wait!"

"The meds don't think so."

"When they start leading the assaults," she snapped, "then they can tell me about it."

"These are some of the most experienced, decorated, well-trained special ops soldiers in the League, Sandy," Ghano had implored her. "And most of that quality is because of you, and what they've done with you, and what you've taught them. You better than anyone should know how good they are. Do you really think that they're so vulnerable without you?"

"It's my call, dammit!" Harshly. "It doesn't matter what the fuck the stupid mission objective is—it's my team, and it's my call! They've got no business interfering like this."

"Sandy." Gently. "This isn't like you. You're usually so full of praise for your guys. You talk about them like they can walk on water." Was that what he thought? Was that really what he thought? "What's troubling you? For the last year you've been tense, you've been moody . . . is it because of the way the war's going? It's not the end of the world, you know—we're not going to have to surrender anything. And no one blames you for anything at all. You've done magnificently. The League couldn't have achieved anything like it has without you and your guys . . ." Sevi Ghano was a nice guy all right, but sometimes, like all the others, he mistook her for a child.

"You're way off target, Sevi." Blandly, and utterly unhelpful. Ghano had sat on the couch beside her. Brushed affectionately at her hair, smoothing her brow.

"Tell me what's the matter, Sandy." His hand rested upon her cheek, smooth and warm. "You'll feel better if you tell me, I promise. I want to help you, I hate seeing you this upset." And he'd leaned down to kiss her on the cheek.

"Blatant manipulation," she'd murmured. Ghano had grinned at her, leaning close.

"Of course." Another kiss, this time upon the lips. Rarely one to refuse an invitation, Sandy had responded.

They'd made love, first on the couch and then moving to Ghano's bunk, as they had numerous times before. It was hardly a regular patient/psychologist relationship, Sandy knew. And she further knew that with Ghano it was mostly because he and the entire psych department dedicated to her study knew that she—and most GIs, come to that—had precious little compunction about whom she screwed, never having been socialised in the art of being picky. Nor taught a common-sense reason to say no. And GIs were nothing if not logical . . . and in that sense, she was just like the others. Which was not to say that Ghano didn't like her—he did. And obviously he enjoyed having sex with her . . . everyone else did, and she had a reputation to uphold. But mostly, he did it because it was the best way to get information from her. She knew this, and in those comfortable, lingering minutes that followed, she usually didn't disappoint him.

Except this time.

"We'll be okay, Cap'n," Tran had told her later that alter-day, after the main-day shift had ended. Seated on the neighbouring bunk, looking puzzled at Sandy's concern. "It's just another damn orbital insertion . . . we were in Tyuz system last month. There's nothing there, even the pinheads say so."

"That's no recommendation," said Mahud from alongside. Shifted an arm more firmly about Sandy's bare shoulders, a casual, affectionate companionship.

"You just be careful," Sandy had told them. Looked across at Raju, sitting at the end of her bunk. Nudged at him with her foot, bare beneath the covering sheet. "Don't trust the pinheads, don't trust command, don't trust anybody except yourselves. I don't like this mission. I don't like it at all."

"Why not?" Raju had asked, as puzzled as Tran. "It looks like a cakewalk." Sandy had stared at the overhead, her jaw tight. How could she tell them? They wouldn't understand. They'd think she was being paranoid. They trusted her in just about everything, but this . . . this was asking too much. And it would distract them from what they needed to do.

"Just be careful," she'd said at last. "Trust me, I have my reasons."

"Sure," Tran had said, casting surreptitious, frowning looks first at Mahud, then at Raju. "Sure Cap'n." Another look at Mahud, when she thought Sandy wasn't looking. Mahud had taken the hint and rolled over, pressing against her body, trailing a curious hand across her flat, bare stomach beneath the sheets. Sandy had sighed, staring up at the overhead again.

"Cap," Mahud had chuckled in her ear, a hand caressing her breast. "You're all tense, Cap. Just relax a bit, huh?"

In time she'd surrendered, that being all she could do. Tran and Raju had moved over several bunks, speaking in mild tones about operational preparations and readiness drills, all the while casting glances over at their sacred Captain, and hoping worriedly that Mahud was doing at least a passable job of taking her mind off things for a while. Everyone knew the Captain had been acting a little strange for some time now. Everyone speculated on what it might be—out of her hearing, of course. Or so they thought. It worried them that she was worried, but for some reason she was incapable or unwilling to share with them her concerns.

Probably, they'd thought, it was yet another strange Kresnov-ism. The Captain had so many strange tastes. Like her books, and her music. And sometimes . . . sometimes she'd spoken to one or another of things, issues and politics and strange, foreign concepts that none of them pretended to understand. They spoke to each other of the Captain's periodic attempts at otherworldly conversation. They agreed that if the Captain thought it was important, then it probably was. But none of them were the Captain, and none of them possessed anything like her designation, so they left it largely alone. Tran alone had expressed a hope that the Captain might find some people among the straights with whom she could speak of such things. And the others had agreed that that would be good but could hardly be considered a priority . . . there was a war on, after all. There always had been.

The Captain's one compulsion that they readily understood was sex—her libidinous reputation was nearly the equal of her martial one, and everyone knew that Captain Cassandra Kresnov was the best fighting soldier in the history of the human race. In bed, that translated into one very big rap, and as such, she could have had her pick of the ship, and chosen at will. But strangely, she preferred to roam mainly within her own small circle of comrades, acquaintances, and the occasional passerby—GIs or straights, she had little observable preference. But, make no mistake about it, not only was the Captain talented, but she was prolific, too. Which, to her companions, had made a certain amount of sense—everything else in her brain appeared to work in overdrive mode, so it was little wonder that her libido should follow the same path. The Captain liked sex when she was happy, and sex when she was sad and, most particularly, sex when she was uptight or frustrated.

This particular alter-day, she had worn Mahud out. Tran, ever conscientious where the Captain was concerned, had insisted Raju do his duty, scowling at him when he looked like he might protest. And so Mahud had departed Sandy's bunk, sparing a brief, friendly ruffle of her hair as she rolled onto the newly arrived Raju, and went to work.

"Three in one day, Cap," he'd told her, "you're not working on your record, are you?"

"Not unless you've got all the men in D platoon lined up outside the hatch," she had replied, humour returned and breathing hard. Raju had found that funny, and laughed. Sandy rested her forehead against his broad shoulder, and chuckled with him, the length of him pressed warm and strong against her naked body, his arms about her in a comfortable embrace.

A nice moment, as she recalled it. She'd always liked that feeling, as much as the actual sex itself. Warmth and affection. A close embrace, body to body, sharing a laugh with a man she might have called her friend. Or comrade, at the very least. And then, she recalled further, Raju had nailed her so hard and so well from behind that her grasping, straining hands had nearly bent the bed frame. A nice moment indeed.

. . . And looked up to find Vanessa still watching her, with the disconcerted recognition of a moment passed, left forgotten. Her time-sense told her that it had only been a few seconds. But she was alarmed to find herself wandering like this, revisiting a time, and a space, and a life that was for her long dead.

And now she was here, dreams of a peaceful civilian existence shattered. Perhaps she'd been stupid to think she could ever leave it all behind so easily. For what would she be without war and conflict? It was the first, last, and only reason that she existed. To think that she could abandon it all for so distant a dream as peaceful domesticity now seemed, in the glare of hindsight, slightly absurd.

But she had always had dreams. Had lain on her bunk, with or without company, and stared at the overhead, wondering at the existence of other people and other lives. It had seemed so magical, by contrast to her own bland, grey world. And the stories she had read, and the music she had listened to, had only stirred her passion for more. Ideology, culture, debate, artistry, ethnicity . . . she had grown fascinated by it all, and the more she had discovered, the more she had wanted to learn.

Sex may have been her favourite recreation, but learning was her passion. It filled her head with wonderful things and gave rise to thoughts and ideas of which she had not previously thought herself capable. After a time she would wander the cramped corridors in the carrier's gut, squeezing past the constant traffic, barely even aware of her surroundings. In her mind, she was far, far away. And it was wonderful.

"Why were they killed?" Vanessa asked. Eyes wide with lingering horror. "How do you know?"

"I saw it coming." Softly. Gazing at the dancing life in the fireplace. "They weren't the first to go mysteriously missing. No documentation . . . I broke in a few times, nearly got caught. I think they suspected. But it was politics."

"What politics?"

"Vanessa . . ." She exhaled wearily. "It's too long. I can't. Not now." Her head was swimming with politics. She needed . . . something else. Humanity. Conversation. The less harmful kind. Vanessa shrugged.

"Hey, sure . . . that's good thinking, I won't ask." And blinked rapidly, still gazing at her. "Were your team anything like you?" Sandy smiled faintly. Repressed a short laugh.

"No. Not at all like me. But they weren't bad people. Mostly. Some were nice—you'd have liked them." To her surprise, Vanessa did not even look doubtful.

"Did you love them?" she asked instead.

The question surprised Sandy. She took several moments before answering.

"I suppose I did," she said then. With faintly pained, distant memory. "Not all of them. We had a turnover ratio . . . they came and went. But I had my closer friends. They were only GIs, but . . . yeah," she nodded, sadness in her eyes, "you could say I loved them."

Vanessa, she saw, was intrigued, wanting to know more, for reasons other than strategic. For what reasons, Sandy could only guess . . . but it felt nice, to be the attention of such innocent interest. She had not spoken to anyone of her past life, not since they'd left her. She felt a sudden, tired, emotional urge to talk to someone. She had not really talked to someone, meaningfully, in . . . she could not remember how long. That told her something in itself.

"They're basically good people, Vanessa," she said. "Different designations from mine, lower numbers . . . you can't tell a GI by the designation, not really, it's just a rough guide. But my guys were smarter than your average GI. More flexible. Their personalities varied more, they had nuances, traits . . . character, I suppose. They were real people, only limited. And they tried, they really did. Like in Goan. You heard about Goan?"

"Course. The first time the League tried to turn it into a proper ground war." A frown. "You were there?"

"I was." She gazed back into the fire, conjuring memories she had not tried to recall for a year at least. Had not wanted to recall. "You remember the fuss about Federation civvie casualties?"

"They said the League basically targeted populated areas for no reason." Sombrely. "League said Federation troops were using populated areas for cover."

"Neither's true," Sandy said. "Federation don't want to admit their evac was all screwed up, that they had enough advanced warning to get nearly all the civvies out in time, but they screwed it. League never targeted civvies on purpose, but they didn't make an effort to avoid it. I wasn't real happy with the scope of what I saw. We were hunting out the last Fed units in the city . . . not real easy. There was plenty of cover, and they were smart. But there were loose pockets of civvies around, hiding in buildings, abandoned rooms, underground shelters . . ."

She sighed. Took a breath. "Anyway, League command told me that couldn't be helped. I ignored them, told my guys we weren't going to call in heavy strikes where civvies were present, we were going to use restraint where possible. They didn't see the point, of course . . . but I said so, so they tried. It mostly worked, I was never sure how much they understood or agreed. They never argued with me. I think they knew when I was set on something.

"But one time . . . we hit a Fed unit. They'd been hiding, I think using some civilians for eyes. We didn't know the civvies were there . . . just saw the Fed outpost, guns and communications, watching the street, set to ambush the next League patrol that went through. So we hit them. A short firefight . . . but someone on their side panicked, started cutting loose with a rapid autocannon, only got off a few shots, but one of them hit a ground floor wall where their civvies had been hiding. Blew the floor out."

Vanessa was staring, meal forgotten. Sandy was unsure where she was going with this. It wasn't necessary to remember it. But it seemed important for some reason she could not, at that moment, entirely fathom. And very relevant to Vanessa's question.

"So we went in there . . ." Memories struck, typically powerful past the faded suppression of tape, and she pressed on with concentrated focus. "There were several rooms they'd been using, had supplies, cooking equipment, a small generator, a whole living space there . . . mostly ripped up where the shell had hit. Ten civvies, mostly family, I think. Two were already dead. Another three injured . . . they'd been in the side room by the outer wall. The other five had been sleeping further away—they were protected. I think these five had been making a meal, there was kitchen stuff and food blasted about the place.

"One of the injured ones was a little girl, about five, I think. She didn't scream or anything. One of my GIs—Chu—was the medical specialist . . . I got her to work on the girl. There was lots of blood. Her mother was screaming. Her little brother was already dead, one of those two. Lots of crying. People thought we'd execute the rest of them, being GIs and all. It was bad."

There was a lump growing painfully in her throat. Vanessa's eyes were wide, fixed in a mute, unblinking stare in the orange flicker of firelight.

"The girl lived for a while, then lost consciousness. Then nothing. And we were still busy. We had to keep a perimeter in case other Feds came along, there was other activity in the sector . . . I'd thought Chu would just go back to work when the girl died. But she just walked over to me, through all this household wreckage and sobbing relatives, and she just . . . she just kept saying, over and over. 'She smiled at me. Cap, she smiled at me,' white faced and staring, like she'd seen a ghost. And I couldn't get her to focus on anything for another half hour . . . I mean Chu had seen dead people before—civilians, children, everything. I hadn't even known she'd had any idea what was special about children, why civvies placed such value on them. I still don't know. But basic psychology says a 39—that was Chu's designation—generally isn't going to have that kind of emotional response, in those circumstances. But I'd hardly seen a GI so affected.

"I still wasn't sure, after it was over. So I took Chu with me up to the ship Captain's quarters the next time I went—I got invited sometimes. And I showed her the pictures of the Captain's children, and some of the vid-messages they'd sent, and the things they'd got up to at school . . . and Chu just broke down crying. Ever since, I always noticed, the only time she took interest in straights was with people who had families . . . every time, she'd ask them about their children. Just little questions. I don't think she understood half the answers. I just think she felt better to know that there were other children out there somewhere who weren't in war zones, and were happy and uninjured."

She paused. Wiped at her eyes, which were threatening to spill over with moisture, and swallowed hard.

"All of which," she continued, "is a very roundabout way of saying that yes, I did love Chu. And some of the others. I loved Chu when she cried. It made me feel less alone."

"Did you feel alone very often?" Vanessa asked quietly.

"Sometimes." She took a deep breath. "Yeah, sometimes I did. But never so alone as when they died. I couldn't stay then. I just . . . couldn't stay in the League. I had to get out."

It had been that, or kill everyone associated with her team's deaths

. . . difficult, even for her. Technically and emotionally. She knew those people. She'd hated them for what they'd done, but had been unsure of the degree of complicity. It was all a part of the system. Everything was. And whatever she did, the system would remain intact, making any violence meaningless.

Besides which, she'd wanted to live.

"So now you know something about me," she said, looking across at Vanessa. Feeling suddenly tired as the events of the day came crashing down on her. She wanted to rest. She wanted to sit here by the fire, and talk of interesting, pleasant, harmless things. Like Vanessa's university course and lifestyle decisions. Like music. Like Vanessa's husband, and what married life was like. Like children. It was possible, she realised with interest, that Vanessa had some of her own. "What happens now?"

"Well . . ." Vanessa stretched slightly, as if suffering her own stiffness, post armour. "I think the Director wanted to have a word with you, once the initial chaos had settled down. Tonight."

Sandy raised an eyebrow. "Naidu's been bumped?"

"Ibrahim's a hands-on kind of guy. I'm surprised you haven't met him earlier. And Naidu's kind of busy right now."

"Suppose he would be." She remembered her meal and wearily set about finishing it before it got cold. The thought of food that good going to waste seemed yet another small tragedy on a night of too many tragedies. She was sick of tragedies. "I'm surprised the city's still functioning."

"Yeah." Vanessa managed a small, wry smile. "Me, too."

# CHAPTER 9

The night air was cool up on the rooftop. Wooden railings ringed the patio, and city light dimmed the stars to a few scattered, bright points. Trees rose up from the courtyard below. Shifted gently in a cold gust of wind, a soft rustling of leaves.

She could see the street from here as she leaned against the railing, absently shifting spectrums from one to another as the night took colour and form. The street was unusual . . . paved with stone, reminiscent of ancient techniques. The houses beyond were large, spacious, and open to the air. Balconies and trees. Wooden shutters, brightly painted, stone walls and coloured plaster. Beyond, the rising spire of a church tower, stone with a Christian cross, and a genuine brass bell. It looked, felt, and smelled like a Spanish-Colonial township. Authentic did not begin to describe it.

Beyond, and all about, at varied distances, the grand towers rose soaring into the night sky, alive with light and colour. The faint hum and whine of air traffic, ever present, but distant. It was a different world, this neighbourhood, nestled in comfortable seclusion amid the towers, shielded by its lovely stone walls and throwback architecture and the profusion of spreading branches from the thoroughly modern world beyond. Sealed by electronic barriers, a centralised network of scanners and security software that monitored every millimetre under its jurisdiction.

Along a nearby street a car was humming. She could hear its engine and the thrumming of tires on flagstones. The faint glow of lights reflecting off surrounding stonework, a glimmer on the greenery. Turned and faded, Sandy shifting to network connections to track it, absently monitoring its progress along the winding streets.

Tanusha had many such neighbourhoods, she knew. They were exclusive, to say the least. Tower views were commonplace among the citizenry. Ground level, customised private houses were much rarer, and reserved for the truly privileged, or the simply lucky. And the neighbourhoods varied in style and character. This one was Spanish, others reflected other Earth cultures, direct copies, representations from historical records and artistic recreations. There were Japanese sectors, Chinese, Indian, Italian, German, Thai . . . she remembered meaning to visit the Thai section sometime after her first arrival. Lovely wooden houses on stilts, stylised carvings, step-over doorways to keep the evil spirits out, statues and ornamentation, open balconies overlooking the network of canals that spread from the Shoban River tributaries, overhung with leafy branches, a spiderwork of clear reflections on a bright and cloudless day . . .

Tanusha had many museums and art galleries, but the neighbourhoods were both. People paid enormous amounts to live in such accommodation simply because it was nice there. Secure regions like this one also made perfect exclusive zones for VIP accommodation, difficult to infiltrate through the winding streets and limited public access, and therefore easy to defend. Thus the cultural character was maintained as a part of the city's basic infrastructure. It was much, much better than a museum, Sandy thought, gazing about at the peaked tile roofs and high, shuttered windows. People lived here. Culture was not something to hang on a wall or keep in a glass case. Culture was to live, to breathe, to touch and feel. As little as she knew of such things, she believed very strongly that this was true. And sometimes, such as right at this moment, she yearned for it. She yearned so badly she could taste it.

A guard patrolled the garden path below, beneath the tree's spreading branches. Flower beds lined his path and water tinkled into a broad pond. Beneath the surface ponderous red shapes slowly swam. The guard stepped up to the verandah. Slow, measured footsteps sounded on the wooden boarding below.

Sandy sensed the man behind her well before he reached the adjoining doorway. A quick race through the network hookups showed her a form, an image, and then a face. The door behind her opened and footsteps scuffed the patio.

"Mr. Ibrahim, I presume," Sandy said without turning. Behind her, CSA director Shan Ibrahim closed the door with a gentle clack. Wooden door, with patterned glass insets. Very unmodern. Another part of this wonderful cultural allusion.

"Hello, Cassandra." Accented voice, mild and calm. The footsteps approached her and Sandy visualised his size and build from the sound. Old reflex. With the gun at her side and the harness beneath her jacket, it was all coming back to her.

The man leaned on the railing beside her, hands apart, weight dispersed. A moment of silent breathing, gazing out at the dim outlines of roofs and trees, illuminated in patches by streetlights and an orange glow from the windows. Beyond, a scatter of air traffic wove between the looming towers, winking and multicoloured lights in lazy motion.

"The night must look different to you," Ibrahim said then. Which surprised her, and she glanced across. Ibrahim's features were as strikingly Arabic as his name and accent. Brown skin, a large, hawkish nose, and prominent cheekbones. The small pointed beard accentuated the sharpness of his chin. And his eyes, as he gazed out at the murmuring night, were deep brown, brimming with focused intelligence. Strikingly handsome, Sandy thought him. Barely a glance and she was impressed. It did not happen to her often.

"Everything can look different," she replied. "It depends on my mood." Ibrahim gave a faint, imperceptible shake of his head.

"I prefer the night as it is," he said. "There's nothing more beautiful than a contrast of light." Unbidden, Sandy thought of a painting she'd seen in the Tanushan Gallery of Art. Broken fingers of sunlight spilling through clouds.

"I agree," she replied. "Not every visual shift I do is functional. I can find some beautiful combinations sometimes."

Ibrahim nodded to himself, as if considering that. And then he looked at her. His eyes registered no surprise, and he took no time to assimilate her, almost as if, Sandy thought with a faint chill, he felt he already knew her personally.

"I'm here to offer you a deal," he said then. "You probably guessed that." Sandy managed to resist rolling her eyes, and stared away at the distant towers instead.

"Look," she said somewhat testily, "I don't even know what my status is. One minute I'm threatened with being shipped off to Earth, and the next I'm told the city's shiny new security codes have granted me some kind of special status, and I find people throwing firearms at me and telling me to defend the President."

"Our investigative teams have traced some promising leads back to a major biotech corporation," Ibrahim stated calmly, as if he hadn't heard her. "We suspect others may be involved, but we have no proof yet. Recent security measures give the CSA powers of entry and arrest in order to uncover evidence. I have a team standing by at this very moment, organising the raid. I want you to help them."

For a long moment Sandy did not move. In her mind, several loose ends clicked resoundingly into place. And she turned, straightening, leaning on her left arm as she looked directly at him.

"And why should I do that?"

"I can get you legal documentation," Ibrahim said flatly, "signed by myself and the President. It'll guarantee your rights as a citizen of Callay." For a moment Sandy thought her heart might have stopped. Her breath caught in her throat.

"It won't be worth the paper it's written on if Guderjaal doesn't sign it," she thought to say, her mouth working on autopilot as her brain raced.

"He'll sign it, too. The security lockdown makes it possible. You can talk to Guderjaal if you don't believe me—I already have. But you have to do it now, because later won't be any good for us."

Good God. What were they asking of her? What did they expect her to do? And why? There were sure to be catches.

"Do I keep my privacy," she asked, a touch breathlessly, "or will I be public?"

Ibrahim nodded. "As private as the laws allow. Your case still falls under state security provisions, Callayan citizen or not. Making you public knowledge would be dangerous."

Sandy stared at him. "And the politicians?"

"They do not advise the CSA on security matters. If they did, the emergency provisions would oblige me to ignore them if I found them unhelpful. In your case, you can be assured that I would find it most unhelpful. And contrary to Tanusha's most immediate security needs.

"But you have to help us, Cassandra." Firmly, leaning imperceptibly forward. "I know that your treatment these past two weeks has at times been less than perfect. I apologise for that, as CSA Director I have many distasteful political necessities to contend with. But we need you now, Cassandra. And I believe you may need us."

His lidded dark eyes held a very direct, very determined meaning.

And she felt her heart skip a beat. A cool breeze gusted and whipped the hair from her brow.

"You know," she said quietly. He gave a brief nod.

"CSA Intelligence is perhaps more advanced in matters of League operations than many of our politicians are aware of. I have made sure of it during my tenure. We know that only GIs command GIs. For an operation like this, only a top-level GI would have been utilised in command. And from postanalysis of your own actions at the Parliament it was decided that even you, with your undoubted capabilities, could not have made certain tactical decisions as quickly as you did without some degree of prior knowledge, or at least educated guesswork, as to the operation's next moves."

Sandy exhaled hard, leaning both hands on the railing, and gazed out into the night. Ibrahim waited a moment longer before continuing.

"Your actions have displayed to us clearly that you have no loyalty toward or involvement with those involved in this plot. But you told Lieutenant Rice just now that you were very close with your former comrades. And that you blame your superiors for having them killed. That was why you left, was it not?"

There was peace out in the cool, murmuring night, amid the lighted towers and the soft thrum of traffic. She sought it, yearned for it, gazing into the vastness. But she was reminded only of other possibilities, of who might possibly be hiding out there. Her past, waiting for her, somewhere amid those fifty-seven million Tanushans. And she nodded briefly to Ibrahim's question.

"I would not seek to harm such a person, Cassandra. Or persons. Lower-designation GIs do what they are ordered. I do not believe such a person could be held responsible for such actions. I only wish them stopped, prevented from visiting more harm. As I believe you do. But on present evidence, GIs within this FIA mission are considered expendable. There must be some doubt that any of your ex-comrades will survive the mission, if left to the FIA. Or if they do, and are transported back to the League when it is all over, they may well meet the same fate as your other comrades. Murdered by their superiors."

Her jaw trembled. She couldn't believe it. They were all dead. She knew they were. Maybe . . . maybe. . . . Her mind raced, desperately seeking alternative possibilities. Maybe someone had copied her patterns. Someone in Intel, perhaps, or one of her minders. She'd published such things, occasionally, in electronic form . . . but that was GI-specific strategy. Straights had trouble internalising so much high-speed multidimensional graphical detail all at once. It took a GI to internalise the complexities, to plot them, to make them work in the field. And she'd *seen* it firsthand. Had run through the Parliament corridors, had made contact with the enemy, and had *seen* them respond in exactly the patterns she'd laid out for GIs of that designation. . . . She dropped her head, eyes closed. Ibrahim waited, with silent patience.

Possibilities collided, and she felt trapped between them, crushed and breathless. Her old life, a Dark Star comrade still alive, and here in Tanusha. And Ibrahim, Vanessa, the whole Tanushan government and security apparatus, suddenly desperate and trusting in their need for her assistance. A chance. A huge chance. Trust, perhaps asylum, perhaps strong enough to override even Federal laws . . . someone had tried to kill the President, for God's sake. On security issues of critical importance to both the Federation and member worlds, Federation concerns trumped all challengers. But here, Tanusha's threat was greater. If they needed her badly enough, even the Feds couldn't drag her away if the CSA were determined enough to keep her. Under present circumstances, however long they lasted. From the chaos the city had descended into since the strike, "present circumstances" could last a fair time.

She'd wanted this. It was, in fact, quite possibly a better scenario than she'd previously envisaged, when she'd first arrived in the Federation and built a new identity for herself. This meant she could be herself. Be real and accepted . . . as much as she could expect to be. She'd wanted civilian life, a civilian identity and all the other things civilians took for granted. A life free from war. A life filled with inconsequential pleasures, like friendship, entertainment, evenings out on the town, taking in the sights.

And now, once again, her old life had intruded. And she almost regretted it. And, and . . . oh God, the thought hit a nerve like few had ever hit before, and a pain speared behind her eyes. And damn, she felt guilty for it. For leaving, when possibly—it seemed—not all of her team were dead. And for having such trouble reconciling her new, desperately desired life, with the old military one. She ought to be overjoyed to hear one of her teammates was still alive . . . dammit, she *was* overjoyed. And confused. And scared, and . . . and nearly every other emotion she'd ever felt or imagined, all at once, and all so sudden and unexpected . . .

She breathed in long, deep breaths, hands tight around the smooth wooden rail. Voices below, guards talking in low, murmured tones. The flitting, erratic pulse of bat sonar, weaving somewhere above the trees in pursuit of insects. And she knew then what she had to do, knew she had so little choice. Like a piece of flotsam racing downstream, she would go where the river took her.

"I'll help you," she murmured. Ibrahim watched in silence. Measuring that response with dark, penetrating eyes. "But you have to promise you'll do everything you can not to harm anyone out there who's just following orders. Anyone League."

"I have one hundred twenty million lives under my care, Cassandra," Ibrahim replied, in quiet, measured tones. "Fifty-seven million of them in Tanusha. When it comes to their security, I'm afraid I am not in a position to promise anything."

"You can try," she whispered. Ibrahim just watched her. She spared him a glance, trying to keep the pleading from her eyes . . . and was uncertain if she succeeded. Ibrahim did not sigh or fidget. He only considered. And finally he nodded, shortly and without reservation.

"I can try," he said. "And I will. In the meantime, if you are to help us, you will serve according to the needs of the CSA, and only the CSA. No other government agency will have authority over your actions. Do you understand?" She nodded weakly. "You have knowledge of League and FIA connections to Tanushan biotech corporations. There is a raid planned for tomorrow morning. I want you on it. Can you manage that?"

CSA SWAT. Civilian operations. To an ex–Dark Star captain, hardly intimidating. She took another deep breath in the cool, murmuring night.

"Sure." What was the civilian expression? "Piece of cake."

# CHAPTER 10

The CSA flyer shuddered roughly through the predawn air. Sandy frowned, leaning forward from her holding-brace behind the pilot's seat, scanning out the canopy side. Could make out the faint outlines of scattered cloud above, barely distinct against the faint glow of the eastern sky. Tanushan weather, so frequently idyllic, could change fast. The cloud was torn and broken, frayed at the edges like wet tissue paper. Again the flyer shuddered and bounced.

The pilot craned her head round to look at her. "Be thankful we're going in before dawn," she said loudly over the dull keening of engines. Shudder and bump, something metal clacked and rattled in the back. Indicated with a gloved finger the gathering cloud, fractured shards across the flat span of sky . . . like sea ice breaking up, Sandy thought, viewed from below the surface.

"Damn northerly stream," the pilot half shouted, guiding the flyer one-handed through a gentle leftward bank and pointing with the other. "Ocean's only fifty clicks *that* way," jabbing with the finger back toward the west, "warm southerly currents meet the cold northerlies . . . you get these rapid weather changes. Things just blow up with no warning a few hundred Ks out, maybe a few thousand. This is nothing. This is just the on-shore flow . . . wait three or four hours, it'll be lightning city and pouring rain."

She levelled out of the turn, rectangles matching, passing through on the navscreen. Bump and wobble as they flattened out, and Sandy gripped the overhead more firmly with a gloved fist. The tops of towers soaring by, spire lights and roof lights ablaze, tall and majestic beneath the ragged ceiling of cloud. Incredible sight. The looming towertops sprawled off for many kilometres in all directions above an intricate carpet of ground light. Another wobble, pulling her arm-grip tight, more equipment rattling in the back.

"How strong's the wind?" she shouted to the pilot to be heard above the earphones.

"Sixty, sixty-five knots. It's not the speed, it's these damn towers," another indicating finger as the flyer curved through yet another one-handed turn. "Turn a steady stream into soup. It's like flying in a washing machine. I'd go lower, but it's not in the profile."

In the left seat, the copilot looked a lot more occupied than the pilot, eyes shaded and interfacing something complicated. Navcomp interface. Copilots were always busiest, inbound. Rifle at her side and headset com-plug in her ear, it was all feeling very familiar to Sandy. Not to mention head-to-toe ablative body armour, a familiar, bracing weight that was no weight at all.

She half turned to glance back at the hold, never losing the all-important grip. The rest of SWAT Four were locked in two facing rows down either side, armoured and armed, just like her. Helmeted, like her, some checking equipment or weapons, others talking. One or two glanced her way, disinterestedly curious, or appearing to be . . .

"Arvi!" shouted Lieutenant Rice from the commander's post behind and to Sandy's left. Barely an armspan opposite, Special Agent

Arvid Singh glanced up from his graphic-slate expectantly. "Haven't you memorised that damn thing yet?" Singh grinned, a good-natured flash of white teeth within a young, brown, thin-bearded face.

"Don't mind me, chief, I'm a little bit stupid." Some laughter down the rows, and Vanessa half glared at him, lock-strapped into her swivel seat.

"No argument here," she replied.

Sandy had had the introductions, hours earlier. Vanessa's team, SWAT Four, armed and armoured civilians, for those rare occasions where civilian law enforcement required something more than tasers and wrist-tape. She'd done a brief, half-hour cram of SWAT operationals, jacked into a database at CSA headquarters, and had been suitably impressed—CSA SWAT followed a basically practical, professional approach centred on training fundamentals and top-line technology. It wasn't flashy, but civilian operations rarely were, and the recorded track record looked solid. The last thing she wanted was a last-minute detachment to an overambitious unit determined to stretch themselves beyond their basic capabilities. Vanessa, she noted, had the initials KISS rather flamboyantly emblazoned in black letters on her armoured shoulder—Keep It Simple, Stupid. Although she suspected Vanessa enjoyed the more suggestive interpretation also.

Vanessa tapped her mike function, swivelling fully about to face her troops. "Okay you guys, listen up. Final thoughts. We're after data. If Tetsu's into illegal biotech, we want the evidence. Data has priority, we get the lockdowns in place early, secure the terminals, let the automateds do the job, and wait for the Intel geeks to arrive and sift.

"Don't discount the human element. We're not carrying live ammo for nothing. Remember, Tetsu encryption codes were used to purchase the flyers that launched the attack on the President. Yes, we want data connecting Tetsu to the attackers, if it exists, but don't forget the basic point—if there's a direct connection, we've no idea who might be home when we come knocking. For all we know, the building itself

might be harbouring armed GIs . . . we doubt it, Intel suggests otherwise from surveillance, but we're not taking any risks. Intel want us
data focused—*I* want us people focused. Data won't put a bullet in
your head. Any questions?"

There were none. No one looked particularly worried, Sandy noted.
They checked equipment, weapons, com-gear, armour tensions, and visor
readings, occasionally exchanging brief, professional remarks. Singh,
Sandy noted, had something emblazoned in Sanskrit across his helmet
above the visorplate. A man named Devakul had a similar blaze, this time
in Thai. And there were others, too . . . she wished her language skills
were better. Another thing to work on at some stage. Vanessa's was one
of the few in English—a smiley face surrounded by the words "have a nice
day." Above what would be, when lowered, a fearsome visage of armoured
visorplate and breather, in frowning, deadly intent.

An access signal registered in Sandy's inner ear . . . she frowned
and allowed the linkup, a brief crackling *pop*! in her eardrum.

"*It's me*," said Vanessa's voice in her ear. Sandy spared a look at
Vanessa, who had swivelled her chair back to her command post displays, monitoring while she conversed in internal formulation without
apparent effort. Sandy regripped the overhead, and scanned back out
the cockpit windows as the towers slid by.

"*What's up?*"

"*HQ called in five minutes back, they found a shuttle in the Verdrahn
region tucked in among the hills . . . that's about five thousand kilometres
away. They say it looks to have come in about five weeks ago.*"

"*Big shuttle?*"

"*Capacity about one hundred and twenty. Enough for all the GIs who hit
the President, and all the FIA involved in your abduction too, if it turns out
to be the same bunch. Not that we're allowed to speculate that the FIA and the
League are working together on anything . . .*"

"*No. Not even when it's true.*" Her mind was racing.

"*Especially when it's true. What d'you think? Five weeks ring any bells?*"

*"I've only been in town about two weeks total, Vanessa. They got here three weeks before I did. If this whole thing is about me, they had some serious advance warning."*

*"True. Raises the question of how they're getting out again."*

*"A smaller shuttle,"* Sandy replied sourly, *"once they've let their GIs kill themselves off."*

*"But all of them?"* Vanessa queried.

*"Well I suppose that's the big question, isn't it?"* The flyer bumped again, and things rattled ominously in the back.

So it was definitely a large-scale infiltration. A capital-O Operation, in every sense. One hundred and twenty was a very large shuttle. She knew all the models personally, and the physical constraints by which such large-capacity assault shuttles operated. They were not used lightly in a military environment. In a civilian environment they were not used at all. Legally. But the security agencies on both sides of the conflict had precious little respect for interstellar law.

"Two minutes," Vanessa shouted in the back, which started a flurry of final preps. Sandy scanned out the canopy, adjusting visual patterns for maximum effect. Scattered air traffic moved along various skylanes, gently curving past the lighted towers, running lights blinking. She hooked briefly into navcomp reception, found the target closing, a declining sequence of numbers. From behind came the power surge of activating armour, com-systems, and tracking units, familiar sensations.

"LT," the pilot said calmly over radio frequency, voice now active in Sandy's ear.

"Go, Sunset," Vanessa replied, calmly doing a final weapons check to Sandy's right.

"Hover LZ has a bad crosswind—be careful on the pancake."

"Roger that Sunset. Team Four, affirm and copy." The calls came in, one at a time. An altitude dip and curving around the next looming tower, a flash of window light slipping close by to the left and suddenly the target was there, ten o'clock and coming about. One minute.

Sandy switched her links to scan, multiple sources, ground-fixed on neighbouring towers. Usual security, all unsuspecting. Clearance came in from those observers, and everything went green. The flyer continued its innocuous course along the registered lane, and the tower ahead swung gently by as they curved left across it. The rooftop was an intriguingly aesthetic mix of a large dome, a spire antenna, and a landing pad.

Very obvious, that landing pad, squarely illuminated in the ostentatious lighting from the surrounding floods and the deep, golden glow from within the dome . . . function rooms for important guests, luxurious beyond imagining—the Intel previews had said so. The Intel previews had also detailed the security provisions at great length—CSA had helped set the regulations governing their use and operation, after all. For people foolish enough simply to land on the rooftop pad without authorisation, there were obvious and extensive precautions. But desperate times allowed for desperate measures, and when the tactical briefing had begun, Sandy had been quite surprised. And impressed. These guys didn't mess around.

"Go go go," said an unannounced voice on directional com, and the flyer came about with a hard starboard turn, breaking lanes with a flaring of navigation alarms, quickly overridden. Thrust flared as the acceleration kicked in, Sandy braced firmly, left fist gripping the overhead and feet widely spread, rifle gripped in her right fist, having done the final checks in advance of final approach, as was her habit. She always liked to take a look, if possible. She looked now, connections hooked in, watching and scanning, thinking ahead. Counting down.

Reached zero, and a thin red line from a nearby towertop targeted a point alongside the landing pad, clearly visible with a spectrum shift. By the landing pad, something flashed, and caught fire. Another line, and a big surge of power as a highly charged electrical system dissolved into flame . . . bang, a sudden eruption of fire from beside the pad, mushrooming skyward.

"Flamer," Sandy announced, watching it rise. "Very pretty." The pad was rushing up then suddenly dropping away as the flyer flared, the pilot kicking the thrusters forward and the G forces shoving them down. *Clack*, and a sudden roar from outside, the rear doors fanning open. Cold wind rushed in, a swirling backdraft. Sandy felt the familiar calm descending, smooth and unhurried.

Then the pad was rushing up below, the rearmost team members unhooked and jumping, vanishing into the cold, gleaming night. The rest departed in an orderly rush, Vanessa following them out and Sandy surging after, a guiding hand along the overhead rail and then out . . . a moment of dizzying fall, then hit hard and rolling to a firing crouch, team members fanning out across the pad with purposeful haste as the flyer howled and thrust backwash hit them with hurricane force. Then faded, a dark, sleekly cylindrical shape, paired thruster fans angling forward as it accelerated away into the night.

Sandy got up and walked slowly forward. Hardly a textbook modern assault technique, but the other eleven troops were rushing about their allotted tasks and she was out of the coordination loop. So she did the one thing everyone trusted her to do—kept the rifle tucked to her armoured shoulder and scanned the garden-lined pad-departure zones for anyone looking to shoot at them.

Troops sprinted and covered alternately through the clearing wind-blown smoke from the laser strikes. Several went to one doorway, several to another, others crouched in support, weapons levelled. Another pair erected a receptor tripod, the big dish unfolding like a flower toward a nearby towertop. Sandy waited behind, anticipating movements as she moved to the pad perimeter, keeping her firelines clear. It dimly occurred to her that the wind was very strong and very cold, and that the view was truly spectacular. The eastern glow had grown to a clear orange line rimed with blue.

A percussive thump and the twin doors blew apart, a simultaneous blast of flying glass and frames, and the first troops disappeared into the smoke. Sandy ran, hurdling obstructing greenery, then through the smoking right-hand doorway.

Scanned the broad, decorated marble atrium, slowing to an unhurried jog as troops behind quickly laid cabling through the wrecked doorway and sprinted to the corner console, right where the Intel schematics said it would be. Fast communication and terse commands as they hooked in, laser com from the near tower feeding penetration codes to the outside dish and direct to the terminal, bypassing the tower's impenetrable encryption barriers completely.

Luxurious entrance corridors abruptly turned a dull, emergency red, and a loud, male voice said very firmly over the intercom, "This is a CSA raid! Remain where you are!" over and over again.

Nothing like physical penetration to render fancy software obsolete, Sandy found herself thinking as she jogged smoothly down across the marble atrium, tall, high, mirrorlike polish on every side. Sometimes those software jocks got far too full of themselves.

Got a frequency patch on the security layout even as she approached the T-junction . . . empty ahead, but she slowed up and scanned for wall reflections on the marble before cornering, knowing better than to trust unsecured links. A trailing trooper covered left as she went right—Hiraki, she remembered. Both clear. From back down the hall came the sound of SWAT Six landing.

She waved Hiraki forward, covering as he raced across the left junction. Confusion on the links, invading programs overriding old controls, locking things down, preventing information transfer . . . another minute and the entire system would be locked. But that would do nothing to stop a well-placed axe through a terminal. Thus the haste. Hiraki arrived and covered, and she sprinted forward toward that side door, sliding in on one knee to slow herself on the slippery marble. Then up and with one kick the door simply exploded open, dual-reinforced fibrous alloy locks and all, lock fragments scattering. Rolled through and covered right as Hiraki angled left across above her. And froze for a moment, taking in their new surroundings.

The dome. It loomed high above, held with minimal support and almost entirely transparent. Above, the underlit patchwork of silvery cloud against a darkened sky. Opposite, the dome fell to the tower's side, presenting 120 degrees of open, uninterrupted views across the dazzling city skyline. And laid out beneath their present walkway-level was a broad circular floor—crowds of tables, a performer's stage, a step-down lounge, and bar a dance floor, all decoratively segmented by lush palms and other greenery. The floor was huge—Sandy estimated seating for at least three hundred, with much room to spare. All silent and dimly lit now. And a good eight metres below their present position.

Hiraki wordlessly produced his rappelling hook and clamped it onto the railing, with no time to bother with stairs. With even less, Sandy gestured for him to cover, half hurdled the rail, and pushed off, sighting a landing spot as she did. Fell for several long seconds and pushed out as she hit. *Bam*! as she smashed a table to pieces, hit and rolled, coming up to a firing crouch immediately and scanning for hostiles. Seconds later, a whirring screech of rope from above, then Hiraki dropped down behind her. Cut the rope and moved up beside her, weapon levelled. Spared a brief glance at the decent-sized wooden table she had reduced to kindling, legs exploded outwards and surface spit down the middle.

"I can't believe you did that," he murmured, beneath mike tolerance. "Such a lovely table."

"They can bill me," Sandy murmured, and moved forward, weaving smoothly between the tables. Hiraki followed his own line, closer to the stage, creating a crossfire angle. Heart thumping and half smiling, Sandy realised she was enjoying herself. What a violent, destruction-loving creature she was. The half-smile grew a little broader.

Elevators at the far wall, stairs beyond. Sandy reached them first and dropped fast down the broad staircase, round the bend and down to the next level, covering the open left, then spinning right, weapon levelled on an open hallway. A security robot sat motionless on silent wheels, immobilised by the invader software. "Remain where you are," the voice continued over the intercom. The robot obeyed, tracking her with dark, suspicious scanners.

Hiraki arrived and Sandy moved off past the immobilised robot, a quick scan confirming it as harmless. Hiraki covered the rear as they advanced down the grand, well-lit hallway toward the locked staff sections.

*"On the floor!"* she heard someone yell over the intercom, and *"CSA!"* That was Singh and Bjornssen, her links told her, probably with an early rising employee. After a raise, Sandy thought as she found the red-badged Staff Only door and punched it clean off its hinges with a ferocious front kick. Sparks flashed and alarms sounded as she entered with rifle levelled, quickly suppressed by racing attack-element functions. Down a narrow corridor at high speed, smashing doorways left and right with ruthless force, Hiraki following, scanning what she'd exposed.

More intercom shouting, some terse conversation—the ground floor teams had run into some bigwigs on their way up who were demanding answers to problematic questions. She hammered the last locked door and spun through—a quick weapons scan showed no tampering, just banks of stacked computer hardware inset in the walls with comfortable chairs before fancy access screen/interface modules.

Flipped the protective cover on the interface unit hooked to her armour webbing, jacked herself in, and tuned through the frequencies as the attack elements told her the required adjustment . . . flash, and she was in, leaning against the seat back as the information flows rushed over her, branchways locked down, massive database entry points, multipoint storage . . . huge, huge system. Enormous didn't even begin to describe it.

"Is it okay?" Hiraki called from the doorway behind, braced in comfortable cover position by the wreck she'd made of the double-locked alloy door.

"I think so," she replied, mike deactivated to avoid channel clutter. A further scan, racing at mind-blurring speed, searching for telltale activity that the attack elements should have painted nice and clearly . . . "No access or transfers that I can see." Her mouth was working on autopilot, her attention racing rapidly elsewhere. "Have to check the AI for anything preprogrammed, though."

"Nothing in the other rooms," Hiraki told her. "Hardware and equipment, maintenance units, a security station. As advertised."

Sandy nodded absently. In one ear, arguments continued with the folk downstairs, who probably had master codes that could halt this search very quickly if they got close enough. Vanessa was stalling them, reading the warrant. Another, nearby link opened, multilevel and intricate . . .

"Hello," said a voice from the walls, "you must be a GI."

"Oh great," Hiraki muttered, "the bloody AI's come out to play."

"Is this a problem?" asked the mildly androgynous voice. "I sense that your activities are legal, I have taken no obstructive measures but to safeguard the rights of the Tetsu Corporation according to the corporate constitution and recent Tanushan law."

"I thank you for your cooperation," Sandy murmured, still racing. "You've performed quite admirably under difficult circumstances, and I'm sure the Tetsu board will appreciate your efforts." Final sweep . . . a scan of associated linkages . . . it was no diversion. The Tetsu network AI seemed to genuinely want to talk. It wasn't usual, not on networks of this size. Network admin AIs generally only answered to their respective corporate heads and kept all nonessential contact with those messy, awkward outsiders to a minimum. Sandy suspected that most of them found the outside world rather boring.

"That's exceedingly polite of you," the AI said, genuinely appreciative where a human might be sarcastic. "I hadn't expected that from a GI. What model are you?" Small talk. God.

"It's classified," Sandy replied, unhooking herself and winding the

cord back into the interface. Suspicious, as she turned to look at
Hiraki, of coincidence of the AI's sudden appearance with that of the
Tetsu bigwigs downstairs. Hiraki spared her a sardonic glance, mostly
lost behind his faceplate, then focused back down the corridor. Still,
she had to hold this position for now, and there was nothing else to do.
"My name's Cassandra," she told it . . . it would know that anyway,
monitoring their communications. "What's yours?"

"Cody," said the AI. "Amusingly suggestive, yes?"

"Definitively." As always, it was difficult to tell exactly what AIs
were thinking. It did amuse her, though. "As you've probably guessed,
we're looking for some information, Cody. Has there been any transfer
or deletion of information during the last several minutes?"

"Not that I'm aware of." Sounding slightly puzzled. "Why did you
knock all the doors down? They're very difficult to fix, you know." In
the physical, outsider world, where things were not constructed from
electronic code to be reassembled at will. Sandy nearly smiled.

"It's considerate of you to think of that, but I was instructed to
make interface as quickly as possible in case any information was lost."

"Well, I don't control the entire system, you know. I only monitor
it . . . I think you could call me a librarian. I'd offer to check for you if
you wished, but I really must await instructions from the board. I'm
not sure of the legal situation regarding any of this." Sandy held up a
placating hand, which would doubtless register on one scanning unit
or another.

"No, waiting would be correct. I hope that our infiltration software
is no threat to your systems?"

"Oh no, it's perfectly harmless to me, thank you for asking. It's
rather fascinating, actually . . . do you know who wrote it?"

The smile broke Sandy's control. "No. But I'm sure you'll have lots
of fun trying to figure it out."

"I'm sure I will." With considerable enthusiasm. Old cliché that it
was, AIs just loved processing data, the more complicated the better.

She'd heard of some AIs actually constructing their own nonessential databases of analytical processes on data processing on various levels of manifestation . . . "philosophy," certain intellectuals had called it. Other expressions of spatial relationships were defined as "art."

And she suffered another twinge of sour amusement that it was AIs, of utterly inhuman and mechanical construct, that should be popularly upheld as representing the "nobility of sentience," while GIs—human imitations—were regarded with such fear and loathing. Perhaps, she thought, it wasn't that people were scared of nonhuman sentience at all. Perhaps they feared that she was too much like them, not too little.

"Garden is secured," Hiraki announced into his mike at her signal, weapon still levelled down the corridor through which they'd come, strewn with pieces of broken doors and security frames.

"*Roger. Garden is secured*," came the affirmation.

"Cody," Sandy said, "you won't tell anyone that I'm a GI, will you? It's a security secret at the moment, with the lockdown legislation in place."

"Sure," replied the disembodied voice from the walls. Monitor screens were blank, save for a few operation lights on the various interface stations. Nothing to suggest a living, thinking sentience, hiding somewhere in the surrounding network. "But you understand that I'll have to tell Mr. Milanovic, the Tetsu executive chairman. He's my boss, you know. He's just downstairs now, waiting for permission to come up."

"That's okay," said Sandy. "I think I'm going to tell him myself."

Milanovic was not helpful and pointedly refused to talk to any lowly SWAT grunt, choosing instead to wait until someone "important" arrived. Looking on disdainfully as more armour and weapons invaded *his* pleasantly civilised building, while his varied advisors hovered at his elbow and communicated on secure, silent uplinks that Sandy could have monitored if she'd wanted, but she was legal now, and felt it incumbent upon her at least to go through the motions of legality, even if she wasn't entirely sure what that meant yet. After several minutes' arguing with a wall of suited, patronising sneers, Vanessa gave up trying and had them herded into a private office section with tight-lipped disregard of their outraged protests, explaining several more times in increasingly dark tones that the building facilities were now *quarantined*, you understand, and left them there with Zago to guard the door. Zago was a one hundred and ninety centimetres tall African who was built like a starship haulage container. In pre-op, Sandy had found him intelligent, funny, and charmingly good natured. She now discovered that he did a very convincing job of hiding those qualities when needful. Arguments from the suits ceased, and Vanessa departed with Sandy in tow, determined to personally effect the quarantine before the herds of CSA Intel, investigators, and others descended from the heavens and found fault with her procedures. Intel, Sandy gathered, had little faith in SWAT's intellectual subtlety on various procedures, and Vanessa was determined not to give them any further ammunition.

There was little to be found on database. The storage units were so huge even Sandy, with her dramatically enhanced data-processing capability, had few ideas where to start. Cody did, and eagerly awaited legal instruction to carry out a search through his beloved data for offending and illegal material (a notion that appeared to intrigue him), but legal instruction, besides shutting off all unauthorised access or transfer, was yet to arrive, so there was little else to do with the local network systems. That left physical storage.

"Hey Sandy," Bjornssen said as they entered the sixty-fifth-floor lab, "need a spare?" Standing beside a transparent cylinder of clear, red-tinged liquid, within which an extremely human-looking leg hung suspended. Vanessa gave him a dark look, and clumped off past rows of other cylinders toward the stowage lockers. Sandy made a more graceful armoured progress to Bjornssen's side, and peered at the limb.

"Won't do me any good," she said mildly. "It's made for you. My brain doesn't speak the same language. You stick that on me it'll be useless."

"What is the red stuff?" asked Sharma, moving further along the row, gazing at yet more suspended body parts with morbid fascination, heavy rifle balanced over her armoured shoulder.

Sandy thought back over what little she knew of human biosynth. "Bio-environment, I guess. See the monitors?" Pointing a gloved finger at the cap seal on each cylinder end. "I guess it's a way of acclimatising each part before attachment. That's a full synthetic-biological environment in there, lots of micro-thingys floating about. I guess that's the red tinge."

"Micro-thingys," said Bjornssen, raising a blonde eyebrow in her direction. "That's a technical term, is it?"

"I'm a grunt, Sven, not a biotechnician. Besides, this is supposed to be based on your biology—it's got nothing to do with me."

"Yes, but you are the GI," Sharma replied with a theatrical head-tilt, "you are supposed to know these things. I mean, logically, just as Sven, being a regular organic human, can doubtless recite the technical terms for each and every part of his own physical anatomy."

"I was just asking," Bjornssen replied, hands up, signalling a strategic withdrawal. Sandy thought that wise. Indian women were good with words. Some were lethal. Bjornssen evidently had the sense to know when he was outmatched. Uplinked, Sandy sensed an active probe in the regional security net and turned to see Vanessa fiddling a direct connection to a wall panel between rows of cold stowage racks in sliding shelves.

"That any good?" Sandy asked. Vanessa made a face, tapping buttons.

"Sure. Deny all access to uncleared company personnel. What good's it going to do if the FIA's got people in senior middle management on the payroll?" Disconnected her insert plug and folded the coil to a loop, one end hooked into the collar socket where the helmet connection would normally go. Walked along the aisle of stowage racks, checking lighted lock displays with a critical eye. Paused at one, tapped in a code, and yanked at the shelf. It slid open, and Sandy strolled over to look.

Beneath clear, hard plastic were circular partitions. In each, things appeared to be growing. Micro-things, in weird patterns and colours.

"Nano?" Vanessa wondered.

"More likely synth," Sandy replied, shifting to maximum zoom . . . it didn't help much, micro was micro and her zoom didn't even get close. "That's where the money is these days."

"Yeah, it's also where the restrictions are. I don't like this security much, doubt it's going to pass inspection."

"What would? If the FIA were helping get League tech in this far?" With a questioning look at Vanessa, vision doing a fast readjustment. Vanessa gave an exasperated shrug.

"*You* can tell the powers that be their grand campaign for the preservation of natural human biology is doomed to failure no matter what they do. I just collect my pay cheques." And gazed back down at the shelf-display. "I can't even see the difference. Looks like a bunch of regular cell cultures to me."

"That's the point." Some streaked across their circular solution-dishes in straight lines, others in fuzzy masses, some colourful, some bland. "If you could tell the difference, it wouldn't work. This is the important stuff, though . . . big structures are important, but for serious synthetic biology it's all these small systems that really matter. Anyone can make a replica human limb—making it function like a real limb is the real trick. And that's all microsystems. Where the League's real edge is, of course." Silence for a moment as Vanessa considered that, but for the clumping of armoured footsteps in further parts of the lab as Sharma and Bjornssen continued their once-over.

"How much of this kind of stuff would they have got from you?"

"Plenty." She was nearly surprised that she could think on it so calmly. But she was armed, armoured, and operational, which meant calm came naturally. "Nerve endings, feedback mechanisms . . . the whole self-regulatory system, it's all micro. Can't study it on dead war casualties—you need a live subject. And my neurology's different from any other GI's. Interacts differently with my physical systems. Using me for an active comparison against what they've already gathered from other GIs . . . yeah." She shrugged, mostly invisible within the armour. "Invaluable, I guess." She looked up. Found Vanessa looking at her, slightly incredulous.

"Pretty expensive for a grunt, aren't you?"

Sandy managed a faint smile in return.

"I'm worth it." The smile faded. "At least the FIA seem to think so."

"The last time a BT company cornered a major market segment like that was Zhangliang Inc. fifty years ago with self-replication programming. That's corporate folklore. They got such a monopoly the Federation government had to split the company. They created a whole new market field almost overnight. Trillions of Feddie dollars. And they wonder if BT corps fiddle around the restrictions at all . . . Christ, it doesn't take a genius when you figure the money. And the fear of someone else getting there first."

Sandy sighed. "I dunno. If it weren't for the FIA, maybe the restrictions would work."

"Centrally imposed restrictions haven't had a huge record of success in market economies. Decentralisation creates wealth. Wealth rules."

"And you think about this a lot?" Looking at the small SWAT lieutenant curiously.

Vanessa smiled. "I did an MBA remember? It's a hard conclusion to escape."

"I don't know." Glumly, stretching her achingly stiff shoulders. "Human systems exist to serve human ideals and principles—they always have."

"The systems determine the ideals, Sandy," Vanessa said firmly. "That's humans. We're adaptive, we don't cling indefinitely to things that don't work in new environments."

"That's ideological determinism," Sandy replied. And gave her another curious look. "You're arguing like you're from the League."

Vanessa smiled. "And you like you're from the Federation. Fancy that."

She completed a physical inspection of several floors of security systems, searching for blind triggers that weren't hooked to the central network. Official personnel were descending in droves and the corridors were increasingly filled with departmentals, some in suits, others in Labs & Research white coats and lugging gearbags of analysis equipment. She watched the people with as much attention and more interest than the security systems, noting their uniforms, official or otherwise, their gear, their manner, ID tags, and general efficiency. Civilian personnel. She'd never seen so many, not working on the job like this. Not while armoured and armed in the aftermath of a raid. But they seemed efficient enough and spared her barely a glance in the corridors, evidently accustomed to working in the presence of SWAT.

Up on the executive floors, her uplinks showed the meetings with Milanovic and the Tetsu bigwigs were intensifying. Already the upper landing pads were a constant traffic snarl of incoming and outgoing government flyers and cruisers. About them, and on the surrounding networks, media were clustering like carrion eaters on the scene of a fresh kill. They kept their distance for now—the hunters were still feeding—but that would not last. The prospect made her nervous. And impatient, as she completed yet another section of corridor, past labs and test-spaces, squeezing past a large piece of equipment several whitecoats were wheeling between offices.

"Ricey," she radioed on basic SWAT freq, "how long's this interrogation going to last?"

"*Dunno*," came the voice in her earpiece, "*could be hours. There's the whole CSA Intel to get through, then the specs from tech-gov . . .*" That, Sandy had gathered, was the department in charge of enforcing biotech restrictions. "*. . . then cross-exam from the evidence we find, if any, and then the corporate squad might want to grill them about cashflow technicalities and* the like. *That's how they catch half this illegal stuff when they do—it shows up in the books somewhere."*

"That sounds like it could take days." The lab corridors opened into a floor entrance foyer, big elevators and electronic displays for guidance. A secure transparent wall, centred by a scan-equipped door, blocked the labs from new arrivals. Big, gold letters on the fake-marble walls opposite the elevators read TETSU LIFE SCIENCES. And below it, in more subdued lettering, Research Division. Several suits and whitecoats clustered there beyond the secure-wall, deep in conversation.

*"It's been known to."* With the flippant disregard she'd expect of a SWAT grunt for Intel chicanery.

Sandy triggered the secure-door with a mental uplink signal, the side panel light blinked green and beeped. Several of the whitecoats glanced her way as the transparent door swung . . . beyond the glass in the office adjoining the foyer, she noted, several more suits were going through desks and drawers. Beyond sprawled the city, darkening beneath black morning clouds. So much plexiglass, she pondered, breaking up the marble and hard walls. Tanushans loved their views.

"We don't have days. I've got some questions I'd like to ask now."

*"Um, yeah, well, clever folk in Intel can get real touchy about their territory . . . I'd suggest you wait until there's a break in the schedule."*

"Ibrahim didn't put me on this job so I could wait my turn." Paused by a water fountain and bent for a sip . . . not an easy manoeuvre in armour.

*"Sandy, Intel know you're here, Ibrahim told them . . . I'm sure they'll invite you up when they're ready . . ."*

"At the speed the FIA could be moving, any wasted time is too much." Leaning one glove-armoured hand on the drinking fountain, watching the suits stripping the office behind adjoining glass walls. "Ibrahim put me here to make use of my judgement. Do you want to come with me, or should I just go in there alone?" That last because it was prudent, and she had no wish to be a loose cannon . . . such things went down badly in civilian and military environments both.

Vanessa gave an exasperated snort. *"Look, can you wait just five minutes?"*

"No." Headed for the elevator. Prudence did not, however, impact upon her sense of efficiency. "Get there when you can. Don't worry, I won't kill anyone."

*"Gee, you promise?"*

The elevator paused several times on the way up, admitting or expelling passengers. Some wore less formal civvies—some government departments, she knew, were less strict on dress codes than others. Most of the less formal wore salwar kameez or saris. Exceptions, she guessed, were granted on cultural grounds above most else. All the civvies kept a respectful distance from the sinister-looking armoured figure in the elevator's rear corner. Which was only prudent.

There were three CSA agents in the car when it hit the main Executive Level—Investigations, she guessed from the chatter, which concerned legal technicalities that went entirely over her head. She gestured them ahead of her when the doors opened, and followed. This elevator foyer was no bigger, but decorative . . . hell, it was patterned glass and wood panelling on the walls, polished floors, tasteful corridors, and a number of intent-looking personnel on the move. Uplinked to the general location, she guessed a direction and followed the three suits to the left. They all turned into a broad meeting room . . . a glimpse as she passed of a huge, gleaming table for perhaps twenty, massive graphical display screens for presentations . . . the ostentation told its own story—of a corporate culture not ashamed to openly display such profligate wealth. Everything gleamed and caught the eye, from polished windows to paintings on the walls, a small sculpture upon a miniature table inset in a corner . . . she turned another corner and was in the main northside hall, broad and panelled, big glass doors at the far end that led to the Executive Office.

And who said civilian societies didn't recognise rank, she thought sourly as she advanced. The whole grand passageway was constructed like a temple, stairs ascending to the grand altar. Kneel before your God. Overcast morning light gleamed grey beyond the glass doors ahead, silhouetting the two CSA guards who flanked it. And those would be the great lord's guardian angels, she reckoned. Both men, tall, broad, and impassive. "Heavies," in civvie lingo.

"Any problem?" one of them asked as she approached with a clump of armoured footsteps on the broad, polished floor.

"I'm Cassidy," she told them. Even Ibrahim wasn't using her real name about the CSA. The old identity served well enough. The civilian one. "I've come to see Milanovic." Stopped before them. They stared at her closely. Both a full head taller, despite her armour.

"You're Cassidy." The shaved-headed agent. Like he didn't believe her. She gave him a look. To his credit, he didn't flinch. Maybe he really *didn't* believe her.

"I've got some questions," she said calmly. "Ibrahim's business." That unfroze them, after a pause. One reported into his headset mike, terse and businesslike. Both continued to stare at her. A moment later the big doors opened and a new agent appeared—young and European with slicked black hair. To her irritation, he stood before her and let the doors shut behind him. His gaze was just as wary as those of the two guards.

"You're Cassidy?"

No, I'm the Porn-a-Sim cyber hump-bunny of the month. Are you deaf?

"Yes," she said instead. The man's gaze furrowed, as if slightly incredulous. Or more than slightly. A half-exasperated grin escaped his control then was quickly swallowed. Sandy watched this procession of expressions, halfway between curiosity and the unpleasant, sinking feeling that things here were a hell of a lot more complicated than they ought to be.

"And what do you want?" the young agent asked, resuming a fair approximation of a straight face. He *was* deaf.

"I have questions for Milanovic," she replied. She was not often afflicted by impatience. But this was different. Urgent. "I'm on this raid because Ibrahim put me here personally, I need to put these questions to him and I need to do it fast."

"Look, um . . . Ms. Cassidy." Scratching his jaw, as if wondering how to put it. "There's, um, kind of a busy schedule right now, as you might see. . . ." She glanced past him and the glass doors. The office beyond opened onto an immense span of city-view windows and was crammed with people, sitting and standing, milling and talking in groups, conferencing around data screens inside and outside the main office. "I'm afraid you're really just going to have to wait your turn. Everyone's business is equally important here."

"Tell that to Ibrahim."

"Lady, we *all* work for Ibrahim. Take a number." Sandy stared at him. In Dark Star she had rank on her shoulder to get past these obstacles. Plus no one messed with Dark Star, let alone a Captain. And if that failed, she could simply push her way in—Dark Star were expected to be slightly crazy, and no one was stupid enough to retaliate with like force—they'd just throw their hands up with resigned disgust. If she tried that here, someone might just be stupid enough to try to stop her. Which would not do at all. And she couldn't just contact Ibrahim. He was no doubt busy, and it surely would do her own credibility no good to be calling on the boss at the first sign of an obstacle . . . Civilians. How the bloody hell did one *deal* with protocol nonsense like this?

"What's your name, kid?" came Vanessa's voice from back down the hall, above the muffled thump of approaching armour, a fast, light stride. The young agent frowned over Sandy's shoulder.

"My name is Agent Patziano," with an emphasis suggesting a dislike at being called "kid." "Lieutenant . . . ?"

"Rice," Vanessa drawled, "I led the raid that got you armchair wonders in here without getting your pretty suits creased. How'd you like to feature on my report to Krishnaswali—all about how you blocked Ibrahim's special addition to my team from doing the job she was personally assigned by him to perform? I reckon that'd hit Ibrahim's vision within about five minutes of my submission."

Patziano stared at her. The towering guards to either side offered no comment. Vanessa stopped before him, and gave a pleasant smile. "Well?"

Patziano blinked and looked at Sandy. Sandy waited. She was good at that, given something to wait for.

"I'll, um . . ." A quick, nervous glance back over his shoulder at the milling crowds in the office beyond.

"You realise," Vanessa said pleasantly, "that you're standing toe-to-toe with the most dangerous killing machine in the known universe and telling her to go jump in a lake?" Patziano blinked again. "Kid, you don't need a medal, you need a brain transplant." He stared at Sandy. Sandy tried to look innocent. Back at Vanessa. Vanessa flicked her head toward the crowds. Patziano swallowed.

"I'll just . . . um . . . go and tell them . . ."

"Just let us in, huh?" He blinked again and nodded. An invisible signal, and the glass doors opened. An audio channel triggered Sandy's uplink reception as they followed Patziano inside . . . Vanessa's frequency. She opened it.

"*Fear and greed, Sandy,*" came Vanessa's voice in her ear as they walked. "*In the world of civvies, those are the two best levers. Promotions, reputations, personal advancement, those are the weak spots. But you gotta make it personal, don't let him hide behind his rank. . . . In the military it's all impersonal, here you've gotta figure the difference. It's all who you know and what they think of you.*"

"*Most dangerous killing machine in the known universe?*" Sandy formulated in silent reply, with mild indignation.

"*GIs are more dangerous than straight humans,*" Vanessa replied matter-of-factly, "*and you're the most dangerous GI.*"

"Oh." Glumly, as Patziano opened the interior office doors and let the pair of armoured SWAT operatives inside. "*I suppose I am, aren't I?*"

Milanovic, she noted, was seated on a large leather sofa before a panoramic vista that stretched about the entire office in a giant semi-circle. Up here at the tower's peak, the structure tapered, allowing for wrap-around views. A procession of towers under an increasingly ominous sky, a view so clear and sharp she could almost feel the chill wind.

Advisors and other executives conferred in low tones about the room, examining their data-slates with full uplinks running, arguing heatedly with various CSA suits about them. This giant melee was just the beginning, sorting out the order of battle. The real action, Sandy guessed, would start later, when each side retired to private quarters to scheme and counterscheme ad infinitum. That part would doubtless go on for months. Or probably years.

She moved in Milanovic's direction, shouldering daintily past suits who started in alarm to find a pair of armoured women pushing into the room. The junior execs and advisors who flanked the Tetsu chairman on the sofa and stood before the windows looked up from a group of CSA questioners seated opposite, several of whom turned.

"What's the problem?" one asked, half-rising from her seat. Armour meant trouble, and was evidently rarely seen in analysis and briefings.

"No problem," Sandy said, "I'm Cassidy, I've got some questions." Some incredulous looks from CSA suits.

"Excuse me," one said testily, "you can't just come in here and . . ."

"Yes she can," said a new voice at her side. Sandy glanced across and found Naidu there. "Top priority, if she believes it to be so . . . Mr. Milanovic, do you mind?"

Milanovic returned a cold stare. A heavy-set man with a thick neck and sharp features under black, wavy hair.

"How many levels of executive security clearance do you have within your personnel structure?" Sandy asked him.

"Fourteen," Milanovic said blankly.

"What designation, format, and serial code?" Milanovic glanced aside at an aide . . .

"Vector-star, Triple HT Overlock, serial code command Eight-Star-Ninety." A young woman from behind the sofa, data-slate in one hand. "Subnumeracy is classified, private Tetsu property protected even under emergency legislation . . ."

"That's yet to be decided," a CSA agent objected. "We've never tested this legislation on subnumeracy serial codings . . ."

"No matter," Sandy interrupted, beginning to get some idea why so many people were here in the room. She knew some basics of corporate law and civilian security legislation, and in a peaceful place like Tanusha it was all untested . . . the legal uncertainties would run all the way down. Not for the first time she suffered the disorienting realisation of just how far over her head so much of this situation went . . . "Are you certified secured against anything in the K-Nova series? Or the Hex–2s?"

The young woman blinked. "That's . . . not commonly found around here." Looking slightly bewildered.

"Software's not my strong point," Naidu said from beside her. Watching the Tetsu network expert's face with sharp, narrowed eyes. "What are K-Novas and Hex–2s?" Sandy halted her reply on sudden inspiration. Looked at the woman.

"You tell him," she said. The Tetsu tech blinked again, uncertainty growing, shifted her weight. In this part of the room, beyond the surrounding confusion all was still. Agents watched, eyes mercilessly intent, searching for any unwitting clue. Sandy figured she'd asked a good one.

"Well . . ." the tech said eventually, "they're reputed to be League infiltration programs. I've never seen one." Recovering her confidence with blunt honesty. "They're sometimes talked about . . . industry talk, gossip and rumours, mostly. Some people even think they're just rumours . . . stories invented by someone."

"They exist," Sandy said calmly, more for the agents' benefit than the Tetsu crowd's. "They're very common in Dark Star. Military construct, direct from League military science labs. There are so many mutations and variations by now that even the designers have lost count, there's only the macro-patterns to identify them."

Several of the agents were looking at *her* now. But she didn't mind that.

"They have carrier-bands," she continued. "Quantum-encryption disguises stored data. It's a parasite program, like a smart virus, runs through large databases like these corporate ones, gathers security data, passwords, encryption, facilitates its own movement further and further into the network, and passes all data out hidden in regular traffic. Nearly impossible to detect."

"There's not a parasite program Cody can't trace," Milanovic objected with a dark frown. "League biotechnology is well beyond Federation, but they have no such infotech advantage."

"Um . . . actually, sir," the young tech nervously intervened, "that may be true, but there's a lot of military and security apparatus–funded programming activity, especially in the quantum and AI fields, that has diverged very sharply over the last eighty years or so . . . they've had almost no contact with each other. They've been kept very secret because Federation/League relations were bad from about then, so there's been no cross-pollination, and both streams of research have become very alien to each other. . . . The result is they can't really stop ours, and we can't really stop theirs."

"So I take it," Sandy said, "that you're not proofed?"

The tech grimaced. "Well, it is fairly hard to be proofed against something we've never seen and is generally beyond the technology of our best net corporates to counter."

"Considering the degree of League biotech infiltration in Tanusha," one agent said, "I find that a pretty remarkable attitude."

"There has been no infiltration of League agents or data into Tetsu Consolidated," one of the corporates stated blankly. Which no one even bothered to respond to.

"Can you actually stop a K-Nova?" one of the agents asked Sandy.

"Stop, no, I doubt it, not with present Federation resources. Deflect, confuse, block, and generally engage in damage limitation . . . yes. But only if you know it's there, and if you prepare for it. Or you could flush the entire system, but obviously we can't expect them to do that . . . much."

"Systems flush requires the shutdown of essential services," another agent commented. "That'd be as good as admitting there was an infiltration. And of course there's *no* infiltration." Sarcastically. There was, Sandy realised, something unexpected going on. They were coming over to her side. All the CSA, backing this line of attack. It surprised her. Doubtless it surprised them too.

"Wait a minute," said the young Tetsu tech from across the low table, frowning deeply, "if you know all this stuff about League infiltration runners, why haven't you told us? Government departments are legally obligated to pass on any security information to private companies . . ."

"Who ask for assistance," said an agent, "first you have to ask . . ."

"No way. Matters of national security are the Callayan government's job to predict, research, and counter . . ."

"And the enforcement of biotech policy is a matter of individual corporate responsibility, to be monitored by tech-gov . . ."

"How *do* you know all this?" Milanovic interrupted. Arms heavily folded across his broad chest. His dark eyes were narrowed, staring straight at Sandy. "A SWAT agent. Not even an officer." So he could read the shoulder pips. "Who the hell *are* you? Barging in against the initial wishes of even your own people?" With a glare at the agents seated across from him. Looking for leverage, Sandy reckoned. Divisions within the CSA. Splits. Politics, to be exploited at higher levels. Parliament, Senate reviews, elected reps . . .

"You underestimate SWAT, Mr. Milanovic," said Naidu, coming to the rescue. "They read much intelligence on League capabilities— that is one of Callay's primary threats."

"Have you made any attempt," Sandy cut in, "to defend, isolate, locate, or otherwise search for such League infiltration software?"

"I told you," the tech retorted with growing frustration, "no one in Tanusha's sure these programs even exist. How can we defend against them?"

"Thank you," Sandy said. Took Naidu's arm with a gloved hand (carefully) and led him over to an empty area by the huge, floor-to-ceiling windows. To her surprise, several other agents gave up their strategic seats and hurried over to join them, forming yet another cluster in the spacious office. Beyond the plexiglass, Tanusha sprawled, the lights of the airborne traffic flashing beneath the dark and wind-torn ceiling of cloud.

"There's no way they haven't heard of K-Novas or Hex–2s," she told Naidu, her voice just loud enough to carry to the several others who gathered close by. From the lack of carrying, recognisable sound from about the room, she knew it had been suppressed . . . portable devices could do that, neutralise voice-width sound by counterpulse so that soft voices would not carry more than three or four metres—even to bio-enhanced hearing, that being the main danger. "It's more than just a rumour, it's standard knowledge for League Intel ops. If they're aware of League biotech policy they'll know the infiltration software."

"Do you know?" Naidu asked the agent at Sandy's armoured elbow.

"I know Hex and Nova, how they're used and some running examples, but the details are impossible . . . I doubt even the FIA know. Ms. Cassidy," turning to Sandy, "we *really* need to have a long talk. I can't *believe* no one thought to mention that side of your knowledge to me."

"April," Naidu said with deadpan irony, "meet Ying Tuo, CSA Network Security head." They shook hands carefully. "We only got her cleared from custody last night, Tuo." With mild reprimand. "You'll all get your chance eventually."

"Do you think you could find traces?" Tuo pressed her. A tall man, she had to look up to meet his gaze. She considered.

"Maybe. I'm more interested to see what action they've taken against that infiltration. If there's a League or FIA plant somewhere in Tetsu, or both, I'm guessing someone will have got hands-on with that system somewhere. That's what we can find traces of." Tuo's eyes lit up, nodding fast in comprehension.

"Of course. Can you help us look?" Earnestly. Sandy blinked, glanced around, and found Vanessa standing nearby, watching the small scrum she'd attracted with a vaguely raised eyebrow. Vanessa shrugged offhandedly.

"Sure," she told Tuo. "I'll work on com relays and theft-translations. That has to be how they're using corporate encryption to move around Tanusha." And where she was also, she knew, most likely to find traces of any FIA/League activity in Tanusha itself . . . personnel traces, active com codes. The means to trace covert people hiding in Tanusha. Possibly. Her heart beat harder at the prospect. "Can you fit me in?"

Tuo grinned. "Only if you can fight your way through all the techs who'll want to meet you." Gave her a slap on her armoured shoulder and left quickly to organise yet more personnel. Sandy looked quizzically at Naidu, uncertain what had just happened. Naidu gave her a rumpled smile.

"Agent Cassidy. Welcome to the CSA."


"Seems weird that the League would be helping their biggest enemies find ways to counter their greatest technological advantage," Singh commented from the back seat of the big government cruiser.

Four SWAT agents sat in full armour, crammed into the cruiser's undersized seating, designed for unarmoured bodies. Seatbelts stretched across powered armourplate. The SWAT flyer in which they'd arrived was unable to make it back to the rooftop pad, which was now crowded with official vehicles. And the media had now surrounded the tower, watching from rooftop vantages and circling aircars and flyers far above the official skylanes, monitoring rooftop traffic through telescopic lenses. There were SWAT experts the media could conceivably contact, a friendly young Intel woman had explained to Sandy, who might count armoured bodies, read personalised helmet markings, and wonder who the extra trooper was in SWAT Four. Thus the civilian aircar, which departed from the internal bay midway up the tower's side.

Data analysis had lasted all morning, and it was now approaching midday, although any notion of sunshine remained securely hidden behind darkening clouds and sporadic showers. There had been traces of collusion by Tetsu middle management. From those traces Sandy had been able to guess what the League programs they were accessing might have been. She'd passed on her hunch and suggestions to the CSA specialists, and they would now track the problem for as long as it took. Now, attached to SWAT with a vaguely defined brief referring to "assistance and advice," she was headed back to Headquarters.

"League's full of weird ideas, Arvi," Vanessa replied, gloved hands on the cruiser's controls, following a gentle, predetermined course between towers. A nearby flicker of lightning lit up the darkened sky, a blue flare across a nearby tower's windows. "It's a weird idea kind of place."

"Old history," said Sandy, eyes wandering to a spectacular looking mosque in a leafy suburb below, fantastic patterns on its blue and gold tile domes. "Like Old China, back on Earth. Used to be a reclusive country. Didn't like democracy, didn't like market economies, didn't even like the proper rule of law. Which meant they were totally impoverished, of course, and getting trodden on by every major World power with big enough boots. So to make themselves more powerful they adopted what were then known as 'Western practices,' like markets and legal systems, basic capitalism. They thought the only way to fight the West was to adopt their greatest strengths and make them Chinese strengths too. And they got enormously powerful doing that, and in the process inevitably turned into a democracy over time, because the old totalitarianisms just weren't capable of handling the modern market system effectively. At which point you have two major powers, China and the West—or most notably the United States of America—looking at each other and realising, hey, we're both capitalist, we're both democratic, what's left to fight about?

"The League sees itself as the West and the Federation as Old China. The FIA accepts biotech advancements to even the League's advantage. But biotech was what the war was about in the first place, or mostly. So if both sides end up with similar attitudes to biotech, what's left to fight about?"

Vanessa snorted in amusement. "Conquest by ideological stealth. That's cunning, really . . . they talk about that a lot over there?"

"Oh yeah," Sandy sighed wearily, "it's a tireless refrain. What they never mention is that China had the last laugh. Markets and democracy didn't make them more Western at all—if anything it ended up making the West more Chinese. And Indian. Which was a good thing obviously, but a lot of Westerners thought it was their so-called victory coming back to bite them."

"You *are* pretty well read," Vanessa said approvingly. Sandy smiled. "I do try."

"Two Western white people in the front seat, I notice," Hiraki commented. "Asiatics in the back."

"That's a clear illustration of *female* superiority over men," Vanessa retorted. "Race has nothing to do with it."

"The new colonialism," Hiraki commented. "Perhaps we should start a revolution."

"Don't be crazy," said Singh, "where would I get pussy?"

"A good question even now," Vanessa told him, smiling.

"You're *so* mean, LT."

"I'm always available, Arvid," Sandy thought to venture. Glancing over the seat back at him. Singh blinked.

"Available for what?"

"Pussy." With her best, dazzlingly clear-eyed gaze. Singh blinked again.

"This must be what the male spider feels like," he commented after a moment, "just before the female mounts and then eats him." Sandy grinned. "Both extremely aroused and *really* fucking frightened."

She had to laugh. And found herself pondering just what it *would* take to get the handsome young Indian into bed.

"Guys," Vanessa announced from the driver's seat, "reintroductions." Having watched that exchange with considerable amusement. "This is Cassandra Kresnov. She's done a job with us, that makes her at least an honorary SWAT Four now, although she may have cause to regret that later."

"True," said Hiraki.

"Cassandra, this is Hitoru 'The Knife' Hiraki. It's a stupid nickname, I know, but he insists on it. Be nice and he might show you his tattoos one day."

"I live in hope," Sandy told him, extending a gloved hand past the seat back, which he shook.

"I don't even like the nickname," he said calmly. "I am merely surrounded by those who would trivialise and demean an artist such as myself for the sake of mere amusement. I pity them."

"And *that*," Vanessa continued with amusement, "is Arvid Singh, the resident village idiot. Don't let the beard fool you—puberty's still many years away." Sandy leaned around and shook his hand.

"And beside you," said Singh, pointing at Vanessa, "is our beloved squad leader Vanessa Rice, once married and three times divorced . . ."

"Watch it," said Vanessa.

". . . if that's possible," Singh continued, unperturbed. "She's vicious at poker, terrible at mahjong . . ."

"Am not."

". . . and is the only person in SWAT Four who actually makes more sense when she's drunk." Vanessa fought back a smile. "Just don't call her 'Midge,' or she'll hurt you."

"Hi," Sandy said, and held out her hand. Vanessa took it. Glanced at her sideways for a moment, as if suddenly realising exactly whose hand she was shaking. "I'm Cassandra Kresnov. When I'm not eating human flesh and decapitating small furry animals, I like listening to music, reading books, and fucking." A cheer from Singh. Vanessa's eyebrows went up.

"Don't get any ideas, LT," said Singh.

Sandy blinked, and looked at Vanessa, Vanessa looked annoyed, removing her hand to grasp the controls.

"Yes, I am," she replied to Sandy's unspoken question shortly. "My husband's a man, though." Which struck Sandy as interesting. Interesting that Vanessa hadn't told her, and interesting that she hadn't guessed anyway. Which was biased thinking, she realised even as she thought it. There was no guarantee that Vanessa's sexuality made any observable difference to her behaviour. As if a Dark Star GI was going to be any good at picking up such things among straights anyway, whatever her intellect.

"Wish I was like that too sometimes," she replied with amusement. "Half the population gone to waste." Vanessa grinned somewhat self-consciously.

"Got that right."

"Why do GIs even have sexual preferences?" Singh asked, incurably curious. He was starting to remind Sandy of Tran.

"She's an imprint, you moron," Vanessa replied testily before Sandy could speak. "Her neural structure is copied directly from a human subject. Everything we've got, she's got."

A hard shudder as the cruiser hit a rough patch where the wind reflected off a nearby tower. Navcomp flickered and beeped, warning of more ahead, displaying topography sections in 3D, their projected course weaving in and out. It was much smoother down here at midlevel than up among the towertops, though. Another flash of lightning. The veil of rain was much closer, blotting out all visibility several towers to their left.

"Some I knew were gay," Sandy affirmed. "Mostly bi, for some reason, rarely single preference. About the same as the usual average though, all told." Sudden communication signal, blinking urgently at the edge of her consciousness. She accessed cautiously. Read the heading code in a flash . . . Tetsu Consolidated, full encryption. Curious, she hooked it up.

*"Cassandra Kresnov?"* asked a recently familiar voice, linked impressively to her inner ear. Clear signal, very clean. Focus and isolate, she concentrated her reply.

*"This is Cody, am I right?"*

*"That is correct, yes. I hope I'm not disturbing you?"*

*"No. Please go ahead."*

*"Very well . . . I have a message for you."* Sandy frowned. Aware that from the back of the cruiser, someone had asked her a question. Vanessa was looking at her. Told Singh that she was accessing, looking curious.

*"Who is the message from, Cody?"*

*"I don't know."* The frown grew deeper. *"Shall I tell you the message? I'm sure it is meant for you, and I'd like to know what it means."*

*"Yes, please tell me the message."*

*"Very well. Message reads, 'Tell Sandy I miss her.' End message."* Suddenly Sandy felt strangely, inexplicably cold. Several interminably long seconds crawled by. Hair prickled on the back of her neck.

*"Where did this message come from, Cody?"*

*"I don't know."* A cold, tense feeling tightened her stomach. *"Do you know what this message means? I am very puzzled about its location, since I can usually detect such things. It has aroused my curiosity."*

*"No. No Cody, I'm not certain what it means."* A brief pause.

*"Was I correct in assuming that the message was intended for you?"*

*"Yes."* The cold feeling grew worse. A shudder as the cruiser gently turned, and then rain was hammering over the windshield, obliterating all visibility, turning the entire world to wet, sheeting grey. *"Yes, I think this message probably was intended for me. If I come to understand what*

*it means, I'll be sure to inform you.*" A shudder on the transmission as lightning flickered and leapt, illuminating the dark shadow of a nearby tower through the pouring rain. "*Thank you for passing this on to me.*"

"*You're welcome. I'll be very interested. Good-bye.*" The connection cut out. Sandy stared into the blinding grey, her head suddenly empty of sound.

"Sandy?" Vanessa asked. The navcomp feed now displayed a lighted space across Vanessa's side of the windshield, a comprehensive head-up display. The course curved away in front, and Vanessa followed it with a gentle shift of her hands. Numbers flickered and changed—speed, altitude, and associateds. "What did the AI want?"

Vanessa, Sandy realised, must have some very fancy enhancements to know who was calling her.

"Gave me a message," she said, staring vacantly into space. Tell Sandy I miss her. Sandy. The only people who might miss her, and who had once called her Sandy, were dead. She'd thought. Until just yesterday.

"What kind of message?"

Cody hadn't known where the message had come from. Tracing and analysing data was Cody's specialty. Until that moment she hadn't been certain if it was *possible* to send messages to an AI of Cody's sophistication and not have the location pinpointed. Damn right Cody was curious. It was a ghost.

The word gave her a shiver. "Trick" occurred to her abruptly . . . but Cody had been very principled, very thoughtful, and was simply not allowed to behave in such a manner. Not likely, no. The message was very real, her instincts told her. Her mind raced.

"Cassandra?"

Of course they were watching the CSA's movements. Somehow they'd found out she was working with them. Or someone had. Well. She took a deep breath. She'd suspected. Now she knew. And the abrupt certainty hit her with an unexpected, jarring force.

She stared across at Vanessa, snapping abruptly back to reality. Vanessa looked concerned, watching but glancing back at the display.

What could she tell her? Suddenly her mouth was reluctant and her throat was tight. It was alarming. She was on the right side, she knew she was. There was the promise of a new life held out before her. Citizenship and equal rights. And her beliefs . . . she thought back to her conversation with Ibrahim, and found it suddenly difficult to recall what she'd told him.

She'd believed in . . . peace? That the war had all been pointless and the League had been wrong to start it? What had any of that mattered, when she was with her team? Happiness had been a few days of uneventful transit, a few bottles and a game of poker down in the ship's bowels. Maybe a vid, maybe a VR sim, and afterwards she and one of the guys could have some fun in her bunk or his . . .

All gone then, when League command had decided her group had outlived its usefulness and, with the war winding down, had in fact become a liability. . . . What had she been thinking, before that time? That they would come with her? Oh God, she'd been so stupid . . . they didn't share her politics, didn't share her drive, her passionate intellect. They simply didn't care—League was good, Federation was bad, and that was the end of it. The war had created them, given them a home and a life, and a meaning to it all. They had a purpose, however little they'd understood it, and it had been enough. Strangely, so strangely, they'd been happy.

She'd wanted to save them, wanted it so badly. But they didn't want to be saved, and it had nearly torn her apart. Please *God*, let one of them still be alive. *Tell Sandy I miss her.* She felt cold all over, hair on end and stomach in knots . . . they were going to break her heart all over again. Vanessa was still waiting for an answer.

"I think," she said hoarsely, in a voice that was suddenly reluctant to work, "I think . . . it might be someone I knew." Pause. "A GI."

"A *GI*?" Vanessa stared at her. The cruiser shuddered, buffeting through a new patch of turbulence. "What was the message?"

# CHAPTER 11

**"T**ell Sandy I miss her."

She stood before Director Ibrahim's desk in his personal office, fully armoured but for weapons and helmet left outside. Under the harness and compression feedback, she knew she was beginning to stink, but there hadn't yet been an opportunity to change. Vanessa stood at ease beside her, watching with curiosity.

"Sandy being yourself," Ibrahim said with a gesture. His eyes were narrowed but otherwise expressionless. If he was irritated at the interruption to his massively overloaded schedule, it did not show.

"Yessir." A deep breath. "My team called me Sandy, for short." And Vanessa had at some point or other adopted the same name. When had that happened?

"And you have no reason to suspect the Tetsu AI—Cody?"

She blinked herself back to the present moment.

"Nossir. In the brief exchanges we had, Cody seemed all above-board."

"He's got no record," Vanessa added. "His design schematics are first rate, his psyche evaluations give him a continuous record of triple-clearance—his last evaluation was thirteen weeks ago. And he used a regional direct channel to contact her, so I was able to register the linkup myself from the driver's seat. He seems textbook, by all indications."

Ibrahim thought about it, deep brown eyes burning with intelligence. The office was surprisingly spartan—simple, efficient, and functional. Any view from the window was obliterated by grey sheets of rain. There were the predictable flags on the walls and photographs on the desk, but the rest was bookshelves, a terminal with interface equipment, and some framed photos on the walls. A tall, leafy plant by the door looked shamefully extravagant. Sandy wondered if it felt guilty.

"Who," Ibrahim said then, "do you think it could be? Specifically." Some question that was.

"I don't know, sir." She felt slightly dizzy, standing there, in a way that had nothing to do with recent exertions. It was a wild, crazy possibility. One she'd been more than half expecting, logically. As had Ibrahim, having seen the reconstruction sim of the Parliament attack, and drawing the same conclusions about its origin that she had. She was good at that. Being logical. There was a natural disconnect, in her brain, between logic and emotion. Something she'd learned, she was sure, rather than been designed with. But to have it actually happen, to be confronted head on by the terrible, wonderful, earth-shaking possibility . . . her head spun and her knees felt weak. "I still don't understand how it's possible that one of them might be alive. I saw the Intel reports. Secret ones that I wasn't supposed to see—I hacked into them. It was very comprehensive. The entire target was detonated with all of them aboard. The whole thing was one big GI trap, and they were all on board when it blew. That's what the reports said, and I can't conceive of how they could be wrong."

"I understand that, Cassandra," Ibrahim replied patiently, "but the question remains—who do you think it could be? Assuming that at least one of them *did* survive?" The question shook her. Assuming . . . good Lord, did he realise what he was asking her to do? It was no simple hypothetical, not for her. It was too painful.

"I'm not sure, sir." Her throat was unaccountably tight. It made her voice waver just a little. She didn't think either Ibrahim or Vanessa would miss it. "It could have been any of them."

"But only from your team?"

"Yessir. No one else called me Sandy." No one else would have dared.

"You don't have to 'sir' me in this room, Cassandra. This isn't the military."

Deep breath. Strange that now, after the raid and dressed head to toe in battle armour, the old reflexes should start returning to her. She gave an affirmative nod. Ibrahim frowned, considering her closely. For a moment she suspected he might offer her a seat, and maybe a glass of water.

"The message suggests someone particularly close to you," he said instead. Unable to pass up a position of advantage, Sandy reckoned. Her estimation of the man rose another notch, however she might have wished things otherwise. "Particularly considering the potential jeopardy in which his or her mission may have been placed by contacting you. Which of them particularly might have left such a message for you?"

"There were several." She really, really didn't want to talk about it now. Helping Ibrahim to find them . . . he had the resources to help her do it, and thus she'd agreed to the deal. Now the debt was due. He wanted answers, about them, about whoever it might be, out there on the run. And she was no longer certain that his priorities and hers coincided. "Chu. Mahud. Tran. Raju. Dobrov . . . maybe." Not really the affectionate type, Dobrov. Certainly Sergei wasn't. She doubted "Stark" had ever had a thought that sentimental in his entire short life.

"So you were close with quite a few of them, then?"

"A few of them, yes." Ibrahim paused, considering that.

"Sexual relations?" he asked then. Sandy thought she could see where that was going.

"Sir, I wouldn't want you to be misled—sexual relations among Dark Star GIs indicate very little, emotionally speaking. We fucked pretty much everyone." Ibrahim's lips pursed slightly, as if restraining a smile. And he nodded his understanding.

"But even so," he persisted, "some sexual relations are more significant than others, yes?"

Sandy nodded. "Definitely . . . but I'd be very reluctant to characterise any of my relationships with my troops in the manner you're suggesting. Sex was recreation. It was affectionate, definitely—maybe even more than that on occasions—but then sharing a game of cards can be affectionate too. I was never 'in love' with any of my troops, if that is your meaning. And they were simply not capable of reciprocating, however much they liked me. The concept was largely beyond their comprehension."

"Are you sure about that?"

There was something about the way the question was phrased, so mildly put, that gave her another cold chill. But . . .

"Yes, very sure," she said, as firmly as she could manage. "I spoke with them about similar things on many occasions, feeling them out, seeing how much they understood or were able to learn." She took a deep breath, wondering how to make him understand. And decided she was up to her neck at this point anyway and should take the plunge.

"My guys enjoyed having sex with me, certainly—they'd damn well queue up for it, actually. It was my reputation, you see—they respected me so damn much, because I was their ideal of soldierhood and selfless service to the League. Sex was an opportunity for them to express that respect . . . they equated it with affection, you see, it's all the same thing among GIs. They don't discriminate much between different kinds of emotions—there's just good, bad, and indifferent. But that's as far as it went."

"Damn hard life, girl," Vanessa commented from her side. Sandy nearly smiled. Threw a grateful glance Vanessa's way, and saw her faint amusement.

"Irritating as hell, sometimes," she replied. "They all wanted so damn much to please me that I wasn't allowed to do anything in return . . . nothing more annoying than a guy who doesn't know what he wants."

Vanessa shook her head. "Jesus, some people will complain about anything."

Sandy bit her lip to keep the smile in check. It didn't seem the right time for levity. But she couldn't help but be thankful to Vanessa for trying.

Ibrahim just looked at her. Possibly a little annoyed, Sandy thought, by Vanessa's intervention, mild though it was. A show of support when he was trying to be firm.

"Cassandra," he said then, leaning his full weight back into the chair as he considered her. "You've been very honest with me in all our direct dealings thus far, and I appreciate that, I truly do. I know this is difficult for you." Sandy couldn't help but tense, sensing what was coming.

"But I want you to answer just one more thing for me, as honestly as you can." Pause, deep brown eyes gazing directly into hers. "If this were in fact one of your old squadmates, would you feel a conflict of interests?"

"In what sense do you mean, sir?"

"In the sense that you continue to feel greater loyalty towards your old comrades than you do towards Callay and the CSA."

Sandy locked stares with him. His brown eyes hawklike. Her jaw nearly trembled, but she tightened it with a hard clench, refusing weakness. Not now. Not before a man of such obvious capability, who would assuredly put all personal interests well behind the necessities of duty. And who homed in on the core of every issue with the accuracy of a tac-suit armscomp.

"Sir, I can't lie to you, and you wouldn't believe me anyway. Obviously, if any of my old team are here in Tanusha, I feel obligated by emotion and duty to help them. I believe that I can best do this by helping them to escape their present circumstance and join me here in Tanusha."

"To defect."

"Yes, sir." The wrong reflex, she remembered again. Right now, she didn't care. She was what she was, and it came naturally.

"Do you think this likely?" In a calm, even tone that suggested neither disbelief nor hope.

"I do, sir." With a calm nod. The armour held her posture firm and kept her body language invisible. She was grateful for it. "I've told you that my comrades respected me enormously, especially my opinions. And that the League murdered . . . at least some of them." God, she just wasn't sure, she no longer knew for certain, and for a brief moment the confusion threatened to throw her head into a spin. "If there were any survivors, it could only be one or two." With as much certainty as she could muster. Hoping she was wrong. But in hope, too, lay danger.

"And you believe you can convince them?"

"Yessir. I can't go back to the League. I've passed on too much information to you now, for one thing. That makes me a traitor. I've no loyalty to the League anyway. I never did have. I don't believe in their cause, or their ideals, least of all their war. That's why I'm here now and not there. And that being my situation, my only chance in helping my comrades . . . would be to find them and convince them to change sides.

"Sir . . ." she cut in before Ibrahim could reply, ". . . they weren't bad people at all. My guys." With creeping desperation. Wanting to lean forward on his desk, shove it into his face . . . but that did not seem wise, under the circumstances. "I actually *liked* them, if that recommendation means anything to you. Not all of them, maybe, but some of them. . . . They'd never do anything indecent or uncivilised, I swear it. And their loyalty was never so much to the League . . . they served the League because it was all they'd ever known. They understood very little of the actual reasons behind the war, and cared even less. Their loyalty was far more to me than to the League, it always was. I believe it still is now."

"The deaths of twenty lower-model GIs in the Parliament attack seems a pretty clear indication of where her loyalties are *not*," Vanessa said quietly. It was a brave thing to say, Sandy knew, given the circumstances. Ibrahim's impassive gaze shifted to the other woman. A faint tilt of the head, as if to concede the point. With tangible relief, Sandy felt the knot in her stomach unwind a notch.

"And those lower-model GIs," he resumed, eyes returning to her own. "You appear to have had little sympathy for their plight."

"There wasn't very much to feel for, sir. I didn't socialise with them because they generally didn't socialise." Deep breath. "They had blank stares. They gave . . . give . . . single syllable answers to questions. I'm sure you get the picture." Ibrahim nodded.

"It's the existence of the lower models that forced me to question the wisdom of League biotech policy in the first place," she continued. "They had a nasty habit of reinterpreting their orders into the most simplistic, linear execution possible. It got a lot of them killed, but that wasn't the problem—the problem was that where civilians were concerned, or collateral of any kind, they'd often just go straight through it rather than take the extra trouble. I had shouting matches with command about it. I told them that regs—that's what the lower models were called—that regs shouldn't be used around civvies, but command's idea was that regs should be used in preference to human soldiers wherever high losses were a probability. League didn't have the manpower to sustain losses, as you know—that's why GIs were invented in the first place.

"So no, I didn't shed many tears over dead regs—my unit called them dregs. They don't value their own lives very much, as the attack on the President shows. And so I find it hard to value theirs, particularly."

It was, she knew, an important factor in her own intellectual awakening. Her guys hadn't liked the regs much either, but the straights frequently hadn't made the distinction between her and them. A GI was just a GI, many had said, and they regarded her accordingly.

It had been alarming that otherwise intelligent, sensible people had failed to make the distinction between her intelligent, thoughtful, creative self and a GI reg. It made her question who she really was. What a GI was and was meant to be, and for what purpose. And what the hell good was a fascination with music and books when your only life's purpose was to fight and kill? Something about that situation had failed to make sense. She had wondered why.

In hindsight, she should have reached the conclusion that she had much, much earlier. But her guys had needed her. Where would Tran have been without someone to answer her questions? Mahud, without someone to iron out his occasional neuroses? Stark, without someone to rein in his occasionally dangerous, single-minded impulses? And Raju, who was so damn good in bed that it just wasn't funny, and who she sometimes missed like crazy, partly because of that and partly because he was just such a nice guy . . .

She missed him now . . . and suddenly wondered if the message had in fact been from Raju, if he was in fact here in Tanusha right at this minute. And wanted very badly to see him smile again, the way he often did at one of her jokes during a liberty, and have him tell her she was funny and smart, and show her just how he thought of her by inviting her to his bunk and driving her nuts for half an hour . . . the old routine.

Dear God, she actually missed it. She'd sworn she never would, but here she was, pining for it all back before any of this crazy, complicated, painful business had ever happened. Had she been wrong to dream of a better life in the first place? Had that been unreasonably selfish or just dangerously misguided? She was, after all, just a GI. Pain, violence, and loss had been her lot in life. Possibly there *was* nothing else, and the GI regs were actually the smarter because they accepted their fate and didn't torment themselves with impossible, futile dreams that would only end in tragic disappointment.

Ibrahim's gaze shifted to the far wall for a lingering moment, lips faintly pursed above his sharp goatee. Considering. Sandy felt the knot in her stomach rewind itself, a slow, painful tightening.

"The reports I've had back from Tetsu so far indicate some significant progress," he said. "Your own name was mentioned prominently by Agents Tuo and Naidu, whose opinions I greatly respect." Again he fixed her with his calm, dark gaze. "You appear to have made yourself very useful. . . . Mr. Tuo in particular has requested future access to your experience. He believes you may have much additional knowledge that could be of use across a range of other network-related issues. But that can wait for another day, and another crisis.

"I'm keeping you with Lieutenant Rice for the time being . . . you have no experience with investigations, and I need to put you somewhere you feel comfortable, in a familiar environment. Further, the two of you seem to be on each other's wavelength to some extent." He looked at Vanessa. "Would that be a correct assessment?"

Vanessa nodded. "I think so." Gave a brief, appraising glance at Sandy. "She's drastically overqualified for this line of work, and I'm not entirely sure I should be the one giving her orders in any combat situation . . . but I'll be happy to keep her on with us, if that's what you require."

"It is. Lieutenant Rice, take her home, and both of you get some rest. I might have allowed you to stay on at the Tetsu site with the investigators if it hadn't been for Milanovic's suspicion and the imminent arrival of a number of SIB investigators . . . attached to the Senate, you'll remember," with a significant glance at Sandy, "and therefore outside the CSA's command structure. I would rather not have Milanovic knowing of your identity at this moment, Cassandra . . . and to be blunt, the SIB are a security risk. Have nothing to do with them. Your authority rests with the CSA, not the SIB and their political masters. That is an order."

"Yessir." More politicking. She wondered how an apparently practical man like Ibrahim dealt with such things on a daily basis. It seemed impossibly frustrating, not to mention counterproductive. "When will I be needed again?"

"Soon enough, Ms. Kresnov." With sombre certainty. "Soon enough."


"He knows more he's not telling us," Hiraki said from the back seat of the cruiser. Rain spattered across the windshield, streaking in the slipstream. A dark, wet tower glided by, lines of ground traffic moving slowly along rain-darkened streets below. Trees and parks a thick, dark green, now sodden. Dark clouds still loomed low overhead, a deep grey ceiling above the reaching towertops.

"He's the boss. That's his privilege," Vanessa replied from the driver's seat—a different cruiser this time, taken from HQ reserves. Evidently the investigators they'd taken the last one from had been perturbed that their own had reclaimed it. "If you don't like it, get promoted."

Silence from the back. Singh had taken a different route home following their delayed debriefing with the rest of SWAT Four. Hiraki came along because some enterprising pair from Investigations had borrowed his CSA-issued transport without asking . . . there was a shortage, the present crisis having stretched every department's resources well beyond the planned-for limit. Public transport, Vanessa informed him, could get him home within ten minutes from her apartment. Hiraki had snorted. SWAT did not use public transport, Sandy gathered. It offended rapid-reaction sensibilities. She pitied the pair of investigators when Hiraki caught up with them again.

"How's CSA's working relationship with the SIB?" she asked, stretching her legs within the comfortable cargo-greens someone had found in her size. The casual ops-jacket, too, was warm and comfortable, if old and somewhat tattered. Darker rectangles coloured the shoulders where old unit patches had been removed. She wondered absently whom it had belonged to.

"What working relationship?" Hiraki commented from the back. Sandy glanced at him. His expression showed deadly contempt.

"That bad, huh?"

"Worse," said Vanessa, watching the navscreen. "We're not on speaking terms." Sandy didn't know what to make of that. Vanessa saw her expression and gave a crooked grin. "Yep, I feel the same way—it's a ridiculous situation. But that's politics."

"What's so bad about the SIB?"

"It depends on the year," said Hiraki dryly. "Right now the President has political problems with the Senate. Union Party has no majority there. Independents have the balance of power. The SIB report to the Senate. It is supposed to be a safety measure to keep the lines of Command and Control separate from the CSA's. The result is that the SIB end up the political tool of the President's opponents. Which is why Ibrahim had to remove you from Tetsu before they got there. I'm sure they know about you by now, given that their masters on the Security Panel do. I'd bet they've already expressed their displeasure about your inclusion in the CSA's investigations. They're already unhappy that the emergency legislation has put most additional powers into the CSA's hands and not their own. Antibiotech senators will be breathing down their necks where you are concerned. I'm sure there would have been trouble had you stayed at Tetsu."

Sandy stared out at the glisteningly wet, grey city, trying to take it all in. A separate law enforcement agency being led around by the nose by knee-jerk political factions? That did not sound very safe.

"Hitoru's the political pundit around here," Vanessa explained. "I always said politics attracted the most dangerous people." Sandy glanced back at Hiraki. He appeared complimented, smiling openly.

"But the CSA can keep a lid on it, right?" she asked Hiraki. "They've got emergency powers. Surely the politicians will be too preoccupied with finding the FIA to worry about me? I mean, there's a crisis here." Hiraki's smile grew broader. When some people smiled, Sandy had noticed, it softened their expression. Hiraki only looked more dangerous. He was, she remembered Vanessa's assessment before the Tetsu raid, SWAT Four's most effective pure combat soldier. Yet he followed politics. Her curiosity ratcheted up another several notches.

"Never underestimate the capacity of populist politicians for stupidity." Sandy leaned around further, not liking the sound of that at all.

"They can't *all* be populists, surely?"

Hiraki just looked at her, deadly amused.

"Cassandra. This city runs itself. An organ of commerce, of flawless planning. Like a work of art. Look around you."

She looked. A pair of soaring towers gliding past. A bend of windswept river beyond. Green suburbs. Clustered high-rises giving way to urbane suburbia, and back to high-rises again. Organised disorder. Predictable unpredictability. The belt servo gave her a sharp, protesting tug. She tugged back. The servo screeched and quit tugging.

"Nothing much happens here," Hiraki told her. "People worry far more about their children's school grades and where to eat for dinner than the big issues of politics. The city was designed with precisely that in mind. And if the politicians cannot connect with the voters on issues of substance, they will resort to issues of less substance. Populism. Emotionalism. Occasionally even extremism. It is the utopia conundrum. Disconnection from reality. I pray that Heaven is nothing like the utopia the Christians and Muslims believe it to be. The human species is simply not equipped to cope with such boredom. We should go mad. The evidence is sitting in the Callayan Parliament."

Sandy shot a hard glance at Vanessa, not at all happy with that assessment. Vanessa sighed.

"It's not that bad. Hitoru's such a pessimist, but he's got a point." Which, if intended to comfort, failed miserably.

Another minute of cruising the turbulent, gusty skylanes, and they began to descend. A wide, decelerating curve around one tall tower, losing altitude, roadways and a ground-level neighbourhood sliding past below, glimpses of modern architecture beneath a sprawling patchwork of wet trees. Some midsized buildings ahead then, taller than the surrounding single-residences, but dwarfed by the nearest towers. The navcomp trajectories turned away in front, leading them in.

Sandy peered out at the neighbourhood, scanning the layout as they lost height. Not a historical reconstruction, but aesthetically modern, as only Tanushan planners knew how. Streets connected gridwise, walkways and parks, blurring perimeter boundaries, a meandering stretch of lightrail, a maglev line stretching by in the near distance, a station stop by the looming side of a sports stadium. A stretch of main street sliding below the window, thoroughfare traffic, fancy shops and people out walking . . . pleasantly low-key, and gleaming in water slick grey beneath the overcast sky.

Then the buildings were coming up to one side, and the cruiser came around in a near hover, revealing a parking space on a lowered section of roof sheltered by a simple stretched awning. Vanessa guided them in on manual-assist, found a parking spot by a cream-white Boxer with stylish rear fins. Sandy noted that all the vehicles looked similar though.

"Government apartments," Vanessa told her as they got out, hefting sports bags filled with gear and gesturing toward the variously parked aircars—big, powerful, and stylishly well appointed. "All government employees here, the whole building. Good for security. Keeps the rents down, too."

In another city, Sandy reflected as the cruiser's doors whined shut and locked, government employees would never have to pay rent on government accommodation. Not so in free-market Tanusha, though. Although wages were generally high enough that "budget accommodation" was something of a local oxymoron. Tanushans didn't have budgets, they had expenditures.

"Are all the SWAT guys here?" she asked as they walked across the covered tarmac, cold wind pulling at clothes and hair, bags hefted over their shoulders.

"No, they're all over the place . . . bad security to have everyone together. More important is that people generally want to choose where they live, it's a perk of the job. I chose here."

Vanessa walked with a slight natural swagger, Sandy was noticing. Controlled energy, tending toward exuberance if it weren't for the discipline. Vanessa, she guessed, had probably been a real handful in her childhood. And repressed a smile, trying to imagine Vanessa as a child.

The unit minder let them in with the required thumb and retina scans, Sandy passing a more than casual eye over the security arrangements as they walked down the main corridor. Vanessa saw her looking and made a wry face.

"Nothing an RPG couldn't solve," she said. "But at least we get a warning." Sandy nodded, tuning through local frequencies and links. In the age of modern assault techniques and enhanced personnel, it was about all that civilian security measures were really good for—compelling an attacker to use forceful, explosive means of entry and thus give warning to the target. As Vanessa said, no armourplast door was going to hold against grenades. Walls and ceiling were little better . . . and laser technology was rather useful these days.

Unsurprisingly, Vanessa's room was on the top floor near the landing pads, convenient for fast response. And it was nice, too, she thought as she deposited her bag by the central table. A big room, with wide windows leading onto a balcony, sofas, and a TV. Vanessa heading to the side kitchen and going through the fridge.

"Make yourself comfortable," she called as Hiraki settled onto the sofa with the ease of familiarity. "I'll get us some brunch. . . . I hope you like Chinese."

"The people or the food?" Hiraki asked from the sofa. Vanessa gave him a reprimanding look over the refrigerator door. Private joke, Sandy thought, strolling to the windows and stretching.

Only ten storeys up, but the view over the neighbourhood was lovely. There was a big, amazing-looking church with tall spires rising well above the trees. And a mosque nearby with patterned domes. A further cluster of taller apartments with rooftop parking. A sports field, puddled and sodden, lakes and gardens adjoining. And everywhere there were trees, a thick green carpet of them, overlaying houses, roads, and gardens alike.

"What's this place called?" Sandy asked, nurturing her rekindled curiosity with an effort. It took her mind off other things.

"This is Santiello," Vanessa replied, putting food containers into the microwave. "That's Ranajit over that way," pointing out past the church, "and Mananakorn over to the right there," pointing across. "Junshi's back behind you."

"Problem neighbourhood," Hiraki added, stretched out very comfortably on Vanessa's sofa. "Junshi, I mean. Lots of Chinese gambling and black market trading. Triads."

"Crap," Vanessa retorted. "Hitoru's just a redneck. I think Junshi's quite nice."

"Seven gang murders last quarter," Hiraki replied, unperturbed.

"Out of a population of a hundred thousand, that's not so terrible." Vanessa rummaged for cups, some other appliance grumbling behind her. "So long as it's only other gang members they kill, who cares?" Emerged from the kitchen with three cups, steam rising.

Coffee, Sandy realised as she accepted the cup gratefully. Took a welcome, hot sip, feeling herself unwinding, just a little, standing before the windows and taking in the view. Lightning flickered somewhere not far away. Second storm front, Sandy reckoned from the direction.

Vanessa settled herself before the phone in the corner with a heavy sigh and dialled an automatic number. Sipped her coffee while it connected. In profile, her nose was slim and slightly pointed at the end. With her attractive wavy, short brown hair recently washed and falling loosely, and her pleasant brown eyes, she looked about as far from the typical civilian notion of a SWAT unit commander as was possible.

"Hi Sav," she said as the call came through and a man's face appeared on the screen. Brown skinned and handsome, Sandy noted.

"Vanessa," he said. A note to his voice that reflected neither surprise nor joy. And Sandy turned away, an offer of privacy. Hiraki, she noted, made no such gesture.

"Just called to say I'm fine, everything went great, no dramas."

"Good." He nodded unenthusiastically. "That's good. Those your squadmates with you?"

"Yeah, they're just having a coffee. How's work?"

"Fine. Everything's great, no dramas." It sounded somewhat tense. Sandy glanced at Hiraki, lounged comfortably in the sofa, looking uncharitably amused. On him, the expression looked like a knife slowly drawn from its sheath.

A few minutes later Vanessa disconnected. Slumped backwards with a deep sigh, gazing reluctantly at the blank screen. Still standing, Sandy decided it safest to remain silent. Many civilian relationships remained beyond her understanding.

"You're only going with him because he's hung like a donkey," Hiraki commented mildly, "you said it yourself." Vanessa shot him a dark look.

"I was drunk, you moron."

Hiraki's smile grew broader, and sharper.

"The LT's boyfriend doesn't like her work," he explained lazily to Sandy. "He's old-fashioned. Doesn't find armour very sexy. I think Rupa would say, 'sexist fucker.'" Sandy recalled Rupa Sharma from the raid . . . tall, lean, and pragmatically unadorned, usual for an Indian civilian woman. Very unlike the glamorous, decorative-types she'd seen. You couldn't generalise about anyone in civilian society, she was realising.

"I thought they were selectively drowned at birth these days," she murmured, sipping her coffee.

Vanessa turned the dark look on her. "Jesus," she muttered, "no fucking privacy around here."

Sandy shook her head faintly. "Ignore me. I'm not in a good mood."
"Two of us," Vanessa replied, staring back at the blank phone-screen.
"You could always divorce him again," Hiraki offered.
"Just shut up."

Rain lashed down. Sandy stood outside on the balcony, partly sheltered by the building as the wind howled and blew. Gusted, cold and hard at her face, tossing hair. Nothing of the view was visible, totally hidden behind impenetrable walls of rain. Lightning flashed the greyness to blue, vivid and sharp. Howling gusts blew everything sideways in sheets.

She felt both lost and found. Numb to anything but the roaring wind, cold and ferocious, and the sudden crackle and boom of thunder, a buzzing rattle on the windows behind her. Such awesome power. She closed her eyes and lost herself in the storm, neither rejoicing nor dreading, merely . . . there. Accepting. Like a welcome long-lost companion.

Vanessa and Hiraki were inside, warm and dry. But she . . . she belonged out here somehow. On the outside, in the cold, where the storm thrashed and howled with a fury that was not rage but identity. The storm held no anger, no intent, no purpose—it merely did what it did because that was what it was. A storm. And Sandy understood exactly what that meant. She'd been there.

She knew that one of her people was here, just felt it for a fact, bone deep. Here in Tanusha, on the other side of events. One of her squadmates. The number of possibilities was not large. Out there somewhere in the storm. She wondered what he, or she, was doing. Why he was here. How he had survived. And, most troubling of all, if she had abandoned him, leaving as she had.

She remembered being told. Remembered it as vividly as the attempt on the President's life yesterday . . . had it only been yesterday? Events and traumas, one on top of another, the images mixed and recurred in her brain with no regard for chronology. But the deaths of her team held a special place amid her memories of horror.

It had taken a great effort to keep her from killing Colonel Dravid when he told her, simply smashing his head to pulp against the nearest bulkhead. That had passed, replaced by grief and loss and the most help-less, soul-destroying loneliness she had ever imagined. If not for her books, and her music, and her passionate interest in things non-martial, she was certain she would have suicided. In a world where even her own side had never entirely trusted her, there had been nothing and no one else to care about. They had been her life. In the physical, tangible envi-ronment in which she spent her days, they had been all there was.

She had known it was no accident. Had even suspected something of the sort, thus her earlier warnings to them, trying to prepare them for something that they would not believe if she came straight out and told them. Old things that she had been gathering over the last few years, on and off, but in that last year in earnest—Intel reports, inter-departmental communiqués, briefings, news feeds, technical and polit-ical analyses, and various other intelligence sources that stretched well beyond the immediate concerns of her profession.

It had created a picture, piece by piece, that meshed with much of what she knew from her own tactical analyses of the unfolding war and the nature of many of her targets. The League's use of GIs, and the rea-soning behind it all. The juggling of factional interests by the League Parliament. The salves to various interest groups. The concerns of an administration only one year from new elections, for whom the war had not gone well, and who were facing the ignominious prospect of a treaty and a permanent cease-fire with none of their stated goals achieved.

The cessation of hostilities would mean that the security legisla-tion, which had kept so much of the military's activities from public scrutiny, would be null and void. Already there had been debates about reintegration, soldiers coming home, the creation of new jobs and new lives for the veterans. And for the GIs . . . obviously the GI regs were good for no other life and had no desire to leave the military, which was their home. With the veterans returned to civilian life, lower-model, mainstream GIs would continue to account for a significant portion of the armed forces, maintaining a vigilant watch for the day when the League needed to mobilise again.

Of the higher models there had been very little mention. There were very few of them, after all. Just her own team of sixteen, and five others like them. Casualties had gone unreplaced for six months by that point—replacements had simply stopped arriving. Her squad had been down to eleven, including herself, when everything ended. Several others had been less fortunate. And two . . . two had mysteriously vanished—departed on raids and never returned. Sandy had never received what she considered a credible explanation for the disappearances. They had made her suspicious, to say the least.

And had started her wondering what would happen if they attempted to reintegrate higher-model GIs back into civil society. The civil rights groups would panic, would demand constant surveillance, psychiatric examinations, personal locators . . . like a group of released criminals. The same watchdogs of the League citizenry who demanded the construction of GIs in the first place, to safeguard the great and noble dreams of the civilisation, and against all the earnest arguments of academics, moralists, and freethinkers who argued that you couldn't realise ideals of freedom by creating an underclass of slaves, while the majority progressives had argued that you *could*, and that the overbearing, blind conservatism of the Federation monolith had forced such actions on them, and it was that or allow the League to go under . . . some choice, for the breeding pit of idealist extremism that the League had become, in those heady, prewar days.

Had the war been won, perhaps things would have been different. League politicians, and the general populace, might have recognised their indebtedness to those beings that their technology, and their stubborn insistence on freedom of action, had created. But the war had been lost, or at least the Federation had achieved a stalemate, precisely as intended. And then . . . what to do with the GIs?

The public assumption had been that there *were* no precisely human-level GIs . . . the statutes governing GI creation dictated a less than fully developed nervous system. Many suggested this was a kindness, that a GI should genuinely enjoy his work and not be troubled by the enticements of possible alternatives. Sandy knew this to be hypocrisy. They only wanted to keep their creations under control. Which was why *she* was such a secret, and why knowledge of her model type was strictly limited, and why every straight who worked in close consultation with her had to pass a half dozen psych tests and be sworn to utter secrecy . . . most of the people she passed in the corridors of a carrier had no idea exactly what she was. And she, of course, was not allowed to tell them.

She had often wondered why. A casual, musing thought, once upon a time, when her brain was not otherwise occupied by more important, military matters. But her misgivings had grown as her interests had grown, and her hobbies . . . and, yes, her sexual appetite. Merely curious at first, then thoughtful, then sceptical. And finally, after what she now readily acknowledged had been far too long, downright suspicious.

GIs were a means to an end. League citizens might feel proud of the technological achievement, and perhaps even grateful to their creations for the job they did, but no one wanted to live next door to one. GIs would help secure the League's golden future. That was the only goal that mattered. No one worried about what happened to the tools once the job was finished. But with the cease-fire looming, many of the legislative barriers that had shielded the League populace from knowledge of her existence would have come under threat. And her troops, although not designed to her creative standards, were still beyond the publicly admitted threshold. They themselves had not been aware of this, being conscious of little beyond their own narrow world—civilian life and politics had been mostly beyond their ready comprehension, and therefore beyond their interest.

What would a government do whose decisions had allowed GI creation to go beyond the prescribed limits? And why had there been only one of her type constructed in the first place?

Lightning flashed, bright and near, lighting up the sky. Sandy gazed unblinking, her retinas adjusting automatically to the flash. Probing with numb, self-destructive determination into this most sensitive problem of her own existence while the thunder crashed and boomed and the very building seemed to shake beneath her feet.

GI construction was difficult, yes. Particularly the brain. Imprint models were followed, but detail was a hugely technical matter. Lesser detail was achievable with reliable results. Greater detail was another matter. Truly human-scale detail . . . extraordinarily difficult, particularly with all the required enhancements and linkages that would allow her to function effectively in her predesignated role. It must have taken them thousands of tries. Perhaps hundreds of thousands. Perhaps millions. But it was achievable, obviously, and she was the proof. And if they'd truly wished for more like her, in specialised roles, then they could have accomplished that. But they had not.

Sandy suspected dissention within upper-level League command. Had occasionally caught the faint whiff of displeasure in a regional commander's orders overturned, or sideways promotions, or rumours of strained relations between particular officers whose politics she had become astutely accurate at guessing.

She herself had been controversial. Her backers had wanted more like her, but settled for what they were given—compromise, the stuff of politics. And so she remained a unique test subject as much as a functional element. Probably they had expected she would not exceed the average GI lifespan by anywhere near as much as she had, thus saving them the embarrassment of ever having to admit her existence. But her talents for survival had exceeded even the highest expectations and fourteen years from her inception, she remained stubbornly, inconveniently alive.

Even in peacetime, though, secrets remained—particularly in the years, even decades, directly following a conflict in which neither side had genuinely disarmed. She could have remained. One soldier alone was not much trouble to hide from the prying eyes of civilian watchdogs and regulators. But five fully rostered and fully operational experimental model GI teams?

Safer if they died in combat.

She felt cold now, standing on the balcony of Vanessa's apartment. Cold in a way that had nothing to do with the howling wind.

She could have done something. She'd seen it coming, after all. And yet here she was, alive, while they were not. Before that raid she'd known, but even then hadn't felt entirely certain, even knowing her own logical, tactical capabilities, and feeling every alarm bell ringing . . . she remembered the feeling well, even now. She should have stopped it. But her own guys would never have believed her, and there was no order, no chain of command through which she could have worked that would have achieved the desired result. She had no say in selecting objectives, only in how to achieve them once selected.

She had known, and done nothing. And had never realised the consequences until she'd lost everything. Leaving the League, betraying all that her life had been up to that point, had seemed so easy then. So why not before? Dammit, she should have told them, pleaded with them in private, and once she'd convinced them, orchestrated a mutiny, or a rebellion . . .

Unthinkable, even now. She was fooling herself to think that it could ever have happened, tormenting herself unnecessarily. But it did nothing to change the fact that she was alive and they were dead, and she felt responsible. More than responsible. She felt guilty.

Please God let one of them still be alive. Just one. She wanted it so badly that it hurt.

Another rattle on the glass behind her, but this time it was the door opening and closing, then Vanessa was standing beside her. A good ten centimetres shorter, though she herself was barely 170. Dark hair tossed about in the wind, arms wrapped around herself for warmth.

"Either you're madly in love with chaos," Vanessa said loudly over the storm, "or you're having some very dark thoughts." Sandy searched but had no reply available. "Want to talk about it?"

"Can't." A small sigh. "Sorry."

"Can't or won't?"

"What's the difference?"

Vanessa looked at her critically. "You know, for a glorified pocket calculator, you can be pretty stubborn sometimes." Sandy blinked. The corner of her mouth twitched briefly. Thunder rumbled again, then boomed, a deep bass vibrato.

"Where were you born, Vanessa?" Vanessa paused, seeming surprised at the question.

"Hospital five Ks from here." Frowning, face framed by gusting dark hair. "Why?"

"And you don't remember anything about it?"

Vanessa thought about it, then half grinned, looking puzzled.

"Us straights can't remember back that far, Sandy. Brain's not developed enough, never stores anything it takes in. What about you, you remember anything from when you were . . . whatever you were?"

"Nup. Not a thing. I don't remember most of my training, and only bits and pieces of my first . . . maybe five years in actual combat. My first real memories are of killing people." A sideways glance. "You believe that?"

"Damn." Vanessa was staring. "That's unbelievable." Crackle and boom of thunder, followed by more lightning. The flicker of blue light was continuous now, only the intensity varied. "And despite all that you still managed to turn out a basically decent person. How about that?"

"Why do you think I'm decent—you barely know me?"

"Hey, I'm a SWAT leader. My character judgment's not perfect, but it's better than most." Glaring with good-natured intensity. A common expression for her. "You wanna argue with me?"

Sandy exhaled hard. "I'm better than some straights, I'll give myself that much credit."

"You saved the President's life," Vanessa interjected somewhat sarcastically. "You hadn't killed or even hurt anyone while you were AWOL . . . I don't know how many straights would be able to say that much if they had your capabilities at their disposal for a year."

Which was interesting. She hadn't thought of that.

"From what my briefing reports showed," Vanessa continued with that aggressive, slightly exasperated smile of hers, "you've been pretty much travelling around the place, meeting people, playing tourist, trying to earn an honest wage, touring art galleries and screwing pretty much anyone who's not female." Sandy couldn't help but smile. "More's the pity." The smile grew a little broader.

"And maybe it's stupid of me," Vanessa continued just as forcefully, "but I just don't find you very intimidating."

"Maybe I'm slipping," Sandy suggested wryly.

"That," Vanessa said, levelling a finger at her, "is exactly what I'm talking about." Sandy looked away again into the storm, smile fading. Aware that Vanessa was still watching, looking puzzled.

"I don't remember anywhere near as much as I should," Sandy said, voice barely carrying above a resounding boom of thunder very nearby. "Tape softens the memories, disconnects them from the emotions."

"Right," Vanessa said, nodding, "everyone gets that. Every time some cop in a downtown precinct has to shoot some gangbanger, they get tape to help the trauma. No shame in that—it helps them get on with their lives. Hell, it happens so rarely here, there's no comparison to what you've been through."

"I don't know," Sandy replied. Vanessa blinked as lightning lit the near sky. Sandy's eyelids never flickered. Boom and crash, rolling onward as if tumbling down a long slope. Faded, overlapped by another, more distant rumble. "I don't know how much I really need it. I go into a different state when I'm in combat. I process so much information. I suppose you'd call it surreal. I don't think it ever really impacts me emotionally like it might a straight human." Pause. "Killing people, that is."

Vanessa brushed hair from where it stuck to her lips. Staring, with evident concern.

"And that bothers you?" she asked.

"It fucking scares me," Sandy replied, still gazing outward, arms folded, her shoulder harness tight beneath her jacket. "We still have ethical debates about the overuse of trauma tape. People say that as human beings we're *supposed* to suffer trauma, that it makes us learn and improves our behaviour. So imagine what I am." Pause for more thunder. She made no effort to brush the hair from her face. "I've personally killed hundreds. And it deserves a hell of a lot more trauma than I've ever suffered, tape or no tape. I'm quite certain of that."

She turned to look at Vanessa.

"So you tell me," she said, "am I decent? I don't bloody deserve to be."

Vanessa shook her head, vehemently.

"That's bullshit, Sandy. There are people on both sides who've been in exactly the same situation. It's no one's fault. You're just better at it than they are. And beating yourself up about it means just one more life gone to waste. The situation killed them—personal responsibility means squat."

"At what point did that line get drawn?" Sandy asked. Staring at Vanessa, her gaze unblinking, despite knowing that it made most straights uncomfortable. "I know I'm not legally responsible for anything I did early on—I can't even remember it. At that age, GIs just do what they're told, no choice at all. But later on? Even when I knew the cause was pointless and possibly immoral? I was having doubts for three full years." Pause to let that sink in. "That's a long, long time to keep fighting for something you're not certain you believe in any more."

Vanessa exhaled hard, staring out into the blinding grey veils of rain.

"You did it for your guys, didn't you?"

Sandy glanced down. The cold feeling was stronger than ever. And she didn't know from where this sudden need to confide had come, except that it seemed like the right time, and Vanessa was the first nonbureaucrat she'd been able to talk with about it. Vanessa was the closest thing to a fellow soldier she was likely to find in this entire, civilianised city.

She nodded reluctantly.

"When there's a lot at stake," she said quietly, "then some things just don't bear much questioning. You know?" Looking up, meeting Vanessa's brown, concerned eyes. Hopefully.

Vanessa nodded. "I know. And you might think it's weird, but it's that kind of imperfect logic that gives me hope for you, Sandy. If you were emotionally and logically perfect, you'd scare the hell out of me. I don't like people like that. The people who allow some damn concept of technical logic, or honour code, or whatever they call it, to come before their gut instincts . . ." and she rapped herself hard in the midriff with her knuckles, ". . . those are the ones I'm scared of."

"The people I like are the ones who agonise over things. Who *get* affected. Who care, Sandy, that's what it comes down to. You care." Vanessa shivered, wrapping her arms more tightly about herself. "Hell, if you didn't care, you'd be sitting inside where it's warm, and not dragging my skinny butt out here into the cold to see what's wrong."

"You didn't have to come out," Sandy said, not unkindly.

"Bullshit I didn't. You're in my team now. I'm your squad commander, remember?" Sandy nodded, considering that. "So come inside, huh? Before some lightning bolt turns the end of your life into the ultimate anticlimax."

Sandy smiled. It *would* be a damn silly way to go, after everything else. Vanessa put a hand on her shoulder, and squeezed.

"If it means anything to you, I actually like you." Sandy looked at her in surprise. Vanessa looked very sincere. And she felt a sudden, unfamiliar emotion and her throat was suddenly tight again, but for a different reason. "And it's not just 'cause I like girls, either." Sandy smiled, painfully. Put a hand on Vanessa's.

"Thanks," she said.

"You don't have to hug a gay woman if you don't want to," Vanessa said slyly, "but I'd recommend it." Sandy's smile grew broader, and when Vanessa put her arms around her, she returned the embrace gladly enough. Vanessa was small, and not at all broad, but she didn't feel particularly delicate either.

Sandy took a deep breath. The embrace felt nice, in the way that she'd always enjoyed such affectionate gestures, rare as they'd been. And she decided that all her concerns could wait another hour or two. Everything could wait. She let the breath out, feeling measurably better.

"So," she said with forced playfulness, "you think I'm sexy, do ya?"

"Don't tease," Vanessa retorted against her shoulder. "I'm very vulnerable."

# CHAPTER 12

"Ow." She sat straight-backed and topless before the balcony view through the windows, legs crossed firmly beneath her, maintaining rigid muscle pressure. Vanessa sat behind on a footstool-cushion and dug small, hard fingers into Sandy's shoulders and neck.

"Ow yourself," Vanessa retorted. "You're practically made of steel, you can't tell me that hurts."

"Until you get a full body-transplant," Sandy replied, "I'll keep my own council on what hurts and what doesn't, thank you. Besides, you've got full arm augmentation—I can feel it."

"Which makes me nearly a hundredth as strong as you." Thumbs pressing hard behind the top of her shoulderblade. Tension resisted. And fled pleasantly. Another hard twinge, muscle knots slowly coming undone. That was what hurt, not Vanessa's pressure. But it was a good pain, and she enjoyed it. Rhythmic Latino drumming reverberated from the room speakers—Vanessa's favourite music, she insisted. Brazilian rumba, Spanish flamenco, Argentinean tango . . . and not a Hispanic bone in her body, she insisted further. The guitars sounded wonderful, the drumming hypnotic and set her swaying invisibly, irresistibly from side to side. The male baritone quavered and cried, full of passion. The massage relaxed her shoulders, the gentle loosening spread downward through her body. Beyond the windows and the balcony railing green suburbs glistened wetly beneath the grey sky. Lightning flickered in the middle distant. For the first time in what seemed like an age, she felt calm and relaxed, and basically happy.

Vanessa's fingers worked down to her left shoulder joint, probing more gently. The red line of recent incision formed an angry, perfect circle about the joint.

"How's that feel?" Vanessa asked with concern. Sandy shook her head.

"It's fine. Harder—that's too soft, I can't feel that." Stretching her spine, shoulders back, ankles pulled in tightly beneath her buttocks. Vanessa's fingers pressed harder, muscles twinged, tendons releasing, and she felt the whole combination of arm, shoulder, and shoulder blade across to spine begin to loosen further. She flexed again, a ripple of muscle across her shoulders, a wriggle of spine.

"Wow." Vanessa worked at the shoulder joint, feeling about the circumference with penetrating fingertips. "Wish I had shoulders like yours. And hips. You're nearly as broad as a man."

"I'll choose to take that as a compliment," Sandy returned, eyes half closed as she held her posture firm, "even though I'm deeply offended."

"Why should you be offended?" said Vanessa. "I hadn't thought your sensibilities would be so shallow as us superficial civvies."

"Oh crap, I like being a woman. Here grab." She held her left arm up over her head. Vanessa took the wrist and pulled across. Sandy winced as the joint stretched, and muscles popped loose down her left side, knots melting away. "I like looking good, I like the way my body's put together even though it's occasionally been inconvenient in an armour harness, and I definitely like multiple sexual positions and multiple orgasms. I also like my breasts, even though they do me no good whatsoever as a soldier and I've often wondered why they even gave me any, except that the people who thought me up were men and couldn't stand the idea of their most advanced GI being flat chested. Harder." Vanessa pulled more and the stretching became intense. Vanessa had arm augmentations all right. No unaugmented human packed that much power with so little leverage, male or female, let alone a Vanessa-sized female. "Luckily I'm strong enough that it makes no difference if I've got them or not. But I'm thankful for it. How superficial is that? Enough." Vanessa let go and started work on the other shoulder.

"Multiple orgasms?"

"Yep."

"That wasn't planned, was it?"

Sandy repressed a smile. "No. Just developed that way I guess. Funny things, brains, synthetic or otherwise. Can't ever tell how they're going to grow."

"How many are we talking about here?"

"What, orgasms?"

"No, Sandy, blackhead warts." Sarcastically. "Of course orgasms, what else d'you think I'd be so interested in?"

"Why?" Challengingly, flexing the right shoulder now as Vanessa worked. "Don't you?"

"God, no." Exasperatedly. "Not in this marriage. I guess I did a few times before . . ."

"With men or women?" Suddenly very curious, in spite of herself. Vanessa frowned.

"Women, I think. Mostly. And very rarely then. . . . Come on, how many are we talking about? You didn't answer me."

"Oh . . ." Sandy made a face, thinking about it. "No real limit. It just takes progressively more time to get there until I figure it's no longer worth the effort."

"How much more time?" With great suspicion, pressing hard with the fingers of both hands.

Sandy smiled, guessing the reaction in advance.

"Oh . . . could be a couple of hours on a slow day." The massage stopped.

"You're joking."

Sandy shrugged. "Or ten minutes if I'm in a rush. No matter." Wriggled her shoulder admonishingly. "More." Vanessa resumed work.

"And there were GI companions of yours who could last a couple of hours?"

"Oh no. God, GI men are even worse than straights, takes a great effort to slow down. Mostly. No, if I had a few hours to spare I'd take turns . . ." Strangled sound from Vanessa. Sandy grinned, and tried an unsuccessful glance over her shoulder. "What?"

"You weren't kidding with Ibrahim?"

"No, of course not." Patted Vanessa's hand reassuringly, as if to a slow child. "I'm a GI, Vanessa, I'm not conditioned to get jealous, neither were my comrades. When you can have anyone you want, there's nothing to get jealous about. Pull." Holding the right arm up over her head. Vanessa grabbed and pulled across. More luscious unwinding down her side and back. Something popped near her hip.

"Sounds like fun." With what Sandy thought might be genuine envy.

"Oh it was. I could go into details if you liked?" Vanessa, she thought, might find it entertaining. Most civilians seemed to Sandy woefully inexperienced in such matters.

"No," Vanessa said firmly. "With my sex life like it is now the last thing I need is visions of wild, lustful frolicking in my head."

"You'll change your mind." Windmilling both shoulders together.

"Smug."

"More so by the minute. Now, what I want you to do . . . get that stool out of the way, get a knee into my lower back here," gesturing with one hand, "put a forearm around my shoulders, and pull back hard." Vanessa frowned, pushing aside her footstool seat, knelt on one knee and positioned the other against Sandy's spine, as indicated. Wrapped the forearm across the front of her bare shoulders.

"How hard?"

"Hard as you can."

"Um . . . that's pretty hard, you'd be surprised." Repositioning for a firmer grip, the knee digging in.

"Unless you can break ferrous alloy barehanded, I'll be fine. Go." Straightening her back to its fullest. Vanessa settled once more, braced and yanked back hard. Sandy felt her spine crack, an abrupt wrench through her back muscles, and let out a hiss. Which turned to relief as more tension evaporated and the looseness spread further, into midriff and buttocks.

"Okay?" Vanessa asked, still holding on to prevent her from over-balancing backward.

"Fine." Easing back to upright, flexing some more. "Fantastic. That's much better." The smaller aches and pains were largely gone for the moment. She'd been getting them everywhere lately, both from the usual stiffening reflex and the obvious recent trauma.

"You fit back together pretty well, huh?" Vanessa suggested, reading her mind as she sat back on the footstool and returned to the shoulder massage.

"They get straight amputation human patients back ninety percent functional in a couple of weeks these days. I'm far easier—organic systems are so messy."

"You can generate a lot more power than any straight human," Vanessa pointed out. "Makes any weakness more difficult."

"Yeah, well, I won't be punching holes through ferrocrete any time soon. Head please." Indicating her neck.

"What, like this?" Vanessa wrapped her head with both arms, a basic neck-breaker hold, hands positioned for a fast rotation.

"That'll do. Not so hard, that's my one vaguely vulnerable bit. Don't tell anyone."

"Wow, I found one," Vanessa replied with humour, and pulled her head gently around to the right, increasing pressure gradually. "You mean I could actually hurt a GI doing this hard enough?"

"Um . . ." Sandy considered, face half wrapped in Vanessa's tense arms, ". . . you could strain a neck muscle at a connection . . . the connections are the key, that's where the FIA got me. Muscle bundles come apart at the connection ends and reseal again super-hard. That's why I healed so easily, it's partly designed that way. Bone joints, too. Muscles themselves you can't separate midlength short of an industrial laser. But if I overstrain a connection joint . . . yeah, that can be trouble." Vanessa reversed the pressure, pulling her head the other way. "A guy I served with popped several simultaneously trying to lift something he shouldn't have. Collapsed like a string puppet. But that was silly—he was working on five tons at the time."

"Oh man." Vanessa laughed in disbelief. "What about your throat? That's gotta be vulnerable?"

"Jugular's in the spinal column, I don't have a pulse there. If the windpipe's severed . . . well I don't need as much oxygen. And it's well protected, the main neck tendons here . . ." she tapped with a hand, under Vanessa's arm, ". . . here, feel this." Vanessa released and took Sandy by the throat right-handed. Sandy rolled her head, arched her neck, and tensed up. "Squeeze," she said. Vanessa did. And gasped.

"Oh Jesus. That's like steel." Sandy could barely feel the pressure past her own tension. Tension always reduced sensation, sometimes entirely.

"Stronger. That's the wonder of synthetic myomer, it changes consistency to match the required stresses. Flexible structures are always stronger than fixed and brittle ones." The old basics. She'd explained it many times to straights in the League. Some had received it with more interest than others. "If you put me under a guillotine, you'd only blunt the blade."

"And if you used proper striking technique . . ." Vanessa broke off, as if something was just occurring to her. "Jesus Christ, Sandy, just how dangerous are you? If you can control and release tension at the right moments when hitting something . . ."

Sandy didn't like the tone of her voice, turned to face the small SWAT lieutenant and rested hands on her knees. Looked her directly in the eyes. Vanessa gazed back with no small incredulity.

"What?" Sandy asked, frowning slightly. "What does it matter how much damage I can do? What matters is what I choose to do with it, surely?"

"But, I mean . . ." Vanessa blinked rapidly, as if not knowing quite how to put it, ". . . control's not a problem? I mean . . . so much *power*! It's unbelievable."

Sandy sat back on her haunches, back straight and stretching. Head to one side, considering her for a moment. Deliberate provocation, topless, clad only in SWAT-issue cargo pants, an elastic waistband that barely managed a proper fit over her hips. Vanessa stared back, watching her *eyes*, she noted with that much admiration for Vanessa's self-control. And on that moment's inspiration she got up on her knees, put her hands firmly on Vanessa's knees and parted them wide. Shuffled forward into the space that provided, and moved both hands to Vanessa's slim shoulders. Looked her very directly in the eyes at point-blank range. Vanessa looked back suspiciously, but made no attempt to move or protest the proximity.

"Vanessa." With amusement. Something about the situation just struck her as amusing. The differences that sprung up between herself and every straight she'd ever met, and ever would meet. Such enormous differences. So inescapable, and all-encompassing. And so trivial. "Don't think of me as a body, Vanessa. That's just the package. I'm in here." She tapped her temple with a forefinger. "Just like you're in there." And patted the side of Vanessa's head with her hand. "Can you see me? When you look at me? Or is it just the package?"

Their gazes locked. Blue eyes gazing into brown. So close, Sandy thought, of the eyes and the lovely, almost girlish face before her. So very close. If only distance could measure understanding. If only . . .

"I can see you." Vanessa's voice held the faintest touch of a smile. It showed on her lips. "It's in your eyes."

"And in yours." Smiling crookedly in return. Vanessa held her gaze without effort. Shared her humour, even though she remained uncertain of what precisely was funny. It was rare. So rare, to find a straight . . . a non-GI . . . who would do that. Meet her gaze without flinching. She felt inexplicably warm. "I like you, Vanessa. That's not a GI thing, that's one of those messy, unfathomable human things. I'll never be any more dangerous to those people or things I like and value than you will. I'm only dangerous to those who'd hurt them."

"Yeah, but that's the thing," Vanessa said soberly, her smile fading. Beyond the delicate features, she looked suddenly mature, wise, and calm. A SWAT commander. "Who defines 'threat'? And how? In a civilian world? A lot of things threaten me, Sandy. A review board could threaten my job, internal politics could threaten my standing and reputation, my goddamn husband could threaten my emotional stability and sanity . . . they all could be dangerous, in one way or another. You gonna be dangerous to all of them? In this city? It's not a war any longer, Captain. You're a civilian. Have you had time to figure out yet what kind of civilian you want to be, with your abilities?"

Sandy blinked, softly. "What kind of civilian do you think I'll be?"

"Whatever kind you choose. S'up to you, girl. Who d'you want to be?"

"The kind whom good people feel safe to be around." It was such an obvious answer. It emerged from her lips the instant Vanessa finished the question. Vanessa sighed. Brushed some stray hair back from Sandy's ear.

"Well, that's not so hard, I suppose. In the CSA. And a few other places. But . . ." she glanced aside, lips twisting wryly, ". . . I mean, given what you are . . . there'll always be someone." Looked her back in the eyes again. "I reckon you'll just have to learn to live with it."

"I suppose." It was disheartening to know that Vanessa thought so. But then, she supposed, she already knew as much herself. Vanessa slapped her on the arm.

"Now get your damn tits out of my face. There are worse things in life but I've got work to do." And gave her head a playful shove as she made to get up. Sandy retaliated, a lightning grab and yank at her arm, and Vanessa was abruptly in her arms with a surprised yelp.

"I should warn you though," she added in Vanessa's ear, in what she thought were far more eloquent tones than Vanessa ever managed, "as a GI, there are some things, like being pushed around, that are beneath my dignity."

"How did you do that without breaking my arm?" was all Vanessa wanted to know, grinning broadly at the surprise.

"You still don't trust me, do you?" With mock offence. "I *told* you, it's just how myomer works—below critical density I can't cause damage. It's only when I tense you get the real power."

"But isn't that difficult?" Held off balance and tipped backward in Sandy's embrace, Sandy's chin on her shoulder. "Finding the medium?"

"Halfway between an art and a reflex," Sandy replied. "If you don't know what I'm saying I can't describe it to you. Mostly I'm not even aware I'm doing it. Now, you going to that chair?" Nodding across the room. Vanessa looked.

"Oh no, don't you . . . no!" Protesting loudly as Sandy shifted grips and lifted her effortlessly, gave her a midair heave to get the grip right. "Sandy!" Having at least more sense than to fight. "Sandy, for god-sakes, I'm not your damn toy!" But she was laughing. Sandy carried her comfortably across to the work chair before the terminal and placed her carefully into it, with only the faintest rippling of shoulders and biceps to mark the transfer of weight.

"What were we just talking about?" Sandy asked her, leaning close with mock impatience. "Trust?"

"Trust?" Incredulously. "Trust you how, in respecting my dignity?

Get outta here y'big blonde ox!" And spoiled it by grinning, the SWAT commander evaporated all of a sudden, replaced by the impish little girl. Sandy gave her chair a hard spin and walked away, windmilling her arms.

"I'm one-hundred-and-sixty-eight centimetres, Vanessa," she replied primly, as Vanessa stopped her rotation with a foot against the desk. "I am well proportioned, extremely sexy, and assuredly feminine. I am not an ox."

"Are from where I'm sitting." Activating her terminal with a good show of looking annoyed.

"A mushroom would look tall from where you're sitting."

"Watch it." And tapped again at the keyboard. Frowned distractedly. Tapped again. Sandy sat on the floor before the windows, legs spread wide before her, grabbed one ankle and pulled herself down to it. Another several taps from Vanessa and Sandy caught the brief sense of Vanessa's own transmission code from her interface augment.

"What's up?" Switching legs and pulling hard, hamstrings resisting with irritating force.

"I'm just requesting duty files," Vanessa replied with puzzlement. "It's not coming through."

"A data-glitch in Tanusha. I hadn't thought it possible."

"No, it's no glitch." Even more puzzled. "The request's just not getting through. It's telling me it doesn't recognise my access code."

"Hang on." Leaned low over her right leg, Sandy uplinked to Vanessa's apartment system. Found Vanessa's active link, followed it racing along the network, through the mass of encrypted connections and light-fast traffic. And hit a barrier wall about the various key operational systems within CSA establishment. . . . It was certainly surprising. And very selective, she saw, pulling back to a more suitable range, observing the way the barrier software isolated only those command-and-control elements . . . "That looks official."

"No shit." Tapping more keys in coordination with her own reflexive uplinks with increasing alarm. "I'm not getting interface with Ibrahim. Nothing, nada, zip. Or Parliament. What the fuck's going on?"

Something felt hollow in Sandy's gut. A slow, sinking feeling. And a growing fear. Something she'd missed? Electronic sabotage of the leading government institutions just wasn't possible in a city like Tanusha, it had to be something else . . . she let all seeker programs fly across the network, racing in a myriad electronic directions to search for causes, key fragments, command codes. . . . What was going on? And if something had happened within the government . . .

Vanessa beat her to the next thought, leaping up from her chair and running for the gear bag on the table. Sandy was up a split second later, darting for her discarded shirt and pulling it quickly on, followed by her shoulder harness, as Vanessa pulled firepower from the bag and began checking and loading. Sandy left her automatic systems to search the further areas of the net, turning her attention instead to the local network, the building security, the neighbourhood hookups . . .

"See anything?" Vanessa asked, smacking in a last magazine and tossing the snub-rifle her way. Sandy caught one handed, rechecking her pistol in the holster beneath her hastily shouldered jacket, established interface with the rifle's CPU and sighted briefly along the muzzle without physically looking.

"No. Could come in by air." No way of hacking into those systems behind those recent barriers. And suddenly the apartment looked very vulnerable, the broad open space of windows that overlooked the Santiello streets, and could afford a sniper a comfortable shot from anywhere within that sprawl of city . . .

"Minder," Vanessa once again read her mind. ". . . window polarise, one hundred percent." And the glass faded to near-full blackness. The view remained visible from the inside, though now heavily shaded. From the outside, all would be black. Sandy backed away from the windows toward Vanessa, standing near the door, rifle in hand, eyes wide and alert with dangerous calm. "Sandy? Any idea what just happened? I'm still getting nothing—it's like the entire Tanushan C&C has been branched."

A sudden reception message, internal visual, one of her autos speaking back . . . she accessed, and received a veritable flood of data-visual information, cross-references, and details . . .

"Sandy?" She overloaded for a moment, searching on full concentration.

"Governor's office." Sandy couldn't quite believe it as she said it. Partly because it made so much sense. She hadn't wanted it to make sense. When these kinds of things made sense, in her experience, bad things followed. "It's Governor Dali. That's what we missed. He's taken control of the Parliament."

"He's *what*?" In utter disbelief. "He can't do that! He . . . he's just the Governor! Fuck, it's . . . it's *ceremonial* . . . !"

"Callay is a member world of the Federation," Sandy recited almost wearily, half for her own benefit, just to hear someone say it and make it real. It was so obvious. The most elusive possibilities were always the ones directly under your nose. And mostly because no one ever believed their opponent would have the unmitigated gall to do something so brazenly obvious. "All power rests with the Governor, on the Federation's behalf. The President was nearly assassinated by Dark Star GIs. That involves the possibility of war with the League, which directly concerns the Federation. If Governor Dali feels the present administration is not acting in the best interests of the Federation, he can take over the administration. He has the master codes to all the relevant systems—he can reroute the entire administration through his own offices . . ."

"Why?" Vanessa bit out, tight-jawed and fuming. She no longer looked wary, backed against the wall by the doorway, black, short-nosed firepower clutched comfortably in her right hand. She looked furious. "What's it gain them? What's it gain anyone?"

". . . thus halting," Sandy continued with increasing steadiness as her combat reflex began to assert itself, "any present governmental activities subject to the Governor's review. That means all CSA investigations. Which means the FIA, all the people we're hunting, can now get away scot-free." She shook her head in disbelief, eyes distant with consideration. "It's beautiful really. A piece of art. Attack the President to force the Governor to invoke Federation privilege, and it'll get you all the protection you need from the CSA. If they'd actually killed Neiland, they would have done this yesterday. I just delayed them a day."

"You reckon the CSA's gonna stop just because some mad lunatic Governor says so?"

"Try running an investigation without your master codes," Sandy replied. "He can shut down the whole CSA. He can shut down everything." Vanessa just stared at her with incredulity. "I think if you check through Dali's file and personal staff," Sandy told her, "you'll find there's FIA backgrounds everywhere. Just a hunch. It's all the same thing, Vanessa. The FIA have tentacles everywhere. Trust me, I know."

"Like you knew about all those codes for so long without telling anyone?" Sandy blinked, staring at her, not expecting that. For a moment she was too confused to speak. "Shit, I'm sorry, I didn't mean it like that . . ." with tight-jawed frustration, sparing the darkened, recently familiar apartment another fast once-over, ". . . just . . . Jesus, Sandy," turning back to fix her with a hard, penetrating stare, "figure out where you're at, huh? No more secrets. You're CSA now."

"Then why are we suddenly expecting an attack?" Sandy replied. Registered Vanessa doing a fast security scan of the premises and surrounding vicinity for suspect accesses or monitors . . . no real need, she had it monitored well enough herself. But maybe anyone incoming would know that and wouldn't bother trying.

"Dali's not CSA," Vanessa replied tightly. "Come on, we're leaving." Smacked open the door and spun out, weapon first. Sandy followed, reflexive cover. The corridor was empty. Sandy shut the door behind, Vanessa locked it with an uplink signal, and they went up the stairs at speed. Flattened against the left wall at the top, before the glass wall and doors that led to the rooftop parking lot. Gusting wind blew the garden ferns sideways, light rain spattering against the glass. Beyond the heaving rooftop awning above the parked vehicles, a third storm front darkened the sky, and lightning blazed the surrounding towers in stark relief.

"Where's Ibrahim?" Vanessa muttered, ducking and peering to see as much as she could from her vantage. "He should have called. If Dali's had second thoughts about the way CSA investigations have been running, you're the first person he'll have taken into custody."

"Who'll he get to do it?" Sandy asked, thinking only practically as she eyed the open space between the glass doors and the sheltering cars. Laser snipers had uninterrupted killing range of several kilometres, without regard for deflection shots. Including all surrounding towers, that meant hundreds of possible firing vantages. And who knew what orders had been given? Considering the predictable xenophobia against her within the various arms of Tanushan administration, and particularly in the present chaotic situation . . .

"Dunno." Tight-lipped, eyes darting. "Could be cops, could be plain-clothes, could be SIBs . . . though that's unlikely—they don't like to get their hands dirty much . . . dammit, we've gotta run for it, I don't give them credit for enough organisation to get a sniper in place in advance. No one plays the bureaucracy that fast in Tanusha, "specially not an outsider. If they're sending someone it's by air, which means we're wasting time."

"I'll go." Accessed the door through the local net and opened . . . it clicked and swung open, cold air and raindrops gusting in. Sandy tensed briefly, got a foot against the back wall and exploded forward, out into the cold, hurdled the gardens and then abruptly slid, feet first in under the first of the cars. Came out the other side and crouched between the two, scanning for any sign of hostile targeting. Nothing.

Made a hand signal to Vanessa, braced for covering fire . . . Vanessa ran, somewhat less explosively but fast enough, and this time kept going straight for her vehicle, the door of which was already open, and Sandy could hear the prestart whine above the wind gusting the overhead awning. Sandy glanced about, vision multishaded and tracking, hearing finely tuned, only too aware of how impossible it was, in these surroundings, to pinpoint a hostile target who did not want to be spotted. Beyond the rooftop and all around towers rose skyward, some near, most far. Clear lines of sight between millions of people. Not for the first time she realised just how useless many of her military skills actually were in this environment.

The engines reached an agreeable pitch and she turned and ran, crouched low, skirting around the front to the open passenger door which whined shut as soon as she hit the leather seat.

"See anything?" Vanessa asked, eyeing the generator displays as the greenlines reached red-critical.

"Nothing. Anyone could have, though, if they'd known where to be." And still could, if willing to take out an aircar. But it was unnecessary to point out such obvious things to a SWAT lieutenant.

"Wonders of obscurity," Vanessa replied, pulling back on the control grips as the indicators reached red and the go-lights showed green. A whine of field distortion, vibrating through the seats, and they rose fractionally above the tarmac . . . a warning light reprimanded their lack of seatbelts, quickly killed by Vanessa. "The only way to be really safe is to be hidden. Big FIA advantage over everyone else, that's for sure."

A com-light flashed as they glided forward, turning towards the open space beyond the rooftop pads . . . they both glanced at it. Vanessa recognised the incoming signature.

"Oh great." Hit the receive button . . .

"*Hello Snowcat, this is S–15, repeat, S–15, please deactivate and stand by for further instructions, we are inbound on ETA of thirty seconds.*"

"Negative, S–15," Vanessa replied, easing control grips forward.

"We are outbound, I am awaiting instructions from a direct superior, I am not at liberty to take instruction from any source outside the chain of command, out."

Sandy did a fast air-grid search, locking onto the ID signature of that incoming message . . . found the incoming immediately, still a kilometre away, and patched that location into the cruiser's own nav-comp so Vanessa could see, it was blacked out on regular systems, invisible to everyone but Traffic Central itself.

*"Snowcat, chain of command has been restructured, SIB have been authorised by Callayan C&C to carry full authority over any unit within our jurisdiction. Please stand down."*

Vanessa shut them off.

"Definitely SIB," she said, although the ID already said as much. "Only SIB could talk about an electronic coup like it was a temporary reshuffle." Pushing the controls fully forward, and the aircar accelerated out into open air, a sudden, unobstructed view of wet city suburbs. "Damn. That means the Senate's involved. They've been after Neiland for years. I bet they're ecstatic."

SIBs . . . governed by political opposition within the Senate toward the Neiland government. Alarmed, perhaps, at the emergency legislation that had given the CSA such unprecedented power . . . which they'd used to override xenophobic caution and include a captured League GI in the investigations. The thought gave her a very, very bad feeling, remembering Hiraki's assessment of Tanushan populist politics, and Ibrahim's calm contempt . . . and the SIB had sent a cruiser straight for her within minutes of the takeover being implemented. The bad feeling got worse.

"Vanessa, I've got to get out of here." As the cruiser accelerated toward an adjoining skylane, gathering speed and altitude. "I can't stay with you. CSA and the administration have been protecting me this far . . . now it's all come down, all the people who're so scared of me are going to be after me." Past the combat reflex, she felt a rising, irrepressible dread. Given the opportunity, it could rise to panic. She determined not to give it the chance.

"Out of here how?" Vanessa asked, scanning her navcomp display, adjusting viewpoints for possible paths ahead as she steered one-handed. "If CSA Ops comes back on line we can get a phony ID, give these fools the slip. Then we'll . . ."

"I can't stay with you, Vanessa." Tracking the trailing SIB cruiser on her uplinks to the traffic network. It was closer, but not much. Unless it broke lanes, it wasn't going to catch up—all Tanushan airlanes were the same speed. "Even CSA's not safe any more. Dali's in command. Even Ibrahim can't challenge that directly." Vanessa shot her a hard look.

"Sandy, this isn't the time to go off half-cocked . . ."

"I'm not going to let them lock me up, Vanessa," Sandy said warningly, the fear surfacing with a sudden surge, her heart rate accelerating at the prospect. "Not again. Not ever."

Vanessa blinked, stared back at the navcomp screen, then at the passing towers and surrounding air traffic, increasingly obscured as the slipstream streaked rain across the windshield with growing force. The mist was closing in and lightning flashed closer.

"What then?" she said finally. Voice hard and reluctant, conceding Sandy's point. "I can't lose the tail until Ops comes back online to give me some help."

"I'll jump."

Vanessa stared at her. "You're kidding!" Already Sandy was scanning ahead, searching the topographical displays for the landmark she required beneath the present flight route . . . found a likely site, locked it in, transferred it to the cruiser's navcomp. It bleeped in reception, and Vanessa stared at it.

"Nice little scenic lake, four metres deep—should be plenty."

"Sandy, for chrissakes, there's not an airlane in Tanusha that goes under fifty metres. If you're gonna hit water from that height you may as well just land on the road . . ."

"I could," Sandy cut her off, "but it hurts." Vanessa stared. "And it's too visible." Vanessa kept staring, then back out the windscreen, steering along the new course and muttering under her breath. The lights of a passing tower flashed dimly through the pounding rain. Sandy made certain of the safety and shoved the pistol back firmly into her harness. Zipped up her jacket as far as possible.

"What are you going to do?" Vanessa asked then. Her jaw was tight.

"Keep looking," Sandy replied, securing the interface unit in one pocket and the spare magazines in the other. "I agreed to help Ibrahim catch the people involved in this. As soon as Neiland is reinstated all the old rules will be back again, and I still want my citizenship."

"Cassandra," Vanessa said firmly, demanding her attention. Sandy looked. "Don't do anything stupid. I know you want to catch the bastards who hurt you. I also know that you want to find whoever it was who sent you that message. Don't let it affect your judgment."

Sandy's gaze was fixed and unblinking.

"I've led more combat missions than I can remember, Vanessa," she said. "I'm not prone to letting my emotions get away from me."

"Bullshit," Vanessa said warningly, half watching her, and half watching the course-display on the windscreen. "You're not the same person any more, girl, you said it yourself. You're angry as hell, you're only marginally legal, and you're dangerous enough to pretty much kill whoever you like, if you choose to. You just be damn careful what you decide to do, and think about the consequences. You can come out of this fine if that's how you decide to play it. Or you could end up a fugitive again, and hunted by everyone. Or dead. You just think about what you're really after."

Sandy stared at her. It was, she realised, well worth her consideration. The cruiser banked again, slowly descending.

"I'm not that angry," she said. Even as she said it, she wasn't certain if it was true.

"Sure," Vanessa said sarcastically. "*Sure* you're not. You're so used to attacking everything from logical angles that you don't even realise when you're furious. If it were me, I'd want to rip their guts out. And unlike me, you can actually do that with your bare hands. Sounds pretty romantic sometimes, having that kind of power . . . but girl, you can keep it. I don't want that responsibility. You just be damn careful what you do with it."

It occurred to Sandy, as she stared at Vanessa, that she should have had this conversation with her before now. But this was leaving things far too late. And the lake in question was barely ninety seconds away. There was nothing she could say to Vanessa's assertions that would have made any difference—they sounded dangerously like truth. And Sandy had always greatly valued truth.

"Vanessa . . ." and she paused, suddenly, unaccountably nervous. Glanced downward briefly. Vanessa was looking to her then back to the nav display, frowning.

"What?" she asked. Sandy looked up reluctantly.

"Are you my friend?" Vanessa looked perplexed. "I haven't had many civilian friends. None that meant life or death, anyway. It'd just be nice to know."

"Why would you think I wouldn't be?" Vanessa replied, still puzzled.

Sandy shrugged, still reluctant. Then, "I thought maybe you were too scared of me. Everyone else seems to be." Vanessa shrugged offhandedly.

"I'd be lying if I said I was never nervous. That's human reflex— you can't blame people for that. But when my intellect has complete control of my reflexes, which sometimes happens, then no, I'm not the least bit scared of you. I have a very naive faith in human decency, Sandy. I'm not frightened of people who possess it, and it's very obvious that you do." And she smiled.

"And yes," she added, "I am your friend."

"Good," said Sandy. And managed a slight, wry smile past the deadening calm of combat reflexes. Vanessa showed controlled tension, telltale heat smears and indistinct posture shifts. "I'm glad."

"Tough to smile when your guard's up, is it?" Vanessa asked.

"You noticed."

"What are you even seeing right now? Your eyes are too wide."

"Ricey," Sandy sighed, "we really should have talked more when we had the chance. I've got to go."

"Find another lake," Vanessa suggested.

"Can't. The tail will get suspicious if we fly around in circles." Hooked into the navcomp and timing the course. Thirty seconds. Disconnected the seatbelt. Checked the safety on the snub-rifle and placed it on Vanessa's lap. "Better keep this. I can't carry it about town and you won't want to explain why it's missing."

"You need an override for the door?"

"No, I've got it." Accessed the circuits, silencing the alarm as the central lock went dead. Vanessa looked impressed. "Not bad for a glorified pocket calculator, huh?" Vanessa smiled. And extended a hand.

"Good luck. I'll be hearing from you." Sandy grasped her hand firmly. For a brief, intense moment, their eyes met.

"No question. Do a good cover story, huh?" Vanessa's eyes widened.

"Oh shit, I hadn't thought of that!"

"Start," Sandy told her. Mentally keyed into the door function, and with a sudden deafening howl of slipstream the cold, rain-laden wind invaded the comfortable interior, and the cruiser rocked as Vanessa's hands adjusted the control grips. Sandy's linkup counted down, a brief recalculation of falling trajectories at present velocity, adjusted for wind readings . . . and jumped.

Lost the link with the cruiser several seconds later, but by then it had ceased to matter. Wind howled and everything seemed to float. A regular human might have found it exciting. Or frightening. Sandy felt little beyond the immediate necessity, and focused on nothing more than keeping herself upright. Vision shift found the lake through the blinding rain, and the surrounding park and the local geography in general, all coming at her very fast. But not too fast. She scanned calmly as she fell and time moved at a crawl.

It was a chain of lakes. Pleasure boats were all under cover. Three forested islands. Landscaped grass and gardens. Some water birds gave heat readings. Nothing human sized.

She allowed herself to spin backward, and spread-eagled herself as steadily as she could, facing the invisible sky. Worst thing a human could do, but best for a GI. And hit with a vicious impact, and lost all sense of everything for a moment.

Came back to her senses, half surfaced, waves frothing from her doubtless enormous entry splash. Took a deep breath, starting to tread water, testing her rib cage. Back muscles, shoulders, buttocks, hamstrings, and calves were harder than steel, a powerful, rippling feeling. The back of her skull was stinging numbly where it had whacked the water at several hundred kilometres an hour. Her neck was stiff. She tried to flex as she stayed afloat. Gradually, the hardness dissolved, bit by bit. Melting away, back to regular consistency.

It was probable, she knew, that even spread-eagled she'd hit the lake bottom. She had no way of remembering, but it didn't matter. Her duties had once demanded that she jump from the third-from-top floor of a seventy-storey tower—the only option when the entire floor had been rigged to blow. Her injuries had been minimal then. The car she'd landed on was a write-off.

She could have done it face down, too, she mused as she overarmed her way toward the nearby forested island through the hammering rain, but she didn't want to risk her face. Especially her nose. And half-smiled at the vanity.

The water suddenly shallowed and she climbed quickly ashore, moving fast into the cover of trees. Suitably hidden, she scanned the surrounding park. Her entry must have made a huge noise, clearly audible above rain, wind, and thunder. Thankfully the park was both large and deserted. It was hardly weather for ducks, let alone people.

Once convinced that she had not been heard, and that her interface, pistol, and magazines had survived the impact undamaged, she eased herself into the water on the island's far side and swam for a bit. Then heaved her sodden self over the rocky wall of the lake rim and started walking casually across the grass as yet more thunder rolled and boomed nearby, echoes bouncing off near and distant towers. Water poured from her jacket sleeves and the legs of her jeans. Her shoes squelched on the sodden grass. A pair of ducks eyed her warily from under sheltering wings.

Or she thought they were ducks. Was a Callayan water bird a duck or not? And shook her head impatiently at the irrelevant line of thought. She felt little excitement when the action was happening, but afterwards . . . in all truth, she was little more than an adrenalin junkie. Her thoughts danced and flowed pleasantly and her limbs felt loose and comfortable as she walked. She ought to jump out of moving aircars more often. Nothing like it. She brushed wet hair back from her face and let the falling rain pound it into place as she walked, face tilted toward the darkened sky.

# CHAPTER 13

"And she just jumped out?" Seated behind his enormous, dark wood desk, Governor Dali looked perplexed. Evidently, Vanessa thought disparagingly, he hadn't considered it possible that someone should choose not to heed his instruction.

"Yes, sir." Vanessa stood calmly before the desk, hands clasped behind her. The Governor's senior aide stood to Dali's side, frowning darkly. An African of short, sturdy build, his beard was incongruously thick. Vanessa thought she ought to remember his name from one briefing or another but couldn't. Typical of her political attention span.

"And you made no attempt to stop her?" Dali's voice was melodiously incredulous. Long, brown fingers folded on the desk before him. A long, brown face, hair impeccably parted. The suit was stylish and expensive. Everything about him, and his office, was tastefully conservative. In her duty jacket, worn cargo greens, and sneakers, Vanessa felt decidedly self-conscious.

She shrugged. "What could I have done?" Dali's perplexion grew.

"I do recall that you are the SWAT commander, Lieutenant. You tell me."

"Nothing, sir." Dali stared at her. Vanessa bit the inside of her lip to restrain a smirk. He looked like an owl.

"Nothing?"

"Nothing," Vanessa confirmed.

"You could have pulled your gun on her," opined the short, bearded aide. His accent was strong. African, but not African-Tanushan. Offworlder. Like Dali.

"But I would not have been prepared to pull the trigger," Vanessa said easily. "She knew that. Besides, I'm not actually sure if the gun would have worked on her. Maybe a shot through the eye . . . but the calibre is probably not high enough for her skull. An incapacitation shot elsewhere would only make her angry."

"And so you just let her jump?" Dali seemed to be having great trouble getting his brain around that concept. Bloody bureaucrat.

"Yes, sir."

A pause. Dali seemed to be calculating the implications of this new development for his schemes. And not, by appearances, doing a very good job of it. He looked highly disturbed.

"Where exactly," said the aide, "did she jump?"

"I don't know exactly." Further incredulity. Vanessa smothered another smirk, this one more difficult than the last. "She scrambled the navcomp. I couldn't see where we were because of the rain. And besides, my attention was elsewhere."

"Where else, precisely?" asked the aide with dark suspicion.

"On asking her why she was jumping."

"And what did she say?"

"That she believed you were going to detain her. That she wished to continue with the investigation. She has bad memories of detention. As you could imagine."

"Lieutenant Rice," Dali interjected, leaning forward in a very concerned, very earnest manner, "you do realise that with circumstances being as they are, I myself am now the Acting President of Callay and Tanusha? And that as such, you are obliged to carry out my instructions, through your commander Mr. Ibrahim, as though they had come from President Neiland herself?" Vanessa blinked.

"Yes, of course," she said. Meeting his eye with a mild, unbothered expression. Dali still looked incredulous. Vanessa wondered how he could maintain that expression for so long.

"I am worried, Lieutenant, that you do not appear to comprehend the full gravity of what has transpired. You yourself swore the oath of loyalty that now binds your actions to the will of this office."

Ain't that a giggle, Vanessa thought sourly. Her expression remained deliberately blank.

"Mr. Governor," she said with repressed but building frustration, "the first thing I was taught in training is to only point a weapon at someone if I am prepared to use it. The only people who do otherwise are terrorists." Dali blinked in consternation.

"Lieutenant, surely in your oath you swore to fulfil the orders of your superiors completely and without question? If people were allowed to pick and choose their orders according to personal preference, then where would we be?"

"Even when those orders could at best achieve nothing, and at worst get me killed?" And shut her mouth abruptly, wishing that hadn't come out at quite that volume. Dali's frown remained unaltered.

"We all have our duties, Lieutenant," he told her in a tone of most patronising disapproval, "however unpleasant we may find them."

"I'm going to fuckin' *kill* him," Vanessa muttered to Sharma as they met in the main corridor outside the entrance to the Governor's wing.

"You will have to join the queue," Sharma replied with mild amusement, eyeing the massively armed security by the main doors.

"Death threats have passed the hundred mark and climbing. Gamma Team have got this place completely locked down, Five and Seven are on callup . . . say, do you really feel like doing security for this guy?"

Vanessa eyed the nearby guards, and the steady flow of traffic through the corridor. ID clearance at the entrance points was particularly tight, even for parliamentary staff. She took Sharma's arm and led the tall Indian woman along the corridor toward the inner courtyards.

"We shall do our duty, Rupa," Vanessa overpronounced in Dali's Indian-English.

"That's very good!" Sharma commended her, smiling broadly. "You're finally learning to speak properly."

"Another triumph for the great Indian cultural conquest."

"For goodness sakes, Ricey," Sharma scolded mildly, "just because you Europeans have been foolish enough to misplace your heritage, you shouldn't take your unenlightened frustrations out on me."

"We didn't misplace anything—it's too big to misplace."

"Of course, darling," Sharma soothed. "Have you looked under your bed?"

Vanessa snorted.

"That's the problem with you Indians, Rupa—a ring in your nose, a chip on your shoulder, and a goddamn pole up your ass." Sharma nearly collapsed with laughter and Vanessa had to slow down for Sharma to catch up.

Her purported dislike of things Indian was a fraud and her close friends knew it. The music was wonderful, the food delicious, the people no more or less objectionable than any others . . . and the omnipresent sense of style, colour, and aestheticism played a dominant role in making Tanusha the fascinating city it was. It was just that there were so damn many of them. And the arrogance of numbers could at times become stifling.

"Not to worry," Sharma said with amusement as they approached the end of the gleaming corridor and the light that flooded the far end, "there's now an Indian bad guy in charge. You'll feel right at home—you can blame it all on him."

"That's not fair."

The corridor opened onto the front of the Parliament East Wing. The cross-corridor ran directly across the front of the building, and the two women paused there, hands resting on the heavy safety rail, and gazed out at the view.

Before them was a transparent shield of reinforced glass many storeys high. Just beyond, huge Corinthian pillars supported the front of the building. Vanessa and Sharma were in the eighth-storey cross-corridor. The typically self-indulgent Tanushan architects had designed the entire interior behind the enormous pillars as a cutaway, exposing internal corridors to the outside view, protected by the enormous glass wall in between. Beyond were the Parliament lawns. Off to the far left, and barely visible behind the convergence of pillars, the breathtaking reddish arches and spans of the main Parliament, towering above the wet-green lawns and gardens.

Far across the gardens and the access roads that linked the entire, three-sided Parliament grounds, security staff quartered the lawns and security vehicles cruised the roads. At least one armoured flyer circled somewhere above—Vanessa could dimly hear the familiar keening of multiposter engines through the soundproofed transparent wall. A crush of vehicles had emerged at one access road, blocked by security vehicles with flashing lights as uniformed personnel with bulky sensor equipment searched each one.

"No," she murmured, "I can't pin this one on the Indians. It's those nasty, good-for-nothing offworlders, Rupa. Can't trust 'em. Ship 'em all home I say. No birth visa, no stay."

Sharma managed a weak smile. And for the next minute they gazed at the commotion across the picturesque grounds, and wondered what the hell it all meant.

"You'd think it would all be very easy," Sharma said after a moment with quizzical irony. "Move the centre of administration from that building," pointing off to the Parliament, "to this building. This is too much fuss. There must be a tac-fix." SWAT slang. Vanessa managed her own weak smile.

Sharma's understatement hit the mark very well. It was chaos. The media were in a state of delighted, gleeful panic. The Parliament the same, only without the glee. Neiland supporters screamed for answers, justifications, explanations for this most undemocratic removal (or temporary sidelining, as the official spin now put it) of the democratically elected President. Her own Union Party were howling outrage, threatening legal action, mass popular uprisings and eternal hellfire and damnation. The Settlers First extremists in the Senate were applauding the removal of an "out of touch and dictatorial President." The main opposition Progress Party were not commenting. Neither were the mainstream senators. No wonder, Vanessa thought. They'd helped it happen. They knew about Sandy, as the general public did not. They knew she was helping the CSA in their investigations. They questioned Neiland's judgment following her traumatic recent experience. They questioned what the Federation would have to say about all kinds of things, from Sandy to the investigation into the FIA, and reiterated the dangers of such an investigation, which could uncover too much and cause unbridgeable rifts between the Neiland administration and the Federation Government itself. Such a prospect had politicians of all shades running scared. They feared Neiland's hard line, her practical, no-compromise approach. They wanted her out.

Such were the rumours that now ran through the corridors of power, here in the Parliament complex, and back at CSA HQ, where new lines of command and control were being hastily improvised, and department heads were scrambling for the necessary clearances from their new bureaucratic masters to continue their work. Dali had played the angles. With so many politicians behind him out of fear or for personal advancement, it was difficult to see Neiland getting back in charge any time soon. First a Federation task force would arrive and assess the situation. They would determine if their dutiful little colony had indeed acted against the best interests of the broader Federation, as Dali claimed. Neiland's reappointment would probably follow. But by then the investigation into the FIA infiltrators would have been sufficiently tied up with bureaucratic red tape, and all the incriminating evidence would have been neatly swept under the nearest available carpet.

Well, at least they didn't have Sandy. Vanessa held to that thought, gazing out across the orderly confusion to lawns and gardens that appeared to glow luminescently after the recent rains.

"And I thought this was a democracy," Sharma sighed, breaking their contemplative silence. Urgent footsteps and voices echoed through the corridors behind them. More bureaucratic commotion. Vanessa ignored it. She wished she could ignore it all.

"Not much point in a Governor if he doesn't have override powers," Vanessa replied glumly. "The tyranny of distance. The modern Federation only really came into existence about the time the League was being formed—they wanted to formalise the political structure but needed to keep control of each member world, just in case." It made so much sense at the time. "Governors can't consult with a four-week timelag. They have to be able to act immediately if they reckon the Fed's interests are threatened. But of course the rules were written so long ago that everyone's forgotten them. And they've never been used anywhere, until now. Everyone supposed they were just ceremonial. Symbolic."

"Callay makes history," Sharma said with irony. "Fancy that. Most Callayans don't even read history."

More footsteps in the corridor behind them, but something about these made Vanessa turn. She was only half surprised to see CSA director Ibrahim walking toward them. That he was alone did not surprise her either. Ibrahim needed no guards, and would tolerate no chaperones.

"Lieutenant Rice." Very sombrely, coming to a halt before the pair of them. "Agent Sharma. How is your knee?"

"Um . . . very well," said Sharma past her surprise, "fully healed now." She'd damaged an augmentation implant a month ago in training and had reached active duty status just last week, in time for the raid on the FIA who'd abducted Sandy. Ibrahim not only knew the names of all his staff, he also knew their status. Cybernetic memory and uplinks definitely helped, but Vanessa suspected he'd have known anyway.

She studied him now . . . as always looking slightly uncomfortable in his dark suit. She was so accustomed to seeing Arabic or Indian men in more comfortable salwar kameez or other traditional garb, she wondered why he felt the suit necessary, besides the formal implications of office. Not a tall man—face to face, she did not need to tilt her head far to look him in the eye. But no less imposing for the lack of stature. His eyes now seemed darker than usual, his gaze more penetrating. He did not, Vanessa thought, have the appearance of a man in a good mood. Ibrahim rarely let his mood show, good or bad. If she could tell, then something was very wrong.

"And how is your other team member, Lieutenant?" Very blandly, and very formally. Not Ibrahim's usual tone, whatever his implacable nature. And he glanced up briefly and to either side, clearly indicating that the corridor was being monitored, or at least that he feared so.

"Recuperating and ready for duty," Vanessa replied. "Very hard at work right this minute, I believe." A monitor would be an automated program, set to alert its users only if key suspicious phrases were uttered. Bland, nonspecific conversation was the key. "But then she was always a very hard worker. And very committed. I think she'll be fine." Ibrahim's eyes appeared to flicker in response. A brief, positive gleam, as if a weight had been lifted, a major concern erased. He took a slightly deeper breath than usual before replying.

"That's good. That is very good. I am on my way to see the Governor. You should head back to your unit, Lieutenant, Agent, and await my further instruction." Something about that did not sound right. Vanessa suffered a slow, cold raising of hairs on her scalp and down her spine.

"Sir . . ." and she paused, wondering how to put it. Ibrahim waited patiently. She wanted to uplink directly, but that could be monitored even more efficiently than verbal communication, and would attract more attention. At least verbally she had the option of being obtuse. "Sir, is the present strategic circumstance . . . acceptable?" Ibrahim shook his head, very calmly and with no doubt or hesitation. Vanessa's cold chill got worse. "Are these circumstances . . . likely to change?" Ibrahim nodded with great assurance, and her heart rate accelerated appreciably. "Are you aware that the aforementioned of my . . . hardworking and dedicated agents . . . considers the . . . the . . ." Jesus, bloody word games—one of her great delights in SWAT was the simplicity of just blowing stuff up rather than having to worry about stupid bloody words and diplomatic sophistry, ". . . considers that the present dominant personality in this mess could in fact be playing for the wrong team?" Ibrahim's eyes gleamed. He understood that one all right. Worse, he appeared to find it amusing. Bloody Sunnis—whatever the man's intellectual composure, he just loved a good fight. It was in his genes.

"I believe, Lieutenant, that the mouse is chasing the cat. That your aforementioned agent suspects as much only confirms my opinions." Vanessa blinked.

"What should we do about this?"

"Patience, Lieutenant. The mouse should show great care. The cat will not run forever, and it has very sharp teeth." He inclined his head briefly, the faintest of dangerous smiles playing upon his lips. The expression suited him. "To your unit, Lieutenant. More shall follow. The game has only just begun." He turned and set off with calm, measured strides down the polished corridor, brown leather briefcase in one brown hand. Vanessa and Sharma stood together and watched him go.

"What did he just say?" Sharma murmured beneath her breath.

"Bad news for mice," Vanessa breathed. "Of any colour."

Getting a room in Tanusha was easy—one of the things the CSA had given her, along with her pistol, was a cashcard. Transaction databases could hypothetically be accessed, Sandy pondered while waiting in the foyer of the Chennai International, despite the illegality. But the CSA card was foundationally encrypted, which was a very common custom job by Tanushan standards, but entirely impenetrable. The benefit of a very basic format with minimal complication. What many data-illiterate people did not realise was that technological advancement meant simplicity, not complexity.

The woman behind the desk handed her card back with an obligatory smile.

"Thank you," Sandy said and tucked the card back into her wallet. CSA issue also. She was careful not to reveal that besides the card, the wallet was empty.

All any records searcher would find on a scan of hotel databases, she thought as the glass-sided elevator whisked her soundlessly upward above the broad atrium floor, was the name she had given the receptionist. Even that could not be verified by the card-entry—personal verification was a thumb scan on the card itself, ensuring she was the only person who could use it. Otherwise, the card was self-contained. If tampered with, it self-destructed, so the stored-value was guaranteed as genuine. Only a recharge would register on the network to any searcher . . . otherwise, there was nothing anyone would know except that a person by the name of Stephanie Dravid was booked into room 903 of the Chennai International Hotel in Anambaro, northwestern Tanusha.

Among the million or so hotel guests in Tanusha on any given night the name would mean nothing. But someone might know. Someone who had known her direct superior in Dark Star and wondered if the similarity between Stephanie and Stephano was merely coincidental. That someone might check the name out of curiosity. If such an accessor used the network codes she thought they would, her own hidden package would activate, and reveal more code, which using further League-issue breakers ought to be simple enough to decode. The answers there ought to provide the searcher she hoped was out there with enough clues to be sure of her identity. And a five-star hotel was a moderately obvious place to stay. So, she mused as the elevator slid to a smooth halt, she'd finally found a use for Colonel Dravid after all.

She hit the lights when she went through the door and checked out the room. When satisfied that it was secure she stripped naked, laid out her clothes on the bed, the shoulder harness conveniently on top, then dropped to the floor and started stretching.

It was painful. She held herself in the air, back arched, supported on shoulders and feet. Muscles tensed hard, pulling tightly, rippled under the skin, snakelike, bulging and tightening to density far beyond steel. Sandy gritted her teeth and arched further. Her body trembled, shuddering. She felt the pain grinding along her spine, pulling tight at her hips and the small of her back, wrenching through her thighs, knees, and buttocks. Shot briefly through her stomach, a memory of recent horror . . . she pushed harder, and the pain got worse.

Synth-alloy myomer strained ferociously on ferro-enamelous bone, a creaking, shuddering climax of tension of megaforce scale. She felt as if she might explode. Surely a regular human would, a red smear of shattered organic matter smeared evenly about the walls and ceiling. A high-speed train crash would have involved similar force. A small asteroidal impact. She held herself like that until the clinging, grinding, grating stiffness had completely dissolved, and then collapsed to the floor with a gasp. Rolled onto her stomach, muscles holding to critical density. They flexed and rippled at the slightest movement, a feeling like a thousand steel fingers massaging her bones. It felt good, in a hard, ungentle sort of way. She lay there for a moment, wriggling and twisting slightly as the tension slowly diffused. She felt like she was melting. Pleasantly. And it reminded her, as always, of the release immediately following orgasm.

She rested her forehead on the carpeted floor for a moment, breathing deeply. Lucky, she reflected with a smile, that she'd learned not to tense so much during sex with straights. The coital embraces she'd frequently exchanged with her Dark Star teammates would have been horribly, messily lethal to any straight, even an enhanced one. She'd been so damn scared of that the first time that she had almost completely failed to enjoy it. Which was the first time that had ever happened, to her memory.

She remembered lying on her bunk during one of her internal planning sessions about leaving the League, and being thankful that she'd learned how to handle that situation, or leaving might not have seemed worth the price. That amused her now, smiling to herself with her cheek to the carpet. God, she could be shallow sometimes. Telling Ibrahim of her high ideals, her political inspiration, her reasoned humanity . . . damn, give her good food, nice surroundings, and a decent, hard shag at least five times a week, and she was happy. Let the universe rot, she just wanted to get nailed . . .

She rolled onto her back and sprawled there, gone completely limp, waiting for her muscles to recover. Trying to think of who that had been, her first non-GI bunk-partner. Not Sevi Ghano. Oh yes . . . she suddenly remembered, through a haze of indistinct recall that suggested it had been a long while ago. She'd been . . . nine. It'd taken her four years of active duty to even get to know any straights besides the Intel, command, and psych officers.

Only she hadn't known this guy very well . . . the name escaped her, but he'd been command crew on one of the assault ships. They'd briefed and debriefed together, shared input . . . and she'd become curious enough to want to do something about it. He'd been giving her looks, too, which might have been inspiration. So they'd gone straight back to his quarters and had it out.

She smiled again, remembering. She'd been terrified. Kept interrupting to ask if he was okay, refusing to embrace him in case of injury, not wanting to be on top in case she bucked too hard, not wanting to be on the bottom in case she flexed her legs too much, and above all, *desperately* wanting not to come in case she locked him in tight, orgasmic grip, and found herself in bed with a mass of red, pulpy tissue and broken bones.

God. Even now she suppressed a shudder through the humour. The control she'd guaranteed Vanessa applied only to sane and lucid moments . . . which, in her experience, often ruled out sex.

But the spirit of adventure had driven them on, along with his assurances that he trusted her and wasn't frightened (fool, she remembered thinking), and they'd finally settled on doggy style, which seemed safest. . . . Sandy found herself laughing aloud at the memory, shaking lightly as she lay on her back on the floor. Even then, she'd *still* had an orgasm. Mahud had once remarked that you only needed to sneeze and the Cap'n would come. Not that GIs ever sneezed, but it had been funny at the time.

At which thought she got up, went to the shower, and took care of that particular urge for the next few minutes. Emerged after a good half hour's further soaking, wrapped in the white hotel bathrobe, and sat on her bed to gaze out over the nighttime city view.

Her trick with the name at the front desk was a long shot, at best. But the possibility that Dali would have compelled certain sections of the CSA to look for her, however unwilling—or maybe the regular police, or those irritating SIBs—made her cautious about accessing the net herself. Her codes were difficult to recognise, she knew, but even so, some of the local people were evidently very good. Technology might not matter to them. They might just have an attack of intuition.

Damn Dali. She wondered if Ibrahim had guessed by now that Dali was probably a part of the FIA operation, whether he actually realised it or not. FIA. Federal Intelligence Agency. Dali's face on the TV . . . "Federate concerns must lawfully take precedence over regional and state concerns . . ." She wondered how they'd roped him in. Dali's personal background was readily available on any number of Tanushan netsites . . . pure bureaucracy, from Indian civil service on Earth to Federal, not an uncommon leap by any means. Nothing to suspect FIA ties. The Governor's personal diplomatic staff, though, were less visible, and their background data was not readily available at all. She wondered who was really in charge in the Governor's office. If Dali truly made his own decisions. Or if he was merely following orders through a more obscure conduit that did not necessarily lead directly back to the Federal Government, but rather to FIA command and associated interests. They did have a very large say in the appointment and function of Federal Governors throughout the Federation, after all. She knew they did. She'd read the documents.

And now, thanks to the tyranny of distance, it was going to be at least a month until the situation resolved itself in the form of a Federal delegation from Earth.

She was, as Raju once used to say, really in the shit this time. Raju. She wondered if he was here. If any of them were. She missed him suddenly. She missed them all. She hoped like hell they were looking for her, and guessing she would no longer be staying with the CSA under present circumstances, and searching those most obvious of alternative accommodations . . . five-star hotels. A logical thought process for one of her guys. The Captain. Loose in a civvie city, with ample credit and her usual expensive tastes. Five-star hotels indeed. She nearly smiled.

She sat on the edge of her bed and considered the city view. It was staggering, as always. Far below was a broad courtyard, at the foot of the building, with what looked like a food court, rides for the children. Beyond, streets, shopping, endless avenues of blazing light, and people strolling. As if nothing had happened, the government had not been disconnected and all was right in the world.

Something else caught her eye, perhaps a kilometre off to the right, on the far side of a broad, grassy park, not unlike the one in which she had crash-landed just that afternoon. Commotion on the street beyond, visible only because of the park and the lack of intervening buildings. Masses of people, flags waving, lights blazing, holographic, pyrotechnic and otherwise. Police lights, too, staccato flashes of red and blue that danced across the park and glared off nearby windows. A protest march. Blocking traffic. Doubtless the traffic planners were furious.

She sat and watched them pass for the next half hour, and still the column did not end. At various other spots across the city vista, she spotted other commotions, flashing lights and the odd circling aircar with security or special media clearance. The numbers of security flyers airborne seemed far greater, too, than she recalled having seen before. Back at the march, the crowds seemed even thicker, spilling onto the lawns of the park as they marched. She zoomed to full maximum, and studied the ordinary Tanushans, of many different ethnicities and modes of dress, marching, shouting, sometimes even dancing. No surprise there. If enough Tanushans got together in one spot, it usually turned into a party. The fact they were marching at all did surprise her, though. And so many. The apolitical city . . . how many times had she heard that since she'd arrived? And yet there they were, out in the streets, blocking the traffic and doubtless sending the automated traffic systems into fits of inspired improvisation.

Had she done this? The possibility was stunning. No. No, she really didn't think she had. These people didn't know she existed, even if the politicians did. No. The universe had finally come to Tanusha, and indeed to all of Callay. The politics of humanity were finally knocking on their door. And she severely doubted, with a feeling somewhere between sadness and relief, that they would ever be quite the same again.

She was awoken by a knock on the door. Pistol in hand and automatically angling across the room with stiff-armed precision. The time was 3:38. Night light filled the room through the windows.

"Minder, who is at the door?" Night light turned to coloured shades, abruptly distinct, as the room transformed around her.

"There is no one at the door," the minder informed her in a pleasant, unworried voice. Sandy considered a fast scan of the hotel networks, and decided against it.

"Who just knocked at the door?"

"I am not equipped to answer that question," the minder said. "Would you like me to call the front desk?"

"No," Sandy murmured. "Shade the windows." The night light faded to black as the windows lost their transparency. To Sandy's combat-activated vision it made no difference. She pulled the covers aside, rolled smoothly off the bed, and dropped to the floor, fully dressed except for her shoes. Moved forward to angle the pistol up at the door, propped on an elbow.

"Minder," she repeated, "is there anyone at the door?"

"There is no one at the door," the minder replied. Sandy knew better than to trust it. Mentally accessed the door control, and fed it the correct code . . . which was readable for a network observer, but she preferred that to opening the door herself. The door swung open, and showed her an empty corridor wall.

She rolled forward, propped her back against the hall side. And ducked her head out and back, barely long enough to flash her eyes left and right. Delay-stored and processed those images, and found that the minder was right. Moved cautiously out into the corridor, back to the wall by her doorway. Using her peripheral vision to scan both directions while staring directly at the wall opposite.

There was a piece of paper on the floor outside the door. She spared it a brief consideration. It was harmless—and a quick vision shift showed it free of contaminants. A single-word message, "downstairs."

Well, she had asked for it, she supposed. Whoever they were. Downstairs it was. But first she went inside to put on her shoes.

From only nine storeys up she took the stairs. Faint heat traces showed on the steps, pressure marks, but indistinct. Someone had been wearing suitable shoes.

Emerged onto the second-floor balcony overlooking the atrium, beside the elevators. Tucked her pistol away as she went to the head of the main staircase, scanning the atrium. Two staffers were on duty at the main desk. A lone woman crossed the broad patterned carpet, past the smoothly carved wooden elephants. Besides her, the elephants and an idle luggage robot, the atrium was as empty as she'd have expected at this early hour.

She descended the curving staircase, all senses primed. The water tinkling in the atrium fountain assaulted her eardrums, a sound like smashing glass. She noted the desk staff's demeanour. Even heat distribution, steady pulses. Not alarmed. She performed a brief, casual turn at the bottom of the staircase then walked to the desk. The woman on duty looked up with a customer-friendly smile.

"Hi, I'm Stephanie Dravid from room 903. Have there been any messages left for me?" The woman appeared surprised.

"Er . . . yes, just ten minutes ago a handsome young man left you . . ." She searched for a piece of notepaper. ". . . this." Producing the paper, Sandy took it. "He said his name was Mahud."

Despite her control Sandy's heart nearly stopped. Resumed again, a fast, desperate thudding. Her fingers unfolded the notepaper, unhesitating. It was an address, written in pen. 113 Jardeja Road, Jardeja. She flashed the woman a smile.

"Thank you." She pocketed the paper as she walked off, headed for the main exit. A quick scan of a city directory would have been safe enough, being a heavily travelled route, but she decided against it. She walked out the sliding main doors of the Chennai International Hotel and into the cold Tanushan night.

Jardeja, the maglev station display told her, was in the northern development zone. Uninhabited. Somehow that didn't surprise her.

She took the maglev to the nearest stop. From there, a connecting lightrail line performed a loop out near to the inhabited perimeter. From there she started walking.

Meticulously planned city that it was, Tanusha's perimeter construction progressed in neatly outlined zones. At one point, a single main tower stood tall and proud, agleam with sophisticated lighting. To the south, metropolitan Tanusha, a seamless feast for the eye. To the north, all construction.

Sandy walked along a deserted street under a recently completed ped-cover. An aircab stand stood new and empty. Work holes dotted the pavement, surrounded by barriers of orange safety tape—traffic control infrastructure being laid. The small-scale buildings to either side looked like regular, middle-density urban zoning, much like Vanessa's suburb of Santiello. That part of it anyway. Already, though, the large trees had been transplanted to line the roadside, missing in sections where the crews had not yet reached.

All looked eerie and silent in the sporadic, yellow streetlight. Sandy's footsteps would have echoed, if she'd let them. She walked in the shadow of the ped-cover, hands buried deep in jacket pockets as she stepped around sections of incomplete paving, breath frosting in the cold night air.

She took a shortcut across an open courtyard, surrounded by the multiple levels of a shopping complex and what would soon be outdoor cafe seating. For sale signs and exhibition schedules stood by the empty glass shopfronts. It was dark away from the streets. She kept her vision tuned for any sign of movement as she walked. Some birds had made a nest in a nearby tree. A red line of tiny paw-prints across a walkway marked the recent passing of an urban bunbun. Bats flitted overhead sporadically. Their sonar pulses felt strange to her ears. One species, she'd discovered, gave her a bad twitch, a signature that felt uncomfortably similar to a Federate-model personnel hand-tracker. Thankfully that species was uncommon. These were chasing insects. If she concentrated, she could hear the thrumming of leathery wings.

A sign by a pathway displayed a local map. 113 Jardeja Road was clearly marked—it was a major tower. She glanced up. The tower loomed overhead, standard height for A-level Tanushan office space. That meant enormous. It looked complete, but no interior lights showed, only exterior navigation lights.

Interesting. With combat reflexes raised, she allowed herself no more than that one, mildly curious thought. She did not ponder the possible identity of the man who had left her the message, or what it might mean. She knew it would distract her. She pulled the pistol from its holster, deactivated the safety, and continued.

113 Jardeja Road was, in typically Tanushan fashion, designed for style rather than security, although both were evident. Multilevel shopping malls stood deserted in the pale yellow streetlight opposite, newly installed windows blank and empty. Pedestrian walkways linked malls with the tower, in anticipation of the crowds, shoppers, and retail commerce to come. In other districts workers toiled all night on generous benefits. Only weeks from opening, this subregion about Jardeja Road was slowly approaching completion. Things progressed more leisurely here. At this hour all was deserted

Everything was linked below ground, through the usual maze of malls, walkways, and shopping thoroughfares that proliferated about Tanusha's commercial districts. Sandy got in through a road underpass, the only barrier some red tape and a warning sign. Beyond, the floor was bare concrete, messy with sand and recent construction. She walked softly, pistol in hand, vision-scanning the way ahead.

Past empty recesses that would soon be shop-stalls, dark and echoing. Many were under development, shelves, counters, and displays installed. Unadorned glass in the windows, reflecting no light. All dark and off-limits to casual wanderers.

Several corners and bare corridors brought her to a web of security tape, making a red plastic wall of the way ahead. She paused, squatting against one wall, pistol ready. Parted the tape with the other hand, scanning on multiple spectrums. Beyond the tape were laser-trips, a series of red lines across the floor at knee height. Those were easy. The molecule-sniffer implanted in the wall beyond wasn't.

She hooked into the local network, a quick rush of data-sensation

. . . frequency was bad here, underground, and the network incomplete, but she could get in as quietly as the League infiltration keys in her implants had ever allowed her to. Found the correct security branch and made a fast, clean access past the unimpressive civilian barriers, turning off the relevant systems. Quietly and without fuss or alarm, the red lines on the floor vanished. Sandy ripped the tape aside and strolled through. No alarm.

More perils of an integrated network, she thought as she moved silently down the corridor beyond. If all systems were connected, then all systems could be accessed, legally or not. Military systems were frequently independent. It made info-networking a problem, but where security systems were concerned it was more important that they simply performed their job of preventing unauthorised access. The convenience of the user had to be balanced against the need to inconvenience the opposition. The latter was clearly more important.

Up a long flight of steps from what she guessed would eventually become a food court and she was in the tower's main entrance foyer. Paused, scanning the broad, open floor. Tall glass on all sides, a huge, typically ostentatious space. Dark, but for the pale yellow streetlight beyond the glass, a splash of colour across the broad, shiny floor.

An infrared scan moved across a nearby wall, and Sandy aimed her pistol . . . security droid, she guessed by the steadiness of the light, and the speed that it moved. Headed this way. She moved quickly and soundlessly across the floor, heading for a point where the foyer gave way to tall, marble walls and broad glass elevators. She jogged toward the stairway entrance. The door was locked. She hacked the system and opened it in barely three seconds flat. A long, steady climb up flight after flight. No more security though, which made things faster. If someone was using this tower as some kind of base, or was merely occupying it temporarily, they would probably be at the top. It had the best strategic view. And long drops were of little concern to a GI.

Ten minutes later she was at the top. The top-level doors had not yet been installed. She stepped calmly through the opening, pistol tracking, all senses keen . . . nothing. She was standing in the middle of the big, open, entirely deserted top floor. Up here at the tower's narrower top the windows went around in a broad, 360-degree circle. Beyond the yellow-specked darkness of Jardeja, and the shadows of middle-distant, neighbouring towers, the lights of Tanusha proper sprawled with undimmed brilliance. Her shadow cast along the bare floor behind her at a hundred different angles, half of the window-circle alive with colour.

She moved soundlessly across the deserted floor, turning in slow, gentle circles. Alert for traps—the floor rigged to blow, soldiers suspended above a window outside, ready to drop in and surprise her. She breathed through her nose, but smelt no explosive, no recent working of relevant tools. Her vision showed nothing but bare floor and windows . . . and a doorway that led to the roof. She headed that way, moving cautiously. In Dark Star, she would have gone up out a window, or blasted through the ceiling, anything to avoid the deathtrap of a single entrance. But this was not Dark Star. Everything was different.

The door was newly installed. Safe, her vision told her. She opened it fast, dropping to a knee, pistol straight-armed up the stairs. Empty stairwell. She followed it up, covering each turn, moving fast and without sound. Paused at the step by the door, listening. Tuned to the clear navibeacon, a pulse from directly above. Active trackers, part of the aerial traffic network. And recalled the radio tower she'd observed from the ground. Formed that mental picture clearly and pushed open the door.

Stood back from the doorway, cool in the night breeze. Braced for fire, crouching low, back to the wall a metre from the doorframe—a high-calibre weapon and a good guess from its wielder could have nailed her through the wall, and thus have lost the initiative. He who fired first against Sandy, and missed, was dead. One of her guys would have known that. One of her guys would be unlikely to take the risk.

"Mahud!" she shouted. The stairwell interior made her voice echo, and pinpointing impossible. "Are you out there?"

"Course I'm bloody out here!" a male voice replied, high above. "Where else would I be?"

Combat nerves or not, Sandy's heart nearly stopped. She felt cold all over. Her skin prickled. The voice sounded familiar. She could hardly believe her ears.

"I'm coming out!" she called. "If you shoot me, I'll be very angry!"

"What do you think I am?" came the reply. "Stupid?"

Sandy stepped out from the doorway. The tower rooftop was mostly flat, and mostly empty. Some nearby plant-holders suggested the beginnings of a garden. Railing ringed the perimeter. And in the middle, a broad gridwork transmission tower fenced with wire and warning signs.

Up on a platform near the top sat a man. A long way up, legs swinging, leaning on the protective rail within the tower structure. Sandy stared, vision zooming . . . oh God. Night breeze ruffled hair about her face as she stared upward, pistol dangling limply by her side. For a long, long moment, she could not move.

Abruptly she sheathed the pistol in the shoulder holster, walked briskly to the tower, and leapt . . . cleared the fencing comfortably with a grab at the metal cross-supports, and swung herself inside to the personnel ladder. Scrambled up at high speed, feet and hands flying over the rungs. Past one level, then another, approaching the third . . .

And stopped, half emerged onto the top platform, staring at the man sitting directly before her. Light brown skin. Youthful, handsome features. An interesting nose . . . she recalled, in a daze, that she had always thought so. Dressed in civvies, jeans and sports jacket, neatly groomed, the weight of a hand weapon in one pocket . . . God, he looked like a Tanushan yuppie. His eyes were unblinking, intent.

And slowly a broad, delighted smile spread across his face. Sandy swung around the ladder grip, slid in beside, and hugged him, ferociously hard. Mahud hugged her back. For a long time they sat on cold, bare metal, locked together with force enough to bend steel, alone in the cool night air. Sandy's heart hammered frantically against her ribs. Combat reflexes all dissolved, barely able to breathe past the lump in her throat.

"God," she gasped eventually, her voice tight, almost trembling. "I thought you were dead." Her voice cracked, tears blurring her vision.

"I'm not dead," he told her, chin against her shoulder. Sounding almost calm, by comparison. And stating the obvious, Sandy realised, as always. She nearly laughed, but her throat seized up. She hugged him harder, a forceful rippling of shoulders and biceps, and felt a similar, steely tension in return. It'd been so long since she'd felt that from anyone but herself. She hadn't realised how much she'd missed it.

She released him, and he followed suit. Sat back, staring him in the eyes, hands on his shoulders. Accumulated moisture spilled down her cheeks. Mahud was still grinning. Wiped the tears away with firm, gentle fingers.

"You're crying," he stated. Sandy bit back a laugh with great effort. She felt totally unstable.

"I'm so glad to see you," she explained. Mahud nodded knowingly, still grinning. Brushed hair back from her forehead with great affection.

"Damn, you're pretty," he said. "I'd nearly forgotten how pretty you are." Sandy did laugh.

"What about you? You look like some local millionaire's son," she tugged at the collar of his jacket. "What a stud!"

He kissed her firmly on the lips. Sandy responded, kissing back deeply, wrapping her arms about him as his went about her, pulling each other close once more. It felt warm, and passionate, and desperately emotional, and it was a while before she could bear to stop.

"Damn, this is hardly the place for a reunion," she gasped as they finally parted, and rested her head on his shoulder.

"We could go someplace warm," he suggested. Sandy laughed again, holding him close.

"Maybe later." A pause, as the issues at hand began to sink back in. "Dammit Mahud, what are you even *doing* here? And how the hell are you still alive? I didn't fucking *believe* them when they told me everyone was dead, I hacked their files, I stole codes, I looked at *everything*! The entire fucking C&C thought you were dead. They'd *confirmed* it."

Mahud sighed, resting his cheek on her hair. For a long moment he didn't reply. Sandy waited, struggling between impatience and the pleasure it gave her just to hold him a little longer.

"You won't be mad at me if I tell you?" he asked finally.

"Mad at you?" Sandy pulled away, staring him in the eyes. He looked very sombre, she thought. Almost thoughtful. From Mahud, that wasn't expected. Not that he was stupid. Just that . . . well, he was a GI. GI—43AU, she remembered his designation. In the higher range—not that that was a reliable indication of anything, intelligence-wise. He could be damn smart sometimes. He just wasn't much given to thoughtful introspection. Apart from herself, very few were. "What could I possibly be mad about?"

"Kiss me again and I'll tell you." Which also surprised her. Subtle humour. She gazed at him, her mind spinning in circles, her world turned on its head once more . . . she'd lost track of how many times that had happened in the past forty-eight hours alone. She was so used to being in control, and this . . . this just wasn't fair.

"It is you, isn't it, Mahud?" she asked a little warily. "League admin haven't made some copy or something?" Mahud laughed outright, reaching into his shirtfront and pulling out a small symbol on a chain . . . a silver crescent moon. A quick zoom showed his name engraved on the surface.

"You gave it to me when the Indians were celebrating the month of Shravan," he told her, smiling broadly at the memory. "You said it wasn't exactly a *rakhi*, and I wasn't exactly your brother, but I was the closest thing to it so I might as well have it anyway." Sandy looked at it for a long moment. Remembering. And looked up.

"And you remember what I told you about it?"

"That the crescent moon was an Arabic symbol, and since my

human ancestry is based on Arabic people, I ought to have it so it would remind me of my human origins."

"And what did you think of that?"

Mahud gave a wry, self-deprecating grin.

"I thought you were nuts." Grinning wide as she smiled. "I mean, I'm a bloody GI. I don't *have* any ancestry. They just give us features and skin colours and names to make us fit in. It's just a bloody custom job."

"And what do you think now?"

Mahud's smile faded slightly. "I don't know. I think I know what you were trying to say. I don't know if I agree with it, but I think I know why you said it."

"Mahud . . ." Sandy grasped his hands with her own, holding them tightly, "what the hell happened to you? Are you the only one here?"

"Yes." Mahud nodded sadly. "I'm the only one."

"What happened?" Sandy's hands gripped his own, hard enough to damage. Mahud's fingers flexed slightly in reply, steely tension. "What happened to everyone?"

Mahud sighed, looking down at her hands. Reluctant. Somewhere in the broad, city-lit night, a flicker of lightning.

"All right." Another sigh. "All right, I'll tell you."

"The guys were worried when you warned them, you know," Mahud began, sitting propped against the railing, his fingers toying idly with the silver crescent on the chain about his neck. Sandy sat opposite, watching him. The platform was barely two metres wide, a cold metal grid. About them was empty space, cold and whistling in all directions. Suspended in empty air, far above the city. Even the towertop looked small and far below. Most Tanushans would only ever see such views from the windows of aircars, and even then rarely from these lofty altitudes.

"We talked about it," Mahud continued. He sounded bleak, almost distant. Against the empty, limitless night, his voice seemed strangely small. "Tran was worried. She kept saying that she wished you hadn't been dragged off the mission, and wondering why they'd done it . . . Stark told her to shut up—you know what he was like. But Tran . . ." he shrugged.

Sandy nodded faintly. "I know."

"Yeah." Mahud looked down at the crescent, turning it over and over in his fingers. "She was . . . anyway, we got to position, made the approach, no big deal . . . then Stark tells us his orders have changed, and we're to keep a reserve team on the destroyer while the main team proceeds to target. Backup, he says." Looking at her quizzically.

Sandy felt cold in a way that had nothing to do with the wind. She never used backup. The team was a single, integrated unit. Backup only divided forces. Backup was what generals did, not special ops unit commanders. In a small team, it didn't make any tactical sense.

Mahud took a deep breath. "We asked him about it. He said he's Captain now, and we'd never have questioned you about it. Tran says that's because you'd never have ordered us to do it. Pizano says, yeah, that's great Stark, but you ain't Sandy. Stark tells everyone to shut up and obey orders." He shrugged. "So we do. I mean, what are we going to do?" Looking at Sandy questioningly. Faintly desperate.

Sandy nodded. "Stark was a good officer," she murmured. "You did right." It was only half true. Stark had been an excellent second. She would never have trusted him with command of a unit, though, least of all hers. He knew the rulebook backwards, right down to the punctuation, and followed it religiously. She'd worn armour more flexible than Sergei. Every tactical sim she'd played him at, she'd ripped him apart.

"So," Mahud continued, with difficulty, "me, Chu, Rogers, and Pesivich get left behind . . . we take the second boat, hold off in support as the first boat goes in . . ." He paused, swallowed hard, clearly struggling. Not meeting her eyes.

"They blew the whole rig, didn't they," Sandy said softly. "That's what the reports said." Mahud nodded.

"Yeah." A deep breath. Sandy felt the pain in her throat once more, just watching him. His eyes were moist, too. "Yeah, it blew real fast. Reactor rig, one small bang, then the fusion went . . . thermonuclear. Big shockwave." He coughed. "Lot of effort for one team."

"They were worth it," Sandy said quietly. "They were worth a whole fucking station." Mahud nodded. A lone aircar passed, a middle-distant whine above the background hum of city noise. Cruising a high lane, but still some distance below their perch.

"Shockwave messed us up a bit," he continued then. Gazing out at the city lights spread wide and far below. "The destroyer never came. We found out later they'd blown it. Never saw it ourselves . . . our scanners whited out at the blast. This other ship picked us up."

Sandy felt her jaw tense, a tight, involuntary reaction.

"What other ship?"

"League ship. Cruiser, Kali-class. Never found the name. Don't know if it had one. Didn't really care at the time." Sandy knew what that meant.

"Spook?"

"Yeah." Mahud nodded absently, face profiled against a gleam of light. Youthful and handsome, like any GI. So familiar. Sandy watched him, entranced. "Big spook. Had military people on board though. Treated us real nice. Gave us tape, said how sorry they were, how they wished they'd only gotten there a bit earlier and maybe saved the destroyer at least . . . said it was a big Fed trap, the rig was bait, the "Kowloon" was hiding on the system blindside, timed on high V approach, closed after the rig blew and nailed the destroyer when they tried to run, never had a chance, they'd had it all worked out. But they hadn't managed to target the destroyer and the second boat simultane-ously, so they missed us on the first pass and the spook scared them off before they could come about."

Sandy bit her lip. Wondering how much of that terribly conven-ient story Mahud had believed. But not wanting to interrupt him now. Wanting the full story before she tried to spring anything onto him.

"They blew the boat after they picked us up," Mahud continued, "left the wreckage floating. Made it look like a high V strike, used Federate ammo, the works. They said they wanted everyone to think we were all dead. They said they had a special mission for us. Something that'd give us a chance to get back at the Feds, get revenge for Tran and Raju and everyone. Everyone thought that sounded good. Really good.

"We kept asking them about you, wanting them to get you to join us. They said you were needed where you were. Said we couldn't even send messages, that you had to think we were all dead, too, just like everyone else. No one liked that. Chu especially. She called them stupid, said if we were going to do a good job on this we'd need you along with us. She said that if it was that damn important, they ought to put their best leader onto it."

Sandy listened helplessly. Mahud didn't say anything more, just stared out into the cold, empty night.

"What happened?" she prompted him softly. Mahud looked at her. She could see the pain in his eyes. The fear. A straight might have missed it, not knowing GIs, and not knowing how the likes of Mahud would hide it. But she could always tell.

"Cap'n, I didn't know what to do," he whispered. His voice barely carried above the gentle keening of wind through the tower struts. Beneath them, the metal gave a slight shiver, as if at the cold. "They said it was important. I mean, they weren't just officers . . . they were real, real heavy brass, you know? Suits, too, not just soldiers."

Sandy nodded faintly. The picture was forming very clearly in her head, and it was not a pleasant one. She gazed sadly at Mahud, imagining his confusion. His fear. And damning all her ex so-called superiors to the hottest, nastiest hell that any of the motherworld's ancient cultures had ever devised.

"Chu got reassigned," Mahud continued, hoarsely. "She was real pissed. I should have said no . . . should have protested or something but . . . but they were *officers*." His gaze was almost desperate. "I mean,

I could never . . . not the way you did, all those times. And I wanted to hurt the Feds. I really missed the guys and they said I was going to be able to really get some payback, and that sounded real good.

"So we went to some station somewhere, I didn't even know where that was. We trained a lot. There were a bunch of midtwenties there, nothing worth talking to. We trained with them a lot—me, Rogers, and Pesivich. They weren't that bright, but they got it done. Barely. We stayed there a long time. Then this thing came up and we get assigned this mission. This is the big one, they tell us. Payback. Kill the President of Callay. I got command over Rogers and Pesivich, they stayed behind. And the regs, they get stupid-tape. They come out of that and suddenly they're all determined to get themselves killed. That wasn't fun . . . I mean, they're only regs, but still . . ."

He broke off. Sandy let the silence linger for a moment, absorbing that information.

Then, "So this whole thing . . . you're not top chief, right?"

He shook his head. "No, that's an FIA guy." Looking back to her, unworried at what would have been treason just twenty-four hours earlier. "You know about it, right?"

"Most, yeah. So you just came down planetside, stayed low, moved around under cover from all these shady types the FIA have in the corporations here, and plan a way to kill the President?"

"Pretty much. Nearly worked, too. Probably would have if I'd been there myself. Damn regs just got themselves smeared."

"I'm damn glad you weren't there."

Mahud shrugged. "Yeah, well . . . I'm not a suicide type. The brass weren't stupid enough to ask me. And the stupid-tape won't work on me anyway, I'm a 43."

"That's not what I meant," Sandy said. Mahud looked at her. Her gaze was very firm, very direct. His expression turned puzzled. "I meant that if you'd been on that op I might have ended up killing you, too. Or you me."

Mahud blinked. And stared, eyes suddenly widening. Questioning disbelief. Sandy nodded confirmation. Mahud's eyes grew even wider and his jaw dropped. For a long moment he just sat there, totally rigid.

"Oh fuck!" he said then loudly. "What the fuck were you doing there?"

"I was in the President's convoy. Fourth car." A further realisation dawned in Mahud's eyes, horrified.

"Fourth? You mean after it crashed . . . ?"

"I got out. I got free and I got armed. I ran a counter against their sensors. They had me on a lower drugs dose than they thought they had . . ."

"How many'd you get?" With expectant trepidation.

"Twenty-one." Mahud looked far from surprised. She was almost flattered.

"Jesus, no wonder it fell apart . . ." and stared back at her, almost accusatory. "What the hell were you doing in the President's convoy?"

Sandy cocked her head to one side, calmly surveying him as she leaned against the railing. Brought up a knee, and hooked her arm around it.

"Mahud, what do you think I'm doing in Tanusha?" He blinked.

"You're asking *me*?" With evident disbelief. Sandy frowned.

"Who else would I ask?"

"Why the hell do you think I'm sitting here with you now?" he retorted. "I want to know, Sandy. I want to know why you went AWOL."

Sandy blinked. Trying to figure exactly what Mahud knew about it all. What he might have been told. What they might have tried to convince him of and what he might have believed. She suddenly wondered at her wisdom in sitting here so unafraid, thinking that nothing had changed between them. She wondered many other things, too.

"What did they tell you?" she asked then. Mahud looked perplexed. For a moment, as he gazed at her, he looked almost . . . lost. Confused. Frightened, she guessed, of the possible answers to this most pressing of questions. It could turn his world upside down. It could tear down everything that he had ever believed in. Or perhaps . . . perhaps, she thought, that had already happened. Perhaps that had happened when he'd first been told that she'd left the League.

"I didn't believe them at first," he said. His voice sounded small. "I didn't think you'd ever have done it. But . . . it was pretty clear eventually that they weren't kidding. They didn't try to make us hate you or anything, I reckon they knew it'd never happen . . . they just said you'd cracked. They said . . ." He took a deep breath. "They said that we'd all always known you'd been . . . different . . . that they'd been scared you were a bit mentally unstable for a while now, and that when you'd been told we were dead, you'd cracked.

"Hell, they even apologised to us, admitted they were partly to blame . . . but they said they hadn't given up on getting you back, once you'd gotten over it . . ." He stopped, seeing that Sandy was shaking her head.

"No, Mahud." She looked at him sadly. "I left because they're a pack of lying, murdering bastards. I left because I knew that if I'd stayed, I'd have ended up killing them all, and getting killed in the process."

Mahud blinked, looking . . . blank. Utterly expressionless. Stunned. Sandy folded her other leg beneath her, leaning forward on her upraised knee.

"Mahud, what's the purpose of this op?"

"To kill the President," he said faintly.

Sandy shook her head, eyes narrowed dangerously.

"No, beyond that. What's the FIA doing here?" No response. "They're covering up the operation they've had here for ages now, the research agreement they've had with Tanushan biotech firms. Why did they leave it so late?"

Mahud's eyes remained blank. To Sandy's night-adjusted vision, he looked almost pale. GIs rarely looked pale. He shook his head very faintly at her question.

"Because they knew I was here. Somehow they found out I was coming to Tanusha. The Tanushan project had never had an opportunity to study a live GI before. Regs, maybe, but nothing like me. They left it so late because they wanted to grab me, and study me. And that's what they did." She leaned forward, staring him intently in the eyes. Her voice was hard.

"That's how I got captured, Mahud. I was free before that, living as a civilian. Your strike on the President gave the Governor an excuse to use his override powers and block all ongoing CSA investigations subject to Federal review, that's all it did. The Governor's in the FIA's pocket, you understand? He's one of them, or as good as. Are you following this? Do you realise what this means?"

Mahud's eyes reflected only desperation. He shook his head. Sandy leaned forward a little more, her body tense.

"Mahud, the League doesn't give a stuff about me, about you, about any of us. Maybe they did once, but that all changed when the war started going badly. We became a liability. This whole ridiculous business in this city was about sending me to some Tanushan biotech firm for study, like a lab rat. That's all I meant to them. And as for Sergei's orders and that rig explosion, that was no Federation trap, that was a League trap . . . they set us up, Mahud. They set up their own people and they killed us, they killed Tran, they killed Raju . . ."

"*No!!*" Mahud shouted, leaping to his feet, trembling all over . . . Sandy leapt up, too, facing him, every muscle tensed. Her eyes were blazing.

"Why the *fuck* do you think I left, man?!" she hissed to his face. "Don't you remember me trying to warn you? Don't you remember how upset I was?"

"Then why didn't you tell us *then*?"

"Because you wouldn't have believed me, just like you don't want to believe me now!"

Mahud spun away, clutching the safety railing. In the clear, cold night came the groaning sound of metal bending.

"I'm not a traitor, Mahud. And I'm as sane as I ever was, probably more so. You know that I'm not disloyal, you know how much I can be trusted. You know more than anyone left alive. I left the League because the League murdered my friends. I thought they'd murdered all of you. I thought you'd have wanted me to live, that . . . that you'd have wanted me to be happy, and there were all these things I'd always wanted to see, and I just had to get away. Mahud, I had to leave."

She broke off, pained and trembling, staring at Mahud's back. Scared of what he might do, or think. That she might have found him, only to lose him again so quickly.

"Come on, Mahud," she said more quietly. Pleading. "You must have suspected something. That I just happened to be left out of the raid, that they wouldn't tell me anything . . . they knew I was suspicious. They knew I wouldn't have bought it. And if I'd started dissenting with you guys around, they couldn't have got rid of me without going through all of you, and that would have been nearly impossible. They wanted to save a few of you for special purposes, Mahud, they wanted the most loyal and dedicated, and that was always you . . . Pesivich and Rogers, too. And Chu, but Chu couldn't tie her shoelaces without my instruction, so they screwed up there . . . and they needed Stark to lead the raid, otherwise they would have kept him, too . . . but Tran asked too many questions, Raju was too irreverent, Keelo was too arrogant, Neddy was a troublemaker . . . it all fits. Doesn't it."

"No." Mahud turned about. Looked her in the eye. His jaw was tight and he kept his composure with an effort. "I can't believe that. You'll always be Captain to me, Sandy, but . . . but I can't believe that. I just can't."

It was more forthright than she'd ever have expected from Mahud. He had grown up a lot since she'd last seen him. Six years old, she remembered him. A year would make a lot of difference. He no longer accepted everything she said as automatic truth. Not without evidence.

She took off her jacket. Unclipped the shoulder holster and

dropped it to the metal floor, pistol heavy. Untucked her shirt and pulled it up over her head. And stood topless before him, cold night wind against her bare skin. Mahud stared at the sharp, red lines about her shoulder joints. At the sharper, thick red mark that encircled her waist, just below her navel.

She turned about in a slow circle, arms held out from her sides. Showing him the long, red scar up the centre of her spine, where skin had been flayed from bone and muscle, peeled away, leaving all bare beneath. Completed her circle, and stood silently facing him, shirt in hand.

Mahud wore much the same expression as she had previously seen on civilians confronted suddenly by the death of a loved one. Utterly stricken.

"This is what your FIA man did to me," she told him quietly. Her voice was trembling. "I'm betting it's the same guy you mentioned. I remember him clearly. They cut me up on a table, Mahud. I was screaming. Even the buffers broke down, I never knew pain until that . . . that . . ." She met his eyes, her own vision blurring.

"Sandy." Mahud reached out a hand to her face, stepping forward. Tears rolled freely down his cheeks. There was terror in his eyes. "Oh God, Sandy. I'm . . . I'm so sorry." He was crying, quite openly. Sandy had never seen that before, from a GI other than herself. Chu had shed tears. Mahud was sobbing. "I didn't know, Sandy, I didn't know . . ."

He buried his face against her hair, shoulders heaving. Hands reluctant to touch her, as if scared of her offence, or anger. . . . Sandy put her arms around him and held him tightly. He hugged her back, sobbing into her hair as the wind blew cold upon her bare skin, and the incision scars throbbed a dull, prickling pain at the temperature change. About them, and from far below, the city murmured.

# CHAPTER 14

Sunlight through the window of Mahud's apartment. Sandy lay in bed, gazing out at a bright gleam of light reflecting off a glass tower face. The gentle murmur of morning traffic, muted through the glass.

She wondered. Wondered what Vanessa was doing. What Neiland would no doubt be scheming. What Judge Guderjaal would do, faced by legal challenge to Dali's actions. And what Dali was up to, pretending to run a government for which he—if she read him correctly—possessed little expertise. Not to mention the totally unexpected and growing political activism from the general Callayan public, which in itself had certain politicians hopping frantically either to define or to obscure their favoured positions . . .

Probably, she thought, she ought to check the news or tune in to some local network connection to see how far the protests had spread during the night, and what the various politicians generally suspected of supporting the Governor were now saying, faced with mounting outrage from the public and thus the populist media. But the bed was comfortable, her eyelids heavy, and her mind wandered unavoidably to other, less grave matters.

She rolled gently onto her other side. Mahud's young, soft features nestled against the pillow. A firm, proportioned build that was very pleasing to her eye. Light brown skin. He looked peaceful. She watched him for a while, head upon the pillow alongside. Thinking everything . . . and nothing, a strange, calm confusion of emotion and possibility. His eyes blinked open, gazing directly into hers. Immediately aware and alert, as if he had never been asleep.

"You're staring at me," he said. Sandy shook her head against the pillow.

"I'm not staring."

His lips widened into a slight smile. "What would you call it then?"

"I wouldn't call it anything. I just like looking at you. You're nice to look at." Mahud's smile grew wider. He put a hand to her side beneath the sheets, feeling down to her hip. Sandy grabbed his arm and rolled over, pulling him up close behind her, the arm coming around her as she desired. Mahud got the idea and pulled her close, a smooth, warm weight pressed up against her bare back. His breath stirred at her hair. Sandy smiled, and gave a long, satisfied sigh.

"I suppose you've been getting nailed a lot as a civilian," Mahud suggested. Sandy restrained a laugh, and it came out as a giggle instead. She bit her lip, mortified.

"I'm just so very talented, Mahud, I even make a better civilian than most civilians." Mahud ran his hand down across her hard, flat stomach.

"You're just weird, Cap. I actually found the word for you—it's called 'nymphomaniac.' I found it in a dictionary."

Sandy snorted. "Must have been one of those damn lousy Chinese–English dictionaries," she retorted. "A nymphomaniac is a woman whose uncontrollable sexual urges dominate every facet of her personality to the point of dysfunction. It's actually a throwback to the prediaspora days when male and female gender roles were so wildly different that the sexual politics became very extreme, and sex was considered the defining element of interpersonal relationships between men and women, in some societies to the exclusion of much else.

"My sexuality's just a matter of getting horny a lot, that's just the way my brain is. There's nothing cultural or psychological about it at all."

A silence from Mahud. Then, "I thought that's what it meant."

Sandy gave him a frowning look over her shoulder. "That was in the dictionary?"

He shrugged. "Pretty much."

"What were you doing reading dictionaries anyway?" she asked with a smile as she resettled herself, a comfortable wriggle of buttocks against Mahud's pelvis. Felt movement there, which perked her interest considerably. He shrugged again.

"We were going undercover. I'd never done an op like that before. I read up on lots of civilian stuff. Kept running into words I didn't know. That kind of thing." Sandy thought about that for a moment. Gazing out at the spreading gleam of sunlight, a slow crawl across tower glass. Busy morning air traffic, cruising and gliding the skylanes. Towers stretching off into the distance.

"D'you like this city?" she asked him then.

"Yeah." A short, comfortable pause. Sandy could almost feel him thinking without seeing his face. She'd almost forgotten how well she knew him. How well she'd known all of them. "Yeah, I do. I think I understand a bit more why you were always so interested in civilian stuff. I mean . . . no, it's an interesting place. I'd like to see more of it."

"It's not just civilian stuff," she replied, matching her palm to the back of his hand, absently toying. "That's an artificial distinction, civilian stuff, military stuff. It's all the same thing. What we do . . . did, anyway, was a result of what went on here. Any military is just a reflection of civilian society, Mahud. We're no different." Mahud rested his mouth on the back of her head. Blew softly into her hair, a gentle sigh.

"Damn you're smart," he murmured. "I don't see any of that stuff. I just see towers and things, and people dress different and act different."

"D'you like that?"

"Yeah. I think so. I mean, I don't really get the point of a lot of it . . . and, I mean, they waste so much time on stuff, y'know? They need to get themselves organised or something, this whole city's running way below capacity."

"But leisure time's a part of the economic system," Sandy replied, still fiddling. Mahud shook his hand clear, but Sandy retrapped it, entwining fingers. "It's an incentive for people to work harder, so they can play harder. Entertainment's worth more cash than a full fleet expenditure each year in this city. And it recharges brain cells. People here do knowledge-based work. They use their brains a lot, not like weapons drill where everything's automatic. They need more time off to recharge or they burn out. So it's all just as sensible as military systems really, it's just a different focus.

"They're creating wealth here. We're just what they spend it on, like one of their infrastructure projects. We don't create anything. We just kill things."

She could feel Mahud tense behind her. His hand stopped resisting her attentions.

"But the war . . . I mean, the war was . . ." He trailed off. Sandy sighed. It was too much, she realised. Too much to dump on him like this. He respected her too much. Respected her opinions, valued her judgments. Trusted her, more than she would have considered healthy if their positions had been reversed. It was a great responsibility. She felt compelled to live up to it and show some compassion for the moment.

"We did okay in the war," she sighed, rubbing his arm affectionately. "We did fine."

Mahud tightened his arm about her, pulling her firmly back against his chest. His naked body pressed against her. Warm breath in her ear, face rested against her hair, watching the span of visible sky.

They lay together for several lingering, unspeaking minutes, watching as the sun-gleam crawled to higher panes of tower glass and the air traffic soared and murmured.

It felt very nice, that company, Sandy considered, warm against his skin and the soft, covering sheets. Perhaps too nice. Other thoughts swam to mind unbidden. Urgent and pressing. She sighed, feeling very, very reluctant.

"What?" Mahud murmured by her ear.

"Just . . . everything." An executive coupe slid by on a near lane, wide, curved, and shark-looking. Her right eye tracked and zoomed, reflexive curiosity on a model she had not seen before. Impressive-looking design. Very Tanushan. "I mean, what are you going to do?"

A brief, unhappy silence from Mahud.

Then, "We have to talk about that now?"

"When else should we talk about it?"

"Come on Cap, this is good downtime. I'm not expected to be anywhere until midday. We can't move around when we're trying to lay low. And now you're here." He trailed a hand back down her stomach again. "Don't spoil it."

"Mahud, are you going to keep working with these people?" The hand strayed lower, reaching between her thighs. "Hey." Sandy's voice was firm, although she made no attempt to move his hand. "I'm serious."

"Me too." The fingers probed, gently stroking. Sandy winced. He knew exactly what she liked, and how. Bastard. She twisted half about within the covers, and gave him a very flat, very sombre stare. Mahud looked pained. The fingers withdrew. He sighed.

"Mahud," she said gently. Firmly. "What are you going to do?" A moment of brief thought.

"What do you think I should do?"

"Mahud, I can't be your Captain forever. You know what I'd like to see you do—I'd hope you'd leave these bastards and stay here with me. But it has to be your decision."

"You said Dali wants to lock you up," he pointed out. "You want me locked up with you?"

"Dali won't be in power for long. Six weeks at most. Hiding for six weeks is easy when everyone from the head of the CSA down are all determined not to find me."

Mahud stared at her, realisation dawning slowly in his eyes, what she was asking. His look was disbelieving.

"You want me to become a *civilian*?"

"You make it sound like a disease."

"Jesus Cap, I . . . I dunno." Very unconvinced. Sandy rolled over to face him, head on the pillow alongside. "I'm a soldier." With pained conviction. "I don't *know* anything else."

"I'm with SWAT right now. It's practically the same thing, just the uniform's different. I mean, I was kind of hoping for a nice, quiet programming job, but hell, I'll take what I can get." Mahud looked very dubious. And worried. And confused.

"Oh come on, Mahud!" Exasperated, she put her hands on his shoulders, looking him intently in the eyes. "You can't go back to the League. They killed our guys. Murdered them. How can you . . . ?"

"That's what you say," Mahud interrupted stubbornly.

Sandy's eyebrows arched. "You don't believe me?"

The confused look gave way to exasperation.

"Christ, Cap . . . I know your stuff about the reasons for this op is true, it all fits. What they did to you sucks." His eyes were fixed on hers, full of emotion. "But the other thing . . . that's a lot to ask. You know that."

Sandy did know that. He was right. It was a lot to ask of him. Probably too much.

"Hell with that then," she said, climbing on top and straddling him, gazing into his eyes. "What about you, you want to keep working for these people? Knowing what you know now?"

He looked up at her kind of distantly, as if remembering things.

The pain never left his expression. And she wondered, not for the first time, exactly what it was that he was thinking.

"No," he said then, very quietly. "But I don't know what else I can do."

"Mahud . . ." she leaned down, forearms to either side of his head. Breasts touching his chest, nearly nose to nose. Her eyes were gleaming. "You can learn to *live*."

Mahud stared. Nearly frightened. Concerned certainly. He looked so vulnerable. She didn't know whether to laugh at his confusion, scream at his indecision, or burst into tears at his poor, helpless expression. Highly trained, lethal combat-GI that he was, he still made her heart melt with his unassuming innocence. She didn't know whether to hug him or hit him.

"It's good here, Mahud," she told him, her eyes alive with enthusiasm. "There are so many things to see! So many new things to learn. Some of the people I've met are really good. Once they realise you won't hurt them, they'll like you. You'll like them, too, I promise. You could probably get a job training them on weapons and tactics— they're pretty good here, but they'd still learn a lot from you. They'd value you. It's completely different from Dark Star. People will respect you for more than just your rank, they'll like you for who you are. You'll never know what it's like until you experience it . . ." She broke off as Mahud began to shake his head helplessly.

"I just don't know if I . . ."

"Shhhhh," Sandy told him, putting a gentle finger to his lips. "Just think about it. You've got a few hours. We can talk about it some more. I'll tell you anything you want to know."

Mahud nodded silently. Not looking any less confused, but now focused more on her than the things she said. She kissed him gently on the lips and pulled back to consider him again affectionately. His eyes were so nice from this range. All of him was. But mostly, it was what she saw on his face, and in his eyes in particular . . . he was Mahud, her comrade, her longtime friend and companion. He understood her rarely. But he was honest and conscientious, and whatever his short-comings, he always tried to do the right thing.

It was more than she could say for many of the straights she'd met. The ones who lacked the courage to confront their flaws. The ones who were smarter and ought to have known better, but didn't. The ones who should have grasped more than a limited, tape-trained mind like Mahud's, the ones who possessed intellectual faculties and training that far exceeded his limited experiences, but failed to put them to any good use. Given more years, and more experiences, she was certain that Mahud could grow in many ways. But even now . . . well, she liked him fine just the way he was.

Impulsively she kissed him again. Like a grown woman petting an irresistibly adorable puppy, the thought occurred to her and she nearly laughed. Smothered it with another kiss, and another. Mahud was hardly responding as she might have hoped. She paused, gazing down at him from a more comfortable range.

"Sandy?" His voice was quiet.

"What?"

"I'm scared." She nodded, with a small, sad sigh.

"I know." And settled down on top of him, wrapping him firmly in a warm, comfortable embrace, his arms enfolding her in return. "We all get scared sometimes. I know it's tough. But sometimes we just don't get a choice."

"Will you look out for me?"

"Of course," she murmured gladly against his shoulder. "I'll always look out for you. We've got something no civilian can understand. Probably no straight either. I'll always be there for you. Don't ever doubt it."

They made love amid the tangled sheets as the golden morning spilled across the room and gleamed on the windows. Perhaps, Sandy managed to think as their bodies locked pleasantly together, she had been too prescriptive, too commanding, too Captain-like in her approach . . . and recalled having told him, just moments before, that he would need to make up his own mind, and that she could not be his Captain forever.

It was true, to a point. But for him to go back to the League, especially now that he knew what he did, could be suicide. They might monitor his changed behaviour, piece together the clues, and decide him to be a liability, like all the others. There *was* no choice. The path was already chosen.

And then Mahud rolled her over and gazed wonderingly into her eyes as he entered deep inside her and it was a full ten minutes before another single, coherent thought crossed her mind.

Vanessa Rice sat on the sofa in her Santiello apartment, watching the news on TV while eating an early lunch of samosas and sauce. She wore her operational fatigues, drab-green slacks with pockets, utility belt, T-shirt under her regulation jacket. Her field boots were the second-smallest size the CSA had on inventory. Her guys often asked her which school-cadet she'd borrowed them from. She frequently replied by leaving a boot-print on one or another backside.

The TV news spoke of absolutely nothing but the present constitutional crisis and the tumultuous events that surrounded it. There were legal experts dissecting the constitution, political debates between Union and Progress Party representatives over whether Dali was justified in taking his extraordinary step, and much excited speculation as to how it all fitted into the picture of the broader investigation into the "Parliament Massacre," as it was now being called.

Vanessa found it disturbing to watch, and spent much of her meal frowning as she chewed. It was disturbing because it revealed just how little the media actually knew about any of these matters. She lost count of the number of times that CSA operational policy was misrepresented, or the extent of the President's powers exaggerated, or events in the Federation/League conflict taken way out of historical and political context.

Vanessa had never considered herself much of a political expert. Only now, watching the media's feeble efforts to make sense of the turmoil, did she realise just how much political knowledge she possessed and took completely for granted. It was a part of her everyday awareness as a SWAT unit leader. Political differences spilled into civil rights council debates, which in turn governed how much force she could use under specific situations, which in turn determined many of her operational considerations. It governed privacy laws, thus controlling CSA taps on network sources. It governed legal and procedural rules, the evidence required for an arrest and the legal framework within which her unit's operations were contained. However much she tried to focus solely on the tactical concerns, she could never entirely escape the political context. Strange how she'd always ignored the implications, and derided politics as something that neither concerned nor interested her.

And the media, she thought as she bit into another crispy samosa, was about fifty percent business-oriented. Everyone knew that. Business or "human interest." Truth was, as Hiraki had said, nothing much ever really happened in Tanusha. The stock market rose, the city expanded, high-life celebrities went to court over divorce proceedings and occasionally some underworld types killed each other in brief, spectacular gun battles, some of which Vanessa had seen firsthand— three she had participated in directly. But none of this had prepared the local media for the sudden explosion in constitutional, legal, and historical complexity that everyone was presently up to their necks in. Some of the interviewer's questions were laughable.

No damn wonder she'd wanted to join SWAT, Vanessa thought sourly as she finished her last samosa, wiping her fingers on her fatigue pants. It was a refuge from entrepreneurial greed and blind self-importance. A place where respect was earned, not bought, and big issues really mattered. Vanessa loved Tanusha, but sometimes she longed for a population transplant.

Her audio implant beeped warningly and she pulled a headset from a jacket pocket. Equalised through the implant, finding the matching frequency . . . and frowning when she failed to recognise it. Serious encryption. Seriously clever too, and subtle . . . she searched, but found no clue to its origin. Audio only though. It should be safe. She received and felt the pattern tune into alignment with a tangible, melding click . . .

"*Nice implant Ricey,*" said a familiar voice in her ear. "*I think I recognise the pattern. When did you get it done?*"

"Cassandra?" She sat fully upright, silencing the TV. "Is this connection safe?"

"*Should be. I'll take my network interface back to the League and ask for a refund if it isn't.*" She sounded, Vanessa thought, to be in a most inappropriate good humour. "*What are you doing?*"

"Right now?"

"*Yep. I'm sitting by a window watching the view, if that's any help.*"

"I'm watching TV and I've just finished eating lunch," Vanessa replied, feeling slightly perplexed. "Where the hell are you? And more importantly, why are you in such a ridiculously good mood?"

"*Just got nailed,*" the GI replied. Vanessa could hear the grin in her voice and laughed in surprise. "*You should try it sometime.*"

"I'd love to." With great sarcasm. "I only saw you about twenty hours ago—your genitals must work like a heat-seeking missile." Happy laughter from the other end. "Who with?" A short sigh. Prelude, Vanessa thought, to something more sober.

"*His name's Mahud. I was his squad commander back in Dark Star.*"

"Oh." Humour faded. "So he's a GI?"

"*Yeah. High model. Nice guy, you'd like him.*"

"I'm sure. Tell me everything."

"*Is that a tactical request, or do you just want to get off?*"

Vanessa smiled. "Business first. The rest can wait."

"*If you say so. Well first, obviously, he survived what the rest of my team*" *didn't. Seems my superiors wanted to keep a few higher models for special operations during peacetime. Like this one. He was the main tactical coordinator on the attack to kill the President.*" Wow. Vanessa felt the breath catch in her throat. And wondered, in an instant of sudden fear, if Cassandra Kresnov was truly as sensible and stable as she seemed in person.

"*He knew nothing about me,*" Sandy said firmly, as if reading her mind through the linkup. "*He's a very loyal guy. He's never known anything but service to the League. I've tried to fill him in on everything that's been going on, but it's difficult. He's still working with them, lying low. I don't want him to get upset or nervous in case they see his behaviour changing. But he can't leave now without alerting them that I'm onto them.*

"*He knew I was coming here when he accepted the mission. I think that's part of the reason why he wanted to do it, to see me again. He just never guessed I was the reason for the mission in the first place.*"

Vanessa could feel her brain starting to race. The implications were enormous. One of the main people in the FIA operation, potentially about to turn over. Or maybe he could be their mole. Give information to the CSA. Help them capture the bastards. Good God, what an opportunity!

"*He says they DO have infiltrator software in Tetsu—he was using it for a covert search during our raid there, seeing what we were up to. He found some traces of the stuff I was using when I was helping out Intel, searching the database and showing them what to look for . . . League software, he recognised the key-codes immediately, knew there was only one person who could use it like that. Which is how he knew to send Cody the message.*"

"Do you trust him?" Vanessa asked.

A pause.

"*Where I'm concerned, yes. With my life.*" Another pause. A deep breath. "*The rest of it, politically . . . I dunno. I don't want him to get hurt, Ricey. I only just found him again. I can't put him into anything too dangerous.*"

Vanessa could hear the emotion in her voice. Jesus. Who would have thought that the League's most dangerous, advanced GI ever brought to life would turn out to be such a mass of emotional dramas?

She knew what she ought to do. What the CSA would no doubt like to do, given the chance. Use this Mahud to give them the rest of the FIA team on a platter, no matter what else it cost. Ibrahim would not like it, but Ibrahim knew where his priorities lay. Ibrahim would sacrifice Sandy's friend to get the others, no question. Damn. And she could suddenly see, at that moment, why Sandy had contacted her and not Ibrahim. It was trust that Sandy was showing. Trust in her. But her priorities . . . lay where? What the hell was she going to say?

"Where is he now?" she thought to ask.

*"He's gone out to a rendezvous point. Nothing serious, just a head count and review. I'm at his apartment. Rented under a false name, buried under a mass of encrypted transactions, you'd never find it unless I told you. The encryption they're using lets them make all kinds of network transactions without anyone seeing. Very corporate."*

"Did he tell you whose?"

*"Nope. I'm not pushing. I'm just happy to have found him. He'll have to make his decisions for himself."*

"Yeah . . . no, I agree. Damn. It's a tough one, isn't it?"

*"Tough on you, too . . . hey, I'm sorry to drop this on you, I know it's a problem at your end. Like right now you're wondering if you ought to push me for more information to bust some asses right now, or leave me here and wait to see if I can come through with something more substantial."*

Vanessa sighed. "Yeah. Well shit, I'll have to tell Ibrahim at least as much as you've told me . . ."

*"That's okay, I want you to. Just . . . leave Mahud to me. I need to do this my way. And if I push him before he's ready, he might just bug out on me. Just give me some time, huh?"*

"Sure." Vanessa smiled reluctantly. "Sure I will. I'll recommend that much to the boss, too . . . it's the best lead I've heard of so far. I think he'd recommend you keeping your head down for now. We want the top people. I reckon he'd want you to stay with Mahud until he's ready to give them to you."

"*I hope so.*"

"So," Vanessa sighed. Stretched out her legs, leaning back in the sofa. "You really like this guy, huh?"

"*Not the way you're thinking.*" The humour was back in her voice. "*I think he's more like . . . I dunno, d'you have a brother?*"

"Two of 'em," Vanessa replied with a smile. "Small difference though—I haven't screwed either of them, and I'm not gonna start."

"*Oh hell, you know what I'm like—even if I had a real one I'd probably be screwing him, too.*" Vanessa grinned. "*No, Mahud's . . . he's just nice. I think so, anyway. Maybe he'd scare other people, I don't know. But you'd be surprised just how harmless he can be.*"

"No I wouldn't be, I've got you as a measure."

"*I'm not a good measure, Ricey. I'm not a good indication of anything, GIs least of all.*"

"Yeah, the rest of them probably all make a lot more sense than you do, Cassandra." Another frequency bleeping. Vanessa recognised this one immediately, and her heart rate rose fractionally. "Sandy, I'm getting an emergency call, I gotta go."

"*Sure Ricey . . . take care, huh?*"

"You, too. I'll be seeing you." Click to static. Readjust to new frequency, then a fast, reflexive tuning. It was code, no words, sending as soon as she connected. She noted it down with little surprise, made a few fast, mental translations with the help of her implant, then disconnected as it began to repeat.

She refolded the headset into her jacket pocket, went straight for her gear bag on the table and strode out the door, heavy weight of rifle, armour harness, and attachments thumping against her back as she went.

The shots started when they were only halfway in. Vanessa thudded sideways into the nearest mall-side, the glass shattering with a crash across her armour. The remaining few civilians screamed, ducked, fell, or ran, amid yells from her foremost team to "*Get down*! . . ." another second and she discerned that the shots were not directed at them, and darted forward instead, dodging between panicked and scrambling civvies, yelling at them to keep moving in the other direction, away from the firing.

"*S–5, under fire, random cover, targets are moving.*" That was Kuntoro. Tac-net had him mapped and she figured his position clearly enough as she ran, tac-sim postulating firing positions from available audio and topographical data . . . she dodged past the last of the civvies, Devakul already up and running ahead, armoured, lithe, and weapon-ready, heavy feet pounding over the brick-paved walk, dodging cafe tables and chairs upended in the recent rush. If she'd had time, she would have sworn. It was no place for a firefight. But she had no time . . .

"S–2," she snapped, "move, grid-fiver, seven, level three and four, keep it blocked, we can't let 'em through. . . ." The mall opened to an indoor food court, Devakul skidded for cover behind a corner and potted indoor palm . . . ducked in abruptly as fire blew the palm to bits, tile fragments showering amid shredded greenery as Vanessa cut left, still sprinting, hurdled an umbrella-shaded table that crashed over, then ploughed through an angled shop window that afforded her a right-angled view across the nearest port of the food hall. Saw nothing moving, propped on her left arm amid still-falling debris, rifle ready, fire ripping past Devakul's position . . . Devakul held his rifle around the corner and fired by remote-sight in short, popping bursts. She heard the launcher's muzzle-pop even as she rose, and ducked fractionally before the grenade hit the wall not four metres in front with a shock that nearly knocked her over.

"Central!" she yelled on all fours amid the showering dust and debris, "they are *armed*, full military-spec, get me everything you've got and all civvies *out*! This is a fucking war!" And for her team, "People, watch for civvies, no random firing, this is a shopping district, not a battlefield!" Or at least it had been.

Devakul was still firing amid the blinding dust, she leapt across the line of fire behind him, slid flat behind the raised podium of the central eating area, then popped up to scan between the clustered table legs . . . ducked back as target-warning flashed and fire sent chairs and tables smacking around the open hall like tenpins, plastic and wooden pieces crashing and clattering all about. She rolled behind the podium, headed away from Devakul, then Bjornssen arrived and laid down fire—she popped up, managed a brief burst at the glimpse of a departing figure, hitting nothing.

"Get him! Watch the angles, no rushing!" as Bjornssen hurdled forward through the dust, Singh behind and Devakul after . . . she saw brief movement on her right as she followed, spun fast, and found a very unthreatening man lying flat on a restaurant floor where the glass front had collapsed in on him, looking stunned and terrified. "That way!" she yelled at him, a fast flick to audio, pointing back the way she'd come, then turned and raced after her guys.

Another grenade shattered windows up ahead, Bjornssen ducking and rolling through the smoke . . . more firing on tac-net, the position showed clear on visor and internal-vision, Kuntoro returning fire somewhere on levels up above. She held herself back, more sporadic fire smacking walls and breaking glass up ahead, checking through tac-net and tac-sim, measuring the angles, watching the distances . . . a grenade took out a shopfront ten metres away, window frames collapsing on Singh's helmet with a heavy crash . . . they were falling back to a major thoroughfare, she saw in that moment of frozen time, multilevel shopping that connected to the nearby major hotel where they'd been staying and had apparently been surprised.

"Singh, Dev, first right turn, right flank and hold! Work it forward! S–5, flank left! Don't let them get past tac-C–2!" Heavy fire in front, Bjornssen and Devakul covering for Singh's dash across to the right-hand corridor ahead. "S–2, forward and spread, I want a crossfire on that atrium hall! Box and hold people!"

Ahead Devakul followed Singh's dash and Vanessa ran up through shattered debris and smoke, ploughed headlong through a protruding side display window, kicked her way through mannequins and display shelves into the store proper. And had the surreal experience of running down a fashion store aisle parallel to the mall, full armour thumping the carpet . . . ducked and fell as shots hammered the surrounding walls, kicking clothes out and stands crashing over, hit the ground amid a hail of shredded fabric and wallboard . . . tac-net showed Bjornssen already running at the distraction . . . then all vision blanked as a grenade went off somewhere over her head and brought half the ceiling down.

Up and struggling, some indeterminate split-second later, through flames and smoke, ruptured water pipes and malfunctioning spurts of foam retardant, smashed a damaged partition wall aside with her rifle arm, burning fabrics clinging like so much bonfire ash . . . tac-net showed a target down in the main hall ahead, several troops covering, and now fire zipping up and down from right to left in front of her position.

She scrambled further forward, found the dividing wall to the next shop to the left and kicked it—her foot went through with a massive thud, took a square metre of brick wall with it. She aimed two more kicks to clear space then squeezed through the crumbling hole. Rolled low, now finding herself in a fancy net-interface monitor display shop, and ran at a low crouch between elaborate stands and displays . . . tac-net calculated fire positions, acquired an exact fix from Hiraki's arms-comp (it was Hiraki on the next level up, she gathered), and from that she guessed the required angle for herself. Stopped scrambling by the shop's far wall, crouched and aimed out the display windows, past the holographic interference of window dressing. Outside was the broad mall, ten metres wide, the multilevel, glass atrium overhead and flanked by balcony walks. A man in a dark coat crouched behind the foundation support for the overhead crosswalk, edged close to the corner, weapon ready, unaware he'd been flanked. She shot him, close enough to see the blood spraying as he spun.

Leapt out through the windows in a crash of collapsing glass, rolling on the floor . . . fire whipped past, tac-net showing two other targets further up, sheltering behind the sporadic cover of stone flower boxes before the opposite side of the broad mall's windows. She fired one-handed as she ran, low and crouched, shots erupting fragments and dust about flower boxes and splintering wooden bench seats . . . abruptly outflanked on another angle as the target tried to change cover, shots knocked him flying before Vanessa could adjust. She skidded in behind the overpass support, flipped to audio, full volume . . .

*"This is the CSA! Surrender to arrest now or you will die!"*

The reply was a volley of fire, aimed blindly over a further row of decorative flowerpots and miniature trees. Return fire shredded the greenery in seconds, erupting concrete and tile fragments sharding the air through curtains of dust . . . she noted even as she fired that the last target behind her was down—Kuntoro and Tsing had got him. She hadn't entirely taken her eye off that potentially fatal threat from behind since the firing started, especially not now in the main mall surrounded by overlooking balconies . . .

*"Watch!"* came Hiraki's warning yell a fractional second before something whooshed past at speed and the entire right side of the mall exploded. A shocking confusion of concussion, flame, and debris and she was shooting without targets, more blind fire hammering about . . . dimly realised through the flaming chaos that something was cutting the air like a saw, staccato blue light flaring through the debris as everything it touched exploded . . . she rolled frantically back behind full cover as the light swung her way, and half the ferrocrete support detonated in a spray of flaming wreckage.

Fire converged heading the other way, leaping red tracer, tac-net showed the fix . . . she spun left around the support, locked and firing as the far mall end collapsed beneath the hail. Ran, because that was textbook, directly at the target, spraying fire to cover possible invisibles, adjusting her suited stride to the recoil as she accelerated through the smoke, spreading destruction before her at will. Got far enough forward to see pieces of another bloody corpse where tac-net said the last should be, and slid to a skidding halt amid a confusion of broken chairs, flower banks, and snack vendors, covering the last position of the previous target . . . empty.

"*Cease!*" she yelled, and the carnivorous hail of tracer above her head abruptly vanished. Propped to her knees and scanned on full motion/multilight, easier now things were no longer disintegrating, and saw . . . nothing. Things collapsing in delayed shock, displays, windows, plants, walls . . . smoke everywhere and things burning. Target IDed corpses. Nothing else. Someone had evidently surprised them. There could be more. But nothing that end of the mall had survived that last barrage, so she was one corpse short.

"Missing one." Tac-net showed Sharma, Kuntoro, and Hiraki already converging along the flanks up the far end, and more following—even without her order they blocked the exits. She rose and walked, a clear enough view now to have faith in vis-scan's warnings if surprised. Feet crunched over rubble, avoiding upturned tables and mall-walk attractions not so much bullet riddled as eviscerated. No sign. A measured, steady pace up the centre of the wreckage, rifle braced, a visor display warning of barely 220 rounds left in the magazine. The dismembered corpse was strewn about something that looked like a V–9 APL. Anti Personnel Laser. Not merely military, but frontline. That had been the blue light. What had made the five-metre crater at the mall wall back there she didn't care to guess.

Blood-trail, she saw then, through the drifting smoke. Heat residue, past the sporadic fires and round-impact spots. Held up a fist, the several marks moving behind in cover formation halted on tac-net, covering with interlocking, integrated fields of fire. Stepped carefully forward, looking right, the location of the blood trail. It made a right turn after barely a metre, and entered a doorway recess. This one was metal framed, and afforded more protection. Another step, and she saw the booted feet sticking out, and a hand limply dangling. Another, and she saw a woman seated, curled up as if for protection. A warm body, and much blood. Vis-scan detected no pulse on IR. A short, snubbish machine gun lay alongside, muzzle warm. Something unidentifiable in her lap, small and apparently plastic. Or something like.

"Got one," she said calmly, rifle levelled unerringly. "Hit and unmoving. Something in her lap. Could be a bomb." Tac-net showed more of her team sweeping, covering. She heard their comments, terse and brief. Someone's horror at discovering several civvies, huddled in a corner. But there were always some. Vis-scan read her voice, analysed the visuals, and went into threat assessment without her urging. And came up negative on the bomb.

She paused. Trust it? Only if she was feeling suicidal. She wasn't. Took another step forward across the mall. Another. Bjornssen went past behind, ignoring her target, covering further up the mall. Smoke drifted, fires burning, localised fire retardant hissing, adding to the clouding mist. A situation light blinked on her lower side-visor, someone off-net wanting an update.

"Hitoru," she said calmly, "talk to central for me would you?" He did, the blinking stopped. Another step. The pool of blood beneath the curled woman had grown larger. The body fractionally cooler. And the black, flat plastic whatever-it-was had a bullet hole in it. She knew some forms of bomb didn't mind that. But it lessened the odds drastically, and she closed the remaining distance. At close range she could look down on it, beyond the woman's obscuring hand and folds of her long coat. Definitely no bomb. More like . . . data storage? "I got it, Hitoru. I'm clear here."

Knelt on one knee—squatting was mostly impossible in armour— and pulled the flat plastic square from the woman's unresisting hand. Noted only one bullet hole, and that only in the stomach. Apparently. Grabbed the woman's face in one armoured hand, pulled the jaw open . . . foam, saliva, general unpleasantness—self-inflicted, probably in capsule form. Jesus.

"*Lieutenant?*" Krishnaswali's voice, invited now on tac-net. "*Vanessa, what happened?*"

"I just wrote off a mall." With forced humour. Only realising now as she spoke just how hard her heart was hammering. She felt suddenly out of breath. "I hope that's okay."

"*Fuck the mall,*" said the CSA's head-SWAT, with typically clear pronunciation. "*What happened?*"

"Um . . . well," she took a deep breath. The woman's blank eyes stared into hers. European, not unattractive and now very dead. The unsteadiness deepened. "They had basically a military arsenal holed up around here somewhere . . . God knows how in a hotel district . . . and they basically blew up the mall." Krishnaswali at least did not need to ask if her team was okay—he had all the vitals in front of him. "And I got a dead girl here I'm guessing might have been in charge, she took a nonfatal round, crawled off to try and do something to what looks like a data-storage unit, then it looks like she topped herself. So it's not just GIs that are expendable, looks like."

"*Do you have the DSU?*"

"It's got a bullet hole in it," she said, holding it up for closer examination. "But yeah, I got it." There was some kind of ID patch on the side of it, maybe a fingerprint patch. "Looks like she might have been trying to erase it or something."

"*I'm guessing Intel will be very interested in looking at that. Please keep it relatively undisturbed. And the bodies. We'll pick up the pieces.*"

Vanessa gazed bleakly about through the smoke, and wondered if Krishnaswali realised just how literally appropriate those words were.

The coffee should have tasted good. She usually liked Naidu's coffee. But this tasted sour in her mouth. Her tongue tasted of sweat, bile, and that slightly acrid inside-the-helmet smell that hung around after having worn armour for too long.

"Not good?" Naidu asked with dismay, seeing her expression.

"It's fine." Wincing slightly and wrinkling her nose. "It's just the taste in my mouth that stinks."

"Indians should neither make nor drink coffee," Krishnaswali added from his seat over by the window blinds, long legs crossed, cradling a steaming cup of tea in his lap. "Very bad form."

Naidu said something derisive in a language Vanessa didn't know . . . Telugu, maybe. Or possibly Tamil. Naidu was Old Earth, born in Bangalore. Krishnaswali was Tanushan born and bred, less than half Naidu's age. He held to a notion of Old India Naidu found pathetically unrealistic, and typical of offworld romanticism of the "mother country" they'd never visited and knew only from stories and news-bytes. Whatever he'd said, Krishnaswali only smiled and sipped carefully at his tea past his handsome, clipped moustache. Naidu gave Vanessa's shoulder an affectionate pat and walked back around the side of the main desk.

They were gathered in Naidu's main fifth-floor office amid the networking maze that was Intel. A nice office, large and roomy, blinds drawn across the broad windows that otherwise overlooked the CSA compound interior. Krishnaswali occupied a comfortable spot on the big-cushioned sofa by the windows. Hiraki and Kuntoro at the back of the room, behind Vanessa. At the front of the room various Intel Agents gathered about Naidu's desk, now crowded with scanning and other electronic gadgetry Vanessa's SWAT-grunt training supplied neither recognition nor interest for. The centre of their attentions was a single black, hard-shelled rectangle, pierced off centre by a single high-velocity bullet hole.

Vanessa stood in the centre of the room, coffee in hand, and surveyed the group with bland interest. Naidu, Intel Chief, at one side, looking even more rumpled than usual, suit and unbuttoned shirt collar in disarray, a cup of his own coffee steaming in hand. Zhong and Suarez crouched over the desk in fascinated absorption—both Intel techs, hardware, software, security gadgetry in general. Chopra standing over them, supervising—with a planetary and military security brief, he usually complained Tanusha had little need for him and spent his time researching things happening in the war just ended far away. Now his eyes gleamed with delight and he positively bounced with enthusiasm.

As usual, Vanessa reflected, sipping determinedly at the sour coffee, she was the only woman in the room. No, not usual. Just all too damn frequent. She'd learned long ago not to unleash that particular frustration upon her male colleagues, it wasn't their fault. Just the fault of an Indian-Arabic-African prominent society where women aimed for "sophistication" and anything vaguely sweaty was "men's work." The CSA was very sweaty. Academia, politics, education, and general civil services, on the other hand, were crawling with women. They thought it natural. And protested with vague, generalised indignation about "mad scientists" whenever someone presented the latest piece of League research that stated clearly it was not.

League scientists were well ahead of Federation research on such things. They did, Vanessa reflected wryly, have at least that much right—science in behavioural fields did move much faster when not held down by the weight of cultural bias and expectation. Sandy, she supposed, was proof enough of that. And it annoyed her, no question. She remembered further what Sandy had said, after the Tetsu raid, about how she sometimes argued like she was from the League, while Sandy felt more comfortable with Federation values. And she wondered, really, where she belonged. Where she would be, if she'd had the good or bad fortune to be born elsewhere within the vast domain of human civilisation. Cultural silliness often exasperated her. She was too pragmatic. But then, if all the pragmatists gathered in the League and the romantics in the Federation, that would only breed extremism, surely? Maybe she was meant to be here. Maybe Tanusha, Callay, and the Federation needed her where she was. But sometimes she wondered.

Zago interrupted her dazed, half-sighted contemplation by

opening the door. The men about the desk glanced up briefly, then returned to their work as Zago made for Vanessa.

"Ricey," he said, trying to keep his deep voice low and not quite managing it, "we've got three mis-ops—two will need full refit, I've got full specs on mech if you need 'em."

"How's Arvid?" she asked, not really caring about the team's maintenance problems right then, however tight the rotation schedule. Arvid Singh had been very near the fireball when the HE grenade had struck the mall side, and the APL barrage that followed hadn't helped. As soon as his helmet had come off, he'd gone into severe shock, pale, shaking, and breathing with difficulty. No one held it against him. It happened. After that barrage, she was amazed Singh was the only one.

"He's okay. Docs say the tape will help, could take a few days though. He might have relapses, might not." A shrug of broad shoulders within his patched and rumpled duty jacket. "Should be okay. Just have to see."

Vanessa glanced up at him. A long way up, even for her. Zago was massive, at over one hundred ninety centimetres and nearly one thirty kilos. Jet black and handsome. Married with five kids. Pity, she'd always thought. The sexiest man in her unit by far. Brute force, she knew, with self-directed sarcasm, was her big weakness. Muscle was irresistible. Size turned her on. God help her.

"How about you?"

Zago flashed a charming wry smile. "Hey, no holes, no damage."

"Arvid's just as tough as you," Vanessa said sombrely, her gaze unwavering. "It's just his turn, that's all."

Zago's face fell. "I know. I didn't mean it like that."

"I know." She patted him on the arm. "I know you didn't."

"Why don't you take a seat, Lieutenant?" Naidu suggested, over the murmured conversing around the main desk. "Surely even SWAT lieutenants rest occasionally?"

"She never sits," Hiraki replied from the back of the room, eyeing her with calm, impassive eyes. Naidu frowned in concern. Zago flashed him a warning look. Naidu raised his eyebrows and turned his attention back to the desktop. Vanessa ignored them all, gazing ahead blankly, gently sipping at her sour coffee, trying to get a reasonable semblance of taste back. Zago stepped behind her, put his arms comfortably about her, and pulled her back against his broad chest. Too tall even to rest his chin on the top of her head. She rested her head back with a sigh and closed her eyes.

Recalled unbidden Sandy's arms about her, a playful embrace. So much smaller than Zago. And infinitely more powerful. Yet she'd felt safe then, if indignant, like she felt safe now. And restrained a half-smile at the memory. She'd been thinking about Sandy a lot lately. A crazy development in an otherwise sane life, that was certain. A friendship with an AWOL League GI. It was nuts. And yet somehow . . . it worked. She sighed, and opened her eyes to gaze at the wall above the men's heads. And hoped like hell the occasionally undisciplined portion of her brain that registered such things would remember that she was presently married, that Sandy only liked men, and that totally regardless, any kind of "relationship" with a person who was regarded in some circles as not even technically human was definitely not a good idea under any circumstances . . .

And she recalled the power in those bare shoulder muscles flexing, the steel-hard tension of the neck tendons beneath her hand, and felt any slight sense of attraction dissipate very fast. Good, she thought to herself with some relief. Just remember what she is, you idiot. That'll keep your groin in check.

"Yeah," Suarez said from his crouch behind the desk equipment with rising excitement. "Yeah, that's definitely it, you've got it." Zhong grinned in triumph, focused with intense concentration on the small control screen of what looked like a las-grid reader—an automated digi-decipherer, the small finger probe held closely suspended over an opened portion of the flat black rectangle. Code raced across another smaller monitor screen amid the pile, and other readouts flickered confusingly.

"Oh man!" Suarez gasped breathlessly, switching stares between graphical construct and raw codage screens. "Sweet Mother Mary that's a P-H class gridrunner . . . look here, that's an execution bracket suite, right there . . ."

"English!" Naidu snapped, "I speak nine languages more or less fluently but techno-babble is not one of them."

"Oh . . ." Suarez blinked, staring about, eyes then darting back to his precious screens, ". . . well, it's not a retarded series nine like I thought, it's multilock compatible, it can replicate remotely across any Dexxie-type grid . . ."

"Oh," Naidu exclaimed, "that's much easier, I understand it all now . . ."

"Um, sir," broke in Chopra, a thin, bookish, dark-skinned man in a tweedy jacket too large for his narrow shoulders, "if I might, sir . . ." He licked his lips in nervous excitement, fidgeting fingers interlocked. "This is definitely an imprinted matrix like we thought, it is unalterable, hardwired software, you . . . you cannot alter the basic imprinted code. The entire matrix unit will erase itself and . . . and probably your infiltrator software, too, I might think it likely." Blinked rapidly, and licked his lips again, eyes darting back to the readout screens.

"An . . . an infiltrator team such as this FIA group might be issued with such a unit within their possession with which to access particular mainframe security systems. A unit such as this could provide breakthrough codes, that such an infiltrator team could perhaps utilise to provide themselves with cover for their personnel and their operations within the broader systematic network . . ."

"You're talking about this network?" Naidu asked. Pointing to the floor, meaning the entire, monstrous expanse of Tanushan info-net.

"Yes, sir." A small nod. "The Tanushan infotech infrastructure."

"Why put those codes onto an imprinted matrix?"

"So they cannot be lost, infiltrated, or stolen. This is a key to the city of Tanusha." Vanessa blinked. Zago's arms were suddenly loose. But for the rapid flicker of visual data scattering across the desktop screens, the office was still.

"But if they're under biotech corporate network protection," Naidu said slowly, frowning sharply under heavy brows, "they're already safe. Especially if they're being protected from within the Governor's office, even if not specifically by the Governor himself. Why a separate key? For what function?"

Chopra heaved a deep breath. "That, I am not certain . . ."

"This is government encryption," came Zhong's voice from the desk. His vacant stare told Vanessa he was uplinked and accessing, doubtless rerouting various analytical data functions on CSA central mainframe toward this particular unravelling of code from the small, black rectangle on the desk. "This imprint software was made in a government facility. Local Tanushan, no question."

Vanessa glanced hard at Naidu. The Intel Chief's lips twisted into a grimace. Coffee held forgotten in one absent hand.

"Dali?" Vanessa ventured. "Dali made this software and . . . and what? Gave it to the FIA?" Naidu ignored her.

Chopra gave her a distracted glance. "Of course." In a condescending tone reserved for ignorant SWAT lieutenants who blurted the obvious. "But not Dali. One of his several FIA-trained and -appointed aides. Their files are fake, but I have resources." Smugly.

"So what's the damn stuff do?" She freed herself from Zago's unresisting arms, walked over, and leaned on the desk, staring down at the maze of minor cables, hookups, and laser-brace, the reader scanning the rectangle's interior. "What's the software for?" No reply from the absorbed Zhong and Suarez.

"I would guess the Plexus grid," said Chopra. Sounding increasingly smug, with the air of one well pleased finally to be presented with an opportunity to demonstrate his life's work and skills. "Access to the Tanushan information network was, as Mr. Naidu rightly pointed out, already guaranteed by the FIA's plants in this city's biotech industries. But the info-network is only one level of electronic security any infiltrating team must penetrate to make good. Far more important is the Plexus grid—Callay is a planet like any other, Lieutenant, with advanced planetary defences and navigation systems. I would guess that this unit should provide the FIA team with access to the Plexus grid, and thus the means to monitor and if necessary control their evacuation details via any incoming ships. This would of course require the assistance of . . ."

"Yeah yeah, I gotcha Pops." Chopra blinked. Gave her a disapproving look, then turned his attention back to the monitor screens. "So that was what that FIA woman was trying to do before she killed herself. Erase it." With a glance across at Naidu. "That'd imply it's not the only one."

"No." Naidu ran a hand through his unkempt hair. "They'd have a redundancy. But we've now limited their options severely. They can't be flexible with their extraction now. They have to keep whoever uses the other unit in reserve. They can't afford to lose the second one."

"Why didn't this one erase?"

"Bullet hole," said Zhong absently, eyes distant as he uplinked through a massive data-load. "Lucky shot."

"Lucky indeed," Naidu rumbled. "About damn time we had a bit of luck go our way." Straightened himself, nearly spilling the coffee as he remembered it just in time. "I have to brief the boss—tell me if anything significant comes up." And gave Vanessa's shoulder an approving shake as he past. "Terrific job, Lieutenant. You too Agents, all of you." And he left, on his way to Ibrahim's office.

"So," said Kuntoro, walking up to a place beside Vanessa, looking down at the inoffensive rectangle on the desk. "LT saves the world, hmm?" Put an arm about her shoulders and squeezed. Vanessa made a face.

"Lucky," she snorted. Wishing they would leave off patting her for a moment, and treat her like they would any one of the other heroic

SWAT stud-commanders after a successful op. Kuntoro let go, only for Zago to move up behind and ruffle her hair with both big hands, as if to a small child. Dammit. She could handle being female in a majority-male environment. She was at peace with being small. But being "cute" was a curse. If they'd merely wanted to fuck her, that was one thing. But rank and her reputation for volatility ensured they didn't . . . well, not actively anyway. Instead there was this, halfway between informal affection (which was her own damn fault for encouraging between her troops as part of her natural command style) and professional respect. She didn't look like a SWAT commander—she looked like a kitten. Being mistaken for one made her fume. Thus the reputation. And if she made too big a fuss about it, it would create tension and uncertainty, which was her responsibility as commander to prevent. She was stuck with all of it and she knew it.

"So what happens now?" she asked nobody in particular, ignoring them all as she stared at the mess of gear upon the desk.

"Well," said Chopra, enjoying his own cleverness on this subject as he bent squinting beside Zhong, watching the monitor screens, "there is a chance that an examination of this data will allow us to determine how the FIA are managing to infiltrate the Plexus grid, thus perhaps allowing us to detect any extraction vessel that infiltrates our spacelanes . . ."

"No, I know that," Vanessa interrupted. "I mean what happens to Dali?" Chopra blinked. Glanced up at her.

"Does that matter?"

"What d'you mean, does that matter? How can we catch the damn FIA if their buddies in the Governor's Office are running the whole damn government?"

"Lieutenant," Chopra said with sarcasm, "the last thing we need is to turn this into a political event. If we can discern the correct codes and perform a proper intelligence job of it, we should certainly be able to carry on our work without the active knowledge or interference from the Governor's Office . . ."

"Fuckin' horseshit." With increasing temper. Chopra blinked. "We're not getting anywhere without a clear-cut chain of command. I can't function without it. SWAT can't. It's not optional." Chopra coughed. Wetted his lips nervously. Evidently not accustomed to such intimidatory behaviour from attractive European females who barely came up to his shoulder.

"Well," he said, with more caution, "with any luck, if we play our cards correctly, the services of SWAT will no longer be required and we can do the rest through proactive Intelligence-guided network operations without a need for further violence."

"Huh." She folded her arms hard. "If you believe that, I've got a nice pyramid scheme you might like to invest in."

"The present government are our lords and masters," said Krishnaswali. Vanessa turned and glared at him. He sat as he'd been sitting the past half hour, long legs crossed, calmly sipping his tea. "We swore an oath to uphold the lawful government. Right now, that means Dali."

"My team didn't nearly just get its ass shot off for Mr-fucking-Dali!" Vanessa retorted. "Arvid's not lying down there in sickbay being force-fed trauma tape for Mr. Dali! I swore an oath to serve and protect the people of Callay and Tanusha, *not* Federal Governor Dali!"

"Then change the law," Krishnaswali said. Met Vanessa's glare impassively above the rim of his teacup, taking another calm sip.

"How?"

The CSA's head SWAT officer shrugged. "Don't ask me, I'm a grunt. Ask the Chief."

"I don't have access to the . . ." and trailed off as something occurred to her, her eyes widening slightly, past the hard thumping in her chest.

"Naidu does," said Hiraki from the back of the room. Vanessa looked at him, seated with equal calm to Krishnaswali, but coolly disciplined to his superior's languid professionalism. The look in his heavily slanted eyes was hard. "Ibrahim knows. He must remove Dali.

We cannot catch the FIA with him in power." With a conceding nod to his commander. "Chief Justice Guderjaal does have the power to remove Dali if the laws by which he came to power have been broken. There was insufficient evidence before. Now, there is the box." He nodded toward the desk, where Zhong and Suarez were still crouched and working, oblivious to the debate going on around them. Vanessa's eyes widened further.

"Jees . . . if we could trace the origins directly back to Dali and show Guderjaal the proof . . ."

Hiraki nodded. His expression was dangerous.

"Naidu will inform Investigations. They will trace. We will act when the time comes."

"But . . . but . . ." Chopra had straightened behind the desk, his expression somewhat horrified, "but . . . I mean, by all means, justice must be done and justice surely lies in the hands of Mr. Guderjaal . . . but Mr. Guderjaal does not possess the Governor's key-codes! He cannot remove the Governor's key-codes at will. He . . . he must . . ."

"He must empower us to take them from him," Hiraki finished. "By force if he resists." Silence in the office. Screenlight flickered on drawn blinds. Krishnaswali sipped at his tea.

"Good show," he murmured. "Wouldn't miss it."

# CHAPTER 15

It was a Friday, as Callayan calendars went. Sandy gazed down on the evening crowds along Ramprakash Road in Velan. The train was crowded, the carriage a mass of stylish clothes and hairstyles, glittering jewellery and flamboyant extravagance. The wide road they cruised above was even more colourful. Everywhere were lights, flashing holographic displays erupting along the broad sidewalk, flaring down the sides of buildings from twenty storeys high.

President Pital Ramprakash, Sandy remembered hearing, had been a connoisseur of expensive parties, the more extravagant the better. He would have been very proud, she thought now as she gazed down at the street that now bore his name. There were other roads like it around Tanusha, but Ramprakash Road was the one with the reputation. Road traffic was heavy and the wide sidewalks were crammed with a constant, flowing mass of humanity. The train made a stop, exchanged one crowd of people for another and moved on silently. Did the same at the next stop, and the next, and still Ramprakash Road continued, with not a bend along the way.

Finally they came to her stop, and she eased past her neighbour and into the shouldering masses in the aisle. Emerged onto the platform connecting to a main pedestrian walkway running parallel to the rail line. It, too, was crowded, and she merged carefully into the semi-orderly flow. Marvelled at the aesthetic planning as she walked by the pedestrian rail, at the way walks and elevated rail lines merged into the streetside buildings, and at the clever use made of open spaces and transparent materials. And even here there was always a view, she realised as she walked, trailing a hand along the railing. Tanusha was definitely the least claustrophobic mega-city she'd ever seen.

A level below, walkways crossed the road every few hundred metres. She headed for one, down a broad stairway, past a busker with some form of robotic mimic/sculpture that amused a gaggle of watching pedestrians, and crossed the road. Down into the teeming street amid the shouts and laughter of excited nightlifers, the whine of car engines and the thump-and-shrill of many-sourced music. Colour assaulted her vision, shiny-smooth outfits in synthetic or leather, wild hair in many colours, short skirts, transparent skirts, heels, high boots, traditional outfits of many different cultures . . . all walking shoulder to shoulder amid the flaring lights and displays, soaking in the energy.

Despite her serious business, Sandy found time to be fascinated. There were nightclubs, restaurants, holographic cinema complexes, bars, VR gaming joints, full immersion VR with plush interiors, and loud signs that offered "simulated sensory experiences beyond your wildest dreams . . ." Sandy wasn't sure about that—some of her dreams were pretty wild, but she got the idea. Display screens broadcast the action inside as living advertisements—massed dancers on nightclub floors, dizzying robot battles on sims, movie-clips, lasciviously dressed couples or groups doing lascivious things. . . . Olfactory replicators throwing "real time" food smells into the sidewalk air outside the fancy restaurants with the intention of making the mouth water . . . it worked, too. Sandy firmly told her stomach to be still and moved on through the pressing crowds.

"The Waterhole," the club was called. There was a patterned glass atrium, several storeys high, a double layer of walled glass and, falling between, a shimmering curtain of water. Hologram light flickered and danced across the glass-painted palms, swirling figures, dancers, patterns, alive as falling water. A queue lined at the double brass doors, and Sandy walked along it, through a clutch of oncoming pedestrians, a very drunk, hysterically laughing group she took to be a work party, and shouldered up to the front. The two big, turbaned Sikhs looked stonily at her . . . she drew the CSA badge from her jacket, waited as the nearest bouncer's eye-enhancement tracked the S-seal, nodded, and unclipped the rope to let her pass.

"Are you on duty?" he asked curiously, as some annoyed exclamations rose from the queue.

"Would it matter?" she asked pleasantly.

"No, of course not. But we just like to know . . . you know . . ."

"Nothing's happening," she assured him. "I just arranged to meet someone on business. Lucky you," and gave the big man a pat on a bulging bicep as she passed, tucking the badge back into her jacket.

She wondered, as she passed through the water-wall, what kind of regular jobs those two bouncers would have. And what kind of business they'd be concerned about . . . she knew there was some underworld activity in Tanusha. Naturally they'd be concerned about any security actions going down in their club. She wished Vanessa was with her.

Through a hallway, corridors branching to either side, then out into the main club. . . . The place was massive, the ceiling over ten metres high. The entire joint was shaped like a giant arch, with herself at the apex looking down. Aisles curved away to either side of her past lines of table-booths, low walled and stylish, screened by palms and greenery. The tables circled the dance floor in ascending rings, shielded by an excess of flashing dance-light and by the balcony roof overhead. The balcony ran right around the walls, and beyond the side rails more tables. Out on the dance floor, a surging mass of humanity, waving arms and tossing heads, illuminated in lightning flashes of kaleidoscopic brilliance in the inky darkness. On the far wall, a good eighty metres away, a stage, and a band. What they were playing, Sandy did not know, but it was loud, techno, aggressively rhythmic, and it reverberated in her bones. The combined assault of light, sound, and vibration was almost overpowering, and she reflexively modulated reception as she went down the central aisle. Retinas adjusted for multiple intensity shifts, hearing tuned down the thumping bass and cut disruption . . . she couldn't help but stare at the throbbing masses on the dance floor, though. She guessed maybe twelve hundred people, all pressed together, blending in motion, staccato movement in the flashing lights. Around the tables another three or four hundred, talking, drinking, eating . . . the damn place was a restaurant, too. More hundreds on the top balcony . . . maybe twenty-four hundred people all told. Jesus.

She walked along a side aisle, past tables of diners, clubbers coming the other way. Then up a staircase by the side wall. The balcony was much the same, except that the aisles were stepped down more steeply, giving each table row a good view of the dance floor. Along the highest aisle, vision tracking, sidestepping waiters with piled trays of food and drinks, she caught a brief transmission, a flashburst from nearby . . . eyes flicked across and found him at a table further along the aisle, at the very top of the arch. He'd seen her first evidently. She smiled as she finally approached.

"Hello, darling." Mahud rose to meet her and she kissed him firmly on the lips, like one lover to another. "Lovely place."

"Yes, dear," he deadpanned past a creeping smile. They sat. "You wanna eat?"

"No no no," she said, "you're supposed to compliment me on how I look, that's how civilians do it." Mahud frowned.

"You're wearing jeans and a jacket. That's not very impressive," with an indication to the dance floor.

"I didn't say you had to mean it," Sandy replied with amusement, "you just have to say it."

"Why don't you compliment me then?" He did, Sandy reflected, look rather flash in his colourful sports jacket, track pants, and expensive walker shoes. It was a particular, legitimate look, one of thousands in Tanusha. Someone must be advising him on what to wear, she decided.

"Because the man's supposed to compliment the woman first."

"No," he levelled a finger at her, dance floor pyrotechnics half-lighting his grin, outlining his jaw and cheek, "you've got that wrong. I've seen plenty of women going after men like they've got bull's-eyes on their crotches."

"I know, but that's not the traditional custom. I'm trying to teach you the basics . . . then you can start the advanced course." He half frowned at her.

"What's the advanced course?"

"We point you at some girl out on that dance floor, and we see if you can get her into bed without offending her." A perplexed look from Mahud.

"Have sex with a straight? What if I hurt her?"

"You mean you never did?" Sandy asked, eyes widening.

"No way . . . you were the only one, Cap. You see, I told you you were a nymphomaniac . . ."

"That's crap, I know Raju did." Enjoying this exchange immensely. "Who the hell was it . . . oh yeah, you remember Lieutenant Li, armoury monitor?"

"Raju would screw anything," Mahud said with a dismissive wave of his hand. "Hell, he was nearly as bad as you." Sandy gaped at him, mock horrified. "My point is that most *normal* GIs, Cap, stuck entirely with other GIs. Straights are all soft and squishy . . . you'd have to have a serious zipper malfunction to want to screw straights, Cap. Raju was a walking penis."

"What does that make me?" Mahud grinned at her. Leaned forward and dusted something imaginary from her shoulder . . . took that imaginary thing between his fingers and peered at it curiously.

"Pubic hair," he identified it for her benefit. Sandy kicked him under the table—softly, to avoid breaking anything if she missed. But she was impressed at the humour. And very pleased. The Mahud she remembered from Dark Star would never have made a joke like that. Could never. The subtlety would have been utterly beyond him. He was learning, evidently. Seeing the world in a new light. It was expanding his mind, and as Sandy sat there looking at him she just felt . . . happy. It was just so wonderful to have him back.

"So," she said. The sound was good, up on the balcony. She could clearly sense the nearby hum of repression acoustics, damping the dance floor cacophony down to something manageable. "What's the occasion?"

"The occasion," Mahud replied, "is that we're moving out shortly." Sandy frowned. Looked closely at him, searching for clues. There were none to be found in his calm, handsome brown eyes. He held her gaze without effort, matter-of-fact.

"Moving out?"

"That's what my superior says. Tomorrow. Something's going down."

"What kind of something?" She didn't like it. Didn't like relying on Mahud's tenuous grasp of events. "Is the operation winding up?" Mahud shrugged.

"Pretty much. But something's happening. It's an emergency withdrawal plan . . . a whole lot of stuff I don't understand, but I think the CSA's getting close. Apparently we've lost one of our Read Only Matrixes. Infiltration for the Plexus grid. Some SWAT raid."

"When?" Eyes unblinking.

"Few hours ago." He gestured to a passing waiter, and ordered two glasses of champagne. Flash of memory, champagne in a bunk-party, smuggled aboard. A good memory. "That's why I wanted to talk to you. We've been put on isolation stand down until tomorrow. I don't know if we're leaving tomorrow or not . . . but we're doing something tomorrow. Morning, I think."

"Mahud." Firmly, leaning forward on the table. Not liking the deep, cold feeling in her stomach. "Mahud . . . what about what we talked about? Are you going to stay with these people?"

He inhaled deeply. Held it for a long moment, looking at the tabletop, at his hands there, splayed upon the smooth surface. Sandy wanted to hold those hands, to touch him, to help him in whatever he needed her help in . . . but sensed that this was not the right time. Nor, perhaps, was it the right man.

He exhaled, long and deep.

"No." He looked up, and his eyes met hers. Mild, as if the decision gave him no trouble at all. "No, I won't go with them. That's why I called you here. I want to help you. If you bring these guys in, you'll get your citizenship from the CSA. I want to help you get them."

For one of the very few times in her life, Sandy could not think of anything to say. Her eyes locked with his in a kind of hypnotic bond that neither of them seemed able to break. The two champagne glasses arrived, and the waiter departed. Sandy tried to regather her racing thoughts. It was difficult.

"You feel you can do that?" she asked him very quietly.

A nod. "I'll be on the inside, they won't suspect a thing. We've got interface levels they don't, we can interface without them knowing anything. I can keep you updated on what's going on, and you can tell the CSA. We'll get them."

"Mahud . . . that's not what I'm asking. I know you can do it technically. But . . . I mean, do you *like* these guys?" A disbelieving frown.

"*Like* them? They're FIA." Like that explained everything. Which it did, she supposed with dazed logic.

"So . . . I mean, you wouldn't have a problem . . . bringing them down?" Betray was not a word she wanted to use. He had always been so loyal. He answered with an emphatic shake of the head.

"Cap, they've made it plenty plain they don't like me. I don't like them either. They just keep me around to do the job. And I stick around because I was ordered to do what they say."

"It'll mean breaking that order, Mahud." Still quietly. It was a hell of a thing to ask of any GI. Especially Mahud. "It'll mean going AWOL. Leaving the League. Being branded a traitor, probably. Can you do that?"

She gazed at him, oblivious to the pounding music, and the epileptic pandemonium of lights from the dance floor. And was surprised when it was he who reached across the table, and held her hands firmly in his own.

"Cap . . . what'd they *do* to you?" Looking her over, eyes narrowed with powerful feeling. "They cut you up, Sandy. I've been thinking about it, and . . . I mean, I just can't *stop* thinking about it. And I helped them do it."

"No you didn't . . ." but he held up a hand, forestalling her protest.

"Bullshit. Of course I did. I planned the assault that gave them cover . . . cover to distribute their damn database they'd gotten from cutting you up, then hide everything so no one would ever find where it went. I've *been* doing that, that's what they've been up to just now. I go into their meetings, wherever they are, and that's what they've been doing.

"And . . . and I've been thinking, Sandy." His eyes were intent, more forceful than she'd ever seen of him. Like he was taking charge. It was definitely a first and his gaze held her mesmerised. "I've been thinking . . . I mean, what's it all for, anyway? I used to love the League so much, but you know what I really loved? It was you guys, you, Raju, Tran, Chu . . . that was why I loved the League. Because being a part of the League made me a part of you guys . . . and that was what it was all about.

"So what the fuck am I doing here? Helping them cut you up? Trying to kill the damn President . . . I mean, why? You like her, right?"

Sandy nodded mutely. Frightened to speak, lest this strange, take-charge Mahud suddenly evaporate, like some holographic trick of the dancefloor lights. His hands were warm and strong.

"This is service to the League?" he continued, eyes burning with sudden conviction. "I mean . . . sure, it's service, I'm sure they need it, but . . . but fuck it, what about me? I've fought for them for four years . . . and that's gnatshit next to your time, I know . . . but it's about damn time they gave something back . . . and this isn't what I had in mind. They can't seriously ask me to choose between you and them, I mean . . . hell, there's no contest. There never was."

"You're going to do this for me?" Sandy asked quietly. Mahud shook his head warily.

"You're going to turn this around," he said in a faintly accusatory tone, "I know you Cap, you'll turn it around so you'll make it look like I'm not thinking for myself again . . . it's not like that." Passionately, his hands tightening upon her own. "I want to do it because I'm figuring where my priorities are. And that's wherever I goddamn say they are. You're my priority. You see? It's not just you . . . it's just that I've suddenly figured out where the damn League's priorities end and mine begin. I'm figuring what *I* want to do. You get that?"

"Yeah." Sandy nodded, eyes gleaming with sad, quiet pride. "I get you. It's one of the biggest things they never took into account when they made us, Mahud. Developing sentiences rarely hold to the same perspectives for long in their formative years. Among straights, kids change perspectives and opinions far faster than adults. If we live long enough, we start questioning things. Straights were changed by the war, their personalities altered by the experience. But we're still building personality at that stage. And small readjustments can reorient our value systems one-eighty degrees in those early stages. We're kids, Mahud. Really. For kids, rebelling is natural. It's part of growing up."

"I'd like to grow up, Cap," Mahud murmured, squeezing her hands. "With you." Sandy smiled weakly, her eyes moist. Took a hand and pressed it to her lips.

"I'd like that too."


Half an hour before sunrise Shan Ibrahim strode across the rooftop landing pad of the doghouse. The wind blew cold, engines howled in the floodlit night. SWAT teams crouched, intent on last-minute consultation. Four special-purpose SWAT flyers squatted diagonally on the pads, dark, angular, and brooding. Ground crews hurried purposefully about the massive engine nacelles on preflight duties, or stood with headset and complist, running through final checks with the flight crews.

Captain Hayland saw the Director approach and walked across to meet him.

"Morning, sir. Four airframes prepped and ready. Takeoff in ten mikes." Ibrahim acknowledged with a nod, listening to the operational chatter on his headset.

"Weather looks bad today, Philip," he said over the keening engines, "I want Eagles Five and Six on five-minute standby for the duration, recovery turnaround asap."

"I'm already on it. You've got the frequencies?"

"I have." He gave Hayland a pat on the arm as he walked past, headed for the nearest SWAT unit. Lieutenant Vanessa Rice sat on the deck, talking to one of her troops—Agent Devakul, Ibrahim saw— rifle propped butt down at her side, and nearly as tall as she was, seated. Saw him coming and rose smoothly to her feet, mirrored by the others, a whining clatter of armour and heavy weapons.

"How much sleep did you get?" was his first question, glancing about to include them all in his query.

"They got six hours, average," Rice replied. Her attractive, fine features looked incongruously delicate above the solid bulk of her armoured shoulders. "I had about three, but hey, that's my lot in life."

"Poor baby," said Agent Sharma from nearby. Rice smiled. She looked subdued, Ibrahim thought, eyeing her critically. Subdued, but relaxed. The other teams looked tense, businesslike. SWAT Four looked quite calm by comparison. Ibrahim knew very well that Rice could take much of the credit for that—her team adored her and followed her positive example with relentless dedication. Today, he needed them. He needed people whose loyalty he could rely on. He trusted Rice. Her priorities were moral more than technical. Today he needed that of his closest people more than he ever had before.

"You're good for it?" he pressed.

"Wouldn't be here if I wasn't," Rice replied. Ibrahim gave her a smack on one armoured arm.

"You're in Eagle One with me. Load up." SWAT Four moved out with barely a comment, and Ibrahim walked on to the next team, doing the circuit. A minute later N'Darie intercepted him as he strode toward his flyer.

"Chief, I've just had a message straight from Dali. He wants direct uplink access, says he needs to be kept abreast of any new developments." Another man might have cursed. Ibrahim thought about it for a moment as they walked, readjusting the com-interface at his belt then rezipping his navy-blue CSA jacket.

"Tell him we are concerned about the integrity of all outsourced links," he said then, half shouting over the engines. "Tell him we have evidence that throws that integrity into doubt and we're concerned about leaks. Give him secondhand reports by the minute, as he requires. No direct access." N'Darie frowned, walking fast to keep up.

"And when he protests?"

"Quote him regulations," Ibrahim said blandly as they passed the port nacelle. "Any regulations. And for Allah's own good sake, say *nothing* of Kresnov or her information source. Imply nothing, suggest nothing." N'Darie nodded her complete understanding.

"I'll keep everything as tight as I can. This won't be easy."

"No," Ibrahim agreed as they reached the rear doors, "it won't be at all easy. We shall do the best we can." N'Darie left, and Ibrahim climbed the rear ramp into the main hold where SWAT Four were already hooked in and waiting.

It was, Ibrahim was well aware, a most delicate set of circumstances. By far the most delicate of his professional career, and probably of the CSA's entire history. He knew that the quarry was about to act. It was both a problem to be solved and an opportunity to be exploited. But the present commander-in-chief was most likely a part of the problem, and his aides were almost certainly directing the quarry personally, whether Dali knew of it or not. How to conduct an operation against the interests of the acting President and not let the Acting President know about it? It would not, as his second had stated, be easy.

He sank into the command chair with a sharply exhaled breath. Did his restraints, ran his bank of display graphics through a systems check, as about him the rest of the command crew did similar, announcing various systems' status and safeing their connections.

The FT–750 was a bigger flyer than those used on SWAT's standard operations, with extended range and payload plus impressive multirole capabilities. SWAT Four had room enough for weapons-drill amid the harness straps and storage lockers toward the rear. The front half was pure Command and Control, multiple observation posts, systems interface, communications, surveillance, all run by their regular people, familiar faces beneath headsets and eyewear, bathed in screen light. CSA flyers had been on standard patrol above the Tanushan skylanes every hour since the attack on the President. No one on the ground would notice the change. This was just another standard rotation . . . only the payload was somewhat altered.

Surrounded by the familiar competent preparations, Ibrahim allowed himself to reflect upon the circumstances that had brought him to this moment. It was so very easy to forget the convoluted history that lay behind the recent turbulent events. Of the two great powers of humanity, and their differing perceptions of what it meant to be human. The League, believing in science as the saviour, charting a new direction for the species. They were the self-appointed trail-blazers. The visionaries. The ones who had attained a new enlighten-ment, out among the new worlds, the new frontiers of human civilisa-tion. They had escaped the shackles of Earth-bound conservatism to pursue their vision far from the intellectual censorship of the Federa-tion. For the great minds behind the League, a ban on scientific research and development was akin to a ban on subversive political ide-ologies. It was censorship, plain and simple, and they steadfastly believed in intellectual freedom in all its varied dimensions. For its preservation, no cost was too great.

And then there was the Federation. The League accused Federation worlds of being mere puppets of Old Earth, children clutching to the apron strings. But that, Ibrahim knew, was a massive oversimplifica-tion. In the Federation, cultural roots remained critical. One only need spend a few days in Tanusha, walking among the historical recreations of its many districts, to see the importance Tanushans placed upon remembering the old, preserving it, living it. The future was not com-plete without a past. And without a clear understanding of one's past, there could be no clear perception of one's future.

Ibrahim could recall with great clarity the various lines and verse from the Koran, and even the Afghani and Iranian folk tales, that his parents had read to him when he was a boy. The tales of morality, of pur-pose and human dignity. He did not believe such things were insignifi-cant. He did not believe it was right or good for any human society to erase such things from its collective memory and start anew. The path had been walked upon for thousands and thousands of years. There was no "new beginning." There was only the next stretch of path, winding ever onward, building the future upon the foundations of the past.

The League, of course, saw this as a clear sign of flawed intellect. Cul-ture, they reasoned, was so frequently the prison walls within which reason was trapped. And like missionaries of old, they spread their word, the word of reason, to where it was most needed. Knowledge, before which the old ignorance and superstitions would dissolve like ice beneath the summer sun. They were the enlightened. It was their mission and their purpose to bring their enlightenment to all of humanity. And once they saw the light, surely, surely reason and logic would follow.

Even now, as the rear doors closed, and the engine noise faded to a muted whine, Ibrahim had to suppress a shudder of disgust. He was by nature so very, very wary of a Great Cause. There had been people of his own religion, and from his own region of the Old World, who had once had a Great Cause of their own. They had not been so different from himself in many ways, had believed many of the same things and shared the same tastes and values, but with no sense of tolerance or moderation. Their Great Cause had brought much bloodshed and suffering, and all these hundreds of years later their legacy was not one of pride, but of shame.

The League also believed in a great many good, decent things. They were the progressives, the freethinkers, the radicals of their day. History favoured such people. They had brought great change, and great innovation, and the present was all the greater for their inspiration. But now, Ibrahim believed, the pendulum had swung too far. The Great Cause had become merely an ideology, and ideology, Ibrahim knew only too well, was the antithesis of reason. He was student enough of history, especially that of his own cultural roots, to know that for a very certain fact.

And it was Kresnov, he thought now, who had brought it all into focus for him in these recent, difficult days. Kresnov, who supposedly represented the pinnacle of the League's technological advancement. She was theirs, in body if not in spirit. And yet she had abandoned them, after they had abandoned *her*. They valued what Kresnov was, but they did not value her. Nor did they value the others of her kind, her friends among them.

It was the Cause. In the face of a Great Cause, the individual was always the first to suffer. The Great Cause consumed individuals as a Southern Plains tornado consumed trees. It did not matter that the Cause was in the name of humanity itself—any such mass ideology, even that conducted in the name of individual rights and freedoms, would sacrifice anyone and anything to further its own grand purpose.

The contradiction was, as always, quite stunning. Especially when this adventure was carried out in the name of logic and reason. But that was not the worst of it. Most ironic of all, to Ibrahim's mind, was that Kresnov was far more akin, in spirit and personality, to the Federation than ever she had been to the League. She questioned the questioners. She sought to understand the Cause. To dissect and examine the ideology, the reasoning that had given birth to her, the Cause that was her own very existence.

Seeking her roots, she had found them here, in a place that would never have seen fit to create her in the first place. Had found a welcome of sorts. People who acknowledged her individuality, however much it frightened them. Individual rights, after all, were the main grounds upon which the Federation opposed GIs in the first place—all sentient beings had inalienable individual rights, and so the creation of a being whose innate abilities extended beyond what society's rights were prepared to grant another individual . . . would be an automatic breach. The Federation believed all people were equal. To create a person who was both more equal (with enhanced capabilities) and less equal (with predesignated social roles) threatened all the shared values upon which the Federation was based.

That any GI *was* an individual and *had* rights was something that most Callayans, and Federation people generally, would concede, however reluctantly. That was the greatest irony of all. The League championed Kresnov because she was "good for humanity," but ignored her humanity in the process. The Federation opposed Kresnov because she was "bad for humanity," but in doing so nonetheless recognised her as a real person.

This insight left Ibrahim in no doubt of which side he was committed to, heart and soul. And it made him realise, in a sudden flash of clarity, that he did not oppose the existence of those like Kresnov because it was "bad for humanity" but because it was bad for Kresnov. He felt great pity for her. Hers was not an easy lot. She had never had any choice but to be what she was, and it quite simply was not fair. He did not hate her for the great destruction she had doubtless wrought upon members of the Federation in her past. He only wished that she could one day find some peace, and the happiness that she so obviously craved. She was in the right place for it, that was certain. And here, unlike in the League, she would never be asked to do anything that another human would not do herself.

Equality. It was the oldest of human ideals. And those who forgot their past were doomed to forget why it had become such a grand ideal in the first place.

The rising engine roar cut into Ibrahim's thoughts as, with a deep thrumming of thruster fans, the flyer lifted smoothly from the pad.

"I just hope our GI's got her head screwed on straight about her buddy," Agent Chow said over local intercom, the flyer rocking slightly as it climbed clear of the surrounding buildings. There were no windows along the fuselage, but everyone had taken this trip so often that it made no difference.

"Don't sweat it," Vargas replied, eyes fixed on his monitor bank. "She's the only hook we've got right now, just go with it."

"No backup either," Chow muttered. "I don't like it."

"She'll be fine," came Rice's voice, switching from her usual TacCom frequency. "You can trust her—she's a pro."

"Her professionalism isn't my problem," Chow replied. "I just want to know the same thing I always want to know if we're working with someone new—when the shit goes down, whose side is she on?"

"I said you can trust her," Rice repeated firmly.

"LT, this is her long-lost buddy here," Chow retorted as the thrust changed direction, acceleration building. "She may like us plenty, she may be trustworthy as hell, but if that were your best friend with his head on the block, and you had to choose us or him, what would *you* do if you were her?"

Silence from Rice. Chow was a complainer by nature, but on this occasion he was right. They all knew it.

"Then let's just make certain it doesn't come down to a choice," Ibrahim told them all very calmly. He didn't mind constructive conversation on the job. And there had been so little time to prepare, his people's minds were still catching up with the issues at hand. "The goal is to get them both out of this alive and healthy. As long as our goals remain concurrent, we're all on the same side. That's the task."

At that moment, the subject of controversy onboard Eagle One was figuring out the intricacies of Tanusha's road rules.

Sandy was on a motorcycle. Her cashcard had given her ample credit for the rental and her CSA badge had convinced the rental operator of her competence. That she'd never ridden one before in her life was a minor detail she had neglected to mention.

She was cruising now along a highway that her link-access map identified as Rama Five, ablaze with streetlight in the near-dawn. The bike was simple enough to ride—it was a Prabati W–9, hydrogen powered, large, comfortable, and lightweight. Navscreen indicators gave a constant head-up display across the low windshield, a 3D projection that interfaced with the helmet visor. Warning indicators informed her of the relative positioning of surrounding traffic, cars behind, to the sides, and ahead, with highlighted warning zones and projected movements . . . motorcycles were, Sandy had discovered from the rental operator, a bone of contention among Tanushan city planners.

All road traffic was, of course, regulated. Highway and freeway travel was an entirely hands-off affair. Manual operated only on back streets, and even there rarely, all speeds and trajectories monitored on the central grid.

Motorcycles however, unlike cars, would fall over if driven by remote. They needed to remain under rider control at all times. Many planners, the rental operator had told her, wanted them banned from Tanusha . . . "road toll" was an expression that provoked horror and disgust in the planning department. More people were killed in Tanusha each year by lightning strikes than traffic accidents. But most of those deaths, the planners pointed out, involved motorcycle riders and pedestrians.

Sandy leaned through a gentle 100 kph turn, eyeing the road ahead through the alert-sensitive display, trajectories and ranges shifting unobtrusively across her visor. Repressed an amused smile at the regulatory overkill. All those silly graphics just got in the way. She could calculate everything she needed with plain vision. She gave the throttle a gentle nudge toward the 110 kph ceiling, a sudden break in power transmission, the engine whine abruptly fading as the buffers cut in. She didn't like it. Fortunately the bike had an independent CPU with interlink barriers, which would last about three seconds if she wanted them gone. She hoped she wouldn't need it, but she was not in the habit of taking chances with equipment.

Crackle of mild static on audio . . . she winced slightly as the encoded frequency locked in, a brief, squeezing pressure.

"*Cassandra,*" came Ibrahim's voice, internal audio, direct input to her eardrum. It always sounded slightly strange on an unfamiliar frequency, through an unfamiliar code. "*We have your bike on traffic-scan, you're doing the near side of legal down Rama Five, left lane, Hammersley District, confirm?*"

"That's me," she replied aloud, voice muffled to her own ears in the helmet. Silent replies took practice, and vocal ones had the same result. "The speed buffers look a little vulnerable on this thing, just make sure the cops don't start chasing me if I have to break them."

"*I copy that, we'll kill the alert if it comes, but we don't want to tell anyone directly who you are in case we're being hacked . . . nothing will make bad guys more suspicious than an on-duty CSA agent on a motorcycle.*"

It was good thinking, Sandy thought. Like it was good thinking to barrier-monitor the dealership she'd taken it from under CSA identification. The dealer had seemed like a decent guy, but if he flapped his mouth they'd cut him off. Ibrahim's team knew this city's network far better than she did.

*"Any word yet from Angel?"* Angel was her idea—Mahud's code-name. She wondered if he'd appreciate the humour. And thought no, probably not.

"He's still on standby," she replied, edging into a convenient space in the right lane, flash of sensor warning as she crossed the dividing line. Wind roared and flapped at her jacket, pressing her body.

Mahud's situation was tricky. He was alone. He didn't know where his "teammates" were. It was not his operation—he was only along for the ride at this point. When he was wanted, he would be sent to a set of coordinates. What happened then, when and how the team would reassemble from their scattered, covered positions throughout the city, was up to someone else entirely.

Sandy thought she knew who. Remembered cold, hard eyes, shoulder-length dark hair. A pistol levelled at her chest. "Get out of this one, Skin." The interviews they'd conducted on those FIA personnel they'd captured had revealed nothing . . . they claimed Federate business and spun a conveniently simple story about tracking a dangerous League fugitive for "security reasons" that CSA personnel could not be privy to under the regulations . . . and claimed, obviously enough, to be working alone. Whoever that man was, he did not like GIs. Surely he was not happy to be working with one.

She gripped the throttle a little more tightly and tried not to think about it lest her worry for Mahud cloud her judgment. Worry was not something that usually afflicted her on a typical op. But this op was far from typical.

*"You think it's possible they might just leave him behind?"* came Vanessa's voice suddenly in her ear. *"If they're planning on leaving, that is?"*

"Christ almighty," Sandy muttered, "I hope not."

*"But wouldn't that . . ."*

"If they leave him here, Ricey, it won't be alive. I wasn't supposed to survive my procedure. The League might not mind if the Federation have live GIs running around, but the FIA certainly would. They hate our guts, remember? Meaning GIs generally." A brief silence.

"*Forget I said it*," Vanessa said then.

"Already have." She changed lanes leftwards, ignoring the indignant protests from her navscreen, indicating as she decelerated down a turnoff branch. "Any more ideas on what they're after this morning?"

"*A few,*" said Ibrahim. "*I won't trouble you with them now. Our net is deploying quite nicely—you can access on TacCom QB1358 . . . do you need a lead on that? The encryption's very serious.*" A brief moment's concentration as she slowed to a stop, feet down, waiting at a red light.

"No, I'm in already." Clear grid-picture of deployed ground units of CSA personnel, in cars mostly. A few aircars, locked into repetitive transit patterns. And the flyers, Eagles One through Four, well above it all, widely dispersed. Even on grid-scan, the city looked as massive as ever. It took a lot of units to do a decent coverage. "That looks like a busy day for you. I'm glad I'm not coordinating that lot. My response trajectories tend to go through things instead of around them."

"*On this occasion,*" Ibrahim said mildly, "*please refrain.*"

Sandy nearly smiled.

"I'll try." Green light and she squeezed the throttle, curved right and under the freeway bridge, quickly accelerating down the empty road ahead. Even then, buffers curbed the power-application somewhat. She shook her head in mild irritation . . . the bike would be lots of fun without those damn buffers. After a lifetime of soldiering, she was sick to death of pointless rules and restrictions. But then again, she thought, maybe she'd never liked them in the first place. Maybe that was why she was here now in Tanusha and not back in the League, hunkered in some carrier's gut, cleaning her weapons.

"*The traffic's going to get heavy in a few hours,*" Ibrahim said. "*Chances are that if a move's being made, it'll be before or after rush hour.*"

"More traffic will cover their movements," Sandy disagreed. The road was now a tree-lined thoroughfare, shops and sidewalks along both sides. She kept the bike to the suddenly lowered 60 kph buffer limit. Everything looked peaceful beneath the pale streetlight. Here and there were joggers, early risers. Past an open park where some martial arts types were already practising.

"*True. We'll keep an open mind. Tell us when you make contact.*"

"Will do. Ricey, you there?"

"*I'm here,*" came Vanessa's voice.

"What's the latest on the Berndt people?" Berndt was the district in which the recently devastated mall was located. It was on the news.

"*Still no personnel records. It's pretty clear they're offworlders. Beyond that, there's nothing that I haven't already told you.*"

"Were they good?" Decelerating again, indicating for a right turn.

"*I'm not sure. I'm not sure that they'd have done better if they were better soldiers . . . it wasn't much of a situation for them, surprised like that and unarmoured against a SWAT team.*"

"Yeah." She took the turn and cruised at a gentle fifty up the residential roadway. Quiet houses, close and comfortable, nestled among the many trees. Behind the many blank windows, ordinary Tanushans were sleeping. "Considering what hot shit you are as a commander, did you meet much resistance?"

"*Plenty. I can't tell you how goddamn lucky we were.*"

"Then they were good. The bad ones just dissolve." A brief silence. It seemed to Sandy an incongruous conversation, cruising up this dark, leafy back street between darkened houses. Soon the families would be rising, children coming out to play on the first day of weekend, the street filling with comfortable civilian life. No inkling of the woman who had cruised this way only hours before on her motorbike, who she was or what she'd done.

"Are you okay?" she asked then. As gently as she knew how. There was no simple way to speak of such things. No guaranteed approach. Nothing that would change the awful reality.

"*Yeah,*" came the quiet, reluctant response. "*I'm okay at the moment, the adrenalin's still up thanks to your buddy. It's not like I'm feeling sorry for those pricks or anything.*"

"That's good. A bit of vicious, homicidal rage can be a healthy thing, sometimes. Civilians never understand that."

"*A bit of your flippant irony doesn't go astray either, I'm sure.*" Sandy smiled within her helmet. Vanessa's character observations seemed part curiosity, part affection, and part defence mechanism. She had an interesting habit of turning words back against the speaker.

It needed, Sandy realised, a degree of emotional perceptiveness that she herself lacked. Perhaps it was because Vanessa was a civilian. Perhaps because she was a straight. And perhaps her bisexuality gave further insights, created certain multilevelled interactions that others would not have . . . it was a puzzle. It was the kind of puzzle she found so stimulating, here among civilians.

"It sure beats staying entirely serious," she agreed, slowing for a stop sign. Navcomp blinked green, the central grid reading no cross-traffic and the buffers allowed her to accelerate once more.

"*Hey, that's my general philosophy of life,*" Vanessa told her. "*See, I told you we had things in common.*"

"Stop hitting on me, Vanessa. It's very distracting."

Vanessa laughed.

"*The com guy's giving me the windup, Sandy. . . . I forget his name, he's some dweeby little redhead with a bad complexion. I never liked him.*" Sandy grinned, almost able to hear the indignation at the other end. Evidently she knew him well. "*I'll get back to you.*"

"Do that, Ricey. Ciao." The link went dead and there was only the muffled hum of the Prabati's engine, a smooth vibration beneath her. The road ahead was dark and silent. But she no longer felt alone.

Vanessa Rice spared Agent Andy McAllister a sly sideways grin as the connection went dead, grasping the handhold by Chow's navcomp terminal as the flyer gave a slight shudder and sway. McAllister scowled, pretending to be angry. Her gaze shifted across to Gabriella Razo, on the neighbouring terminal. Razo had been looking more and more incredulous as the conversation had progressed. Not, Vanessa thought, a big GI fan. Or she hadn't thought she was.

"Stop thinking 'cold heartless machine,' Gabby, and start thinking 'cool, sexy chick.'" Smiling as Razo's expression remained blank. "She's a nice girl, you'd like her."

Razo gave her an intensely dubious look and concentrated once more upon her monitor.

# CHAPTER 16

The underground parking lot lights shed an artificial glare from the broad, featureless ceiling. Mahud walked soundlessly, eyes scanning. Level 14 was a long way down. On this Saturday evening it was deserted. Nearly.

There was a van in a park beside the exit ramp. Navy blue. The size made sense. He walked toward it, hands in the pockets of his sports jacket, fingers wrapped about the handle of his pistol. The van's suspension was compressed a little. There were heat readings from inside. Multiple sources, he guessed, striding quickly the last several steps, and recognising the man in the driver's seat, past the darkened tinting. Pham, a tall Vietnamese, watching his approach. He slid the side door open and climbed in.

Six of the usual ten were there, plus Pham in the front. They paused in their serious conversation, looking. Mahud dropped himself into an available seat behind the driver, settled sideways with his legs extended, watching the meeting. The four men and two women went back to their discussion. Different from before, Mahud knew. They did not look at him, but they were aware. They always had been. So many weeks with these people and still they looked at him like . . . what was Sandy's expression? Something the cat dragged in? Mahud had never seen a cat, but he got the idea.

"Where's Shimakov?" he thought to ask Pham in the front seat, as the discussion continued behind. Tactical details. Frequencies, barrier protections. It always changed. The corporate encryption protected them from government detection mostly, but things were serious now, and they were taking no chances.

"Coming," replied Pham. It was about as much as Pham ever said to him. His companions weren't much better. Mahud watched them through half-lidded eyes. Sandy, he knew, had some success at reading stress levels on infrared, watching the bloodflow. He himself was not so accomplished. But he could hear the seriousness of their conversation, and see the hardness of their expressions.

"What's the com specs on the van?" he asked Pham, unperturbed by the lack of enthusiasm. He knew that Sandy worried about that, too, wondering how he'd managed for so long serving with these FIA types who so obviously disliked him and all that he was. The thought nearly made him smile. Sandy worried about so many things. Truth was, he didn't care. Sandy had always needed a degree of emotional contact. Mahud only cared that those he liked thought well of him. These people . . . well, at another time, in another place, they would be his enemies. He had killed FIA before. The last thing he wanted was their friendship. He just did the job, as he'd always done, and so long as the FIA did their bit, all was well.

Pham reeled off a technical answer and Mahud accessed the van's CPU. Read sensory equipment, displays, reception, frequency coding . . . it was standard civilian, hired as always under an encrypted alias, briefly modified with their mobile add-ons. It was not particularly sensitive to reception. If he was sensible, he could interface and not be detected. He did so, and received an answering click . . . familiar frequency, familiar connection . . .

"*Mahud, what's going on? I'm getting bored.*" Mahud kept any trace of a smile off his face with an effort.

"*I'm in a van, Cap. In an underground parking lot beneath that big main tower in middle-Tarutao.*" He leaned his head back against the side window, legs crossed and extended, pretending to rest as he waited. The conversation continued, unaware. "*It's a Hindustan Caprice, twelve-seater in the back, navy blue with adjustable window tint. Eight of the regular eleven are here, including me. We're waiting on Shimakov.*"

"*Thank you very much,*" Sandy pronounced. "*You'll make an undercover man yet. Any idea of a target?*"

"*They don't give me the time of day, Cap. I reckon I'll find out when I get there. There's at least one more van, maybe two . . . twenty-five including me, remember? They'll be out there somewhere.*"

"*Thank you for jogging my horribly defective memory Mr. General, Sir.*" The sarcasm was dripping, even in silent-acoustic. Mahud kept the twitch from his lips with difficulty. "*Any hint you might get as to a location would be lovely. You wouldn't believe just how big this city looks until you have to pinpoint a single person or vehicle—it's like finding a grain of sand on a beach. But don't do too much. If you give yourself away it's all worth nothing, you got that?*"

"*Yes, Almighty One.*" Chortling laughter from the other end. No other GI made a sound like that. God she was weird. "*How many of you guys are out there?*"

"*You mean CSA?*"

"*Yeah.*"

"*Heaps. Not so many that they stand out among fifty-seven million people, but enough.*"

"*And what about that political stuff? Guderjaal and Dali, you heard anything about that yet?*"

A brief, almost imperceptible pause.

*"No, I wouldn't be worrying about that. I haven't heard anything, and there's nothing we can do about it anyway."*

They'd spoken about it before, briefly. Sandy, Mahud gathered, had made friends with one of the CSA's best SWAT commanders. She had told Sandy that things were happening at the top level, where command decisions were being made. The President had been removed, but now it looked like the rules that governed that removal might have been broken. And it was up to Supreme Court Justice Guderjaal to decide.

Exactly why Guderjaal had this power, Mahud didn't know. Who was in charge in this stupid city, anyway? What was wrong with having just one commander? Why did they have to spread it out between President, Supreme Court, and Governor? He supposed he ought to have figured this one out by now—it had been the raid he had planned, after all, that had given the Governor the excuse to kick out the President. There were rules for it, apparently. But hadn't Guderjaal approved of it? Guderjaal seemed to be the referee here. So how was he going to change his mind now without feeling stupid? And what the hell was it with a system where the right thing became the wrong thing depending upon the circumstances?

God, it was a nightmare. But it worried him all the same . . . if he and Sandy were relying on CSA people, who were the CSA taking orders from if their leadership was all over the place like this? It was the number one priority in combat operations—the chain of command had to be absolutely transparent and clear-cut. Mahud knew he could always put his life in Sandy's hands. But the CSA? Sandy had said Ibrahim was on their side, but wasn't he supposed to be taking orders from Dali? What if someone removed Ibrahim? Put a friend of Dali's in his place? Would Sandy and her SWAT commander friend be forced to choose whether to obey the new CSA Director or not? And how many CSA people would go with them?

He suspected that Sandy did not think him capable of such analysis. That she thought he did not realise what any of it meant. And perhaps she was right . . . he knew that Sandy's knowledge was much more extensive than his own. But he knew enough for it to worry him. Enough to see the potential flaws and problems in the operation. His commanders hadn't assigned him to this mission for nothing—of the remaining members of their team, he was comfortably their best tactical operator. He did not volunteer as much to Sandy, though. It had been she, after all, who had taught him the first rule of operational engagement—if it's not helpful, don't do it.

"*Got that*," he told her. "*You just be a bit careful, Cap. I don't reckon my position's that much more dangerous than yours.*"

"*I bloody well do, genius. You waste time worrying about me, I'll kick your ass.*"

"*Got that, too*," Mahud replied, repressing another smile. "*I'll tell you when we start moving. Out.*"


Tarutao. Sandy uplinked to a regional directory, scanning the street grid as the freeway lights flashed past on either side. Dark again now. An entire day, cruising and waiting, with pauses for meals at roadside vendors. There had been no news of a decision from Guderjaal. And little more from Mahud, who had been concerned that his apartment was bugged. The entire thing was getting on her nerves.

Tarutao was near enough. There was no great rush. She cruised comfortably in the left lane, settled in her slot behind a clustered string of traffic, nose to bumper, nine cars in a line with barely a metre between them. Cars moved in such coordinated groups here on the freeways. Slipstreaming saved power, so the traffic grid stacked cars in nose-to-tail lines, coasting on autopilot. Crouched comfortably low over her Prabati, she barely needed two-thirds of the usual throttle to keep pace, and the slipstream pressure felt noticeably reduced. A turnoff approached and a car in the middle of the group slid sideways toward the exit. The group closed up, reforming a single, smooth line at 140 kph.

She wished, as she scanned the directory display through the moving graphics on her visor, that they could just send in the cavalry now and grab that van in the parking lot. But as Mahud had said, there were twenty-four of them besides himself, and there would be other vans or cars. And Shimakov was not there. He was the one they wanted, more than anything. He, more than anyone, would know the extent of League/FIA biotech infiltration in Tanusha. He would know how far the cancer had spread.

It was possible they would just make a run for it. There would be a pickup zone somewhere outside of Tanusha. Anywhere on the entire planet would do. The Plexus grid coverage, she'd gathered from further discussion with Ibrahim, was less than perfect to begin with, being a civilian system designed to track commercial freight. It was also designed with established space lanes in mind. Coverage of the planetary surface itself was limited, thanks partly to Tanusha's limited number of population centres from which shuttles would normally launch, and partly to the fact that the system faced mainly outward, away from the planet.

Besides all of which, a planet was a very, very big place. Citysiders, used to universal sensory coverage of their entire environment, sometimes forgot just how big. The less-than-perfect grid had been compromised once. It would be folly to assume they had eliminated all means of further infiltration. A ship, a fast, silent ship, could very conceivably get close enough to launch a shuttle pickup, and get away again, mostly undetected. In all likelihood, such a ship would be in-system now, invisible to all scanners. Sandy knew it was possible. She'd done it herself more times than she could remember. Provided the sensor grid was compromised . . . nothing to it.

Once the FIA got outside of Tanusha and into the vast Callayan wilderness, they would vanish. Another fact sometimes very easy for Tanushans to forget—most of Callay was utterly uninhabited. To sweep an entire planet, and guard against a covert pickup when the security grid was ineffective . . . both were difficult tasks, to say the least. Particularly against this level of expertise. And no one knew what aces Dali and friends still held. The only way to make certain of a capture was to grab them here, inside the city.

Sandy's navscreen flashed, an icon glowing on her visor. There was a vehicle moving into position behind her, joining the slipstream. Sandy indicated, received a clearance, and slid out into the middle lane as the car moved up behind. Wind roared at her arms and shoulders, and she let it slow her down, then eased into place behind the new arrival, rejoining the convoy. More hassle with motorcycles—they broke up the slipstreaming effect created by cars, and not being connected to Central Control there was a risk of collision. Cycles were compelled by law to stay at the rear, and the fines for doing otherwise were harsh.

As to what the FIA were even doing, at this late stage . . . not even Ibrahim professed to know. Ongoing investigations had revealed traces, but nothing substantial. Some biolabs that may or may not have been used for experimental purposes. Some databases that could perhaps have stored illegal information. A biotech manufacturer held for questioning whose production line might have been utilised for the assembly of banned, experimental technologies.

The investigations showed that it was widespread, this activity, and deep rooted. Callayan citizens, offworlders, lifelong Tanushan residents . . . many were implicated but little proven. Everywhere were signs of evidence cleared, data cleansed, damning technologies incinerated or otherwise destroyed. And the operations were all, without exception, hidden within intricate webs of corporate identities and ownership complications that made it very difficult for investigators to determine exactly whom the operation actually belonged to, and where the money came from. Which was typical of Tanushan businesses, with their corporate secrecies and intellectual-property protection precautions.

She glanced upward through the visor as she settled into comfortable range of the new car's rear bumper. Zoom-focused, looking for airborne activity. She couldn't see any flyers, up there beyond the lower, cruising aircars and gleaming towertops. That was probably good. A flyer could close distances very fast—there was no need to circle directly overhead and risk suspicion on the ground. They were up there somewhere, waiting for action. That was comfort enough.

"*Sandy*," came Mahud's voice in her ear, "*we're moving. It's still just the eight of us, no Shimakov. He must be in one of the other vehicles.*"

"Okay, Mahud," she replied calmly within the confines of her helmet, scanning the layout schematic in her head, "I'm nearly there. Keep me informed."

"*Will do.*" The connection went dead. Sandy's jaw tensed unconsciously as she considered. No Shimakov. Mahud usually accompanied Shimakov. Where the hell was he? And what were they up to?

The directory-grid showed the Tarutao boundary ahead. Towers gleamed tall and bright beyond the flashing streetlights. A turnoff flashed past and she indicated for the next one, attempting a triangulation on Mahud's last transmission . . . failed. Evidently Mahud's van had better sensors than that, and anything as obvious as a tracking signal would risk detection. Her mind flashed on, visualising the Eagle One feed on CSA positions, realtime and updated . . . about half of them were closing on Tarutao, covering key junction points, main trunk routes. It looked good. She called up Ibrahim.

"Angel's moving, eight people in the van, Angel included. No Shimakov."

"*Copy that. Do you have positional fix?*"

"Negative." As the turnoff lane opened to her left and she slid into it, a sudden buffeting of slipstream. One of the nine-car convoy also moved over, slowly decelerating, and Sandy nudged the brake as she moved up behind. "I'll get closer, I might be able to hack a frequency ID if I can get a visual."

"*Be careful you don't get seen. That's imperative.*"

"Copy that." Broke connection, slowing as the turnoff left the highway, eased in behind the low, sleek groundcar, wondering just how much confidence Ibrahim really had that a special-ops killer would truly understand covert surveillance. The lights were red and she stopped. Navcomp counted the seconds for her. Green at zero, the car moved on immediate, centrally controlled reflexes and she followed just as fast with a squeeze of throttle.

This road curved at 100 kph through a landscaped zone of lakes and foliage, then in among the buildings and towers of the main Tarutao business district, and the buffers cut the speed down to eighty. Central tower. She scanned and found it, several blocks away. Lights and sidewalk commotion flowed by on either side. Saturday night crowds, partygoers, dinner groups . . . traffic was considerable, and navcomp flashed a warning of slower speeds ahead, bottlenecks building as traffic merged and unmerged, seeking side streets and parking lanes.

Damn. She let the buffers ease her speed down, ignoring throttle setting, and cruised for a while one metre from the rear bumper of the car in front, eyeing the nose-to-tail traffic ahead with distaste while simultaneously scanning her linkup-directory for areas of less congestion. Wondered again at the buffers, and the barrier elements that protected the Prabati's CPU from a simple hack-and-disable. It was tempting.

*"Sandy, we're out of the parking lot, heading northwest along . . . Buschler Road. Bit of traffic, we're ten below speed limit at the moment. Looks like a busy night."*

"Tell me about it. Thirty-second intervals or next turnoff, keep me informed."

*"Copy Sandy."* She called Ibrahim as soon as the connection blanked.

*"Hello Cassandra,"* came a new, male voice on the other end, *"the Director's unable to speak right now. Where's the target?"* Sandy frowned beneath the helmet. Ibrahim not available? What the hell could possibly be more important?

*"Angel is headed northwest up Buschler Road, 10 kays below the speed limit. What's Ibrahim up to?"*

*"Copy on Angel . . . the Director is consulting, he's on the ball, nothing to worry about."* Click and gone.

Sandy thought about that reply and decided in slightly less than half a second that she didn't like it. It was a silly time to start consulting. And she *hated* being told not to worry. Especially by some green civilian kid who sounded barely out of secondary school. She didn't know who Freud was precisely, but she reckoned that was one of his slips. Her vision edged to a reddish tinge and time seemed to slow another notch.

The Eagle One feed showed a CSA unit—a groundcar—headed for approximate rendezvous with Mahud's van . . . she accessed, found their frequency, and called them up.

"A–3, this is Snowcat, please inform me if you get a reading on that van's frequency ID."

"*A–3 copies, Snowcat.*"

The traffic accelerated a bit, she saw the adjoining turnoff approaching and took it, an uninterrupted cruise down a side street and then paused at the entrance to Buschler, indicating. Central control found her a spot, one car slowed, and she moved out into the gap as the navcomp instructed. The tower parking lot was behind her now, Mahud should be somewhere up ahead. But with the regulated traffic flow, overtaking was impossible. She bit her lip, and restrained herself from beating buffer-elements into so much cybertronic wreckage.

Scanned the road further ahead . . . it ran long and straight through this built-up district, office buildings rising high to the sides, blazing light and only sporadic nightlife, here in corporate-central. Traffic lights changing further along . . . if she got caught, she'd drop even further back.

"*Sandy, we're stopped at the lights. Where are you?*"

"I'm just a bit behind you, can't see you yet but I'm getting there. Anything more for me?"

"*If I hack this thing's frequency ID it'll detect me. Safer if you do it from the outside, I think . . . you were always better at it anyway.*"

"That's fine, keep your head down. I . . . wait, I think I see you."

Vision-zoom through the visor over the car in front, another set of lights further ahead, cars stacked up, a mass of red taillights . . . a navy blue rooftop, higher than the surrounding traffic, probably a van. Closing fast.

"Yeah, I've got you . . ." The lights went green . . .

*"Green light."*

"Yep, that's you." Her vision retuned slightly, back to normal light, combat reflex fading a touch. "If I get a fix I'll see if I can get your frequency."

Cruising at 80 kph, sandwiched by traffic, tires thrumming smoothly on a typically laser-planed Tanushan road. Up ahead, the CSA car A–3 turned onto the road behind Mahud's van. Moved over a lane, traffic making way for him. Strange manoeuvre. Maybe they were trying to catch up. They might have traffic override systems that she didn't possess on this rented bike. She called Ibrahim.

"A–3's got him in sight," she said, cruising through the green light of the van's last stop. A car ahead of her moved across to the slower left lane, and Sandy found herself gaining ground, empty street ahead for a hundred metres.

*"Eagle One copies, Snowcat,"* came that same, young male voice in her ear. Still no Ibrahim. She didn't like it. The road angled slightly right, corporate offices giving way to mixed commercial, much busier, pedestrian crowds, bright lights and overpasses, gliding past on all sides. Eyes fixed on the visible top-rear of the navy blue van, she reconsidered the Eagle One feed, saw vehicles shadowing along nearby streets and trunks . . . navcomp flashing then to indicate a vehicle falling back in the right lane, decelerating.

It was A–3, drifting back at 65 kph while she cruised on at 80 . . . something in mind, Sandy thought, frowning, seeing that Buschler ended another kilometre up ahead, and trying to calculate where the van would head next, toward what general destination, and which CSA units would follow . . .

A–3 dropped to level beside her and equalled her speed. Sandy looked across in surprise, not liking such a noncovert manoeuvre that could only stand out on an automated system, and the passenger window dropped on A–3's side . . . and found herself staring down at the muzzle of a pistol that she recognised as a stunner. Chemical pellet, a GI neutraliser. She stared.

*"Snowcat, this is A–3, pull over at the next left turn and halt."* The feed from Eagle One went abruptly dead, terminated. Possibilities raced. The mind overloaded. Came clear, vision shift to combat-scan, thoughts suddenly flat. Calm. Intent and calculating. Time slowed. Fast access, multiple pathways opened, quick penetration, sort-and-scan . . . quick routing down a Traffic Central branch, annihilated A–3's CPU barriers with complete absence of subtlety, hacked the Prabati's own in a second more, locked in . . . *"Snowcat, this is A–3, I repeat . . ."*

Executed. A–3's brakes abruptly locked in a squeal of burning tires, passenger's heads whipped forward as the Prabati's own barriers fell and suddenly, wonderfully, the cycle's performance buffers simply weren't there any more. Sandy gave the throttle a savage twist and the bike exploded up the road with a howl of hydrogen power, spewing white smoke from the wheelspin as she went.

Made the first cross-street before she could take a breath, slammed on the brakes and the massive sports-bike tried to stand on its front wheel, took the corner with a hard lean at 80 kph, her right knee scraping the road as she went. Accelerated out with the rear end sliding, aiming at the narrow gap between two lanes of traffic-filled road, and turned 80 into 200 kph in three seconds flat down the busy Tanushan street. Navcomp screamed at her, screen flashing red, and central comp tried admirably to adjust—she could see the cars moving over in their lanes just before she whistled by in a blur of speed. There wasn't much room between lanes and she swerved across the road to aim up the centre line past oncoming traffic, cars slowing and swerving to avoid as central comp took panicked evasive action. The next light was red, but central stopped the traffic for her and she shot through at a shade under 260 kilometres per hour, the street beyond the traffic lights appearing comparatively clear.

Crouched low over the bike, hands fastened on throttle and clutch with fingers tickling the brakes, the speed was immense, but hardly troublesome. Net-linked, she scanned ahead, sorting through the oncoming web of roads, crossroads, and traffic, analysing each piece of moving data with computer precision. The bike was fast, the traffic chaotic, but in combat mode her brain was far faster. Time moved at a crawl as she calmly, unhurriedly calculated her route, judging angles, speeds, and trajectories, and adjusting her path and velocity accordingly.

Tried to contact Mahud, as she began the long, hard deceleration toward a new, promising turnoff, bodyweight suddenly thrust forward upon her arms as the front suspension compressed. Nothing. No Mahud. Something had gone badly wrong, and the CSA operation was compromised. Everything fucked. And now some CSA elements were after her instead of Mahud, she'd lost the van, lost contact with Ibrahim and Vanessa, running like hell to stay ahead of them all, still free, and thus of some use to Mahud, while hoping against hope that Ibrahim would fight a way through whatever had happened, and reestablish contact. Somewhere past the smothering, intense concentration of combat mode, Sandy felt herself in the perfect mood to kill someone.

Indicated a left turn for central comp's benefit, saw/felt the traffic take evasive action, half slid into the wide, three-lane corner at 90 kph . . . and nearly lost it as she applied hard power and the rear end bucked, threatening to throw her from the saddle. So, she found time to think as she howled up the highway, dodging traffic, she wasn't perfect after all. The bike had its own handling characteristics, and if she ignored them she'd crash. Snaked hard left and then right, another twist of throttle as she grazed past a car-side in a hard right lean, rocketing up past 250 in no time at all and passing the next group of cars so fast they might have been parked. She resolved to pay attention and learn.

Realised then that the navcomp was squawking something else at her . . . cops were after her evidently, even Ibrahim's promise of protection from the local police hadn't happened, God knew what that meant. Someone unwanted was trying to access her communication frequency and she diverted them with absent determination . . . more traffic lights, and the turnoff she'd been aiming for, up to the freeway. Through the lights as cars pulled wide, and up the curving access ramp leaning wide and low, roadway rushing past at nearly 200 . . . then upright and through the narrow gap between car and railing, a flash and gone through her peripheral vision, and then she was on the freeway. Elevated, eight-laned, long, and very flat. Crackle in her inner ear, and then . . .

"*Sandy, you there?*" It was Vanessa, her voice hard with adrenalin. Sandy weaved, once and twice at 240 through traffic, making her way toward the outer right-hand lane.

"Go Ricey." Beyond the roaring of engine, tires, and slipstream she could hardly hear her own voice within the confines of the helmet.

"*Long story short, Sandy . . . Dali intervened, we think the FIA are in on it but some of our guys have gone with him.*" Burst through a metre-wide gap, a hard lean left toward another space . . . "*We lost uplinks and frequencies, we're trying to reestablish . . . SWAT's still with us, but some are on the fence, it's chaos, and we've lost the van. Where are you?*"

"On a freeway." Tight-voiced and tense-stomached at a wide, curving right-hander toward the suddenly available outer lane . . . every car seemed so much closer to the next at these speeds, and large spaces were suddenly very small. "A–3 pulled a gun on me. I'm being chased by cops, I'm not sure about CSA. Get them off me."

Arrived finally at the outer lane and rammed the throttle as far as it went. Head low and body flat behind the windshield, she quickly passed 300 kph and kept climbing. About her, the slipstream was solid as a wall. Everything thundered.

"*We'll try, but I'm not sure if we can—no one seems to know who's in charge. Dali ordered you arrested, Sandy, he knows about the operation. Some of our guys are taking orders direct. We think he's using some internal leverage with some of them . . . Ibrahim's trying to contact them but we're cut out of the system and it'll take some time to reestablish—they've cut us off. Look . . ."* distractedly, as if searching through something, *". . . we'll try and hide you, just don't get caught and try not to kill anyone, huh?"*

"No promises," Sandy snarled, hugging the centre rail through a curving turn at 348 kph. There were no shapes or colours, only motion, a continuous, eye-baffling blur. The sensory assault was vicious. Like her mood.

"Hello Sparrow," said Pham from the seat in front of Mahud, "are you clear?"

*"Sparrow is clear,"* came the reply from the other vehicle. *"Proceeding to target. Good luck."* Pham turned in his seat beside the driver and grinned at those in the back.

"Best insurance in Tanusha," he said.

"Damn right," said Schroeder, checking her weapon. The van cruised up an on-ramp, onto a northern freeway, slowly accelerating to merge with the Saturday evening traffic.

Mahud clenched and unclenched his jaw, gazing sightlessly out through the windshield at the sporadic cruising traffic that wound onward between the soaring towers. He'd lost all contact with Sandy. The corporate com-network on which all FIA units were operating had cut in a new shielding function, which transferred through to the van's systems . . . damn, something had happened, something big, and an emergency system had activated. Something he hadn't known they'd had. Shit.

"What happened to the links?" he asked, keeping his voice deliberately bland. "I can't access my links."

"Just a part of the override," said Emeagi from the back. "Our friends in the Governor's Office are hooked into Tanusha main. We can access anything we want and they can't touch us." His voice was cool, but Mahud could hear the excitement there. And the tension.

"Like having God on your side," Pham added from the front, less restrained than the others. "Unbelievable. The whole damn system is just ours. Nothing they can do about it. Just incredible."

No comment from the driver, Ramez. Nor from the others. The van sped along in the middle of a growing convoy, speeds approaching 140. Blazing tower sides slid smoothly by and the tires hummed in anticipation. Mahud resisted the urge to fiddle with his pistol and said nothing, gazing out at the curving lanes of tail-lighted highway snaking ahead through the city. Toward their target.

The target. Mahud had some ideas about that. This was the final play before withdrawal. The recovery ship was in-system, undetected by the Callayan security grid, such as it was. The shuttle would launch soon. Just one more op and they would be gone, out of Tanusha and toward the shuttle rendezvous, somewhere in the broad, deserted Callayan wilderness. Away from the Federation. Away from Tanusha. Away from Sandy.

Mahud felt a surge of something that might have been . . . fear. It was not an accustomed feeling. Not before an op. But there had never been this much at stake before. He'd never thought that there could be anything more important than life and death, live or die. But it seemed that there was. And the discovery was astonishing.

Sandy sat against a hard, bare wall and gazed sightlessly across the empty expanse of parking lot floor. The Prabati stood idly alongside, its smooth, powerful lines untarnished by its recent high-speed adventure. Artificial lighting gleamed on dark curves, a glint on moulded metal. Not even a scratch. That much to be said for the central Tanushan traffic network's improvisational abilities. And more to be said for the neurally enhanced, meta-synaptic brain that had guided it through the snarled evening traffic where original, organic models would surely have failed.

Failed and died, 300 kays an hour of mangled organic wreckage strewn across the freeway. Wasn't technology wonderful.

Sandy hugged her knees closer to her chest, the ferrocrete ground uncomfortably hard beneath her rear. She could still feel the shuddering thunder of her headlong plunge through traffic. The bike vibrating between her legs. The howl of slipstream. The energy of speed, and sensation, coming at a rush. And her ability to handle it, whatever the stresses. Her jeans were torn at both knees, thanks to those fast, leaning corners. Her exposed kneecaps were skinned and red to look at, but only faintly. Surface skin would shed, but foundational skin required far worse than friction and temperature. Beneath that, kneecaps of ferro-enamelous bone. The road would break before they did. She knew from experience.

She liked being a GI. It was a singular, revelatory thought, and she stared across the empty parking lot, considering that monumental notion and its ground-shaking implications. She liked being able to break things. To jump high and run fast. To process information at speeds that made time appear to crawl, like a quarter-pace video feed. To feel invulnerable.

But increasingly, even in Dark Star, she had distrusted that feeling. The feeling that let her enjoy speed and action. Combat was nothing if not speed and action. It was the drug that hooked lesser GIs. The ultimate experience. The moment upon which the rest of their lives were based. The thing that they lived for, their whole purpose in life. Make them enjoy it and they'll never question what it means. They'll want to do more. And in the absence of independent thought, and with the League's own special brand of "moral guidance," they'll do it willingly until it kills them.

And it had made so much sense. Back then. GIs had special capabilities. How fitting to find one's purpose in life exercising those capabilities. That was what they were there for, after all. It was all so very logical. She leaned her head back against the hard wall, and closed her eyes.

She felt cold. Cold and empty. People were after her. Mahud was in danger. There was chaos everywhere. Being what she was had caused nothing but trouble. Trouble for herself, trouble for Mahud, and trouble for all those civilians killed as part of the operation to bring knowledge of her workings to those underground programs operating here in Tanusha. She attracted trouble like a magnet. She passed through, and people died.

And it was not just politics, not for her. It was . . . everything. Everything that she was. All her thoughts, hopes, and dreams. Every aspect of her personal self, all the things that she'd liked to delude herself were private, and no one else's business but her own. It was all involved, and she'd been deluding herself if she'd ever thought things otherwise. Just another happy little delusion to comfort herself with rather than face the truth.

She was a contrivance. Some humans had created her. Her very existence had huge implications. And most of them, it seemed, were negative. The recognition was so devastating that she felt numb. She couldn't cry, couldn't scream, couldn't fight the truth. There was only emptiness. And the dark, hollow thought that maybe . . . just maybe, her entire life, and all that she'd thought she was, had been built on a lie.

Eyes squeezed shut, she scanned for Mahud through the nearby linkups . . . and found nothing. It was like he'd vanished, cut off from the entire network, like Eagle One and Ibrahim had been cut off when the Governor's Office had used their central control to undermine the operation, bypassing Ibrahim by ordering in units directly to arrest her. God, there was something seriously wrong with the Federal system if this could happen, if Federation agents could take control of the government and use it for their own purposes. Once this was over, and the Federate committee arrived from Earth, the shit would really hit the fan. Callay breaking away from the Federation. Becoming an independent world. As little as she knew about such Federal political machinations, Sandy thought it was possible. And public opinion, once the present scandal fully emerged, might just demand it.

At that precise moment, however, she could not have cared less. She wanted Mahud back, and she wanted him now. Beyond that, the Federation and the League could both just rot and die.

"*Sandy, where are you?*" It was Vanessa. She sounded calmer now.

"Safe," she murmured. Her voice sounded strange to her own ears, loud against the echoing silence. "Parking lot."

"*You okay?*" Reception crackled, distorted through layers of ferrocrete, twelve levels below ground.

"I'm okay." Quietly, hands in her hair, elbows rested on her bare, skinned knees. "What's up?"

"*Well, we've got through to police HQ, we're establishing a subnetwork, new connection points, new encryption. We can talk to a few people now. We've got some contacts at HQ and they've put a hold on your arrest . . . we can't guarantee the same will apply to all units, but it's bought some time. We've got our best people on the network links. We don't think they can find you, but we're not sure . . .*" A hard sigh. "*It's just all fucking insane—it's like the whole CSA just got split straight down the centre and we don't even know who's on which side. We're trying to contact each of them individually to find out. Some are on the fence, others refuse any order that overrides Dali . . . whole heap of goddamn ass-lickers worried about their performance reviews, refusing to break chain of command . . . hell, you get the picture.*"

"Busy little democracy you've got here," Sandy murmured. "Bet it wouldn't happen under a dictatorship."

"*A what?*"

"Old-fashioned idea. Never mind."

"*Anyway, point two: we just had a shooting. Werner Associates, small, independent design and consulting firm . . . guess the industry.*"

"Biotech," Sandy said tiredly, rubbing her eyes.

"*Clever girl. Three dead, one security and two designers, both at different locations, both in their homes. Very orchestrated. Looks like the sweepers are clearing away the last loose ends before they leave, anyone who knows too much or might talk . . . we've got security after what suspects we've got, but the Chief*" *doesn't think we've found any of the top people yet. And your buddy's not likely to be on any home assassination job."*

"You could put out a warning for all biotech industry in Tanusha."

*"Too many people to target with any accuracy and we can't talk to them anyway with our links all fucked up . . . no chance. We just have to keep working."*

"Damn Dali."

*"No kiddin'. We're taking steps in that direction right now."*

"Steps?" Sandy's hands dropped from her face.

*"Solid steps, you understand?"*

"That sounds like fun. If I weren't more occupied elsewhere, I'd volunteer my services."

*"Be patient, Sandy, you'll hear from him. Take care."*

Nothing then but the echoes of cars moving a number of levels above, distant tires on rampways. And silent again.

Steps, Vanessa said. Solid steps. Her trigger fingers itched. If she weren't so concerned for Mahud she'd be over to the Parliament Building *so* fast . . .

# CHAPTER 17

"*S*andy, I'm in Rawalpindi." Sandy's eyes shot open,
jerking fully upright against the wall. Mahud's
sending voice sounded hard and tense. Preoccupied. "*There's
a building here, I don't know which one, it's on Vento Street, it's an
office district. We've parked nearby, we're in two groups, I'm headed
for the top floor, I'll know more when I get there.*"

"*You're out of the van?*" Sandy sent internally, reflex preventing her from voicing her alarm to the open, silent
parking lot. Did a fast race down an adjoining city-link
. . . found Rawalpindi, broadscanned . . . shit, it was
thirty kilometres north and she was leaping onto her bike,
ramming on the helmet, and activating the engine . . .

"*I'm out, we're moving, the van had some kind of countermeasures locked in over the network, it can't track this transmission once I'm outside . . .*" The engine throbbed into life, a
deep-throated, whining growl, display screens flashed to
life. Sandy turned the throttle and accelerated swiftly
across the open ferrocrete, headed for the exit.

"I'll be there as soon as I can," she said, hitting the ramp hard and flying upward, "I'm thirty klicks away—that could be fifteen minutes on these roads . . ."

"*Sandy, I don't think you're going to get here in time, this is a big hit. We've got goddamn floorsweepers here. It's gotta be a civvie target—there's nothing else here. I think it's biotech* . . ." Harsh shriek of tires around the bend, up the next ramp with a vicious thrust of speed, then a hard, wheelspinning U-turn and up the next . . .

"Mahud, when they give you your target, just do it, okay? Don't question it, just do it . . ." She could hardly believe her own ears as she spoke, but her heart was pounding, her mind deadly calm and vision shifting at impossible intensity as the bike roared through slide after slide, climbing levels . . . there was traffic here now, and startled pedestrians, and a near miss past a car-side . . .

"*Kill civvies?*" Utterly disbelieving. "*You want me to kill civilians?*" Somewhere through the knife-edge calm, terror stabbed. A sharp jab of unreasoning, terrifying panic.

"What the fuck else can you do?!" she snarled, a furious explosion as she ripped through a narrow space between car and rampside, spun the rear about to unseen evasions by terrified pedestrians . . .

"*Sandy* . . ." A pause, as if struggling to think of something to say . . .

"Hold on," she told him, leaping off the final ramp and accelerating along the ground floor, snarled with traffic, hurtling up through the narrow gap between cars, locked brakes when some pedestrians didn't move and *clipped* one, hard, as she accelerated past. And through the exit scanners, Central Control halting traffic once more to find space for this mad motorcyclist who was somehow riding outside the speed buffers with a death wish on her mind . . . she howled onto the road, dodging traffic once more at frustratingly low speeds, and searched through her links . . .

No Vanessa. No Ibrahim. There were other, general connections, doubtless she could get some board operator on Eagle One, but she wanted that direct connection, not trusting any others, not trusting the people who would answer . . . solid action, Vanessa had said. A brief jump onto a mainstream news network and scanned through a flashing succession of realtime pictures—trouble at the Parliament once more, security activity, seeming chaos, flyers hovering out of lanes, and unauthorised activity progressing, communications blocked on all sides . . . Guderjaal. Guderjaal had ruled, and Dali's power-grab had been found out of order. Solid action indeed.

She should have been happy. Now, she only thought of all the resources tied up at the Parliament right now, and no one could possibly get to Mahud in time, no one loyal anyway. . . . She left an emergency parcel on Vanessa's frequency, and on Ibrahim's, streaked through more lights, then decelerated for the next turnoff and took it fast, and up the ramp toward the northern freeway, speed rising once more. Clicked back to Mahud.

"Mahud, there's trouble at the Parliament, I . . ."

"*I know, we're moving fast. They think Dali's not going to last another half hour—they want to be gone by then.*"

"No one's going to get to you, Mahud." Her eyes sensed flashing light from behind as she screamed across to the freeway right lane, where traffic was sparsest and speeds faster . . . "I don't think I can get there myself, just don't do anything, all right?"

"*Okay Sandy.*" Flat and sombre.

"You promise?" Fear made its way into her voice, past her control. The flashing blue lights were close behind, matching her at 350 kph, hurtling along the empty right lane as traffic ahead shifted leftwards to avoid them.

"*I promise. Don't crash, huh?*" And gone, with that last, gentle quip. Leaning low over her bike in the roaring velocity, Sandy's throat was tight. Her right fist shook with effort to restrain another savage twist—it would go no further, and if she twisted any harder it would surely break. The lights behind were closer, and over the howl of wind and engine Sandy could hear sirens.

She reached into her jacket, and twisted slightly sideways in the saddle. Pulled her pistol, grasping the left handgrip, and straight-armed the pistol out behind her at 340 kph . . . emptied half the pistol magazine into the chasing police car's hood, reholstered the pistol, and recovered her briefly diminished speed in an instant, bending low to keep entirely out of the slipstream.

Behind her, two stunned police officers sat in their coasting vehicle, watching as the Prabati's taillight grew rapidly smaller in the distance, and wondering how it was possible that their cruiser's CPU was telling them that only the main drive feed was damaged.

She roared away from the freeway at mind-numbing speed, hurtling through the narrow gaps between traffic-filled lanes. Calling Mahud on continuous recycle but getting no response . . . had been getting no response for the last five minutes. Preparations would be beginning, his full concentration required. Terrified beyond words as the cars flashed by and pedestrians jumped back in shock, taking the next corner and accelerating again, a traffic snarl to one side and she switched lanes fast, a hard lean past a protruding taillight as Vento Street approached up ahead, beyond the next set of lights, and she twisted the throttle once more . . .

Central finally misdiagnosed her intentions, not expecting that acceleration approaching the lights, and the car that would have gone past ahead was suddenly right in line . . . brakes locked in a squeal of white smoke, and Sandy's own brakes followed as she spotted the inter-secting trajectories too late, saw the impact coming and leapt clear.

The Prabati W–9 hit the rear left wheel of the passenger car at a shade over 200 kph and disintegrated, the car hammered wildly about as the Prabati's rider flew a full forty metres down the road through the air, arms out, then shoulder rolling as she hit, sliding and tumbling on firmly braced limbs, over and over until she tucked into a tight ball and slammed into the back of a stationary car.

Sandy was up before her head had totally cleared, undoing the helmet and throwing it away as she ran, past staring pedestrians and shouted exclamations, people running the other way, toward the carnage at the intersection. Loose cloth flapped about knees and elbows, ripped clear in the slide. Sprinting fast along the roadway and then onto the sidewalk, flying past yet more pedestrians at inhuman velocity, yet agonisingly, horribly slow. Her right shoulder grated, damaged in that final impact with the car at the end of her slide. Her right hip was neither perfect, and the combination affected her run.

She turned hard onto Vento Street and saw another chaotic gathering of frightened, jabbering people about the base of a building. Flew that way, carved straight through the crowd, up the steps and into the ground floor, where several frightened people shouted at her to stop, that there was shooting upstairs, then she hit the stairwell door and was going up entire flights in single leaps. Somewhere up the stairs, her hand yanked the pistol from its shoulder holster, and took off the safety.

Out then, onto the top floor. Devastation. Through the smoke-thick air, there were desks and chairs strewn and wrecked, office spaces destroyed, partitions, some still burning, riddled with bullets. . . . Sandy's eyes took in the details without effort, analysing the pattern, the grenade blast-type, the calibre of weaponry. She strode, pistol ready and scanning, across the office space. There were bodies. Some dead from range, some executed with a point-blank shot to the head. She counted six. There would be others. Corridors and doors led to labs and filing rooms, storage and research . . . but the stairs to the roof were there, and it was the only path that could possibly matter—she leapt up them in a flash.

More bodies on the rooftop. The shatter-proof glass shattered, twisted frames of doors. She pushed them aside, past the lifeless legs of an FIA man . . . she counted two more who must be FIA, weapons in hand. Several civilians beyond that, hacked by fire as they'd tried to escape. And in the open space by the parking lot, beneath the leading edge of the aircar awning . . .

She sprinted. Slid in beside Mahud, pistol discarded, grabbing him by the jacket and . . . and . . . oh God, he was covered in blood, GI plasma, holes in his jacket, lying on his back and unmoving. Reached frantically into her jacket for her interface lead, reached back and jacked herself in, then behind Mahud's head, feeling for the insert . . . found it, click and merge, barriers weak and the codes . . .

The eyes blinked open. Weakly, and her heart missed a beat.

"Oh thank fucking Christ!" she gasped, and was in tears. Just kneeling there beside him, linked direct, holding him, but scared to touch more. He looked at her, recognition faintly dawning . . . and the lips moved in a slight smile.

"Sandy," he whispered, with evident pleasure. His hand raised feebly toward her and she grasped it tightly. "Sandy."

"Mahud, don't move, there's help on the way, you're going to be all right, Mahud, we're going to fix you up just fine. You hear me?" With panicked desperation, bending over him, hand clasped with her left while her right brushed at his forehead. "You just hang on. You're going to be fine."

"No." A single word. He looked up at her and his brown eyes were smiling. Distantly. There was blood across the side of his jaw, bullet strike. Sandy's mouth opened, but nothing came out.

"T–5, Sandy," he whispered. "Nothing you can do." T–5. Chemical nerve suppressant. A GI killer. Degenerative and irreversible, fired from close range, execution style. Sandy just stared at him. Utterly stricken. His smile grew a little broader. "I got four of those bastards. There's . . . another one behind the car . . . over there."

"Mahud . . ." She was crying. "Why?" she managed to whisper, strangled past the agony of tears. "Why . . . God, why didn't you just do what they said . . . you didn't need to do this!"

He managed a weak, slow nod.

"Did." He let go of her hand. Reached up, and brushed the tears gently from her cheek. His brown eyes were sad, beyond the smile. "Can't live here, Sandy. Too strange. Don't belong here. Can't live here, can't live there."

"But you said . . ." Her voice broke, strangled and sobbing, ". . . you said you would . . . that you'd . . . *Why?*" Pleading. "Oh God, why didn't you just *say?*"

Mahud smiled up at her, a sleepy, sad-eyed smile.

"Love you, Sandy," he whispered in reply. Like it was all the reason in the world. The only reason that had ever mattered. The only reason that ever would. Sandy broke down and wept.

"I love you, too," she managed to whisper, leaning down close, her tears wetting his face as they fell. Like raindrops, soft and gentle. She held him close, sobbing her life away as Mahud slowly died in her arms. About them, the towers loomed tall and gleaming in the cool night sky.

A howling scream of thruster engines and the last flyer departed, a mad flapping of rooftop awnings and decorative hedges. Across the rooftop, green canvas flapped, exposing a sprawled limb beneath, a patch of ground dark with dried blood. Forensics, 3D modellers, and trace-scan technicians roamed the rooftop battleground, examining bodies, shell casings, bullet holes, piecing the scene together. Direct-linked to CSA headquarters, where complicated graphical programs attempted to reassemble the action realtime. With every piece of data, the picture grew clearer, the events slowly pieced together.

Vanessa Rice walked in on the scene from the stairwell, through the shattered doors that had been propped aside, stepping over the bodies. Beyond the grim rooftop activity, and the flash-and-strobe of blue phase-scan, she could hear the sound of sirens and street-level activity from below. Lights flashing off the windows of the building opposite. She spotted the scene commander nearby in conversation with a forensics man and walked that way.

Captain Khurana saw her coming, a small, armoured figure with a weary stride, moving through the ordered commotion, heavy rifle slung over one small shoulder. The forensics man went back to his work, but not without a lingering, respectful glance at the approaching lieutenant. Khurana stroked his impressive, black moustache and drew himself fully upright, thumbs through his belt. Vanessa stopped before him. Looked up at him blandly . . . not even shoulder height on the strapping chief investigator. Dark, sombre eyes considered him from beneath bedraggled, helmet-flattened hair.

"It's not pretty up here, is it?" Khurana said, Indian accent lilting. Looking about at the bodybags and canvas covers.

"Worse down there," Vanessa replied, with a faint indication back toward the stairwell. Looked about, following Khurana's gaze. "Has Kresnov been here?"

"Yes. Her Prabati W–9 is several blocks over there," pointing away past the near buildings. "She finally messed up an intersection, went into the side of a passenger car at about 200. Flew through the air for fifty metres, slid for another fifty, then hit the rear of another car waiting at the next intersection still going at about 100. Got straight up and kept running. Eyewitness reports said she was doing about sixty down the road on foot. She was in a mighty hurry, it looks like. Lucky no one else was hurt."

"Are the people in the car okay?" Vanessa asked, still gazing off across the rooftop.

"Yes, she hit the rear wheel. The impact nearly took the back off the car, though. Those Prabatis are big bikes—you hit something at 200, it gets damaged. If she'd hit the door side, it would have been nasty. But," he added on reflection, "I'm informed that Central Control did excellently well, and it's unlikely that both it and she would have miscalculated by so much. A pity we could not get her to interface directly like the emergency crews do, then there would have been no problem. Damn Dali. How is Dali, anyway?"

Vanessa sighed. Thinking that Khurana liked the sound of his own voice just a bit too much. Broad-shouldered and snappily dressed, he looked like a moonlighting Indian movie star. The moustache looked suspiciously well groomed.

"He's in one piece," she replied wearily, "more's the pity. We had a job talking him and his security down, though. They didn't want to take Guderjaal's word, wanted everything filed in triplicate and stamped. The President helped."

"Yes," said Khurana with heavy irony, "she would, wouldn't she?" Vanessa shrugged. "Where is Dali now?"

"Locked up, I hope." Her eyes fell on a nearby cluster of people, kneeling and scanning, exchanging intent conversation, over the body at their feet. She could guess who that was. "Maybe we could just give him to Sandy for a few minutes," she murmured.

"Sandy?"

"Kresnov. Sandy short for Cassandra." Khurana frowned, following Rice's gaze. And realised.

"Hmm." He stroked his glossy moustache, eyes gone darkly sombre. "I'm sure that would violate a few interplanetary conventions, but I find the notion strangely appealing. I'd only worry for the person who has to clean up the mess after she's finished."

Vanessa nodded absently. Liking Khurana more for that.

"Have you heard from her?" Khurana asked. "Sandy?" Vanessa shook her head.

"Not a word. How long ago was she here?"

"I could not say precisely." Khurana stroked his moustache, frowning to himself as he considered. "Judging from the GI's time of death, I would suggest somewhere between thirty-five and fifty minutes. Forensics think she was here when he died. There was a lot of activity around then, according to eyewitnesses from downstairs." He paused. "And tears on his face, same time-date."

Vanessa turned and stared up at him. Cold emptiness in the pit of her stomach. And a growing lump in her throat. Khurana gazed back at her, grimly curious. Vanessa exhaled, a hiss between clenched teeth.

"Shit," she murmured, and looked back toward the cluster of forensics. For a moment there was no sound but the rooftop activity and the wail of sirens and crowd noise drifting up from street level.

"Friend of yours?" Khurana asked.

"Yeah." Softly. "Isn't that the damnedest thing, I only met her a few days ago. Who'd have thought that?" Khurana looked at her for a long moment. Probably wondering what kind of a person could possibly count a GI as a friend. Vanessa didn't care what he thought. Khurana unhooked his thumbs from his belt.

"Come over here," he said, and walked off toward the cluster of people around the dead GI. Vanessa followed, stepping carefully to avoid treading on anything important. Forensics made a space for him and Vanessa moved up to his side.

The body at their feet was that of a young man. Brown-skinned, of Arabic appearance. Handsome, Vanessa realised, gazing at his face. Peaceful, but for the torn scar of a bullet wound across his jaw. He lay as if at a wake, long and straight, hands folded upon his breast. Sandy's friend. She stood for a long moment at Khurana's side, gazing down at the handsome young man before her. The ache in her throat grew worse and her eyes prickled.

"See here," Khurana said with grim purpose, pointing back toward the nearest aircar in the rooftop parking space, riddled with holes. "He fell over there, covered behind the Ford. We've pieced together that much—that was the second time he was hit. First he killed his three FIA companions—the woman over there and the two men over by the doors," pointing across at the stairwell. About them, several of the forensics had paused in their examinations to listen.

"Our best information is that he refused the assault order. They hit him first, that much is clear. But they failed to kill with the first shots and it cost them their lives . . . hardly surprising, considering what he is. He then took cover behind the Ford and waited for the civilians escaping from below to come up the stairs.

"We have four dead biotech employees—the two there," pointing at the two shapeless, canvas-covered forms between them and the stairwell, "and two over there, behind the cars," turning about and pointing behind, past the parking space overlooking Vento Street. "Those two were last. These two," turning back around, "were killed first, shot from behind."

"It appears that Kresnov's friend here covered the first two civilians to come up the stairs and told them to take cover behind the cars. The second two were caught halfway when the first FIA . . . or our first murderer, I should say . . ." Here his assured, analytical tone turned particularly cold. ". . . reached the top of the stairs and shot them in the back. He was in turn killed by this young man." Indicating the GI. "Thus the third dead FIA man by the stairwell.

"Then there was a firefight, during which this brave young fellow was further wounded, evidently his wounds to this point were troubling him gravely, or else the entire FIA team may well be dead, and he still alive. A pity." He stroked his moustache, looking down at the body. "The FIA then executed the two civilians he had been trying to protect, at point-blank range, and made sure of the GI with a chemical pellet containing something called Terrascovine, or more commonly T–5. Specially formulated chemical to disrupt GI nerve function. Like nerve gas for GIs, since they're largely immune to the chemicals that will kill you or me. Evidently the FIA had anticipated trouble earlier, either from him or from the assault team that struck the President."

A sombre pause. Down on the street another siren, its wail echoing from the surrounding buildings. A clatter of equipment from across the rooftop—a new scanner being set into position.

"The end result of which," Khurana concluded, "is that we are four down on the twenty-four fuckers we are looking for. 'Fucker,'" he added with a mild glance at Vanessa, "being the present investigative jargon for FIA. That leaves us with twenty fuckers still to find and hopefully kill. This young man did a very good, very brave thing. I intend to see to it that he is treated with the respect and dignity he has earned. Did he have any religious inclinations, do you know?"

Vanessa shook her head.

"No," she said tiredly, rubbing her eyes with a gloved hand. "I don't know, but I doubt it. We'll leave all that stuff to Kresnov when we find her. Just don't let any government pricks start poking about for research. She wouldn't take that very well."

"I can imagine," Khurana said soberly. He put a hand on Vanessa's armoured shoulder. "Are you all right? You've been on activation a long time, Lieutenant. Perhaps you should take a rest."

They knew about the Berndt incident, Vanessa realised. Word had been spreading. And now the standoff with Dali, tensions at the Parliament . . . weapons ready and not knowing if Guderjaal's order would be resisted with force . . . God, what an insane situation. Civil war indeed. In the end, she suspected, it had only been the realisation that he would surely lose any confrontation that had forced Dali's hand. He had simply lacked the support among the men and women who carried the guns. So much technology, so much progress, and still it came down to guns. She rubbed her eyes for a while longer, as if to remove the memory of recent days from her brain. Khurana, she realised, was still waiting for a reply.

"No," she sighed, "I'm okay. I can sleep later. It looks like this won't last very much longer, one way or another." The observation met with grim silence on all sides. She lowered her hand, looking blankly ahead, past the gathered forensic experts. All were looking at her, awaiting her words. Even then, she couldn't help but feel some amazement. Being a hero wasn't something she'd ever given much consideration to. She wasn't sure she liked it.

"We have to find Kresnov again," she said to no one in particular. "I don't think she's going to be real happy right now." And immediately felt disgusted at herself for such a glib remark. She knew with a dark certainty what her new friend's present state of mind would be . . . and it was painful to think about. And frightening. Please God, they had to find her, and soon. Before anything irreversibly horrible happened.

"She made direct interface with the GI before he died," said a nearby forensics man. "We found traces. It's possible that she managed to copy some of his codes . . . how good is her interface function?"

Vanessa blinked. "Full neural integration, no messy fiddling between organic and synthetic brain function . . . how good do you *think* she'd be?" There were some incredulous murmurs from the surrounding technicians. It evidently meant something to them.

"Well then," he continued, taking a deep breath, "I think it's possible that she's copied some of this GI's codes. Maybe even enough to get traces of that damn encryption they're using to move around. Maybe enough to track them. If she's as good as you say."

"She is." Vanessa thought about it, arms folded and chin in hand, a gloved finger tapping absently at her jaw. "If she's got any leads, though, she hasn't told us yet."

"Considering what the fuckers did to her friend," Khurana said mildly, "and considering what she is capable of doing to them . . . would you tell anyone?"

"One of the FIA's rifles is missing," a woman added, and paused as Khurana gave her a hard look. "One of the fuckers' rifles, I mean." Khurana looked appeased. "Magazines, too."

"Shit," Vanessa muttered. It looked like trouble. Big trouble. But . . . maybe a solution, too. It was a dark, nasty thought. But a logically sensible one also.

"Good work," Khurana advised his people, "I'll pass it on." And paused as he turned to go, looking at Vanessa. "Do you know this man's name?" Vanessa looked at him. And looked down again at the GI. At the young, handsome face. At the eyes that should have been open, the mouth that should have been smiling. . . . And for a brief, frightening moment, she thought she could feel the faintest ghost of his Captain's grief.

"Mahud," she said quietly. "His name's Mahud."

Khurana spared Mahud one last, lingering glance. Murmured something in Arabic quietly and departed. Vanessa stood where she was, as the forensic team moved off about their various tasks. Arms folded about her small, armoured self, as if to ward off the gathering cold.

*May your light shine with glory in Paradise, Mahud.*

With a reflex unfelt since seventh grade, Vanessa crossed herself with one gloved hand. An unfitting symbol to go with an Islamic thought, perhaps, she considered as she refolded her arms and shivered. But fitting, perhaps, that he whom faith had deserted in life should be embraced by all faiths in death. Upon the young man's cheek, Vanessa felt she could detect the slightest trace of moisture.

Sandy, she thought desperately. Where are you?


Katia Neiland wearily walked the familiar route down the Parliament's central corridor. Armed security were everywhere. Local Parliament guards stood by the ornate major doorways that led to Congress House, weapons at port arms. SWAT personnel strode with brisk purpose across the further end. Harried interns scurried in all directions, rapid footsteps up the huge marble stairs at the far end. And in front and behind her walked four members of Alpha Team in pairs, dark-suited, com-wired, and terminally, professionally suspicious. The usually immaculate red carpet that ran the length of the enormous floor was scuffed beneath the traffic of heavy-duty boots. The huge, ostentatiously ornate hallway echoed with urgent activity.

Katia wanted a bath. Followed by a long rest in her favourite chair back at the Quarters, a relaxing raga on the stereo, and a glass of something strong. Judging from the present circumstances, however, she guessed it would be a while before these wishes could be fulfilled.

An intern gave her a wary, concerned look as he passed. Katia straightened her jacket self-consciously and brushed at her hair with a tired hand. In difficult circumstances the President more than ever needed to appear in control. She flexed shoulders that were aching from too much nervous sitting on the edge of a chair, hunched over a control screen back at the Presidential Quarters while Guderjaal and Ibrahim had attempted negotiation with Dali and aides and SWAT flyers circled the Parliament once more, explicit threat in a situation whose manoeuvres had long since ceased to be subtle.

It had not been easy. There had been communications problems at conveniently inconvenient moments. Threats from Dali to make media announcements regarding the Neiland administration's involvement with a dangerous and unstable League GI who was presently on an uncontrolled, government-approved, vendetta-style rampage through the city. Of illegal and improper contact between President and Adjudicator. Of criminal conduct and abuse of power by the Director of the CSA. Of threats, information theft, grandstanding, and general grave misconduct from the Neiland administration. Of a widespread conspiracy among senior Tanushan parties to undermine the constitution and the rule of law.

In the end, Neiland thought wearily as she matched her stride to the Alpha Team agents in front of her, he had only refrained from acting on those threats because of the realisation that, in the long run, no one really cared. To be sure, there were those in the Progress Party who were only too keen to make political mileage from the already prevalent perception of an arrogant, dictatorial President . . . but out among the general public, such political machinations counted for little.

Dali was a Federal representative. Every citizen in Tanusha understood the pact through which the Federal Governor's presence was tolerated. Callay was one world of the Federate Alliance of Worlds. Membership had considerable benefits. The majority of people on all member worlds believed in the importance of some form of central governing body, overseeing the affairs of all humanity and making sure that the species did not split itself off into separate, alienated groups, who would over a period of centuries become unrecognisable to each other. Dali's presence was the sacrifice that the people of Callay made of their own sovereign independence for the greater good of interstellar human civilisation.

But Dali had broken that trust, and while constitutional law may have been on his side, the vast majority of the Callayan population were not. Membership of the greater human diaspora sounded nice and cosmopolitan to the average citizen, but no one ever expected that Dali would actually *do* anything. He was just supposed to sit there, and placate their good-natured idealism by his presence alone. Taking over the government wasn't what they'd had in mind. Running it under the guidance of shady, FIA-connected advisors certainly wasn't. When they'd used the release of that information as a counterthreat to Dali's own, the end had been neigh. To that point even senior Progress Party members had been distancing themselves from the more rabidly opportunistic of their number.

A good thing, she thought as her entourage accompanied her up the huge central stairway, that there had been no shooting. The Governor had brought his own security with him from Earth, and there had been little doubt of their willingness to use force if ordered. And then there was the assigned wing of Parliamentary Security required by law to guard the acting Head of State, and a certain boot-licking captain who had not switched sides until the game had already played out . . .

It made Katia fume even now. God knew how these people attained their positions. Some in every organisation, Ibrahim had told her, matter-of-fact as ever. Katia could only marvel at his restraint—that damn woman had risked a firefight between people who were supposed to be on the same side simply because she was too chickenshit to deviate so much as a punctuation mark from the damn manual, *and* hadn't wanted stain on her record. Katia strode down the corridor toward the Presidential Office, wondering darkly if there were any legal way for the President to intervene in a certain security officer's performance review . . .

Then she caught sight of the tangle of milling, arguing people in the euphemistically named Garden Room—the waiting room outside her office, for anyone needing to see her on short notice. And nearly stopped in her tracks. Twelve, she counted, her poor secretary trapped behind his desk in the corner, trying to answer calls and sort through a teetering stack of papers while the dozen intruders milled about, arguing loudly. . . . Oh no, Kishen Chandresakar was there, haranguing her Finance and Internal Affairs ministers, and Mahudmita Rafasan hovering on the periphery. All faces turned her way as she entered, escorts dispersing about this safe territory—just when I most need them, Katia thought desperately—and all voices raised in a single, urgent entreaty . . .

"Just bloody wait," she shouted at them, striding through their midst, hands raised in defence. "I've got an ongoing security crisis. Everyone's just going to have to wait another five minutes. Where's Ibrahim?" reaching the doors and looking sharply around.

"He let himself in," called Sarpov, her secretary, from the rear of the crowd.

"Did he now," Katia muttered, opening the door . . .

"Ms. President," interrupted Chandresakar, "I really must speak with you immediately with regards to the . . ."

"There are fifteen dead people at Rawalpindi," Katia cut him off brutally, "gunned down by FIA. We might have more before the night is over. You've got something that tops that?" Staring hard at the Progress Party leader.

Chandresakar glared. "I'll wait," he snapped shortly.

"Maisie," Katia said loudly as she walked through the door, "in here, now." Left the door open for Rafasan to scamper through, closing it behind her.

Ibrahim was waiting by the windows behind her desk, gazing out at the city lights beyond dark shadows of Parliament gardens. One-way armoured glass, Katia recalled soberly, moving directly to her comfortable leather chair. She was in the habit of remembering such details, lately. Sat down with a heavy sigh and leaned right back, closing her eyes. Comfortable, for a brief moment.

Looked up and saw Rafasan waiting, chewing a fingernail and looking anxious as usual. Her normally immaculate sari appeared slightly rumpled, some hair loose about her fringe.

"For God's sake, Maisie," Katia said tiredly, "have a seat and relax. All these bloody people determined to kill themselves worrying. Get yourself a drink if you want one . . . something for you, Shan?"

"Um . . . he doesn't drink, remember?" Rafasan said hesitantly. Walked to the drinks cabinet. Katia had to smile.

"Forgot we had a genuine practising Sunni Muslim in our midst," she sighed. "So many Indonesians and regressive Indians in this place . . . scotch and soda for me, thanks Maisie."

"Well this regressive Indian gratefully accepts your offer," Rafasan said, unstopping a bottle and pouring into ornate glasses. "My nerves are shot to pieces, if I ever see another gun in my life, it shall be far, far too soon."

Rafasan, Katia remembered, had been here at Parliament all along —as legal advisor, she had various consultative functions with branches of the public service, representing the Administration's position on this or that legal matter. She had been here, albeit in another wing, when the flyers had come circling overhead and Guderjaal's decision had been announced. Near enough to hear the shooting certainly, if the worst had happened. Katia sympathised. Firefights, she knew from experience, were no fun at all.

Jesus. How had they got into this situation? Just public servants, all of them. It was a career. This, or medicine, tech-science or law . . . or in Mahudmita's case, both. But no lawyer's résumé ever stated "risked life in hail of bullets." Yet here they were. Public servants with armed protection, directly targeted for selective political violence. The universe, Katia concluded, had gone mad.

"Must have been touchy here for a while," she said to Rafasan.

"Touchy!" Rafasan's voice was unsteady. "That is to put it very mildly . . . I was just terrified. I think I made at least twenty basic grammatical mistakes in my briefing to the Revenue Department . . ."

Katia laughed. Rafasan glanced at her, surprised and pleased at the response. Went back to pouring drinks.

"Of course, it's nothing compared to what you went through . . . Shan, would you like a juice or mineral water?"

"A soda, thank you." From behind Katia's chair, facing away, gazing out of the window.

"Decadent," Katia commented.

"A creeping darkness of the soul," Ibrahim agreed mildly. Walked slowly around the desk as Rafasan brought the drinks over. Katia watched him surreptitiously.

"Thanks, Maisie," she said, reaching for her own drink. And saw Ibrahim rest a brief, absent hand on Rafasan's shoulder as he took his drink then retreated to a chair. Typical of the man, Katia thought. A gentle man, in many ways. A man of simple, forthright concerns. And yet, somewhere in the translation of principle to action, cold, hard purpose set in. The necessity for ruthless action.

The curse of all power, Neiland pondered darkly, sipping her drink. No good could be done without also causing harm. To do good required firm resolve. And firm resolve, inevitably, got people hurt. And she wondered, not for the first time, at the wisdom in her choice of career.

"So what's the latest?" she asked Ibrahim as he settled into the available chair. Ibrahim sipped absently at his drink. His attention seemed elsewhere.

"Well," he said after a slight pause, "Chenkov Biomedical Designs have made some interesting transactions we've dug up on external records. It seems fairly obvious that they were in it up to their ears. There's nothing left of their own records, of course, but we suspect they were a major distributor on the underground network. Evidently they knew something important, or were vulnerable to disclosure for some reason . . . possibly we'll never know. There's not very much left." A brief, silent pause. "But I suppose that hardly matters now."

"And the FIA?"

"We're following all available leads." Wearily. "We've been detaining, questioning, and even arresting a steady stream of people since the Tetsu raid, and some of them are unquestionably involved, but there's just no legal means of obtaining the information from them within the time required, and they're determined not to talk. . . . I think more than a few are afraid for their lives. Which means we have to do everything ourselves from scratch. We've got plenty of leads, and over the time of a normal investigation I would be very confident, but now, working to this deadline . . ." He shook his head. "If I had another five thousand people we might have a chance, but I doubt the expenditures committee would go for it." There was an edge to the sarcasm that Neiland could not remember hearing before from Ibrahim, at any time.

"More difficult than you thought, huh?" Katia asked him solemnly. Ibrahim's eyes locked on hers, a darkly penetrating gaze.

"You have no idea." Sounding nearly exasperated. Which was also a first. "This city . . . there are layers upon layers upon layers. A million different means to conceal your presence or actions, and a million more places to hide. We have become so reliant upon information networks, and so unquestioningly faithful that open information flows are the panacea that guarantees all rights and all goodness in a modern, pluralistic society . . ." He shook his head. Took a deep breath.

"Large-scale institutions created the networks. If you have money and expertise and technology, you can manipulate information as easily as Old Earth societies ever censored the paper press or TV broadcasts. Far more easily, when there are places on the networks where independent monitoring is not allowed. Further regulations could help, but even then . . . there are difficulties. And it's too late for any new regulations to stop the FIA now."

"You never thought you would be advocating Big Brother, did you?" Rafasan inquired wryly.

"No." Ibrahim sipped at his drink. "Never. I wrote papers about it, back in my student days. About the ultimate futility of information controls in an infotech society. I thought then that such controls were a waste of effort and money because they could never succeed. But now . . . I wonder."

"There has always been a strong anarchic streak through the media lobbies in this city," Rafasan added, fingering an elaborate earring. "And through the academic institutions that support their arguments. The panacea of information, the notion that all information is good— it's yet another form of academically inspired ideological utopianism that's just typical of this city. They think information is like water in a desert—you can never have too much. We need a system of account-ability here . . . perhaps my bias toward the libel system reflects my legalistic roots too strongly, but we clearly need to give thought to some kind of control mechanism. It's the broader philosophy that con-cerns me, and we all know the limitations of centrally imposed con-trols, we need a system of personal responsibility enforceable by law . . . oh! I'm sorry, I'm rambling. Too much coffee and adrenalin and my brain thinks it's in court arguing a case . . ." She sipped again at her drink, looking anxious once more.

Katia smiled. "You want to commission a report?" she asked. "We could put together a community study group. You'd chair it, table a recommendation for Parliament to debate." Rafasan blinked. And blinked again.

Then, "Really?"

"Really. That line between censorship and governance is supposed to be invisible, but somehow it keeps tripping people up. This whole mess just shows how much of a rethink we need. I can get you funding by next sitting. Say a week."

Worship shone in Rafasan's eyes. Several months of mind-numbing legalistic debate, semantic hair-splitting, and the concept-redefining techno-legalese—lawyer heaven. Rafasan looked positively emotional with gratitude.

"Oh my." Halfway between bewilderment and excitement. "I've wanted to do something like that since law school. How will I ever . . . ? Oh, perhaps . . ." The eyes became distant as the mind raced on ahead. Her drink hung from absent fingers, temporarily forgotten. Katia looked at Ibrahim. He raised an eyebrow at her, the ghost of a smile upon his lips.

"Living proof," he said, "that the distance between heaven and hell is merely a matter of perspective." Rafasan ignored the jibe, lost in mental calculations. Katia sighed and took a large mouthful from her glass. Swallowed hard.

"So, Shan. What are our chances of catching them?"

"The CSA's chances?" He shrugged, all traces of humour vanished. "Almost none. For the reasons we've been speaking of. They've just vanished. And our best inside contact is now dead."

"No word from Kresnov?" Ibrahim shook his head grimly.

"No. It could be good news. She made direct interface with her friend before he died. His interface possessed certain codes for use in this operation. Theoretically they're not transferable, but considering how well Kresnov knew him over their years together, it is certainly possible that she now has possession of certain leads that we are not privy to."

Neiland considered that for a moment.

"And she hasn't told us." Pointedly. Ibrahim gave a single nod, acknowledging that line of thought. Darkly. For a moment, Katia did not know what to think. "Well, I suppose that would solve a problem for us. Should it eventuate."

"I would like to question someone," said Ibrahim.

"Why should they tell you any more than the bunch we're holding right now have? They're Federal agents, Shan. Their cases all fall under

Federal jurisdiction. As soon as that damn committee gets here, they're gone. No matter what they've done."

The tension about Ibrahim's mouth and brow spoke of certain very dark thoughts passing through the Director's mind. Katia knew exactly how he felt.

"I have a question." It was Rafasan, emerging from her dream-world. She sounded uncharacteristically subdued. Katia nodded.

"Go ahead."

Rafasan took a breath. "If Kresnov does find them . . . and something happens . . ." a long pause. "Do we still need her? Technically speaking?" Katia stared hard at Rafasan. Her legal advisor looked almost ashamed of the question. Katia opened her mouth to retort . . . and shut it. God help her, with Dali gone, and herself back in charge, and the FIA out of the picture one way or another . . . Kresnov's presence would be a huge problem. Knowledge of her existence would assuredly get out. There were too many people who knew already. Questions asked. Interviews requested. Parliament shouting matches, pointed fingers . . . God, political mileage fit for Kishen Chandresakar's wettest of wet dreams. A League GI, employed by the CSA, granted protection and even *citizenship* by the grace of the President herself under undemocratic, unconsultative emergency powers. To say nothing of the outcries from various lunatic biotech conservatives and religious nuts who argued that GIs did not have souls and could never be recognised as sentients by the courts, which meant legal challenge, news show interviews, death threats by the hundred . . . God knew where these people got their financial backing, but she knew damn well it existed. Mosque, Church, and Hindu temple united, an unholy alliance. Not to mention certain insultingly wealthy academics who should have known better but didn't, and wrote bestselling books explaining why.

But if Kresnov were to get herself killed, and die a hero . . . God, she nearly hated herself for thinking it, but it would solve a lot of problems. Not the least of which being that, politically speaking,

Kresnov could theoretically expect more support from the right-wing Progress Party than her own Union Party colleagues. And an awful lot of her own party would number themselves among the most seriously dissatisfied. By Christ, it was going to get complicated.

"Let's just get through the next twenty-four hours, shall we?" she replied finally, with a tired sigh. "It's going to be a nightmare few months ahead, whatever happens."

"Who'd we lose?" asked Petr Shimakov, striding into the plush coffee lounge. People lounged in chairs, weapons on laps, or leaned against the walls. The only light came from several small, shaded lamps. City light gleamed silver through the broad windows that counted for the far wall, towers and traffic. Here on the top level, the street was only six storeys below—disturbingly close, to Shimakov's thinking. But it was the place they had, and it would do.

"Schroeder," said Wong, a tired, cracked voice. Shimakov stared at him, a dark figure, slumped against the wall near the windows. Feeling a cold anger brewing. "Ramesh, Togodo, Pham. All confirmed."

"Fuck," Shimakov pronounced with controlled fury. Deathly silence in the room. "Was it the GI?" The dark shadow that was Wong nodded.

"I don't know what happened. But there was shooting on the roof about twenty seconds before zero-signal. We went early, did the deed with no help from the roof, chased some stragglers up the stairs . . . and Togodo got hit. Right through the chest, real accurate. We just started shooting back . . ." He shrugged. "Suppose we had more firepower. Skin was already real shot up. We hit him with a T–5 to be sure, finished off the last marks, and got the hell out. Guess he bugged out on us. Schroeder said we should have whacked him after the big hit."

Shimakov stood silently in the middle of the room for a long time, unmoving. Thinking that something most certainly did not make sense. Thinking that the Skin just hadn't been smart enough to start a rebellion on his own . . . and whatever he thought about GIs, they just didn't do that. They followed orders. Unless they got instructions from elsewhere.

Had they been doublecrossed? Had Dark Star given him different instructions? No damn way, the Skin had been as dangerous as any Skin was likely to get. It'd helped plan a damn good hit on the President's convoy—no way he or any FIA guy could have done the same, unfamiliar with GI capabilities and operating techniques as they were. It wouldn't have waited until such last-minute desperation before pulling a stunt like this—more likely it would have killed them all in their beds, hunted them down, if that had been its instruction. Or jumped out of the moving van and left a grenade behind.

It didn't make sense, that last-minute, foolhardy change of plans. And the Skin being dead did not make him any more comfortable with the situation. Dead or not, he felt edgy.

"I want full guard on this whole damn building," he told them coldly. "If you think you've got it locked tight now, lock it tighter. We're out of here in two hours, people. I've got the cars on the roof, just two more hours and we're headed out of this damn city. Let's not fuck it up now."

Night-tuned eyes watched through the windows as the agents climbed to their weary feet and moved out. Heat silhouettes on the darkened glass, human shaped, multiple shades of red and orange. One figure stood still in the centre of the room. Facing the window, as if seeing the dark, crouched figure who watched him from afar.

Finally, he turned and left the empty room. The eyes zoomed back a touch, scanning the building layout. Small luxury office building. Six storeys, tucked into the pleasant greenery of the Ringold commercial/residential district. Standard fare for Tanusha's multitude of small design and technology firms—specialised, wealthy, and flexibly creative. A different style from the mega-conglomerates that populated the mega-rises. In Tanusha one did not need to be big to be successful.

Feelers raced down nearby links, probed security barriers, hightech and sensitive. Probed the layout, vision scanning through light reflective glass, making out shapes, patterns, supports, and variations. More links found an architectural display site, open for public viewing . . . found the designer name, and the layout in question, and found a near-match. Accounted for custom alterations . . . and began to put together a picture.

More scanning, a fast zoom toward movement through lower windows. Noted the deployment. Noted the pair of large-capacity aircars on the rooftop pads. And began summing the accumulation of security measures, their weak and strong points, probing cautiously, careful not to trigger any alarms.

Then, when the framework had been constructed, the whole assembled in a workable form, a new link opened. Communications. Within seconds it was answered.

Ibrahim recognised the signal immediately, and made a fast switch onto the frequency.

"Cassandra, where are you?" Urgently, as the CSA cruiser in which he was riding began its curving descent toward HQ, a short, four-minute flight from the Parliament. Overflew what looked like an open-air concert ablaze with waving spotlights that strobed the night sky and teeming crowds . . . past midnight now, and still the city raged. For a moment there was no reply, only the distant, rhythmic thump from below beneath the thrumming whine of engines.

Then, *"I can solve your problem."* A soft, empty voice. Ibrahim stared ahead at the looming side of CSA headquarters. Growing larger, as the engines throbbed on a new, descending note and the horizon gently tilted.

"Cassandra," he tried, "where are you? Which problem?"

*"The problem."*

"Cassandra, why don't you just tell me . . ."

*"It's going to happen, authorised or unauthorised. Which do you want?"*

Silence. Ibrahim closed his eyes, attempting calm. Weighing the options. Attempting dispassionate judgment. Uncertain if it was possible. He had been half expecting this call. Half hoping for it. And dreading it all the same. There were no good possibilities, only bad and worse. A balance of horror.

Another man might have questioned his faith and the God who presided over such futility. But Ibrahim knew that it was in such circumstance that Allah's presence could be most keenly felt. If the world were perfect, there would be no need for Paradise. If the world were perfect, there would be no need of Allah himself. Beyond the calming darkness behind his eyelids, Ibrahim thought of the teachings of his parents and grandparents. Of the wisdom of his God. And prayed that he, of humble thought and deed, should make the right decision in this moment of choice.

He thought of Neiland. The wreckage of aircars upon the Parliament wing rooftops. Bodies sprawled, hacked and shattered. Neiland herself nearly killed. Thought of more recent assassinations, of Chenkov Biomedical. Of Kresnov's dead friend. Of Kresnov herself and the horror she had suffered.

He had seen this coming. This decision. Kresnov's actions. If she went without approval, she would be a fugitive. That would hurt Neiland when news of Kresnov hit the media. Having placed trust in a fugitive GI who proved unstable. It was bad politics. As was capturing the FIA infiltrators, only to lose them as soon as the Earth Committee landed, and took them away for Federate justice. There was nothing for Tanusha there. Nothing for Callay. No justice. No satisfaction. No guarantee that it would not happen again. To do what they had done . . . not just these individual FIA, but the FIA in entirety . . . was unspeakable. It violated law, local and Federal. It violated decency. It violated sanity. For them to get away with it, even to live, and see a Federal jail cell for the rest of their days, would solve nothing. It did not punish the masterminds. They were untouchable, either way. But they needed a message. They needed to know what it cost. For everyone.

Morally, technically, and politically, someone needed to pay.

"Do it," he said simply, in a calm, quiet voice.

"*Copy.*" A brief, silent pause. "*Give my love to Vanessa.*"

Silence again as the link went dead. The aircar cruised lower, locked into close-range approach. Ibrahim gazed out at the gleaming blanket of lights and wondered if things had always been this way, in the end. The way of humans. And the way, sadly, of their Gods. For in the battle of good and evil, even Gods were, in the end, victims of circumstance.

# CHAPTER 18

**P**etr Shimakov was bothered. He sat in the dark, surrounded by office equipment and blank display screens, darkly contemplating the nighttime view of the city that had been his reluctant home for the past weeks.

As missions went, this one had not gone smoothly. He had lost people. More people than he, or his mission planners, had anticipated. The CSA were good . . . he'd been warned so repeatedly in the preparatory briefings. But their abilities should have come to nothing if they were unable to trace the encryptions his team utilised to coordinate their activities about Tanusha. And they *had* been unable. Mostly. But still, with guesswork and ingenuity they had tracked centralised FIA activity to Tetsu Consolidated, had been tipped off to Renaldi's hideout at the Vista Hotel, and had somehow found a way to implicate the Governor's Office so as to allow the Supreme Justice to overrule the Governor's assumption of power.

It was an unsettling number of things to have gone

wrong. And now this, the fiasco at Centa Research, where the Command GI had abruptly gone nuts and killed his own people. The Centa vulnerability had been neutralised. Ninety-five percent of the listed, traceable vulnerabilities had been cleaned away. The rest, without their support structures, would fade and wither without notice. Overall, a successful mission. An achievement. But still it troubled him.

The CSA getting close was one thing. The GI going nuts was another. Both of them together was just plain unsettling. He couldn't see a connection. And was frustrated, even now, at the utter lack of intelligence they'd had of the CSA's operations . . . it was impressive security, far more impressive than their contacts had led him to believe. He'd been promised leaks, insights into CSA investigative initiatives, data-trails. Someone, it seemed, had underestimated the strength of the emergency legislation that had come slamming down after the Parliament strike, and the civilian transparency it had removed from the CSA's operations. And, it seemed, underestimated the iron grip that Director Ibrahim held over the entire organisation.

Damn Ibrahim. His fist clenched against his thigh in frustration. The man had ruthless tendencies, for a civilian. He'd kept the CSA entirely isolated from outside influences and possible security leaks, no easy feat in a city like Tanusha. Now there was no clue as to whether the GI's alarming behaviour was somehow connected to CSA operations, or if they'd been infiltrated, or if it had been a League doublecross . . . he just didn't know. He hated not knowing. It was his job to know. Everything.

Calm. He gazed out at the gleaming night and forced himself toward calm. Calm solved everything. Tape-teach, in early operational days, reinforced the fundamental importance of problem solving . . . calm, he thought, and the reflexes kicked in, old and familiar, and not entirely his own. An implanted reflex. One learned to trust them, with experience. One learned the disaster of not trusting them and resolved to do better.

The calm helped him to think. And he saw the situation clearly enough. The mission was safe. He'd done a difficult job exceedingly well, as his training dictated. And he was not upset about the mission out-come. More about the losses. And the casualties inflicted. Images in news reports. Devastation at the Parliament, bodies strewn about. At Centa Research. At the homes of several of the lesser contacts—loose ends and security vulnerabilities—bodies still cooling, yet to be reported missing. Civilians all. League-inclined, to be sure. But civilians nonetheless.

And there was no avoiding it. For what they had gained, and what was at stake . . . those lives lost seemed trivial by contrast, even his own, if that had been necessary. He sought no thanks for his work. The true heroes, he knew, rarely received the recognition they deserved. For the good of humanity, the Federation had to survive. Survival meant neutralising the GI threat. To neutralise it, one had first to understand it. The knowledge they had gained was now secure. The Tanushan operation would be wound up and operations shifted to regions of greater stability . . . all hell would assuredly break loose now in Tanusha, and further operations were no longer tenable in such an environment. But that, too, was part of the plan.

Shimakov exhaled hard, and gazed at the floor. His superiors in the Core had plans for everything. Plans within plans. Democracies were unstable. So, too, civilian societies in general. Tasked with their defence, knowledge, and expertise needed security from such volatility. Guidance. The FIA provided such, safe from troublesome political meddlings. The greater good, so often lost in the pointless bickering of populist, localist politics.

If only, he thought, it needn't cost so much.

Home. He wanted to go home. To comfortable offices in Ventura One Station and the grand view of Earth from his living-room win-dows. To his wife and child, whom he had not seen in months, and had not spoken to of this mission for previous months before. Justine, an A-Level Intel herself, had not questioned. But Cynthia had.

"Why are you going away, Daddy?"

"To make the world a better place, sweetie. A better place for little girls to grow up in. A place where there still *are* little girls, where mechanised monstrosities haven't taken over because a group of people many light-years away decided that real little girls were suddenly obsolete."

Or, at least, he'd wanted to say that. Security wouldn't allow it. But he believed it all the same, and believed it with a passion. His little Cynthia was waiting for him. He'd helped to make her future a brighter one. In just a few hours he was going home to see her again, and neither FIA nor League betrayals nor crazy, murderous GIs were going to stop him. He tapped his headset mike into life.

"Liu. Status." Static crackle—the connection was down. Damn com-gear, it'd been shorting out the last few days . . . but it was necessary. With the CSA making progress with Tetsu encryption, network communication wasn't always safe any more. He switched frequencies. "Perez, Liu's com's down again. Go check it for him."

Nothing. "Perez?" The room was suddenly cold. An endless second seemed to linger into eternity, his mind abruptly racing, hand reaching unthinkingly for his rifle as he rose from the chair. Crazy GIs. Ambushes. Things that would make a GI turn. GI loyalty being lock solid and almost mechanical, he'd been assured so frequently in preparation . . . and he knew, with a sudden, horrifying jolt, that he'd missed something, something right under his nose . . .

"*Alarm Red!*" he yelled into the mike on general freq. "Everyone get the fuck up here *now* . . . !" A burst of gunfire from the floor above, shuddering impacts and the sound of things breaking. Return fire, multiple, abrupt bursts, voices yelling over the intercom as he bashed through the office door and onto the main office floor, multiple layers of glass working partitions across a broad space of desks and work terminals . . . an explosion, and everything rattled.

"Top floor!" Shimakov roared into the pickup, rushing to a firing crouch behind a partition as an explosion shook the floor and rattled partition windows. "Get up here! Situation!"

"Sir," came a panicky voice back over the speakers, "I think it's just one person, it's come in from the roof . . ." indistinct scrabbling, ". . . that grenade might have got him, hang on . . ." Silence for a short, heart-pounding moment. Shimakov knelt, braced his snub-rifle on the work desk, scanning through the maze of partitions, glass sheeting, and office doorways.

"*Fu*—!" Explosion of shots and static, somewhere across the partitions, cutting off the horrified scream before it had even begun. N'dulu fired, approximate targeting, fire ripping through temporary walls . . .

"*Cease fire!*" Shimakov yelled, and N'Dulu paused, eyes wide and trembling. "No firing unless you have a clear target! Wong!"

"Coming across! People, crossfire, stagger your shots, he'll come through this way . . ." Thunder of footsteps across the office space, figures moving fast, weapons ready.

"Who's in the way?!"

"Have we got clear fire?! Where's Andre . . ." Roar of gunfire, partitions disintegrating.

"Movement at C–3, check your grids!" Shimakov braced and tracked, linkups illuminating the spot, flashing colour . . . someone else fired, *spak! spak!* of bullets ripping soft surfaces and things breaking.

"Do you see her?" Shimakov shouted, no need for com-gear now, everyone on line of sight past the partitions and office gear . . . more movement from behind as people arrived from downstairs . . .

"There!" someone shouted, then a hail of fire, entire partition sections disintegrating, splinters and smoke clouding the air . . . grenade explosion, entire desks flew skyward, fire and smoke blinded, and shots from a different angle through the smoke, fast, controlled bursts. Screams of agony and terror, a dark flash of movement that dove at impossible speed through the burning chaos, like a trick of the light . . . a body smacked through partitions in a hail of bloody fire, another cartwheeling in a spray of blood and tissue, limbs flailing.

Shimakov fired at the shadow's vicinity, as gunfire ripped and screamed all about and the orderly nature of things disintegrated like a haystack in a tornado. Teurez was beside him at one moment, firing madly, then collapsing like a bloody rag as an impossible, horrible precision found her from the middle of that killing hell and ripped her open. A body that might have been Wong's spun abruptly backward across a desktop and vanished from sight. N'Dulu thudded backward into a partition, slid bloodily down as something fast and dark, somewhere in that destructive madness, picked them off, one at a time in rapid succession. Someone ran and dove for new cover, another leapt a partition through the smoke and debris, people dodged and fought as best they could, trying desperately to survive the death that advanced upon them. . . . Another flash of movement across the floor, and then another scream, and voices yelling and screaming in total panic amid the ear-shredding racket of gunfire.

Grenades lobbed and the entire neighbouring section of office space exploded, the shockwave crushing everything that was not already smashed and desks and chairs flew through the air like missiles, crashing down like rain. Shimakov raised up . . . and saw, in brain-dazed slow-motion, a dark, human shape that ran through the burning fires, and hurdled the shattered wreckage, and fired with right-armed precision as it came on, one burst and Yelenova died, another burst and Chan punched backward . . . it came on, eyes like fire, killing as it came, hair astrew and dark against a background wall of flame. Like a vision of hell.

Shimakov spun and ran so fast he was past the next partition and flying down the corridor before he even knew he'd gone. Half crashed into Aziz running in from an adjoining corridor, grabbed him, and staggered onward toward the stairwell.

"Get the fuck out of here!" he screamed at Aziz, who saw the wild terror in his eyes and followed. Pelted full speed up the stairs and onto the roof, then sprinting across the pad, Shimakov fumbling at his belt control as the car doors swung upward and the control lights activated. Near the building's rear he saw a body . . . Levarche, the first dead, before Perez and Liu . . . the names assailed him, all dead, all dead so fast and so horribly, all his people . . .

He hit the driver's seat so hard it hurt, hit the startup and prepped navcomp as the engines began their familiar building whine and Aziz hit the passenger seat, the doors beginning to close, so, so slowly . . .

"Come on!" he yelled at the car, at the numerics that flashed on the displays, green, stupid, and uncomprehending of the mortal threat that loomed.

"Look!" shouted Aziz, pointing back across the pad, and Shimakov fumbled for his rifle, discovering in horror that he'd left it behind, forgotten in his mad escape. He looked through the side window and saw a figure coming toward them across the pad . . . limping, he realised in gasping relief. One of theirs.

"Come on!" yelled Aziz. The figure limped on, trying desperately for speed as the engines approached operational volume, halfway across now and getting nearer . . . going to make it, Shimakov thought desperately, wanting to wait for others but knowing it was impossible . . .

Stutter of gunfire beyond the windows, the limping figure collapsed like a bundle of wet rags, and Aziz cried out in anguish. Beyond, at the top of the stairwell, a chilling dark figure stood, weapon pointed their way. Shimakov stared, waiting for the hail of bullets that would rip through the cabin and kill them both . . . but nothing came. No violent death. Lights blinked green as the engines throbbed. The killer was out of ammo.

Shimakov hauled back on the controls, a throbbing whine as the lifters kicked in, and the cruiser began to rise. Aziz shouted warning, and from the corner of his eye, Shimakov saw a black streak headed their way, moving impossibly fast . . . braced his arms and *thump!*, hit their side and the cruiser rocked. A crash from the rear, a fist smashing through the reinforced window, the cruiser losing altitude as it rocked, another crash and the rear door caved in. In the seat alongside, Aziz hauled his rifle about to angle behind Shimakov's seat.

Fired a long, thunderous burst through the wrecked door, the car shuddering as bullets tore through the side, earsplitting within the enclosed space. . . . Shimakov caught a glimpse in the rearview of the killer swinging away one-handed, avoiding the worst of the fire as Aziz dared not shoot near the rear engine mountings . . . he renewed his efforts at the controls and then they were rising again.

Aziz ran out of ammunition and did a fast reload. Crash and lurch as another blow ripped through the door, and there was suddenly a hole. Weight tipped slightly as the killer reached in. . . . Aziz finished loading and fired again, point-blank. Thunder of impacts and the car rocked . . . and free, suddenly, Aziz howling triumph, the killer nowhere to be seen, knocked flying by that final burst. The cruiser climbed higher and Shimakov spared a fast look around, searching for any trace of the death that stalked them. Saw nothing. No trace. Only an innocent, small, dark-metal object lying in the middle of the rear seat, and his exclamation of relief died a fast death upon his lips.

Ten metres up, and the grenade exploded. Doors blown outward amid an explosive scatter of wreckage, the cruiser staggered, frozen within an expanding halo of flaming debris. Then it fell, a short, inglo- rious plummet to the hard, unyielding pad below, slammed hard and broke. There followed an unmoving silence, where nothing moved but the crackling flames that licked about the ruined chassis. Smoke plumed into the gleaming night sky, a dark, ominous pyre. From far away came the haunting echo of sirens.

Sandy awoke. Things were burning. Nearby things. She could hear the crackle of flames and smell the acrid smoke. Light flickered and danced on her retinas, as she struggled for focus through a haze of uncentred thoughts.

Came clear, finally, upon the night sky. Smoke, a thick, rising plume. It drifted by stars, obscuring the view. Stars. She liked watching stars, the memory occurred to her dimly. Had enjoyed lying in the open, planetside, and watching the stars. In space, stars lost their romance. No. But they were different. Attainable. The unattainable was more romantic. She thought.

She felt, she realised, rather bad. Senses came clearer. Her stomach felt numb. It was a horrible numbness, the numbness of impacts. She remembered. Remembered getting hit, getting that grenade in the cruiser. Remembered impacts, and falling. Then nothing. But she'd known she'd get hit. Had known, and gone for the grenade anyway. Why? And then she remembered Mahud, and the world came crashing in once more.

She lay on her back for a moment longer, listening to the rise and fall of sirens somewhere beyond the crackling flames and the pinging of heated metal. Then she rolled over. That felt bad. That felt very, very bad. With great, concentrated effort she got slowly to her hands and knees. Her midriff refused to cooperate. She felt weak all over. And could feel, as she got her hands properly beneath her, the pulling restriction of puncture wounds across her stomach and lower chest. The sticky feeling was blood. Looking down on the pad beneath her, it was entirely red.

With an even greater effort she pushed up to her knees. And then sank slowly down to her haunches. Sat there, kneeling on the landing pad amid the burning wreckage of the fallen cruiser. There were pieces of it everywhere, littering the pad. A blackened corpse, sprawled over the front dash of the aircar. Two of them, still burning. Humans. Straights. They died so easily. Skin burned, and flesh tore. So fragile. No wonder they created machines of such strength and power. Technology, to overcome their weaknesses. Herself.

As she turned her head slowly she could see another body sprawled face down on the pad. She'd shot him in the back. It had been so easy. And so good, in her fury, and her grief. She'd been mad. Mad like it had often terrified her to think about. They'd cut her up. They'd killed Mahud, the last hope she'd had of salvaging something from all those

years, from that entire, former life. Murdered him, like all those innocent civilians. They'd made her so horribly, grievously angry. And this
was the result.

A cool wind swept the pad, blowing smoke. A howling of distant,
airborne engines. The sirens were closer. Death was everywhere. She
could smell it on the wind. Could feel it in the air. Horror and destruction. She looked back toward the fallen body. Turned herself in its
direction and started crawling.

She did not want this life. It disagreed with everything she'd
wanted to be. With every one of her dreams and aspirations. She'd
wanted to be beyond all of this, she'd wanted it so very badly. And this
was what came of her very best efforts. No matter what she did, or
what she tried, she was a killer. Where she went, death followed. And
her concern for those about her, her love for them, became a killing
rage, when they died, and wreaked vengeance on all. There was no
escape from it—it was all that she was. It had been there from her
inception. It was the founding thought that had given her life, her
entire reason for existence. She could not fight fate. She could not fight
God. The stench of blood and burning flesh filled her nostrils, and this
. . . this, was her life.

Well, she wanted none of it. She wanted it stopped. She wanted an
end to the pain.

The dead man's rifle lay by his outstretched fingertips. She ignored
it and reached for the pistol at the back of his waistband. It was a big,
powerful calibre, plenty effective from close range. She sat down
heavily beside him, her brother in death, clicked off the safety, and
thought about it. Thought of skull thicknesses, and trajectories, and
possible approaches that might or might not work . . . there was a
roaring now in the air and a buffeting of howling wind across the pad,
but in her dazed, pain-filled mind, nothing could deter her from her
purpose. She'd been so determined to do something good in her life,
when she'd come to the Federation. Well, now she would.

Base of the skull, she thought to herself, visualising. It was weakest there, where an external trajectory was unlikely to go. She knelt upright with a great effort against the roaring wind, turned the pistol about in her hands, and put the muzzle into her mouth.

"Sandy!" A distant voice above the thundering gale. "Sandy, for God's sake! Put it down!" Angled it back, pointing upward, not wanting a ricochet that left the job unfinished . . . "Sandy, put the gun down! *now!*"

A popping sound, and something smacked into her side. The jolt was minimal, little more than a distraction. She refocused, gripping the handle more firmly . . . and felt her fingers slipping. Then her vision began to go. Blackness gathered and she tried one last, desperate time to squeeze at the trigger, but her balance was going, the pistol fell from unresponsive hands and the only thing that remained as she thudded limply to the ground was the roaring in her ears.

Dim sounds registered. Echoed faintly. It sounded like a long way away. Everything did. Like looking down a long, long tunnel, blackness all around, and a faint prick of light in the distance . . . growing larger, and brighter, and then she was blinking, blurred light assaulting her vision and making her wince, blinking hard.

Smells. A harsh, familiar smell. It triggered memories. And then, suddenly, it became clearer, with a growing rush of fear and pain. Vision cleared further and she could see the white, antiseptic floor beneath her, and that horrid chemical smell in her nostrils. Working sounds around her. Voices. The beep of monitoring equipment. Numbness all over, impenetrable in her present state. She struggled for her voice as the fear got worse.

"*Help me,*" she managed to whisper hoarsely. Coughed once, a stronger, vocal sound.

"Cassandra," said a nearby voice, unfamiliar, and something else that she lost as fear grew to panic, and she realised herself face down in an operating surgery again, awoken from one nightmare to be dropped headlong into another even worse, strapped, drugged, and immobilised while doctors cut her open again and she could do nothing at all . . .

"*Oh God,*" she managed to say in stronger, shuddering voice. "*Oh God, help me. Don't . . .*" Her voice cracked, sobs of pure fright. "*. . . don't cut me, please don't cut me . . .*" And then there was a man talking to her, but she didn't know him, and didn't want to hear him, she just wanted out of this horrible life, out and gone for good, she couldn't take this, she just couldn't stand it . . .

"Just stop it!" she screamed at them, voice approaching normal as her control reasserted. "Leave me alone, you bastards! Oh God, someone get me out of here! Someone . . . please!" She broke off, sobbing, face down and helpless, locked into place beneath the knives and probes, unable even to look about and see, her head locked into a metal brace and staring immovably at the floor . . .

"Sandy!" A familiar voice, and then someone moving at her side, filling her peripheral vision through the tears. "Sandy, it's me, it's Vanessa."

Worried sounding, and then a face, crouched alongside and peering at her, frightened concern in her eyes. Touched her face with gentle fingers. Desperately worried. The sobs continued, uncontrollable.

"Sandy, it's okay." Leaning close, warm breath upon her face. "You've been hit, Sandy, it's not bad . . . you took some slugs in the stomach and a few in the chest, some of them went through and others were stopped dead by those damn armour-muscles of yours . . . the ones that went through did a bit of damage but these guys've patched most of it. It's just that the ones that went through are lodged in your back and causing problems—that's what they're doing now, they're just getting them out. You hear me? It's nothing serious, they're just taking out a few slugs."

Looking and sounding very worried. The fingers stopped stroking her face and moved to her hair above the head-brace. Warm and comforting. The sobbing receded slightly. Sanity returned. The panic began to fade. She felt weak, drained.

"They've made a couple of incisions in your back," Vanessa continued talking to her, hand stroking her hair, "they've pulled back some skin and they're going after the slugs . . . it's just that it's a bit unfamiliar to them, Sandy. They're pretty sure about the basics, but they wanted you awake in case you started feeling something in your legs or shoulders. That whole spinal region is much more different from humans than the rest of you. They just wanted to be sure they didn't do any damage. Okay?"

Pulled back some skin. She recalled what that meant, what a GI's dermal tissue behaved like, that it could be pulled away from muscle, peeled back in sheets for convenient access . . . oh God, that was what she looked like now, with Vanessa here and watching . . . new panic rose. A new fear.

"Don't look at me," she croaked. Crouching down further to see her face, Vanessa looked worried all over again. "Please. Please don't look."

Understanding dawned in Vanessa's eyes. Sadness.

"Oh Sandy," she sighed. Leaned further forward, and kissed her gently on the cheek. Rested her forehead there, a gentle pressure. Hair tickled softly at her ear. "Sandy, I quite honestly don't give a shit. Actually, it makes me a hell of a lot less squeamish than the organic stuff I've seen. You're much more convenient, not so much of that messy, gooey stuff." A pause. "Shit, I shouldn't be talking about that, should I? Just ignore me, I've been on duty so long my brain's dissolving."

Pulled back to look at her again. New tears were gathering in Sandy's eyes, but for a different reason. Vanessa smiled sadly at her and wiped them away before they could gather and spill.

"Not that it's a pretty sight, mind you," she continued. "But then it's not supposed to be a pretty sight, is it? I mean, if you think I'm going to get scared off because you don't look pretty with your skin missing . . . well, that'd be pretty shallow of me, wouldn't it? I might be small, but I don't reckon I'm shallow . . . although mind you, I'm the best person for crouching down like this because I'm the only one who can get low enough to look you in the face. Oh here, this won't do," wiping away more tears, "veteran combat soldier crying like this. Can't let the rookies in SWAT see this, you'll never live it down. Hurt your promotion chances, too, you never see Ibrahim crying. Mind you, I never see him fucking either, so I don't know if that's much of a bright spot on his part . . ."

It nearly got a smile, and Vanessa's eyes lit up as the lips twitched.

"A-hah! Signs of recovery. You're gonna be fine, just patch everything back together, get you laid a few dozen times by an assortment of handsome hunks of my choosing, and you'll be right as rain in no time. You know that . . ."

"Ricey," Sandy croaked.

"Uh-huh?" Waiting patiently.

"You talk too much." Weakly.

Vanessa grinned. "Well at least you're back to stating the obvious, that's a good start." And paused, smiling. "So how are you feeling now? Better?"

"Better than what?" Sandy retorted weakly. Terror subsided, her voice was no longer so strong. The drugs did that, loosening muscles and vocal cords alike, deadening responses.

"Well okay, forget better. Are you feeling slightly, mildly, averagely, or totally fucked?"

Sandy thought about it for a long moment. Wanted to take a deep breath, but the life support made it unnecessary—she was getting enough air through some damn machine she was hooked up to. And she remembered her diaphragm wasn't in such good shape.

"Totally fucked when I woke up. Then you came along, and now it's only average." Eyes locked on Vanessa's. Vanessa was smiling, emotion in her eyes. "Thanks," Sandy whispered.

"What for?" Vanessa said dismissively, and kissed her again, twisting her head about so that this time it got her firmly on the lips. Sandy blinked. Vanessa pulled away, looking sheepish. "Might not get another chance," she explained.

Sandy managed a weak smile, and Vanessa looked pleased all over again.

"You're a scoundrel," Sandy murmured at her. "Try it again and I'll bite your jaw off."

"Homophobia," Vanessa replied, smiling calmly. "See, you're not perfect after all. You need to be bisexual to be perfect, we appreciate everyone."

"Okay then." Sandy managed with an effort. "Try it again. You never know, I might like it better the second time."

"Tease," Vanessa scolded. "That's a very mean thing to say to me— you know I'll fall head over heels."

Sandy didn't reply. Humour was too much of an effort, now of all times. Conversation was. She only knew that where there had been blackest despair, there was now . . . hope. Not a bright hope. That remained a long way off, like a distant dream. But she no longer felt so empty, and there was something good, something worth looking forward to. Again.

"Sandy?" said a new, male voice into the silence. Someone crouched on her other side, looking at her. "I'm Doctor Li. Li Jianjun. Are you in pain?"

"No," she whispered. Wanting to turn her head, but not unable to. "No, I can't feel much. Just some tingling. The buffers cut off any really bad pain. I feel reflex pain normally, but nothing longer."

"Okay." Doctor Li nodded, taking that in. "Okay Sandy, now the Lieutenant's told you what we're doing . . . I'm sorry you woke up so suddenly. That was our fault, we didn't know how fast it would happen when we brought you back. We overestimated." We, Sandy guessed, meant the other doctors. She thought there were at least four, and probably others advising.

"Now everyone here is biotech, Sandy," said Doctor Li, as if reading her mind. "In fact, we've got probably the best biotech surgeons on the planet here in this room right now. You'll forgive us if we find it all more than a little fascinating . . . but we're not here to study you, Sandy, we're just going to patch you up. The damage isn't great. You should make a full recovery. Now, if you have any questions at any time, about anything, just ask. Okay?"

"Okay," she whispered. Doctor Li gave her a gentle, reassuring pat on the head and regained his feet. "Ricey?"

"Right here." Leaning in close again, with the doctor resuming work.

"Don't leave me."

Vanessa smiled, hand in her hair again, a soft, comforting presence. "Not a chance. No chance at all."

# CHAPTER 19

At 10:16 the next morning, Katia Neiland walked into the private hospital ward. Sandy looked across in surprise, and lowered her paperback. The President walked unescorted across the sun-splashed floor, smiling at her.

"Hi," she said. Stopped by the bedside, a hand upon the visitor's chair.

"Hello." Weary-eyed and fuzzy-headed, her voice remained at best a soft murmur. An eyebrow quirked in mild surprise, looking past the President toward the doorway. Then refocused with gradual, deliberate calm. "Where's your entourage?"

"Leashed in the corridor, sniffing nurses' backsides." Smiling in apparent good humour. "You two make a nice couple."

Sandy glanced across at Vanessa, who lay alongside on the broad hospital bed. Sleeping peacefully, brown curls strewn about a face that seemed to Sandy perhaps incongruously angelic, now that the mischievous energy in her eyes was safely hidden behind gentle, closed eyelids. Dressed in the customary, postarmour tracksuit that had followed her shower, lying comfortably above the covers. Only a small weight on the mattress.

"She was on a thirty-hour rotation including the Berndt Operation," Sandy replied, gazing at the sleeping Lieutenant. "Maybe three hours' sleep in between. Then she had me to attend to all last night. She got to sleep about six hours ago, I reckon she'll wake up in another eight, if she's lucky. It takes it out of you."

"And what about you? Why aren't you sleeping?"

Sandy shrugged faintly. "I hate sleeping under drugs—they're still in my system. I wake up feeling even more tired than when I started. I woke up two hours ago and thought I'd read instead."

"Hmm. What is that?" The President stepped forward and lifted the book in her hand, studying the cover. "Jagdish Singh. Is he any good?"

"Typical Indian drama, lots of marriages, scandals, gratuitous high-fashion, and excuses for fancy costumes . . . it's fun, it passes the time."

Neiland settled back into the visitor's chair with a sigh. Looked about at the broad windows that stretched around the large room, letting in the sunlight. Outside, it was a lovely day. Endless blue sky beyond the reaching towers. The room was well furnished—a deluxe suite. Security required it. And their guest deserved it.

"So," she said, looking back at Sandy. "How are you feeling?"

"Doctors briefed you, I suppose?" Sandy murmured. Neiland nodded. "Well this is where I get grateful I'm not a straight human— I'd be dead five times over. I just feel numb all over. Can't move, can't eat properly, breathing hurts . . ." She shrugged. ". . . I'll be okay."

"Christ, after stopping an automatic burst point-blank, that's something to be thankful for."

"There was a car door in the way," Sandy replied, quiet and hoarse. "Slowed them a bit, flattened them, made them tumble. Uneven impacts, they didn't penetrate as much." Neiland was staring. Sandy managed a faint smile, remembering the line they'd always told straights who asked. "My stomach's rated at fifty percent tougher than a vest. Most of me is."

Neiland reached and took her hand. Held it in both of her own, feeling between fingers and thumb. Probing. Sandy watched, blue eyes gone sombrely curious. Flexed her fingers slightly, a faint ripple of movement beneath Neiland's probing examination. Neiland looked at her, mild amazement in her eyes.

"That's pretty zeeked," she said. Borrowing from her son's vocabulary, Sandy guessed with faint amusement. "Feels completely human. You've even got the same veins . . ." probing with a curious forefinger, tracing a line.

"Cosmetic," Sandy told her.

"Even so." Turned over her palm, as if reading the lines. Felt at the wrist. Frowned as she searched. "No pulse though."

"Lower blood pressure," Sandy murmured. "Much thicker consistency, much more efficient. Keeps up sensory energy mainly. Feedback nerves, temperature, organs. Muscles don't need it, that's mechanical. So I only need about twenty percent the blood that you do." Neiland looked fascinated. "Don't ask me any more. Biology isn't my strong point."

"Biology," Neiland murmured, continuing her examination. "That's what it is really, isn't it? Artificial biology. Nothing mechanical about it."

Sandy made a fist and clenched it, hard. Neiland pulled at it with her fingers. Grabbed with both hands and made an effort, biting her lip. And gave up with a whistled breath. The fist moved not one millimetre.

"It is mechanical," Sandy told her quietly. "So's yours. A hand's just an organic tool. Yours grew from DNA. Mine's synthetic. But it's still just a hand. It just depends on your perspective."

Neiland gazed at her, green eyes locked, hands gentle upon the closed fist.

"Does that bother you?" Sombrely. "Having been made? All this . . ." Fingers probed down her arm, ran up to her shoulder, and rested there. ". . . all put together in pieces. Made in hundreds of high-tech labs. Toiled over by workers, designers. Engineers." Sandy blinked, softly.

"Does it bother you," she replied, "having once been a small collection of cells in a bloody mass attached to the side of a womb?"

"No." Smiling. "It's marvellous. The wonder of birth and growth. But factories, money, and politics . . ." Her gaze was penetrating. "It doesn't bother you?"

"How doesn't bother me," Sandy replied. "Why does. Why bothers me a lot."

Neiland thought about it. Leaned forward, elbows on knees, and rested her chin on her hands, Sandy's hand still lightly grasped in her fingers.

"I'm sorry," she sighed. "It's hardly the perfect time to start getting curious."

Sandy gave a faint shake of her head.

"No, it probably is the perfect time." She rolled her head against the pillow. Looked at Vanessa, head on a separate pillow alongside her own. Still sound asleep. Sandy doubted anything short of a live weapons drill would wake her.

"I've been thinking about it quite a bit," she said, gazing at Vanessa's peaceful face. "It's something that needs thinking about."

"Any conclusions?"

"No." Softly. "Just that I need to think about it some more. Soon."

A silence, Sandy watching Vanessa, Neiland watching them both. There was something very touching in Vanessa's slumber, here at her side. Sandy remembered that Vanessa had once spoken of reflexive fears, human reactions to the theoretical presence of threat. And yet here she was, sleeping soundly alongside, unafraid and unworried. Wanting only to be there because her friend Sandy required it, and there was no second bed in the ward, and Sandy, conscious at the time, had invited her to. Vanessa had climbed up alongside, put her head down, and was asleep within seconds. No qualms, no second thoughts, not even after witnessing firsthand what Sandy was capable of. Not even after having fired the stun pellet that dropped her. She had lain down with full knowledge of what she had been sleeping beside, yet had shown not the slightest trepidation, reasoned or otherwise.

It was a nice feeling. For someone to know full well who and what she was and accept her anyway. Consider her a friend. Someone who would protect rather than harm. Which she would, if it came to that, no question. In fact, she thought with tired, reluctant amusement, Vanessa could probably not have found a safer bed to sleep on in all of Tanusha.

"So," she said tiredly, withdrawing her hand from Neiland's curious grip and putting both hands behind her head with a slow, wincing effort, propping her head. "What's it been like at your end?"

Neiland exhaled, shoulders slumping theatrically. Sandy smiled.

"A mess," the President said, leaning wearily back in the chair. "But that was inevitable. There's a major Senate inquiry being launched, full access, public disclosure . . . just a big, major flap." Ran a hand absently over her dark-red hair, tugged at the rear knot. "The Federal Committee's going to get here in another ten days . . . they're not going to know what hit them. A very sour reception from both sides, I'm feeling. Of course, it remains to be seen just how much of this whole FIA operation they knew about. We'll be demanding a Federal inquiry on their own level with full Callayan representation, but I don't know if anyone's really expecting much. The FIA has too many Federal supporters, too many border worlds are still hawkish on the League . . . you know that story better than I could tell it."

Sandy raised a conceding eyebrow. Flexed stiff, painful shoulders, wincing at the stabs of pain up her back and through her stomach. Tight beneath hard-packed bandages.

"You realise," the President added, "that the media now know you exist?"

Sandy sighed. Nodded painfully. "Yeah. I heard. Figured it would be kind of difficult to cover up at this point." Silence, thinking about that for a moment. "Suppose it was inevitable. Pity. I kind of valued my anonymity."

"Ah," Neiland waved a dismissive hand, "it's not so bad, you'll get used to it." Sandy gave her a very flat look. "Well okay, it'll have its moments. But we've got an action plan in the works. They can't reveal your name or face because that's covered by the security legislation, and we've got feelers out in the underground that suggest they're pretty much on your side. The whole underground crowd are generally League-sympathetic anyway—they hate the FIA. They seem to think you're some kind of white witch or something. So you'll have your supporters. Things shouldn't get too far out of control." She paused. "And things are going to get kind of busy in the next few months. People will have plenty of other things to worry about."

Sandy didn't ask. She already knew enough. The anti-Federation protests. The succession moves. The anti-League backlash. Anti-Federation backlash. The biotech radicals and religious conservatives panicking. The next few months would give everyone a lot to think about. Unfortunately, all of those issues seemed to lead directly back to herself, at some point or other.

She exhaled hard, a tight pulling at her midriff, head pillowed on her hands as she stared at the ceiling. The clear, bright sunlight through the windows made a mockery of such murky complexities. She longed for simplicity again. Just a brief respite from having to double-check every option for traps, pitfalls, and dead-ends. To go where she pleased and not care for consequences. To forget.

"Another thing I wanted to ask you," Neiland said after a long, silent moment. Her voice was quiet. And Sandy felt her spirits drop through the floor as she sensed what was coming.

"Mahud." One single, sombre word, and the blackness hit her hard in the gut. The sunny day turned to brooding dark. "The body's under the tightest security possible, meaning information control as much as anything. There are options here that I want to clear with you now, while I have the chance."

Neiland's tone was professional and steady, but there was sadness in her eyes. Sandy stared blankly at the ceiling.

"The first thing," she continued in that quiet, sombre tone, "is that when the Senate investigation gets into full swing in a few days they will find out about Mahud. There are powers by which they could gain access to his body. Once that happens, it's out of my hands. There could then be forensic investigations and examinations, maybe even some study research . . . it's not allowed, technically, but there are loopholes and arguments for special cases. They've already found plenty with the Parliament strike team. They're not nearly the prize that Mahud would be, though.

"Now I've talked to Guderjaal, and he's prepared to grant you family custody, as effective next-of-kin. Technically it ought to wait until the inquiry finds out, but it's not explicitly spelled out, and that's too bad for them. It also falls under the Federal anti-GI restrictions, which most politicians will find difficult to argue against without getting into hot water with the public, conservative radicals or otherwise. In the meantime, I'm informed that there is a smelter we can hire for government use on short notice that could double as a crematorium. I'm told that's the way it was done in the League, with a recovered body. It can handle a GI's body, and give you his ashes afterward. I know it's not my place to decide for you, but obviously a burial would not work since GI remains mostly do not decay. What do you think?"

Strangely, Sandy did not feel any urge for tears. There was just an empty hollowness, the sense of something just missing. Like she was back on that operating table, under the FIA's knives, losing limbs. A horrible feeling. But she was too drained for grief. Too empty. And maybe, she couldn't help but think, too good at coping with this kind of thing.

No. She hadn't coped well at all last night. Had tried, she recalled dimly, to eat a bullet. She felt no such urge now. It solved nothing, and her waking, sane logic rebelled at the prospect. She knew now, with a grim, fatalistic certainty, that things would go on. She would go on. She had once believed Mahud dead, only to discover otherwise. To have lost him again was agony of a kind that was almost unbearable. But she knew herself too well to believe herself defeated by events. To know herself crushed.

For she could recall, with great, terrible effort, that she had been through worse. It did not seem possible, and for long moments at a time her brain refused to accept that it could be true. But it had been worse, back then, when she'd been told that her entire team was dead. And she had survived and recovered, somewhat, from that devastation. This blow was less, but cumulative. Yet she would survive this one, too.

She was too good at the big picture. It had always been her tactical strong point—her ability to see the broader canvas. To focus beyond the moment, to see the future and the past that anchored the present in place. In mission planning it had enabled her to link together cause and effect, to predict an opponent's movements, and the reasons behind them. In life it enabled her to see further than the immediate trauma, see the possibilities that lay beyond. To see that there was always something worth living for . . . for someone prepared to change her life.

She turned her head and looked again at Vanessa, sleeping like an angel beside her. Pulled a hand from behind her head, and brushed some loose, curling hair away from Vanessa's face. Her sleeping expression registered no response, oblivious to all but her sleeping dreams. Sandy feared they might be bad dreams, but hoped sincerely otherwise.

"I think," she murmured, "that you should do that. He wouldn't want me to give those bastards the satisfaction." Neiland nodded solemnly.

"I'll give the instruction." Pause. "A number of CSA agents have requested to be present at the ceremony." Sandy turned and stared in astonishment.

"Ceremony?"

"They took the FIA's actions very personally," Neiland continued. "Some of them nearly dropped through lack of sleep trying to track them down. The effort was enormous. A Chief Investigator Khurana in particular, Shan tells me. He and his people consider Mahud a hero. He has demanded to be present at the ceremony. I think he'll have a lot of company."

Sandy blinked, swallowing hard against the growing ache in her throat.

"I don't know if a ceremony . . ."

"Of course there'll be a bloody ceremony," Neiland cut her off with gentle firmness. "You need it, they want it, and he bloody well deserves it. Don't you think?"

Sandy nodded, unable to argue with that. Not trusting herself to speak.

"Good." Looking at her with a tired, lopsided smile. "I'm sorry to dump it all on you so soon. It just needed to be done." Sandy nodded, wordlessly. Her head was spinning.

"And after that," Neiland said, "when you've recovered, there's something that Shan wants you to do for him. For everyone."

"What?" she murmured hoarsely.

"Take a vacation." Sandy blinked. And looked at the President, questioningly. A vacation. She couldn't recall ever having been on a vacation. Unless you counted going AWOL. What did one do on a vacation? Was there a procedure?

"Where would I go?" she asked.


The sunlight through the canopy was bright at four thousand meters. Hands rested on sun-warmed controls, a gentle manual, feeling the rise and fall of air currents against the flyer's control surfaces. A buzz of vibration through the molded grips, through the comfortable leather of her seat, a muffled whine of thrusters, broad fan jets, carving the air.

As her eyes filtered the glaring light, Sandy gazed out the enclosing width of canopy at the broad, open country of Callay that lay stretched below. Here the forests had given way to broad, open valleys, patches of bare granite amid the flowing grass and scrub. Rivers flowed, many-tongued and linking, a myriad of sun-glistening causeways. The flyer rocked slightly, air rising in thermals from the rock below. A pressure on the controls and she corrected, a shifting movement as the flyer responded, riding the air that she caressed with her hands.

She was one hundred and forty kilometres southwest of Tanusha and it was a lovely day. Further into the distance was broken and scattered cloud, snow white in the sunlight. There was a song on the radio—a Tanushan station via satellite relay, a rock band, guitars and vocals, something both sad and happy at the same time, pleasant harmony and rising emotion. It had been running around in her head for the last few days, and it was good to be hearing it now. She hummed a soft accompaniment and breathed the deep, long breaths of open space and long distances yet to travel.

She wore casual shorts and a T-shirt scrawled with Urdu script— Vanessa's alma mater, she had gathered, and a common enough sight on the streets of Tanusha. Her bare legs were warm in the midmorning sun. A gentle breeze of air-conditioning kept the temperature cool. She had a backpack with clothes and necessities on the back seat, a decent quantity of credit on her CSA card, and a surfboard that Singh had lent to her at Vanessa's insistence, with a promise that she'd learn to use it. Vanessa had been pleased at the idea, had said that with her coordination she'd be an expert grommet in no time at all. Vanessa, Sandy knew, was trying to find her a hobby. She appreciated the thought.

Well Ricey, she thought to herself past the rising chorus from the radio, the tourist brochures say there's a hundred thousand kilometres of untouched coastline on Callay, not even counting the islands. Maybe some of those waves have my name on them.

The flyer rocked again, displays describing a thermal, upward flowing air in curious, rotating pillars. Another shift of hands, enjoying the sensation, the aircraft loose and free upon the shifting currents of air, responding to her touch. It had been a while since she had last used her pilot's qualifications. One of many military skills, it had been, tape-taught long ago but rarely used, faded with time and lack of practice. But the hands remembered. They held a steady course, while the eyes scanned the displays and her interface made occasional, brief, scanning contact with the flyer CPU, acquiring a feel, a broad sensation of data. Of flying. It felt good, as the sun on her bare limbs felt good, as the vista of rumpled, rocky, folded terrain was good, amid a sea of grass and scrub, and a running gleam of sunlight across the many forks of rivers.

It was good. And it was surreal.

Herself, in a civilian flyer, packed bags like some adventuring Tanushan backpacker escaping from work, or family, or school, to the adventure of the ninety-five percent of the planet where humans were rare and civilisation rarer. It was, she had gathered in recent days, a significant part of Tanushan folklore. Among SWAT and CSA personnel of her acquaintance, stories abounded of "going bush" or "walkabout."

For some, it meant luxury resorts, sunsets by the swimming pool and karaoke barbecues. For others, it was cruises and boats. Vanessa, of course, was a mad-keen scuba diver, who swore that a week among reef fish, coral shelves, and five-metre, curiously intelligent dragonrays was the ultimate solution for urban tension. Hiraki was a keen mountaineer, for whom happiness could be found amid the soaring heights of the Great Tarikashi Shelf, or the equatorial Wilmott Ranges. And the big, burly Bjornssen, she had been surprised to learn, was a dedicated nature enthusiast, who had once spent a month's accumulated leave in the southern Argasuto tundra with his girlfriend, following the hundred-thousand-fold migration of the *twelik*, a kind of native deer. Which must have been quite a sight.

And she herself . . . she would go wherever the winds and thermals would take her. It was a vague thought, partly formed amid the abstracts of sun and landscape and the soaring sensation of flight. And it was most unlike herself. Vague thoughts. Unfocused. Wandering, wherever the winds should blow. She only knew that it was good. And necessary.

The flyer was Ibrahim's idea. A rental. Expensive, she knew, but Ibrahim had dismissed it with an absent wave of a hand. "And remember," he had told her, "the destination is nothing without the journey."

"Islamic?" she had asked.

"Shanish," he had replied. And was gone before she recognised the humour.

The song came to an end. Another began, mellow acoustic. She adjusted the volume, hand gently levering the throttle, searching for a steadier airflow in the mild turbulence. Civilian flyer. Recreational. Cruising at a little over five hundred kilometres per hour, she wasn't about to set any speed records. But it was reliable and easy to fly. And fun, that too. She had the coastal town of Ito fixed firmly in the nav-comp, and the user-friendly pilot displays showed her the way. Ito, she had been told, had nice beaches, good diving, some forested mountains nearby, and a population of barely twenty thousand, most of whom did little more than service the tourist trade. She was certain that Ito would be nice. She was certain that the places beyond Ito would be nice also. She had the flyer on twelve-day rental. She could come and go as she pleased, and the planet did not seem like such a large place after all.

And she felt . . . curious. Soaring in flight, her consciousness somehow free, beyond the moment, the shift of control grips upon yielding air, the crystal sunlight, the vast horizon. Perhaps it was significant, she pondered, this detachment. Perhaps some curious quirk of bio-artificial psychology. Perhaps post-traumatic. Perhaps a rejection of sensory data, a reflex response to recent overload. Most probably it was. All of those things, and more besides.

And maybe . . . maybe she was just tired. Tired of the ponderings. Tired of the questions. Tired of the endless contradictions that made up her existence. And just sick and tired to death that it had to mean *anything*. She felt, perhaps, the most overwhelming and complete urge just to let it be.

She was. She would always be.

*I am.*

The civilian flyer cruised on, a small, significant speck in a vast expanse of sunlit sky. It faded toward a new horizon, bright and clear in the gleaming sun. Time flowed. Life continued.

The city of Tanusha bided its time, and awaited her return.

Joel Shepherd was born in Adelaide, South Australia, in 1974, but when he was seven his family moved to Perth in Western Australia. He studied film and television at Curtin University but realised that what he really wanted to do was write stories. His first manuscript was shortlisted for the George Turner Prize in 1998, and *Crossover* was shortlisted in 1999.

Apart from writing, Joel helps in his mother's business, selling Australian books to international schools in Asia and beyond. This has given him the opportunity to travel widely in Asia and other parts of the world. Joel also writes about women's basketball for an American Internet magazine.

*Crossover* is Joel's first published book.